Cage Life

By Miles Watson

"Walk the mean streets of New York, brushing shoulders with the mob, the molls, and a tough MMA fighter in a debut crime novel, *Cage Life* by Miles Watson. A martial artist and former law enforcement officer, Watson knows his characters and tells a helluva story."

-- Patrick W. Picciarelli, author of *Undercover Cop*

"As one of the best MMA fighters in the world, Mickey Watts knows how to defend a takedown and can get out of the tightest submissions. But when he enters the mob's cage, he learns there is no tapping out."

-- John Dixon, Bram Stoker Award-winning author of *Devil's Pocket*

"Rich language, memorable characters, and sharp dialogue are clearly Watson's stock-in-trade. *Cage Life* takes you on a trip through the world of mixed martial arts and then makes a detour, dropping you smack-dab in the middle of the New York City mob. You're never quite sure what's coming next, a chokehold or a bullet to the back of the head."

-- John Fortunato, Tony Hillerman Prize-winning author of *Dark Reservations*

One Nine Books
OneNineBooks.com

For Mom. She saves the world. A lot.

I forgive you boy. But don't leave town.
-- The Stone Roses

PART I
Chapter One

The roar of the crowd.

It scared me at first. All those voices. All that bloodlust. Somehow they made me feel unprotected. Naked. That's the way the first gladiators used to go into the arena, you know – no helmet, no armor, no shield. Just skin and the knife. They stood there bare-assed with the sun hot on their neck and the steel cold in their hand and the opponent glowering across the way, and all around them the crowd. Screaming.

Ave, Caesar! Morituri te salutemus!

Yeah. It scared me at first. Hearing it in the dressing room my knees used to clack like castanets. Not now.

Now I enjoy it.

The first shows were small. Velodromes in Virginia and Louisiana, parking lots in Iowa and Illinois. The crowds were small and scattered, but what they lacked in size they made up for in volume, and the more I fought, the larger they got. The one in Vegas was my coming-out party. A small arena in a second-rate casino, but packed to the rafters with five thousand people. That was when I began to feel like I'd earned the noise; like maybe it was even my due. See, in this sport, a lot of guys are challenging for the world title after a dozen bouts; I wasn't even in contention, and when the cage door closed on me in Sin City I already had twenty scalps dangling from my belt. It didn't frustrate me; on the contrary, it made me feel worthy of my name. No Watts ever had anything easy. My family was and is the longest distance between two points.

My twenty-fifth fight was in a ballroom in Atlantic City: lights wreathed in cigarette smoke, a close-pressing crowd seated in folding metal chairs, ring-card girls with breasts bought on the installment plan. It was a rough one. When the horn finally sounded, my right eye was pinched shut, my ribs felt like a xylophone struck by a sledgehammer, and I was pretty sure I'd fractured my shin. The referee held my hand up at the end, and as I acknowledged the cheers with a nod that sent sweat and blood spattering onto my feet, I'd wondered if anyone watching knew that my father and grandfather had also fought in this very same venue. Put it all on the pass line and rolled the dice, not for the money and not for the rush, but because fighting was in their marrow. God makes some men wise and others fools, some heroes and some cowards. He made *us* fighters. All of us.

One important difference, though.

They fought in a ring.

I fight in cage.

And there it is ahead of me, a sinister septagonal shape, sitting like an open-air torture chamber under the lights. The place where I earn my keep and my share of concussions, contusions and broken knuckles. But here, on the edge of the ramp, with the fans screaming their heads off on either side of me and my opponent waiting within that thirty-foot prison, I'm still safe among friends. There's Alton Barnes, his face like dusty cordovan beneath the gray-shot beard, doubtlessly turning over every detail of my fight plan in his mind. He was showing me how to throw Muay Thai knees when they were still scabbed from failed attempts to ride a bicycle. Next to him, Massimo Raia, my grappling coach, calm as an assassin and bearing an assassin's expressionless face and glassy-calm stare. And walking ahead, towel flung over the shoulder of his archaic silk cornerman's jacket, his step as sprightly as mine despite his eighty-plus years, is Old Sam Hanshaw, Alton's uncle, the man who taught my father to box. The man who'd once traded punches with Jake LaMotta.

Not a bad group to take to the door with you.

But when that door closes, I'm alone.
A gladiator *always* goes in alone.
I who am about to die salute you.

Chapter Two

The feet of Wilson Kreese are roughly the size of gold bricks, but they move a lot faster.

I discover this when one of them lands on my thigh with a *crack* they can probably hear up in the cheap seats. After the sting of pain comes a dull warm crawly feeling, like somebody slapped a handful of freshly made jam on my leg. I know this feeling well. During my training camp, I sparred twice a week with Muay Thai kickboxers from Amsterdam, and those motherfuckers could *hit*. I hated those sessions, but they had a purpose: toughening me up for what's happening right now.

Alton figured it like this. Kreese knows I hail from a long line of prizefighters. He doesn't think of me as a mixed martial artist, but as a boxer who took some jiu-jitsu classes, and he expects me to fight that way. He *expects* my stance to be wrong, my feet to be planted in such a manner as to leave my legs vulnerable. He said that much at the press conference. And that's precisely what I aim to do. To be the fighter he trained to beat…until it's time to be myself.

But in the meantime, it sure does hurt.

Kreese, of course, is an expert on hurt, and he looks it, from his shaven head to the swastikas tattooed into his kneecaps. His flesh glistens like snow under the glare of the overhead lamps, and he carries his muscle easily, light-footedly, like a predatory beast. I have to take a moment to remind myself beautiful bodies don't win fights, and lugging all that muscle around can be a tiresome gig.

Yet I have to admit there's a fascination in watching this bastard. I know Kreese is one of the best submission grapplers alive. He was doing mixed martial arts back when there were hardly any rules at all. That's how he got his nickname: The Kapsule. His trademark in the old days was an armbar that hyperextended the elbow joint until the capsule connecting the articular surfaces burst from the pressure like a tomato in a microwave. Whether you tapped or didn't tap made no difference to Kreese; he wanted to hear that sucker pop.

Nowadays, of course, they'll kick you out of the League for that sort of shit. Mikhailis Morganstern – that's him at cageside, wearing the smirk and the Saville Row –is working very hard to convince the public mixed martial artists aren't street thugs, but highly trained athletes, no different in their way than wrestlers, boxers, or football players. And by and large, that's true. Trouble is, anyone who gets in fights for a living is *a priori* crazy. Maybe not bark-at-the-moon, keep-severed-feet-in-the-freezer crazy, but a bit crazy nonetheless. Hell, I admit even I might be couple cans short of a six-pack for choosing to get locked in a cage with a guy like Kreese.

And therein lies my problem.

Kreese is *completely* crazy. The terrifying gleam in his eyes is not an effect. What I'm seeing – what all the hundreds of thousands of people across the country are seeing, on their television screens – is not a sane man pretending to be a loon, but a total psycho who has learned how to store up his insanity like steam in a boiler and is now releasing the pressure valve. That's why he does what he does. So he can let go of all that pent-up madness in the one venue on Earth it won't get him arrested.

The cage.

Kreese switches up his stance and blasts me on the inside of my left thigh just below the groin. I respond with a couple of jabs that fall short of the mark, eat another leg kick – *crack!* – then spin out to avoid a third. The aim is to make him overconfident, not cripple myself. He advances after me like a giant crab, with a curious scuttling movement, his hands held high – he's wary of my fists, and he should be. Now his eyes flicker from my face to my feet. Is he looking for the takedown already? He must know

I've got a terrific sprawl. No, it's a feint. He's punching for my chin, and he very nearly finds it. Yeah, he's a grappler, and yeah, he's been to Bangkok to train, but he's also skilled in *panantukan,* a Filipino street fighting art that resembles boxing with the rules removed. It emphasizes switchblade-quick attacks and is especially dangerous in a clinch. But I have no intention of clinching with The Kapsule now. He's too fresh, too strong, and his wrestling is too good. So I slip the right hand and the follow-up and circle back out to the center of the cage.

Kreese comes at me again. This time he's after my left calf. I planted my leg too far forward, and he's taking the bait. The impact of his bare foot sends a sharp silvery pain right into my skull. He grins as I retreat behind a nervous-looking jab. Thinks his plan is falling together. Thinks that he just has to keep whacking away at my legs like a bloody-minded lumberjack until all that remains to do is shout *"Timber!"* and take me to the mat.

He thinks he's won already.

Instead, he's falling into my trap.

Another minute goes by. Two. I've burned up more than half of the five-minute round letting him play the aggressor, and he plays it well. Lightning-fast attacks on my legs, mostly, but also some hard punches I've had to block with my gloves, forearms, biceps. My hard breathing is not a performance: this sumbitch is pushing me, and he knows it. His gaze is glancing down regularly now, looking for a buckle in the knees or a dragging slowness in the feet, any sign that I'm ready for a takedown. And it turns out I am.

Just not in the way he wants.

Kreese telegraphs his lead right leg kick by tensing his whole body for a split-second beforehand. On any other fighter, I might not notice it, but this dude is a walking anatomical sketch; I can see every sinew. Now his right foot is blurring toward my thigh, where it has so often found a home, but something blurs even faster to intercept it. The side of my knee. And as I check his attack, I mount one of my own: a hard kick with the same leg into his right side. I can actually feel the impact of my heel on his hip bone through the waistband of his fighting trunks. He staggers backwards, windmilling for balance, and I bridge the gulf between us with a Superman punch – a leaping right hand that has the whole of my weight behind it and lands squarely on his chin.

Ten thousand people gasp, in unison, and Wilson Kreese hits the cage with a rattle. A beautiful equation, and one I spent three months working out:

Be the guy he wants me to be.

Until it's time to be myself.

Kreese doesn't go down. He's way too strong to be blasted out with a one-two, no matter how powerful. But he's stunned, and I use that moment to seize the sides of his head in a Thai clinch and bring my knee up into his chin.

He takes it.

Tough sonofabitch.

So I give him another.

And another.

And another.

Now he goes down, tumbling forward into me like an elephant with a bullet in the brain. The problem is a guy like Wilson Kreese doesn't *need* his brain. He's had fifty-three combats in the cage, and threading their way through that powerful body is enough muscle memory to o'erflow the minds of a dozen ordinary gladiators. As he falls, he rams his huge bald head into my chest, swings muscle-clad arms around my waist....

And lands right on top of me.

Ever had a bowling ball slammed into your sternum? The feeling is approximately the same. Except bowling balls aren't attached to six feet of angry, delirious psycho. I feel the air explode from my lungs, and for just a second the world flares white. Then it all comes back to me: sight, sound, smell, taste, touch. *Especially* touch. I'm as aware of the smooth texture of the mat beneath my shoulder blades as I am of the hot sweaty pressure of Kreese's forehead on my chest. I'm also aware he's scrambling, if only clumsily, to gain full mount, with his knees opposite my ribs and his ass firmly on my stomach. In that position, my legs are neutralized and my arms can do little more than flail helplessly while he smashes hammerfists and elbows into my face. Almost nobody survives a full mount. Either you get beaten unconscious or the referee steps in to save you when your face begins to look like pie filling. Either way, you chalk up one in the loss column. And I didn't come here to see that particular cherry broken.

I try to trap Kreese within my guard; wrapping my legs around his ribs and my arms around the back of his neck, to pull him close where he can't get the leverage and distance he needs to acquaint his elbow with my nose. He feels the clutch of my limbs and struggles against them. Pressed as close as lovers, I inhale the scent of him, a thick hot powerful odor redolent of horse sweat. His body feels like washed stone, and it must be nearly as heavy. Every breath requires effort. Do I have him? I think I have him. He's trapped, helpless as a fish in a net. But no, wait. He's up to something. He's not trying to free his arms to use on my mug; he's trying to worm them *beneath* me. And he succeeds. But why? *What the fuck is he doing?*

I get an answer a moment later. Wilson rocks his body backwards as if trying to pry me off the mat like a manhole cover; and for a second I feel the air against my back as I'm lifted clear. Then I'm slammed back down, a four-or-five inch drop that feels like ten feet with Kreese atop me. It hurts like hell, but I don't really understand the point of it until he repeats the move four more times. He's chivvying me across the cage the way a man would move a safe up a flight of stairs. He wants me trapped against the fence where he can punish me from the top, and he's already almost halfway there.

Slam. Slam. Slam. Individually the impacts aren't fatal, but they have a cumulative effect, mainly on my lungs. They can't get filled with air when the thing that encases them – me – is being beaten like a bongo. And those drumbeats are winning over the crowd. They are cheering like mad with every impact, and that's probably influencing the hell out of the judges. I wonder what Massimo's face looks like right now, watching this display of improvised matwork. He thought he'd seen it all, he said he'd seen it all, but I doubt he's ever seen –

This. Kreese has performed an arcane wrestling move and has somehow gotten the flats of his feet planted on either side of my hips. He's lifting me over his shoulders. He shouldn't be able to do that from his position, nobody alive should be able to clean-and-jerk my weight at such an awkward angle, but apparently conventional rules don't apply to the monstrosity I'm fighting. I'm going up, up, up – I'm actually seeing over the top of the cage, limbs dangling in open air, this is *bad*, folks – and then suddenly I'm smashing into the cage post so hard I can actually hear the shiver of the chain-link all around me.

This was not in the plan, dammit.

I'm on my back now, with my arms and legs up and flailing, like an overturned turtle. Unlike a turtle, however, I'm not entirely helpless in this position. Every time Kreese leans in to throw a punch at my face, I thrust my feet into his sweat-slick belly and try to tie up his fists with my hands. Emphasis on the word *try*, because every third punch is getting through. A shot to the forehead – *shit!* – a shot between the eyes – *fuck!* – and now a long, looping punch that catches me flush on the ear. *Damn* it. If this doesn't stop soon, the referee will end it. And yet amidst the beating I see my chance bobbing around like a target in a gunsight. Kreese is hot to finish me, so hot he's getting reckless with his hands, sometimes letting them linger within my guard for a split-second after each punch. If he does that once more…just once more….

He does it. And the punch lands – *oof!* But even as I feel the impact I seize hold of his arm with both hands, and with a single snakelike contortion of my body get my legs around it too. Wilson's eyes go wide, and with the speed and power born of panic he lifts, lifts with all his considerable might, trying to straighten his arm, to break away from my grip. He strains until the sweat stands out on his white face in matchstick-sized beads, until the veins in his biceps bulge blue. But it's no good. His lone arm, strong as it is, is not stronger than all four of my limbs, and I'm bending it backward at the elbow. He's caught.

Caught in his own signature finishing move, the armbar.

I can see the realization in his face, and it's not pretty to look at. Wilson Kreese has lost decisions; he's even been disqualified. But he's never been submitted in the whole of his illustrious fifteen-year career. Somehow he always found a way out. But there's no way out now. Either he cries uncle in front of ten thousand people or they get to hear the capsule of his elbow pop.

Tap or snap, Wilson, it's up to you.

We lock gazes. Kreese has oddly beautiful eyes, the color of seawater, and in those eyes I can see it all playing out: disbelief, fury, horror, and finally, acceptance. Not the philosophical kind. The type a man experiences when he looks down the muzzles of the firing squad and grasps that what's happening to him isn't a nightmare or a hallucination, but real. As real as it gets. And with a drawn-out, close-mouthed scream of frustration and pain, he slaps his hand against his thigh in submission.

Are you not entertained?

Chapter Three

Manhattan by limousine is different than Manhattan by foot, subway, or Ford Maverick. It's not that the streets had changed, or the sounds, or the faces I saw mobbing the sidewalk; Eighth Avenue looked more or less the same way it did when I was a knock-kneed boy of eight, arguing with my cousin about who'd best who in a bareknuckle fight between Superman and The Hulk. Doubtless if we'd rolled down the windows the odors would be the same, too – the beery smell of the taverns, the hot scent of frying onions from the pushcarts, the perpetual stink of ozone underlying it all. Linger too long at a red light, and it's for sure some wino with a filthy sponge would stagger over and offer to smear brown water over the windshield for a dollar. *That* hadn't changed.

It's the perspective that's different.

This was the other end of the looking glass.

When I was in my teens, my old man used to take me to fights at the Garden. Don't think he was being generous; he just wanted to show me where my destiny lay. On our way up to the nosebleed section, we'd often pause to watch the glitterati filing into the front row – the men in their thousand-dollar suits and cashmere overcoats, the women in their mink stoles and spike heels. Under the bright lights, you could see the diamonds afire in ears and on fingers, the gold gleaming on necks and wrists. It used to fill me with a kind of hot, restless ache to know that one of those stones could have paid the mortgage on our house. Sometimes I would wrench my gaze from those beautiful women and those sleek, self-satisfied men and study my dad's face in profile – the scar tissue around his eyes, the thrice-busted nose, the satin bowling jacket with the cheap stitching, the size-fourteen hands. He seemed like another form of life entirely.

And I was his son.

Later, out on the sidewalk, I'd watch the *übermensch* swagger up to their limos and stretch Caddies and chauffeured Town Cars, the wind flapping the skirts of the ladies up over their shapely black-stockinged thighs as they climbed inside. It was like watching genies recede back into their bottles. Who were these people? Where did they come from? Where did they go?

What was it like on the other side of the glass?

Now I knew.

For tonight, anyway.

"You're runnin' low on bubbly, Mick. Can't have *that.*"

"No," I said. "We can't."

My cousin uncorked a second bottle of Cristal Rosé, his grin crumpling into a comic scowl when the glittering white foam erupted over his manicure. A handsome guy, Clean – entirely too handsome for his own good. Thick, perfectly barbered hair, black as jet. Marble complexion, brilliant blue eyes, an aquiline nose, and a full-lipped, sensitive-looking mouth that was the biggest case of false advertising since Thalidomide. But it wasn't that, or even his surname – Immaculata – that got him fitted with his particular handle. It was his tendency to avoid the worst consequences of his own actions. The trouble he caused never touched him. No matter what, he stayed Clean.

It was the people around him that got dirty.

Maybe that's why Anne detested him. Worried her boyfriend's mobbed-up cousin was going to drag him into trouble. It was reasonable enough applied to anyone else, but the irony was that since we'd been boys fidgeting through Sunday mass together, it was Clean who had kept me *out* of trouble. As criminal-minded as he'd always been – the guy had organized and run the only floating crap game in the history of our Catholic school – Clean had always insisted on protecting me from my own worst impulses. Always kept me away from his schemes, his dodges, his hustles. And that hadn't been easy. There had been a time when, smoldering with reckless anger, I'd hungered for the life he was leading, I hadn't yet learned to release that anger in the ring and later, the cage, so I released it in school…and on the streets when school was over. The trajectory I'd been following described a course straight into juvenile hall, county jail, state prison, but I hadn't given a damn. It was my cousin – by his teens already an on-the-record associate of the Lucchino Crime Family – who had changed my direction.

I could still remember the day – a lowery, sullen summer afternoon. Leaden skies and spatters of warm rain. Around us a scrapyard – cars with busted-out windshields, heaps of worn-out tires, piles of junk, and a stench of burning rubber and rusted metal that hung over everything like a pall of smoke. A magnetic crane was swinging old yellow taxis into a box crusher, and Clean, an English Oval dangling from one corner of his mouth, pointed with his Budweiser longneck at the four-taloned iron claw as it thumped down greedily on a taxi roof. *You know why my uncle keeps this place, Mick? To get rid of bodies. This ain't a scrapyard, it's a fucking cemetery. There are guys I grew up lookin' at over the dinner table who ended up here. Twenty, thirty years they put in for the Family, but they crossed the wrong guy or they said the wrong thing and* bam, *this is where they ended up. Not even a fuckin' mortician for company.*

The claw had swung the taxi clumsily into the iron box, and almost immediately the hydraulics kicked in, whirring over the protesting groan of the crumpling metal and the sharp crack of the breaking glass. I tried to keep my face indifferent, but I could imagine a body in the trunk – *my* body. It wasn't fear that had washed over me then, not precisely; I knew well enough the odds of reaching your golden years when the mob was your vocation, and I was still too young and too pissed off at God to be much afraid of death. No, what struck me was the *squalidness* of the scene; the shabby, greasy-fingernailed pathos of it. A wino dying of tuberculosis in a cardboard shanty left the world with more dignity than this. It wasn't fitting. It wasn't *right.* And it frightened the hell out of me in a way that the thought of dying itself ever could.

This ain't for you, Mick, Clean had said, sounding much older than his nineteen years. *You're not gonna be no damn wiseguy. Me, it's in my blood – my old man, my uncle, my brothers…I took it in with mama's milk. But your old man's a solid citizen, and you got talent. You're gonna be famous someday, and not John Gotti famous neither. And when you get there, I'm gonna elbow people in the ribs and say, 'See that guy up there with the title belt? He's my fucking* cousin!'

Years ago now, that moment; long years in which I'd dutifully walked the straight and narrow while he'd immersed himself deeper and deeper into the shadowland of the mob; and yet we'd stayed close, a relationship no one but the two of us understood. Not our own families…and certainly not Anne.

I turned to watch her sip champagne. Saw the blonde curls, the smoke-green eyes, and the Bermuda tan as if for the first time. She was wearing a short black cocktail dress, but even naked you knew she was rich. Something in her posture, her languid movements, the inflection of her voice summoned up images of Aspen and Montauk, Cape Cod and Palm Springs – places, at any rate, where nobody banged on your door with a pipe and shouted, *The rent's due, motherfucker!* And I guess that was part of the attraction. With her bulging trust fund and degree from Vassar, Anne was as different from the gum-chewing *cugettes* I'd grown up with as a Ferrari is from a fucking Yugo.

I took her hand and kissed it. Felt the warmth. The smoothness. The strength of her pulse. And forgot all about the feet of Wilson Kreese. "It's a shame it can't always be like this, huh?"

She turned to me and smiled. "Like what?"

"Like right now. This moment, here. Fight's over, we're together, and I don't have to think about real life for a few days."

"This isn't real life?"

"This is fantasy."

"It seems pretty real to me."

"Course it does," Clean said, sucking Cristal off his fingers. "Limo rides ain't nothing special to your girl here. They took her home from the hospital in one."

Anne's curls swung as she turned toward him, eyes glinting combatively. "I forgot to thank you for the wine, Michael. Did you hijack it off a truck?"

"I'm not in the muscle-end of the business, honey."

"Well, you can't be in the brains-end either, so what does that leave?"

Clean opened his mouth to reply, then thought the better of it and sank back into his seat with a complacent grin. I was relieved to see that his hands were still, his Ferragamo shoes flat against the limousine floor. No cocaine in that system yet…but the night was still young.

"By the way, *cugino mio,*" I said. "I need a favor."

"Anything."

"Try and stay out of trouble tonight."

His grin widened. "I always *try.*"

"I'm serious. I've taken all the punches I want to for one evening."

"Mickey, you worry too much."

"And you don't worry enough," Anne told him.

He poured himself yet more champagne and then made it disappear with a flick of the wrist. "Why should I, when I got others to do it for me?"

The limo stopped, and I heard the locks release. The driver came around and opened the door. When I climbed out to the sidewalk, the alcohol seemed to go straight to my head despite the winter chill. Months of hard training had stripped me of all tolerance. I blinked a few times and found myself facing an enormous blockhouse of windowless brick. Saw a great crowd, pinned back by a velvet rope. A square of light by an open steel door. Bouncers with the sleek-yet-menacing look of well-trained attack dogs. We were somewhere in Chelsea, I guessed, or maybe SoHo – one of those neighborhoods that becomes a block party after sundown regardless of the weather. I didn't know; a fighter who is serious about his trade doesn't party much.

We didn't wait in line. Men like Clean never do. A few words, a few bills, and we were inside. Darkness. A long hallway, green-painted, peeling. Heavy mingled scents of cologne, perfume, incense, marijuana. Now flashes of light, stuttering. Sense of space opening up – hard-floored, high-ceilinged. Tremendous heat. Tremendous humidity. Tremendous noise. Walls of speakers. People dancing on them. A dance floor the size of a basketball court, jammed with writhing bodies, bare flesh, sweat-dampened hair. A long L-shaped bar lit by red bulbs, backed by mirrors, the crowd three deep behind the stools, drunk, shouting, exultant. A deejay booth like a small fortress amidst the chaos. Glow sticks blurred in fisted hands like hallucinogenic comet trails.

Maybe it was the contrast between this exultant orgy and the Spartan regimen of the training camp I'd just completed; perhaps it was the adrenaline hangover, or the champagne, or the giddiness of seeing Anne again – my beloved Anne, who didn't know that the win bonus I'd just collected for submitting Kreese would allow me to make the last payment on her engagement ring. All I knew was that I felt the same sense of invincibility and recklessness that I'd seen in Clean when he'd gone a few rounds with the Columbian Nose Fairy. I wanted to rip Anne's little black dress off her body, to take on a trio of bouncers in the center of the dance floor, to climb atop the huge throbbing speakers and tell Manhattan that its son had returned a conqueror. It was silly, childish, stupid, and very hard to resist.

A cage elevator took us up to the V.I.P. lounge. Waitresses in silvery hot pants and high-heeled boots strutted about with drink-loaded trays, while patrons dressed in Brioni and Lacroix lounged on couches of bottle-green leather, showing the same regard for the city's stringent antismoking ordnances as they did for Uncle Sam's tax laws. A smiling hostess, wearing some very good perfume and not much else, led us to a divan whose candle-lit coffee table bore a sign marked RESERVÉ. Both Anne and Clean looked perfectly at ease as they reclined. I, on the other hand, in considering words to describe how I felt, had worked my way up to *imposter* by the time the first round of drinks arrived.

"A toast," Anne said, smiling. "To my boyfriend, the future champion of the world. May he look as good with the belt around his waist as he does stark naked."

"Please don't make me blush," I said.

"Please don't make me *puke,*" Clean said.

We touched glasses and drank. I was halfway to my chair when I saw Clean's arm was still extended, the rim of his glass ablaze with disco light. I straightened, ignoring the pain in my leg. The facetious look on his face had yielded to something else – an expression so solemn that for the moment his features held it, he seemed not merely older but vastly more mature. He hesitated for a moment, glanced at Anne, and then, in a low, emotionally charged tone that cut through the gabble of conversation around us, said, "To my cousin Mickey. The best brother my mother never had."

For just a second, I swear there were tears standing out in his eyes. This was the side of Clean nobody else ever saw and even I, who had been inseparable from him since the age of eleven, glimpsed only rarely. Then, as our glasses clinked a second time, he cleared his throat, forced a grin and said, "Even if he *is* just a punch-drunk, half-breed, fuckin' social climber. Now, if you two will excuse me, I'm gonna go find myself a companion for the evening and give you two some tongue time."

"Why didn't you just bring a girl?" I asked, struggling to keep my own voice light. "Not like you're suffering from a shortage."

"Knowing who you're gonna bang at the start of the night takes all the fun out of it," he replied. "No offense."

"I'm *glad* you came alone," Anne said, sounding somewhat relieved that Clean had reverted back to normal. "I wouldn't want to spend the night making conversation with some bimbo who's frightened of three-syllable words."

"In my line o' work, people who use more than two are usually cops." He dropped a wink and sauntered over to the railing overlooking the dance floor.

We resumed our seats. I put my arm around Anne's shoulders, which were bare despite the weather. "Maybe I have a contact high," she said, resting her head against mine. "But for a moment I thought I heard sincerity in his voice."

"You did."

"It didn't last."

"It makes him uncomfortable. It makes *me* uncomfortable, too."

She kissed the inside of my neck; goosebumps rippled to places on my body I didn't know were subject to them. "Emotionally stunted, are we?"

"Not feeling very stunted at the moment."

"You missed me?"

"Like pancakes. You?"

"So much it hurts." She tested her teeth against my earlobe, and I felt rather than heard myself groan. "In fact, my vote is that we have another drink, and then get the hell out of here and find a flat surface."

"Vertical or horizontal?"

"Why, Mickey Watts, you're a mixed martial artist. You should be able to do it on your feet *or* on the ground."

I was well on my way to proving this when a waitress appeared and set down another round of drinks. Somewhat sheepishly, we disengaged tongues, lips, and hands and sat back on the creaking leather to catch our breath. "Like a couple of teenagers," I said.

Anne shook her head, and with a somewhat superior smile gestured down to the dance floor. "Those are the teenagers."

A group of particularly beautiful women were holding court directly beneath us, their near-perfect bodies rendered flawless by the downward-thrusting glare of the disco lights, which exaggerated the depth of their cleavage and pooled their faces in intriguing shadow. They moved languidly, faces bored and haughty, meeting the envious stares of the women and the admiring gazes of the men with equal indifference. One in particular caught my eye: a shapely redhead in a short sheath dress composed entirely of silver sequins, each of which reflected the light at a slightly different angle, so that the air around her glittered with fairytale luminescence. In that galaxy of female flesh, she moved like a private constellation.

She caught other eyes as well. Clustered at a booth near the floor was a group of *cugines* in their Saturday Night Steppin' Out clothes – floor-length overcoats of black leather, shirts white enough to scald the retina, gold jewelry glimmering on fingers, necks, wrists. The restless violence of their body language told me that they had done considerable traffic with the coke you couldn't buy out of a soda machine. They bellowed for champagne, tossed cash around like confetti, and were loud enough so that scraps of their conversation actually carried through the music to reach up to my ears.

"What's so funny?" Anne said, plucking a Maraschino cherry from the depths of her amaretto sour.

"I was just thinking I could write a hell of an anthropology paper on those clowns."

"What would you call it?"

"'*Regarding Mating Habits of the Common Guinea.*' And speaking of common guineas…"

I glanced over at Clean. He had moved to the railing and was looking speculatively at the redhead, who had succumbed to the mating call and was at that moment miming copulation with a tall, gaunt-faced young man with slicked-back hair and the coldly arrogant expression of a Fascist statue. I knew from experience that Clean no more acknowledged the man's presence than a wolf acknowledges the property rights of a sheep owner, and I felt a faint twinge of unease just below my breastbone. Perhaps he would benefit from a few words of sober discouragement – but no, as I watched, he turned and marched purposefully to the elevator.

"Shit," I said.

"What's wrong?"

"Nothing," I said swiftly. The last thing I wanted was to give Anne more excuses to dislike my cousin. He gave her enough actual reasons as it was. "Just a bit tired. And a bit drunk."

"Lightweight."

"Actually I'm a light heavyweight."

"An up-and-*coming* light heavyweight, so I hear."

"Yeah, well, I'm tired of being up-and-coming," I said, looking into my empty glass. "I've been up-and-coming for years. I want to *get* there."

"Oh, you'll get there, kiddo. You proved that tonight."

"Did you actually watch?"

"I was mostly like this –" She covered her face with her hands and peered out from between a crack in her fingers. "But I saw who won. Never mind that he almost threw you through the fence. What did Mikhailis say to you afterward? Is he going to offer you a contract?"

I felt a brief pulse of irritation at the way she used his first name. Had to remind myself that her family and his knew each other socially. All really rich people in Manhattan know each other socially. They go to the same charity balls, the same fashion shows, the same five-star restaurants. They're part of a closed society, and one of the obligations of membership is constant hobnobbing. Doesn't mean they *like* each other.

Not one bit.

"He offered me a fight," I said. "On his next card, in the spring. He says if I win that one, I can sign on the dotted line."

"Why the wait?"

"He said he isn't convinced I'm the real deal yet. That I have a lot of wins over guys he's never heard of. That Kreese is a big name, but that he's also got a lot of mileage on him, and that I have to beat a dangerous young stud if I want a place at the big boy's table."

"He actually said that?"

"Not in many words, no. But that's what he *meant,* the bastard."

Anne tilted her head in the way she always did when she found either my behavior or my tone inexplicable. "Mickey, why do you hate Mikhailis so much?"

"I don't hate him. He hates me."

"He barely knows you!"

"Ah, but he knows *you*, doesn't he?"

"What's that got to do–"

"He's carrying a torch," I said.

"You're being ridiculous. We dated one summer when I was seventeen. It's ancient history now."

"To you, maybe. Not to him."

I felt rather than heard the cage elevator arrive. Clean emerged with the redhead glittering on his arm, looking insufferably pleased with himself.

They found a nearby table and huddled together in something very much like intimacy.

"That was fast," Anne said.

"About average," I replied uneasily.

Up close, Clean's companion was even more attractive than she had been from afar. Dark red hair pinned up over diminutive ears. Silvery-purple eye shadow. A slim, almost elegant face thrown slightly out of balance by the presence of two voluptuous lips, painted metallic pink. A smooth-muscled dancer's body, untouched by the sun, and dominated by large, superbly shaped breasts, pressing so urgently against the front of her dress it looked as if the sequins might burst.

A woman to die for. A woman to *kill* for.

It was this thought that sent me reluctantly to the railing, where I observed the gaunt-faced man, who was standing at the edge of the dance floor, holding two glasses of champagne and scowling. A young woman sidled up to him, smiling shyly. Gaunt-Face shoved both glasses into her hands, wheeled, and stalked back to his companions at their booth. One of them pointed toward the elevator.

"Oh hell," I said.

Anne got up and joined me. "What are you–?"

Gaunt-Face was already elbowing his way across the floor, two of his friends behind him; a doorman tried to stop them, then seemed to think the better of it and backed away, talking into his radio. A moment later I heard the elevator thrumming. I turned to Clean and called his name. His face was buried in the hollow of the redhead's throat, and his bejeweled left hand was sliding purposefully up her bare thigh. She clasped a hand to the back of his head and looked at me opaquely over his shoulder. In the dim light her eyes seemed all shine and no color – cool, crystalline, not quite human. She was smiling.

"Mickey." Anne's voice, stern as a governess, wrenched me back into the moment. "If he's in trouble, don't you get involved."

The elevator door rattled open like a drawbridge. Gaunt-Face stepped out, hawk-like in profile, his fists bunched at his sides and his lower jaw thrust belligerently forward. His two friends padded after him like attack dogs. It took them a few seconds to spot Clean, and they had just started for his table when I stepped between them.

"Not tonight, boys."

"Mickey..." Anne said.

Gaunt-Face stopped in the manner of a man suddenly confronted with a large and unexpected pile of dung. His face, already drawn into lines of fury, tightened further around fever-bright eyes. "Fuck outta my way."

When I didn't move, Gaunt-Face's head actually twitched with rage. "You don't get out of my face, you're goin' over the goddamn railing!"

"Believe it, asshole," the goon on his left barked. He was short, bull-necked and very dark, with an ample chin that seemed to be supported by a glittering gorget of gold chains. "We can do two as easy as one."

"And I can do three as easy as two," I said.

Gaunt-Face's eyes widened. He thrust his face to within a few inches of mine, so close that the smell of his cologne actually made my eyes water. "You know who the fuck you're dealing with? You know who I *am?*"

"Nope. And I don't give a shit, either."

The attack dog on my right made a disgusted noise and started past me. A moment later he was reeling head-over-heels across the floor, coming to a stop only when an empty chair arrested his momentum. The whole of the lounge was suddenly plunged into a silence all the more deafening for the blare of the music.

"Call it a loss and go," I said.

Gaunt-Face was clearly not a man used to resistance. He tugged at the button of his leather blazer, which parted to reveal the rectangular butt of a semi-automatic pistol, jutting rudely over the edge of his gold belt buckle. He made no move to draw the weapon, simply stood there, holding the jacket open, sneering. "You got a fuckin' problem?"

I looked at the weapon and then at him. I could see the clockwork of veins throbbing in his temples. His sneer seemed to have been branded into his face; all that was missing was a cloud of smoke.

"Ain't so fuckin' tough *now*, are you, you five-dollar-an-hour bit—"

He had scarcely formed the word when my lead right hook smashed into his chin so hard I saw the lower jaw slide sideways like the drawer of a broken cash register, spewing teeth instead of money. He fell as rigidly as a block of stone, knocking the legs from a coffee table as he did, and lay with one leg grotesquely quivering amidst the wreckage.

The ample-chinned goon stared at me in open-mouthed disbelief, droplets of blood glistening on his cheek. All the arrogance had run out of his stare, and his hands spread further in something like supplication. "Do you know what the fuck you just did?"

I looked down at my hand, felt a warm throbbing there, a kind of deep-body satisfaction, such as you experience after a particularly powerful orgasm. Looked up when I saw the second bodyguard had taken his feet and was advancing toward Gaunt-Face's supine body, his eyebrows pinned high on his forehead. "You are one fucking dead son of a bitch," he said tonelessly.

Black-clad bouncers appeared from everywhere. Boots thudded. Walkie-talkies crackled. I took a step back and shook out my hand, staring hard into the bodyguard's eyes.

"Don't call me bitch," I said.

Chapter Four

When I first met Anne, she was deeply ambivalent about me and my profession both.

On the one hand, she hated violence. Didn't dislike it or despise it; fucking *hated* it. Amidst the sophistication and sensuality that made up so much of her being, there was no room for bloodlust, for the primal if vicarious thrill of watching two finely-tuned athletes beat each other like piñatas whilst locked in a steel cage. In the beginning, despite our mutual attraction, she insisted that anyone who was good at fighting must also be a rotten human being and could not possibly occupy a serious place in her life.

On the other hand, over the long period of our courtship, having watched me train and watched me fight, she had developed a grudging respect, even a type of backhand affection, for both the profession of mixed martial arts and its practitioners. The violence was brutal, but it was also balletic, and as a former collegiate swimmer and a very active tennis player, she could appreciate the discipline and the science behind the carnage. So long as it remained in the cage, under the watchful eye of the referee, bound by the rules of the sport and the provenance of the athletic commission, she could tolerate it and – when I was victorious and not too busted-up afterwards – even enjoy it.

So long as it remained in the cage.

I knew I was in trouble when I woke up late the next morning and discovered that I had slept alone. After months of monastic isolation in the icy gloom of the Catskills, with only coaches and sparring partners for company, my loneliness had reached the pitch of frenzy. The only thing that had kept me from going over the wall and thumbing my way back to The Big Apple was the knowledge that Anne was suffering just as keenly and would be just as ecstatic as I was to renew our sex life. Making love to her was the pot of gold at the end of the rainbow, and I had dreamed about it and fantasized about it so incessantly that defeating Wilson Kreese was practically an afterthought in comparison. And yet, there I was, the conquering hero, my body throbbing with sixty days of accumulated frustration, and neither sign nor scent of Anne anywhere.

Of course she had her own place – a luxurious apartment on the Upper East Side, overlooking the Queensboro Bridge – but we spent much of our time in my ramshackle flat in South Brooklyn. Anne called it "homey," and when you come from as much money as she does, I suppose there is a certain charm (the charm of novelty?) in window boxes, inherited furniture, and playing that game where you pretend the intricate patterns of water damage on the ceilings are really a topographical map of Middle Earth.

Evidently, that charm had its limits.

The booze I'd sucked down the previous night was exacting a high price from me now; putting together the events that had landed me in the doghouse was like assembling a puzzle while someone rhythmically beat my skull like a tom-tom. I was still fumbling with the pieces when the telephone on the nightstand began to jangle.

"Anne?"

"Not even close," Clean said. His voice sounded thick somehow, clogged as if he'd never been to bed. "I'm about five minutes out. Meet me in front of your place."

"For what?"

"Just meet me."

The line went dead, and as I reluctantly climbed out of bed and began to pull on my clothing, I cursed Clean and his paranoid ways. Like every other wiseguy in the Five Boroughs, he got most of his cues on how to behave from watching Martin Scorsese films, and he had a strong tendency toward melodrama. Probably he wanted nothing more than to take me to breakfast and give me a thrust-by-thrust account of what he had done to the redhead while I was sleeping, but to the street I went nonetheless. Sticking by my cousin was an old habit, forged by necessity and tempered by genuine affection, and I slipped into it as easily as my leather jacket.

Outside it was gray, wet, and rawly cold; the bitter end of December, when fall is in its grave but winter not yet born. A harsh wind stripped the previous night's drizzle from the branches of the willow trees along the sidewalk and sent it sideways in silvery gusts that stung my bare face and hands. The sun was up, but through the close-pressing cloud remained more of a suggestion than a definite shape. I tried to summon up the feeling of glory that had crowned me like a halo only hours before, but it was like trying to remember a dream, and knowing Anne was angry with me didn't help.

A hulking Buick swung to the curb. There was no neon sign flashing MAFIA THUGS ON DUTY, but the way it settled on its wheels, I knew it had a reinforced frame, a supercharged engine, and probably windows of ballistic glass. Maybe a hidden gun compartment in the dash or console, too. What the anointed called a "work car" and not at all Clean's usual style. I felt a twinge of unease, a twinge that became a full-blown spasm when the door swung open and I got a good look at the driver.

The view through the rain-spattered window had flattered him. He looked like Humpty-Dumpty after the fall – or Mr. Potato Head after someone had shoved a cherry bomb up his ass. Unkempt black hair, coarse as frayed rope. Glowering black eyes. Trollish nose. Pitted olive skin. Right side of his face slashed open at the corner of the mouth, the long-healed scar exposing his yellowed teeth in a permanent death's-head grin. All of him ovate and massive and ugly, three hundred pounds of seething menace crammed into a shitty-looking Members Only jacket and designer jeans that had seen their best days when I was still in Underoos.

I glanced into the backseat. Clean sat slumped behind the driver, pale and haggard-looking in yesterday's clothes, his collar jerked open and his tie missing. He looked at me out of bloodshot eyes but did not speak.

Next to him was another stranger, a powerfully built Italian in a fleece-lined warm-up suit of crimson and black, who gazed at me with heavy-lidded indifference.

"Fuck you waiting for?" The Face said when I hesitated. "Fuckin' engraved invitation?"

His voice was a horrid rasp. I had to obey it or run away. I got in the car. It was moving before I'd even shut the door, the acceleration dislodging an empty can of Budweiser from under the seat. It rolled over a crumpled copy of the *Daily Racing Form* and lay still.

"So," I said to Clean after thirty seconds of silence. "You wanna tell me what this is all about?"

"We got a beef," he said.

I looked down at my right hand. There was a small cut on the knuckle of my middle finger, where my fist had caught the edge of Gaunt-Face's front teeth. "Because of what happened last night? He had a *gun*, for crissake. And he wants to beef with the cops?"

"Not the cops," Clean was staring resolutely out the window. "The *brugad.*"

I felt my breath catch. *Brugad* is a Brooklycino slang word devolved from the Italian *borgata,* meaning neighborhood. It is one of those words defined by its connotation. Clean was not referring to the neighborhood at all, but rather to that organization which had grown out of the neighborhood like a weed growing up through a crack in the asphalt: *La Famiglia*

"Don't even tell me that punk was with somebody," I said.

Another silence fell – so heavy that the squeak-and-drag of the windshield-wipers took on the metronomic quality of a funeral bell.

"All right," I said, my voice rising. "Who's he with? Some half-assed wiseguy wearing fake Ferragamo?"

Clean coughed into the back of his hand. "Bruno."

It took me a moment to process the name. "Bruno *Battaglia?*"

"Yeah."

"The Bruno Battaglia who runs Coney Island?"

"Bruno don't run Coney Island," Clean said. "Just the policy games. And gambling. And—"

"I get it. How connected is this guy to him?"

"They got the same last name," Clean muttered.

"A cousin? A nephew?"

Clean's gaze dropped.

"His *son?* I hit his *son?*"

"Yeah. But don't get upset."

"I'm not upset," I said, sounding extremely upset to my own ears. "I'm just remembering that Bruno Battaglia once killed a guy over a parking space."

"He beat that case," Clean said immediately, and then seemed to realize that this was the wrong thing to say. "But listen, it's been taken care of. I mean, I'm taking care of it."

"Did you talk with your dad?"

"My dad don't have a payphone in his cell, Mickey. Neither does my uncle. I went to Gino – Gino Stillitano. He's the acting skipper of my old man's crew until he gets out. I asked him to sit down with the Battaglias, straighten everything out, so…"

So I don't get whacked, I thought, and then said, "And he said yes?"

Clean did not immediately reply. He was in a strangely familiar pose, staring glumly at the backs of his hands. Just as he had looked all those times outside our principal's office. Except that our principal didn't kill you when you stepped out of line. "Well…you know Gino, Mickey."

"No, I don't."

"Well, he's, ah…kind of a hardass."

"Kind of?" Face said incredulously, bubbles of saliva forming in the well of his cheek as he spoke. "*Kind* of? He's *kind of* a hardass like…like…"

"Like Ted Williams was *kind of* a baseball player," finished the muscular Italian. "Like the Red Baron was *kind of* a fighter pilot. Like Al Capone was—"

"Guys!" Clean said, but his voice had a whining, pleading quality to it I did not like, and when he finally looked me full in the face, he was as shaken as I was beginning to feel. "Gino ain't exactly the type to do something out of the kindness of his heart, but he knows you're my blood, and he's fair in his own mind."

"So was Jeffrey Dahmer," the Italian said.

This remark killed all further conversation and left me alone with my thoughts, which was a very nasty place to be. It was occurring to me that all the martial arts skill in the world wouldn't buy me a second's more time on this planet if the Italian – who looked muscular enough beneath his warm-up suit to bench press a small truck – jammed a .22 against the back of my skull or slung a garotte around my neck. But I dismissed the idea as ridiculous. Clean was my cousin, my *compare,* the flesh of my flesh, and he knew damned well I had thrown that punch to save his bacon. There was no way he would sell me to the Battaglias.

No way in hell.

At some length we pulled up to a run-down garage not far from Rockaway Inlet called Presto Repairs. The garage was wedged between a scrapyard and a weedy lot surrounded by a sagging, rusted length of chain-link fence. A railroad trestle, its rusty stanchions stomping down into the dirty concrete like the legs of a gigantic centipede, threw everything into perpetual shadow.

Face killed the engine and motioned for me to get out. It was extremely cold in the shade but I could feel the sweat beading on my temples and upper lip. Everything around me smelled of metallic decay and engine oil. From the darkened bowels of the garage came a series of mechanical growls and then a clatter of metal. Just barely audible, Frank Sinatra was singing that he was going to live until he died. It sounded like a good proposition.

We entered through a glass door so grimy it was virtually opaque and into a front office with fake wood paneling. Yellow-carbon work orders and credit-card receipts covered the counter, which guarded a coffee machine whose bitter smell could not quite mask the stench of lubricating grease and gasoline. There was no attendant.

"Wait here," Face said abruptly, exiting through a door behind the counter. A clipboard clacked against the door as it closed. The Italian — I remembered now that I had met him once before, and that he answered to Philly Guido — leaned against the counter and lit an ultra low-tar cigarette without taking his gaze off me, his face properly expressionless. He looked like a slightly more handsome version of every gum-chewing *cugine* I had known growing up. I knew without being told that he drove a red Camaro with a plastic saint swinging from the rearview mirror, a used condom in the backseat ashtray, and a five-pound *cornu* in the back window. I knew also that the expression of cold arrogance on his face was not affected, would not budge so much as a millimeter, even if he shot me to death.

The door opened again. Face motioned me in. I followed the fingers, half-wondering if plastic carpeting awaited my feet.

I was greeted by the sight of a tall, fair-skinned, hard-muscled man in an unbuttoned bowling shirt, who was leaning on an old metal desk near a window, arms crossed, a telephone wedged between his chin and his shoulder. His hair was medium brown, thick, and rather long; his features harsh-angled and square-chinned, handsome in a menacing sort of way. His exposed forearms looked brutally powerful. It was difficult to place his age; he might have been a well-preserved forty-five or a battle-tested thirty-six; either way, he no more resembled the stereotype of an Italian gangster than he did a Zulu warrior. When I noticed the embroidered *Gino* on his shirt I felt a momentary surprise.

I glanced quickly about the office. It sported a drop ceiling with bare fluorescent bulbs, more fake-wood paneling, and linoleum floors of dispirited blue-gray. The couches against the walls were Salvation Army castoffs: burnt orange plaid and lizard-green vinyl, with a half-empty water cooler like an end table between them. A second man reclined on the plaid couch with his feet up on a scarred wooden coffee table carelessly heaped with magazines: *Soldier of Fortune, Car & Driver,* and *Guns 'n Ammo.* He glanced up at me from behind umber-tinted lenses and then went back to his own magazine: *The Outdoor Sportsman.*

Gino's eyes were gray and cold as dry ice. They took me in with little apparent interest and then, assisted by a slight nod of the head, gestured Clean and I to sit. With the same slight gesture, he ordered Face out of the room.

"Uh-huh," Stillitano said into the phone. "Uh-huh. It had *better* be." There was a short silence during which he interlocked his fingers and twiddled his thumbs. "I don't give a flying red fuck. If it's thirds it's thirds, and cut the fuckin' excuses. What is this, a charity? Is my name Jerry Lewis? 'Cause you're acting like one of his kids! You want I should put on a telethon for you? Take up a collection?"

I sat down next to Clean on the squeaking vinyl. The man on the other couch did not look up from his magazine. He was in his early forties, medium-sized and round-faced with curly black hair and a bull neck, wearing a collarless, button-down shirt of raw, pearl-colored Italian silk, a Western-style belt buckle, and midnight-blue jeans over expensive cowboy boots. The Boot Hill-meets-Bensonhurst look reminded me of John Travolta in *Urban Cowboy,* but the face was pure Sicily.

Stillitano continued his grumpy discourse. Mostly, he listened. Sometimes he fiddled with a black metal box with a red bulb that was connected to the phone by a thin cord. His voice was deep but smoothly resonant; his speech an odd mix of gangland slang, Brooklycino and business-school jargon. Abruptly he said: "It better not be bullshit," and slammed the phone down on its cradle hard enough to make me jump. Just as abruptly he turned to me and said: "Well? What you got to say for yourself?"

I stared at him. He stared back. There was no expression at all on his face, although this non-expression was a sort-of expression in itself. When I said nothing he barked: "You fuckin' mute?"

"No."

"So talk."

"About what?"

"About what? Clean, I thought you said this kid was smart. He sounds like a fuckin' parrot! What do you mean, about what? About the mess you made of Tommy Battaglia's face! Or don't you remember it?"

My throat closed. I swallowed once, convulsively. I glanced over at Clean for help, but he was staring resolutely ahead, like a cadet or a condemned man. His custom-tailored suit and black patent-leather shoes looked ridiculously out of place in this shabby old office.

"I remember."

"Well, that's good," Gino said. "It's nice to know your memory works even if the rest of your brain is ten pounds of bullshit in a five-pound box." He went around to the other side of the desk and opened a drawer, removing a bottle of Old Crow and a shot glass. "Let me tell you something, tough guy. You have caused me some aggravation this morning. And believe me when I tell you I've got enough of it my life without some asshole cousin of Clean's bringing me more. *Especially* with the Battaglias."

"I'm sorry."

He unscrewed the cap and poured himself some whiskey. "You'd be surprised how many people say that to me. You might also be surprised how little I give a fuck."

"I didn't have a choice. This guy –"

"Tommy."

"This guy Tommy was gonna move on Clean with two of his boys. They were packing, too. I *had* to step in."

"That ain't the way they tell it. According to Bruno, you sucker-punched his kid for no reason."

"That's a lie."

"Of course it's a lie," Gino said, looking mildly surprised. "Tommy starts shit wherever he goes. He's a hophead. Always starting trouble, always fucking somebody up. Except this time, it didn't work out so well for him." He downed the shot, grimaced, and then poured himself another. "According to Bruno, you broke his jaw, knocked out three of his teeth and gave him something called a Level Three concussion. I dunno what the fuck that is, but it sounds bad, and I'm betting not many people can do that with one smack. Aside from myself."

"I'm a professional fighter."

"Well, Bruno Battaglia wants you to retire," he said with a horrible sort of cheerfulness. "You beat up his son, who despite being a world-class douche bag, is almost a made guy, and that's a death penalty offense." Gino paused and let the silence eat at me for a minute. "On the other hand, you only slugged the fuckhead because he was about to tune up

Clean, who is *also* almost a made guy, and who is your cousin and the son of *my* fuckin' boss." Gino sighed and shook his head, the very picture of vexation. "As beefs go, this is sloppy-joe shit. All mushy and oozy. Running all over the plate. Nothing to stick my fucking knife in. So to speak."

"So where does that leave me?"

"Well…" Something that might have been a smile shallowed in one corner of his mouth. "If I had some incentive to lean one way or the other, it wouldn't hurt."

"If you mean money…"

"Actually, for once in my life I do *not* mean money." He downed the shot, then screwed the cap on the bottle and began to unwrap a cigar produced from a scarred-looking humidor on his desk. "What I mean is a situation by which you are worth more to me alive than dead. Follow?"

"No."

"You will. I got a goulash house in Queens called the Grind Joint that the Fairy Prince over here –" He indicated Clean with a contemptuous jerk of his chin.

"—runs for me. You know what a goulash house is? It's like a casino, but without the license. The clientele is strictly street. Associates mostly. Rough trade. Hijackers, shylock muscle, some low-end hitters. The games go all night long. Place like that, there are fights, beefs, that's expected. Trouble is, the people I got working as bouncers ain't exactly known for their restraint. Their idea of breaking up a fight is to empty a fucking automatic into it. That's bad for business. What I need is a cooler. Somebody who can keep things in line without using a gun. You understand what I'm layin' out?"

I had been concentrating on Gino's every word; so much so that the actual meaning of what he was saying didn't hit me for some seconds after he stopped talking.

"You don't mean me."

"Who the fuck do you think I mean?" Gino lighted his cigar and puffed rum-scented smoke like an irritable dragon. "In case you haven't noticed, shithead, I'm holding your marker. Bruno went *ubatz* when he heard what happened to his kid. If I don't cool him out, you wash up on the Jersey shore tomorrow, one limb at a time."

"And I appreciate that, but–"

"You *appreciate* it?" The dark-faced man, who had given no indication that he was even listening, abruptly threw the magazine down on the table and glared at me from behind his tinted lenses. "Listen to me, you punch-drunk cocksucker. You can shove appreciate right up your ass. You don't agree to do whatever Gene says right now, I'll blow your fuckin' brains all over the ceiling."

I stared back at him. If he was hiding a pistol, I couldn't see where; but as threats went, it sounded anything but idle.

"Easy, Nicky," Gino said. "This guy ain't from our world. He maybe don't appreciate the situation he's in."

"He appreciates it," Clean muttered.

Gino's cigar paused halfway to his mouth. He turned to face Clean with a look of exaggerated surprise. "Oh my God, he *isn't* a mannequin. What'd you say, Clean?"

"He appreciates it," Clean repeated. "Don't you, Mickey?"

"Sure," I said.

Nicky continued to glare at me. Even through tinted lenses that stare felt like sunburn on my face; if it hadn't been for long practice going nose-to-nose with my opponents during the referee's instructions, I would never have been able to hold it. At last Gino fell into his chair with a thump and a squeak. "Goooood," he said. "I like it when everybody's on my page. It saves me from having to remove brain from the ceiling. You can leave now. Clean'll take you home, and on the way he can tell you about your new job."

Clean stood up and fetched his cashmere overcoat from off the armrest of the couch. His face was brick red; with humiliation or rage I couldn't tell. I rose on shaky legs and followed him to the door. At the last moment I stopped and turned around.

"One question."

The tip of Gino's cigar flared. "How long?"

"Yeah."

"Until I say stop."

We walked out through the front. Philly Guido and Face were at the table by the cigarette machine, playing a hand of gin. They glanced up without much interest as we walked by. Something about their manner told me their reaction would have been the same if we'd been carried out.

Clean's midnight-black BMW sedan was parked in the back. The fading sunlight looked strangely muted through the tinted windows as we pulled out from under the shadow of the railroad bridge. The fear that had seized me all morning was easing its grip; in its place, a great, fulminating fury was forming. "Why the hell didn't you warn me?"

Clean turned to stare me in the face. The flesh around his right eye was twitching; I could see a vein throbbing in his temple. He unbuttoned his coat, drew a nickel-plated semi-automatic pistol from his waistband and slammed it down on the console so hard that I was surprised it didn't go off. "Warn you? Mickey, you dumb son of a bitch, if you'd said no, I was supposed to *kill* you."

We drove in silence the rest of the way back to my apartment. I got out of the car and closed the door without saying anything else. Clean started forward, caught the red light at the corner, stopped. The Beamer's engine made very little noise against the evening quiet; its tailpipe shivered faintly, blurring the air around it. I walked over and rapped on the tinted window. It slid down with a faint electronic drone.

"Would you really have killed me? If he'd told you to?"

Clean gazed at me steadily until I heard the metallic switch of the traffic light overhead. Then he drove off into the afternoon and left me standing in the street.

Chapter Five

"You did *what?"* Anne shouted.

"I agreed," I said. "What else could I do?"

"You could have told them 'no.'"

"And ended up dead."

"Don't be so damned melodramatic. Clean's your cousin and your best pal. He certainly wasn't going to shoot you."

I thought about telling her that in Clean's world, they always came at you *through* your best pal, but as I hadn't remembered this myself until it was too late, it hardly seemed worth pointing out to Anne. Instead, I turned my gaze away from her and looked out at the fast-rushing waters of the East River. "True or not, I have a debt I have to pay off, and this is the way they want it paid."

We were standing on the Promenade under the Brooklyn Bridge, which was lively with foot traffic despite the wind and cold. The late afternoon sunlight streamed down through the thunderheads over the River, throwing the bridge into grand illumination, as if God himself were trying to point it out to an indifferent world. A white cutter with the blue and orange ensign of the Coast Guard on its bow slid gracefully between concrete pilings, spreading a wedge-shaped wake toward Governor's Island. The two of us stood close against the railing, with our heads bent conspiratorially toward each other; the tourists and Christmas shoppers passing by must have thought we were working towards a kiss.

If only, I thought.

"But this is ridiculous," she said. She was no longer shouting, but her voice had not returned to normal. "Completely and utterly fucking ridiculous!"

"To you, maybe. To them it makes perfect sense."

Corkscrews of blonde hair had blown over Anne's face; she swept them away with an angry gesture and said, in a scornful tone: "Does it make sense to *you?*"

I filled my lungs with frigid air. Here was the barrier, the rock of upbringing and class difference looming up out of the water to shipwreck the precious thing we had between us. Normally, I navigated around it with the utmost care while doing my best to deny its existence; now I could do neither.

"It doesn't have to," I said at last. "The situation is what it is, and I have to deal with it on that level."

"But I don't see *why*. Can't you just—"

"Call the cops?"

"Well, why not? And you better not tell me it's because it violates the Code of the Streets or some such bullshit."

"I don't give a damn about the Code of the Streets. I'm not even sure what it is, nowadays."

"I don't believe you, but go on. Explain."

I hesitated, thinking of a story my grandfather had told me as a child, about probing the soil around Salerno for land mines with his bayonet. Sinking the blade into the earth, waiting for the *clink* that signaled the contact of metal on metal, hoping it did not precede an explosion. "Anne, this may be hard for you to understand, but I'm not the victim here."

"No?"

"No. And I can't act like one. The rules of the world Clean lives in–"

"But you're not *in* that world, Mickey! You never have been!"

I repressed an urge to place my head in my hands. What use was it trying to explain to Anne that it was only *because* of Clean that I had never joined the mob, or that where I came from, the rotten apples and the good ones not only shared the same barrel, but fell from the same tree? "Well, now I'm in it up to my neck. And as long as I'm in it, I have to play by its rules. And Rule Number One is when you're in debt, you pay what you owe."

"You don't owe anyone anything. Clean owes *you* for saving his ass."

"He *did*. But he paid up when he went to Gino and asked for his help. He and I are even."

"You really believe that?"

"Damn it, Anne! It doesn't matter what I believe! What matters is how the system – their system – *works*. Clean owed me; now I owe Gino. And until settle with him, I've got a target on my back. Going to the cops, the FBI, or the Pope isn't going to help me."

Anne turned away from me as if from a blow. In her snowflake-patterned knit cap, powder-blue ski jacket, and buckled white boots, she looked for all the world as if she had come into Manhattan in a one-horse open sleigh, and at the sight of her, climbing out of the Yellow Cab with a joyous sparkle in her green eyes and a smile on those well-loved lips, I had very nearly lost my resolve to tell her what had happened. Now those eyes were pallid with anger and the lips clamped so tightly they looked white. Confession might be good for the soul, but apparently it did fuck-all for human relationships.

"You had to do it, didn't you?" She said quietly. "You couldn't just let the worthless son of a bitch take his lumps. You had to step in and play the hero."

"Anne, he's been my best friend –"

"Since you were kids. Yeah, I know."

"You *don't* know," I said, feeling suddenly desperate. The very flatness of her tone, the disinterested finality in it, scared the hell out of me. "You really don't. You don't know what it was like–"

"To get uprooted from where you'd grown up," she said, in that same bored tone, staring out at the river. "To get transplanted to a neighborhood that was ninety-nine percent Italian and one percent you. To get stuffed into a Catholic school when all you'd known was public. To find out your mother has breast cancer and to never see your father because he's working eighty hours a week to try to pay her medical bills. No, Mickey, I don't understand any of these things. I've heard about them a thousand times, but I don't understand them, because I'm just a poor little rich girl from Greenwich who spends her days in a tanning bed and probably belongs on a reality television show."

"I didn't mean—"

"The hell you didn't. It's right there on your face. Christ, Mick, it's like you despise me because I didn't grow up in a cold-water walkup on West Forty-Eighth Street. Am I supposed to apologize for the fact that my parents weren't poor?"

"Of course not." I said, feeling at once angry and ashamed. "It's just that…well, damn it, we do come from different worlds, and sometimes it's hard to communicate across that gap."

"That's becoming painfully obvious."

"Don't talk like that."

"I say what I feel. And right now I feel like I can't talk to you, because no matter what I say, no matter what I tell you to do, you're just going to go ahead and play this stupid game. You've already made up your mind, and you could give a damn what I say or how I feel about it. Isn't that right?"

"I care a whole hell of a lot how you feel."

"But if I tell you to walk away, to find another way out, you won't listen, will you?"

"There *is* no other way out."

"That you're willing to take."

"Tell me what else I can do."

Anne turned back to me. Her expression had changed. The anger was gone – or if not gone, suppressed. In its place was a sort of wide-eyed, earnest longing that made my heart ache. Taking my gloved hands in hers she said, "Come away with me."

"Away? Where?"

"Anywhere. Anywhere at all. You don't know how to ski. I could take you to Aspen. Or Gstaad, for that matter. Or if you're tired of the cold, we could go to St. Maarten's. My parents have places everywhere, Mick, and they just sit around for most of the year empty. Let's fill 'em up. Let's *go.*"

"What – now?"

"Right now. This very second. You don't even have to pack. I'll buy you a new wardrobe when we get wherever we're going. Just go home and grab your passport. Think about it! In twelve hours we could be anywhere in the world."

For a moment I swam within a hallucination so vivid and detailed it seemed as if I had stumbled into some rip within the fabric of reality and transported myself a thousand miles in the blink of an eye. I was reclining negligently on a beach chair under the blazing sun, watching Anne forage for seashells in the surf. The waves creamed around her ankles, polishing and repolishing the silver slave bracelet I'd bought her, and her wet hair swung down off her shoulders as she knelt, gold mingling with the electric blue of her bikini…

Jesus, it seemed real. I could smell the salt, the suntan oil, the freshly cut limes in the steel bucket by the ice chest. Feel the sun-warmed sand enveloping my bare feet. Taste the beer and hear the metallic *plink* of the steel drums playing beneath the distant cabana. And the most horrible part was that it was not really a fantasy but a sort of preview. Anne could make it happen. Her money could make it happen. All I had to do was say yes.

I shook my head, and the bubble burst. Reality rushed in with the icy wind, the lowery gray sky, the muted roar of the East River. Rich people think anything can be solved with a judicious application of money. So do poor people, of course, but they have the saving grace of ignorance. The rich ought to know better.

"You say that like it would solve everything," I said.

"Tell me why it wouldn't."

"For starters, I'd have to come back."

"I'm not suggesting you move. Just get out of town 'til things blow over."

"Things don't blow over with these people, Anne. Just the opposite. For them, time wounds all heals. And even if that wasn't true…."

The earnest, longing look was fading into disappointment, and the dull sort of fury that comes with it. "Spit it out."

"I can't run."

"Here we go," she said bitterly. "The Code of the Streets."

"It has nothing to do with any of that Hollywood bullshit. It's just me. I can't run. Call it pride, or temperament, or just plain old fucking stupidity, but I've got to stay here and see this through."

She shook her head slowly, deliberately, her eyes now refusing to meet mine. "Well, I guess I have my answer."

"I'm sorry."

"So am I."

She pulled away from me and turned back toward the water, dull-eyed and blank faced. At some length she made a scoffing noise and shook her head, as if she was carrying on argument within her own mind and had just been presented with a particularly unpleasant piece of evidence. Watching her, I remembered a comment by Lyndon Johnson: *I feel like I'm caught in a Texas hailstorm. Can't run, can't hide, can't make it stop.*

"I swear to you, Anne, this will be over before you know it. And it won't affect us. I won't let it."

She shrugged as if the whole matter had suddenly become irrelevant. "Don't make promises you can't keep."

Chapter Six

Clean's BMW coupe was funeral black and polished to a high gloss. When it swung up to the curb before my apartment building just shy of midnight, its tinted windows reflecting rather than admitting the light of the streetlamps, I was reminded briefly of a hearse come to collect the dead. The fact I was alive seemed at that moment a very minor technicality. From what I understand, Charon ain't too partial, and neither, apparently, was the local mob.

I opened the door and, while still standing on the sidewalk, made a thorough visual inspection of the backseat.

"Fuck are you doing?" Clean said.

"Looking for a guy with piano wire."

"Don't be an asshole."

"Oh, I'm sorry," I said, climbing in and slamming the door. "Did I hurt your feelings? Hey, since we're talking about feelings, how do you think it feels to have The Best Brother Your Mother Never Had tell you he was copacetic with blowing your brains out?"

Clean's jaw muscles bunched as he put the car back in gear. "Don't get so fucking self-righteous on me. You've always known exactly who I am and what I did for a living, and you were copacetic with *that* so long as it didn't touch you. Well, now it has. How's it feel to live in a gangster movie, Mick?"

"It sucks."

"Welcome to my world."

"You chose this life. I didn't."

"Maybe not here –" He tapped his forehead with his forefinger. "But you chose it here –" He made a fist with the same hand. "When you knocked out Tommy Battaglia."

"I did that to save your ass!"

"And I appreciate that. But the one's got nothing to do with the other, and you know it. I did what I could for you."

"I don't see you sweating."

"Dammit, Mick, don't act like this doesn't bother me. You think I wanted you mixed up in this shit? I'm the guy who talked you out of going into the *brugad* in the first place – the only really good thing I ever did in my whole goddamn life! You know how proud I been, to know it was *me* got you to realize you didn't have to go that route, that you could make it the *right* way? And now, because I couldn't keep it in my fuckin' pants..." He shook his head as if trying to hurl the thought out one of his ears. "Well, what's done is done. It played out the way it played out, and we both got to live with it."

We drove for a long time in silence, the streetlamps flashing overhead as we whipped through Brooklyn with the speed of a man in a high-performance automobile who regards traffic laws as optional. The contrast between the plush, heated-leather interior of the Beamer, with its blue-lit dashboard and lingering scent of expensive perfume, and the desolate ink-black darkness that surrounded us was almost surreal; I felt as if I were moving through inhospitable depths in a submarine made of glass. At last I said: "Does it bother you at all that it might have 'played out' with my brains on the ceiling of Presto Repairs?"

"Don't pretend you don't know how the streets work, either. You aren't fucking stupid enough to go into a meet with a guy like Gino Stillitano and tell him 'no.' I *knew* you were walking out of there."

"You mean you hoped."

"That, too. At any rate, we're at where we're at. I don't see the point in you acting all cunty about it. Shit, what you're gonna do at this place ain't no different from what you did when you were bouncing doors."

I looked at him.

"All right," he said. "It's a little different. But not much. I mean, it's not like I'm gonna put you in cold. I got a guy who runs the place who's gonna show you the ropes."

"I thought *you* ran the place."

"He, uh, handles the day-to-day. I'm more of a big-picture guy."

"You mean he does all the work and you take all the money."

"That's another thing we got to talk about," he said, tightening his grip on the wheel. We had slipped onto the Clearview Expressway and seemed to be hunting a particular exit into Queens. "Your mouth. In this car, right now, you and I are blood. But once you walk through the door of the Grind Joint you are part of my crew. That means you work for me, you do what I say, and you don't give me any fucking lip. Not to my face and not behind my back either."

"Perish the thought."

"I'm serious. This Life runs on a pecking order, Mick, and you don't violate that if you want to stay breathing. I mean it."

"Oh, I believe you. But I'm new to this, Clean. Aside from you, how the fuck am I going to know whose ass to kick and whose ass to kiss?"

"Kraut will explain everything to you."

"Kraut?"

"That's my day-to-day guy. He's German. His dad was actually some big-time Nazi, if you believe the story. Anyway, he's been busting Gino's balls to get some extra help here, so I'm pretty sure he's happy you're coming on board. As happy as he can be, anyway; he's a pretty grim motherfucker."

"Can't wait to meet him."

"There goes your lip again."

"It's habit."

"Well, you better break it quick, because here we are."

We descended an exit ramp into one of those ill-lit, down-at-heel neighborhoods for which Queens is so rightly famous. Houses with missing shingles, faceless short-rise apartments, dead lawns, trees with twisted limbs, vacant wind-whipped lots, broken streetlights. The only hard colors came from the red-and-white neon signs on a corner bodega, as soon glimpsed as gone. At last we came to a dead-end street illuminated by a single flickering lamp; the houses were surprisingly large but had the weather-beaten pathos of age and neglect. We pulled up before one of them and stopped.

"This is it? Here?"

"What'd you expect? A flashbulb marquee?"

"I guess I didn't know what to expect."

"Get used to that. Because in this place, anything can happen."

He hit a switch and my door unlocked with a *thunk*.

"You're not coming in?" I said.

He shook his head. "Big picture, remember? I only entrée twice a week to go over the books."

"Books? You keep books at an illegal gambling joint? What if the cops show up?"

"The cops." Clean repeated this in such a way that I gathered he feared the possibility of the house being struck by a meteor as an equally likely scenario. "You got a lot to learn about this life, Mickey."

I climbed out of the car and looked up at the old four-story house that loomed before me, vast and solid and sinister with its bricked-over windows and steel door, then turned back to Clean.

"You ain't kidding."

PART II
Chapter Seven

"I think we all know," Baby Joe said slowly, "that the odds of you coming up with four of a kind holding a pair and an ace are pretty fucking steep." His cards were bent in his left hand and his right was white-knuckled around a tumbler of Johnny Walker Black.

"This really ain't my game," Dago Red said. Both of his hands were on the money. "My game is stud."

"Sure," Baby Joe said. "But we ain't playing stud now. Right now the game is straight and you just showed me four fucking deuces."

"So I did."

"You know what the odds are of drawing two cards and coming up with four of a kind when all you got is a pair and an ace kicker?"

"No."

"The odds are one thousand and eighty to one."

Dago Red pursed his lips in a faux-interested fashion. "Is that a fact?" His hands were still on the money. They hadn't moved.

"Yeah, it's a fact."

Red smiled. "I guess I got lucky."

"I guess you did. On account of I had a full house."

"I can see what you had."

Baby Joe drank some scotch. It was hot and airless in the room despite the cold outside, and cigarette smoke hung about us like fog. Joe was sweating the big-beaded sweat of a very fat man. "Can you see the problem I got?"

"The problem you got is you lost," Dago Red said. He drew the pot slowly across the felt until it touched the cash in front of him, never once taking his eyes off Baby Joe. "The problem is you're a sore fuckin' loser."

"I'm always a sore loser when I get cheated."

Gavin was the dealer and looked the part. He had been a pit boss in Atlantic City for years before he was caught skimming and blacklisted. This is not a mark of shame if you move in certain circles. Now he worked at Don Cheech's after-hours club, and he prided himself on being a straight mechanic. This was wise. Stealing from a casino cost you your job. Stealing from Gino Stillitano cost you your life. He said: "You think I'm bottom-dealing you, Joe? Is that it?"

"I ain't sayin' that."

Gavin said nothing but looked a little relieved. He probably didn't give a shit if Baby Joe and Dago Red killed each other as long as he wasn't being accused of dealing from the bottom of the deck. He pushed his chair away from the table to watch the show.

Red tugged at each of his sleeves in turn. Nothing fell out. He smiled. Dago Red had a nasty smile.

"Very fuckin' funny," Baby Joe growled.

Kraut had been watching from the corner of the room with his arms folded across his chest. He was stubble-headed, broken-nosed, and hard-jawed, and he sported a black leather jacket over a longshoreman's turtleneck sweater. His engineer boots thumped on the floor when he moved.

"Outside if there's a beef," he said.

"Oh, there's a beef all right," Baby Joe replied.

"Fuck your beef," Dago Red said. "Who cheated you? Kraut, you see me fucking cheat this *cazzu?*"

Kraut said nothing. He wasn't supposed to take sides. He was supposed to keep the peace. He looked at me expectantly. I had two years of city college; he thought I was a diplomat.

I put down my copy of *The Ring* and stood. It was four in the morning, and I had a headache from too much smoke and not enough sleep. I could hear dance music and women laughing in the next room. But the women never came in here, not even the whores. This room was all men and all business.

There were fights in here almost every night. It was expected given the clientele: shylock muscle, cowboy hijackers, and freelance hitters, the best of whom charged twenty-five hundred a contract. Men on the disorganized edge of organized crime. They drank too much and gambled more than they could afford to lose, and other people's blood made no impression on them. Many had rivalries dating back from juvenile hall or their street gang days, and they weren't about to cease fire because Clean wanted them to.

I hadn't worked at the Grind Joint very long before I discovered that Clean's description of himself as a racketeer rather than a gangster was quite accurate. He may have been a lieutenant in Gino Stillitano's crew, the son of a made guy, the nephew of one of the most powerful captains in the *brugad,* and delayed from getting his button only by virtue of the fact both of those relations were in prison; but he was also considered soft, a sort of mob silver spoon, and that one flaw outweighed all his other crooked virtues. He wasn't one to sit in a room that stank of cigarettes and body odor and too much Paco Rabbane, watching low-rent hoods gamble and argue all night long, or, if they were serious players, for two or three days at a stretch, going on nothing but coffee and cigarettes and greed. When he appeared, it was usually to have a drink and backslap with the higher-ranking associates of his father who sometimes came in with their crews and their girls. They were slumming; there were much classier goulash houses, but they'd come in to see Clean. He was one of them, a rising star. The rest of us were just hired help. And it was up to the hired help to keep guys like Baby Joe and Dago Red from demolishing the place when a game of cards went south.

I said, "Red, don't call him a *cazzu,* okay?"

"He just fucking called me a cheater, didn't he?"

"Joe, don't call him a cheater either."

"Fuck else should I call him?" Joe growled. "He's cheating!"

"He got lucky."

"Lucky?" Joe said. His fat-enfolded eyes were rheumy with blood and bourbon, and the sweat stood out on his stubbly jowls. "This game is a fucking science. You want to see the tables of probability?"

"Why?" Dago Red said. "You got 'em tattooed on your ass?"

Baby Joe stood up so fast his chair fell down behind him. He moved quickly for such a fat man. You have to move quick when you're in the shylock business because your customers do. It got very quiet. Dago Red did not stand. He slid back from the table, one hand on his winnings and the other out of view.

"None of that shit in here," Kraut said. "Outside."

Red smiled. "I ain't going anywhere with this fat fuck."

"He ain't going outside with me," Baby Joe replied, glowering under big bushy eyebrows. "He knows I'll whip his ass."

"Need an extra-large whip to do it," Red said.

They stared at each other. Next door the subwoofers thumped. I could feel the bass through the soles of my boots.

"You gonna do something about this?" Joe said at last, to no one in particular.

"Nobody saw anything funny, Joe," I said. "I'm sorry."

"Yeah, well, youse two don't know the game like I know it."

"We run the game," I said.

"You don't run shit. Who the fuck are you anyway? You only been around a couple months. Don't tell me you run the fucking game. You're a fucking doorman."

I took a deep breath. If I had to roll around on the floor with somebody I preferred it to be Red. He was one-third the size of Joe, and I hated him. Baby Joe I almost liked. "I'm the doorman you're gonna have a beef with in about ten seconds if you don't sit down."

Baby Joe looked at me. His flesh-crammed, brute-jawed face was brick red; a muscle in his jaw worked convulsively. Unless I could knock him out with the first shot, he would flatten me. No skill, just physics. I tried to plan the shot without tensing up. While I was thinking, he shoved what was left of his stash into his pocket and yanked a rumpled suit jacket the size of a pup tent off the back of his chair. "Fuck this," he said. "Fuck all of you."

He slammed the door behind him hard enough to raise the fine silt of cigarette ash on the felt and send it into languid motion under the lights.

Red took his hand out from under the table and reached for his beer. "Sore fuckin' loser."

I said, "I think maybe you oughta go too, Red."

Red's fingers froze along with his face. The wattage of his smile seemed to dim. "I didn't hear that."

"Let me say it again. Take your money and get out."

His eyes were a hot, coppery brown, a shade darker than his hair. They did not blink. His smile was like the expression a junkyard dog makes while watching you approach the fence. "Are *you* sayin' I cheated?"

"I'm saying you're not that lucky."

Red stood up slowly. He was five-foot-seven in two-inch heels and probably weighed a hundred and thirty pounds, but he fought as if he were still in prison. Even when he wasn't carrying, he always had a knife. You had to watch his hands all the time. "You got some balls, boy. I'll see you around maybe."

"Whenever you want, Red. Just not tonight."

"Just not here," Kraut said.

Red glanced over at him, then stuffed his winnings into his pockets and walked out without looking back. He left the door open behind him and the air stirred the smoke and sent it moving. The music was much louder, and it seemed to break the tension.

"Every fuckin' night," Gavin said.

"Shut the fuck up, Gavin," Kraut said. "Was he cheating or wasn't he?"

"If I saw it, I would have called it."

"The fuck you would have. Baby Joe had you shaking in your fucking shoes."

"Like hell he did."

"Guys," I said quietly. "Let it go, okay?"

We stood there, green felt brilliant under the lights where it wasn't covered by empty glasses or overflowing ashtrays or cards. We were all tired, and we still had a good bit of night to go.

"I'll be down at the door," Kraut said, walking out.

Gavin sat back down and put his face in his hands. "I don't need this shit. I really don't."

"It's all right," I told him.

"No, it's not. I been dealing thirty years. I deserve better than this."

"I know you do. But you're stuck with it. We're both stuck with it."

He looked up at me. He was a distinguished-looking man with pale blue eyes, white sideburns, and a dimpled chin. "You think you're stuck? Talk to me in thirty years."

If there had been a window in the room, I would have opened it, let in some of the cold air, some of the rain, but of course there were no windows.

I went into the hallway and shut the door behind me. When Kraut was working the door, I was supposed to make my rounds: bar, tables, dance floor, and then the blackjack and craps and roulette games in the back. In a place like this, trouble could start anywhere over anything, and you had to keep moving.

Although I had learned to despise the place soon after arriving there, I never ceased to admire the ingenuity that had gone into the Grind Joint's construction. From the street, it was indistinguishable from the other houses on the block. Inside, it was a miniature casino, insulated by layers of soundproof foam and protected by two steel doors equipped with portholes. There was a main bar with a small adjoining dance floor, two card rooms, and a large gaming room equipped with roulette wheels, a craps table, and a smaller bar. Kraut, who owned a construction company, had built a strongbox into the office floor, installed a kitchenette, and partitioned the third floor into cramped bedrooms that could be rented by the hour. On a busy night, well over two hundred people passed through the doors, the majority leaving most of their money behind.

Presently there were six women on the dance floor. They danced with each other sensuously to very black dance music. They knew how to dance in high heels, and it was good to watch them. None of them were black, however, and there were no black faces in the crowd. One of many new things that I had learned was that white and black criminals seldom mix. The only black people you ever saw in The Grind Joint were whores or strippers who had entered on somebody's arm. These girls looked alike as sisters with their long-legged, big-breasted bodies, expertly bleached hair and artificial tans. All their breasts were perfectly round and gravity-defying and probably made of the same space-age material as their press-on nails. You had the feeling watching them that if they died, you would not need to embalm them. But it was good to watch them anyway.

One of the ladies kept glancing over at me. Her hair was straight and impossibly blonde, her sequined dress impossibly tight. Her heels brought out the definition of her calf muscles beautifully. She had a gymnast's legs and a gymnast's ass, and she moved them both with equal ability. I was supposed to be making my rounds and not looking at her long legs and her round sequined behind. Almost as if she could feel the weight of my stare, she turned to me and smiled again. I waved for her to come over, and she did. In her heels, she could look me in the eye.

"You don't remember me, do you?" she said.

"No."

There was a certain calculating mischief in her smile. "Couple a months ago in Chelsea. I was dancing with Clean. Tommy Battaglia took exception."

"That was *you?*"

"Mm-hmm."

"That girl was a redhead."

"Newsflash, Brainiac," she said, brushing long, silver-painted nails through her hair. "This is a wig. I like to mix it up a little."

"I didn't recognize you."

"No big deal. You were busy that night."

"Yeah, well. I wish it hadn't happened."

Her smile widened. Her eyes had an odd sheen to them, almost a glaze that made it impossible to make out their color. "I bet Tommy wishes the same thing."

"If wishes were snitches, we'd all be rats."

"That's cute."

"I learned it working here."

"I register no surprise. So, what are you, like a traveling bouncer or something, wandering the earth in search of people to beat up?"

"As it happens, I'm a fighter."

She arched an eyebrow. "What, like a boxer?"

"No, I fight in a cage."

"Mmmm! Like those guys on TV?"

"Yeah."

"Now that *is* interesting." Her voice had changed, gone from playfully insolent to a kind of dulcet purr that made my forearms break out in gooseflesh. "You any good?"

"Ask Tommy Battaglia."

Her lips parted; she wetted them with her tongue and then took a sip of the drink she'd managed to carry without spilling whilst dancing, staring me in the eyes the entire time. The truly horrible thing about this little pantomime was that it appeared to be unconscious rather than a deliberate act of seduction…which made me wonder just how much heat this lass could generate when she really *was* trying.

I tried to think about Anne. She would be fast asleep now. Anne was a late sleeper. She would still be in bed when I got back. I hoped she would be. It was getting harder to persuade her to stay over when she knew I wasn't going to be there. She said if she was going to sleep alone, she would just as soon do it in her own bed. It made perfect sense. A lot of things I did not like were starting to make perfect sense.

"Well," I said, somewhat sharply. "I gotta make my rounds."

"What, you scared of me or something?"

"Yes."

"Why?"

"You're too beautiful for my own good."

I went back to the cardroom, where Gavin was dispiritedly tapping out ashtrays into a plastic garbage can. We did not speak. I sat back down on the couch and picked up my magazine, trying very hard not to acknowledge how violently that girl had my heart beat. Where had I been at when the argument at the table had started? Ah, the article called "The Ten Best Fighters You Never Heard Of." Mostly the author talked about Charlie Burley. My father was not on the list, but he was mentioned in a little sidebar at the bottom of the article called "Runners Up." I wondered how he would have felt about being classified as a runner-up to the best fighters you never heard of. Probably the same way he would feel about me working in an after-hours joint owned by gangsters. I threw the magazine on the floor.

Kraut came in and sat in one of the chairs by the table. Gavin rose stiffly and walked out of the room, shutting the door behind him. Kraut shrugged. A battered chrome flask emerged from his jacket. He unscrewed the cap, took a drink, and handed it to me.

"Thanks," I said.

"How's it going?"

"Quiet, now."

"It was a bad game anyway," Kraut said. He picked up Dago Red's empty glass and put it down, wiping his fingers on his jeans as if he had touched something unclean. We began to pass the flask back and forth. "You notice how fast everybody got out when Dago Red sat down?"

"They don't want to get stabbed if they win."

"We're gonna have to do something about that son of a bitch."

"Clean says we can't ban him. He brings in too much cash."

"He's a good thief. I'm not saying he's not. But he's a pain in the ass. That's why he's never gonna be anything but what he is. Half a goddamn wiseguy." We each took a drink. The whiskey was warm, with a faint metallic taste. "Not that I got much room to talk. I'm half a fucking wiseguy myself. I mean, I gotta take orders from Clean. How pathetic is that?"

"Clean's our boss."

"No," he said flatly. "Clean's nothing. He's a waste. He thinks the Joint is beneath him. He thinks *I'm* beneath him. Mind you, he don't turn up his nose at the money I put in his pocket, but he still thinks this place is like shit on his shoe. You know he's here tonight?"

"No," I said, surprised and slightly hurt in spite of myself. "I haven't seen him."

"Of course you haven't. He came in the back way and holed up in his office with a couple of whores and some coke. We're out here busting our nuts to line his pocket, and he's in that playroom of his getting his joint copped. Some boss, huh?"

I made no reply. Kraut's mouth twisted briefly into a smile. "I guess you don't like it when I badmouth your *compare,* do you?"

"Everybody here does it. I'm used to it."

"That's no answer."

"I guess my loyalty has a certain... momentum."

"Momentum? What, you two not so tight anymore?"

"He agreed to put a bullet in my head."

He shrugged. "*Befehl ist befehl.* That's the Life. You do what you're told when you're told to do it. It was nothing personal."

"Not to him, it wasn't, because this is what he does for a living. But I'm not a professional, Kraut. I'm not even really an amateur. I'm a draftee. The Life isn't my life, and I can't just forget that he agreed to kill me."

Kraut methodically lighted one of his unfiltered cigarettes. "I'm not one to defend Clean, but it seems to me you're attacking him on the one spot where he ain't really wrong. You wanna be pals with a wiseguy, you gotta remember that they *are* a fucking wiseguy. As to everything else, well, if it weren't for him being related to Don Cheech and Vinnie Mac, he wouldn't last five seconds in this business. He's lazy, arrogant, stupid, and fucking weak in the bargain. And yet they stick him here, over me, who built this fucking Joint with his bare hands and has it running like a Swiss watch. But that I can take, 'cause orders are orders. What boils my balls is that Clean acts like this place is some fuckin' purgatory he's gotta deal with until they prick his finger and make him. Like it's some shitty little waystation he's gotta go through to get to where he wants. But you know what? This shitty little waystation is far as I'll ever *go.*"

Kraut drew the heel of his hand over his mouth and sat silently with the flask in his lap, looking at the tips of his engineer boots. Every single thing he had said was true, and he said it all calmly and without bitterness, but wistfully, the way a man speaks about a long-lost love. He was a hands-on guy, a tough guy with good business sense at the street level, and the ability to kill quickly and without remorse if he was crossed, but he was not Italian and ran with Italians, and to them, blood was always thickest. If you were part of a crew and not Italian, you had to be a terrific earner to move up, and Kraut was not a terrific earner. He was solid and stolid. He would put money in your pocket, but he wouldn't make you rich. Loyalty and service meant only so much. It stank, and there was nothing he could do about it.

"We'd better get back out there," he said.

I went down to the craps game. They had recently added a blackjack table in the gaming room, with a real pit boss and stickman and dealers Gavin had brought with him from Atlantic City. Every one of them was blacklisted or had their markers in the wrong pocket and had no other option, no way out but to work it off here, one night at a time, and they were quick and quiet and they did not steal. Watching them was like watching the mechanics in a real casino except that the felt was cigarette-scarred and cheesy, and the Bicycle playing cards they used had long since lost their celluloid snap.

I stood at the back bar for a few minutes, debating another infusion of caffeine but opting for water instead. Linda the Bartender served it to me, silent and unsmiling. The smiles were for the customers. Flirtation was also available if you tipped well. If you had just come off a big score and were feeling really generous, handing out sawbucks for every sandwich and seven-and-seven, she would sit on your lap with the side-swell of one saline-infused breast in your face and let you rest your hand wherever you wanted. Linda had been a stripper, and a good one, but she had reached the advanced age of thirty, and her options were running like sand pouring from a broken hourglass. In a year or two, she would be leading half-assed wiseguys and their third-cousin dentists into the little suite of rooms upstairs to make some real money on her back. It was inevitable. The course she was on was as fixed and unalterable as the trajectory of a bullet, but you could see she did not believe that. No one in the life ever believed it. They saw a dozen, a hundred, a thousand people precede them into the trap, saw how unvarying and pitiless the end was, and with all that fresh in their minds they did the same, of their own free will.

The door burst open, admitting a small group of hijackers from 101st Avenue in Queens. I knew they were fresh from a big score because they had been very loose with their cash from the moment they walked in the door, and they were now very drunk and high and full of themselves. They brought three girls with them, including the platinum blonde who'd made my heart go pitty-pat. She was holding hands with a curly-headed, bullnecked hijacker in a sharkskin suit, laughing as she stumbled along after him. I was surprised how much the sight of this annoyed me.

I sipped my water and thought about Anne. After the scene on the Promenade, her attitude toward me had changed, but not in the way that I had expected. Instead of hostility or pique, she seemed distracted, as if that argument which had convened in her head that icy December day was still in full session and prevented her from concentrating on anything else. Our telephone conversations were riddled with silences, and when we were together, she did not seem to see me, looking instead into a middle distance where I did not exist. On the few occasions we had been to bed, there was a terrible uninvolved quality to her lovemaking that I had never experienced before, and nothing I said to her seemed to help; apologies and assurances both were met with that same preoccupied glance.

A sudden crash shook me, almost gratefully, from my reverie. Sharkskin, his face purple with rage, had taken a crapshooter by the collar and was punching him furiously – savage, lightning-fast uppercuts to the face. The victim had let go of his roll, and a sheaf of sweat-softened bills scattered into the air like confetti. Trying to shield himself and scramble after the money simultaneously, he was doing a poor job of both.

I lunged straight at them, shoving aside patrons with no regard for their dignity. One of Sharkskin's companions, a short, tubby Italian with an Elvis pompadour, was shrugging off his jacket with the grand gestures of a prizefighter slipping out of his robe; another, blond with a scarred eyebrow, pulled at the walnut handle of the .38 tucked into his waistband.

"Motherfucker!" Sharkskin raged in a huge, terrifying voice, his every word punctuated by another blow of his fist. *"You! Talk! To! Me! Like! That! I'll! Fuckin'! Kill! You!"*

A very pretty brunette in enormous hooker-heels stumbled too close and promptly caught his elbow directly in her left eye, sending her sprawling to the floor. Pompadour was slipping on a pair of brass knuckles when I hit him with a hard overhand right to the cheekbone that had the whole of my bodyweight behind it. He hit the floor in a heap, the knuckles clattering beside him.

Scarbrow turned toward me, clearing the pistol from his waistband with a clumsy jerk. My knee found his groin, and his eyes widened in cartoon agony as my hand closed around his wrist and then slammed the gun-wielding hand to the edge of the craps table. As the revolver clattered to the felt, I seized him in a Thai clinch and brought my knee up again, this time catching him square in his now-downturned face. I felt his nose gave away like a fortune cookie, and he collapsed bonelessly into a fast-spreading puddle of his own blood.

The room was now a mass of sweating, struggling, shouting bodies, half of whom were trying to flee, the other half fighting over the ten- and twenty-dollar bills that had scattered over the floor. A woman in a sweat-plastered cocktail dress and runny makeup crawled on hands and knees, stuffing crumpled bills down between her breasts while two crapshooters swung wildly at each other over her head. The platinum blonde, holding her shoes in one hand and her purse in the other, watched all of this from a corner with a hardened expression, as if she had expected nothing more.

Sharkskin had beaten his victim to all fours and turned on me. The veins in his neck and temples stood out like electrical cables under a carpet; spittle ran from his mouth and down the lapel of his jacket in a slobbering stream. "You wanna fuck with me?" he screamed. "You wanna do that?"

Something flashed over the back of his skull with a sickening, meaty *crack*, clearly audible over the din. The expression on Sharkskin's face crumpled from murderous rage to slack-jawed unconsciousness, and he hit the floor like a felled tree. Kraut loomed over him, wielding a long sap secured to his wrist by a leather thong.

We stood in the middle of the room, breathing hard, glancing around for signs of further resistance. There were none. The room looked as if it had been struck by a typhoon: cards, poker chips, ashtrays, overturned bar stools and chairs, shattered glass, crumpled bills, and high-heeled shoes scattered everywhere. Among the groaning, feebly moving bodies, I recognized one of the stickmen, who had been struck in the face with a bottle and was crawling around, bleeding badly from a gash on the bridge of his nose.

"Every night," Kraut breathed. He spotted Scarbrow's revolver on the table, picked it up, and shoved it into his pocket. "Every fuckin' night."

In the corner, the blonde put her heels down on the floor and carefully stepped into them. She righted a chair and sat down, fumbling with a cigarette. I went over to her. "Are you all right?"

She surprised me by smiling. "You know, that's twice I met you now and twice you punched out the guy I was dancing with. I think maybe you just don't like me dancing with other guys."

"Maybe you should pick better partners."

"You got somebody in mind, slugger?" She smiled over the cigarette. She had wonderful lips; her teeth had recently been bleached. "That was some fast work you guys did. Tell you the truth, I thought you were gonna get killed."

"People who play with guns usually can't fight. Anyway, I don't always come out on top."

"That's okay. I like it just fine from the bottom."

Her voice was low and just a bit hoarse, whether naturally or from too much shouting over loud music I could not know, but it was sexy all the same. Behind us, the dark-haired girl, still sobbing, was lifted slowly to her feet. "Look, I gotta go," she said, staring me straight in the eye. "We gotta take her home. But I could meet you later."

I felt something stirring that was not supposed to when I was on the job.

"I'd like that," I said. "But I'm seeing somebody."

"Uh-huh."

"It's kind of exclusive."

She nodded the way a person nods when they think you are doing something incredibly foolish but don't want to offend you by saying so. "Cute *and* monogamous. Your girlfriend's a lucky lady. You're Mickey, right?"

"Yeah."

"I'm Tina."

"Nice to meet you, Tina."

She smiled with her perfect teeth. "You're polite for someone who breaks jaws." She stubbed out her cigarette, picked up her sequined purse, and stood up. "Well, if you need a drink sometime, Mickey, I got one."

"I'll remember that."

Tina put her hand on my shoulder and leaned down and kissed me on the mouth. Her tongue was cool, and it tasted like white wine and chartreuse and menthol.

"Now you'll remember *me*," she said. I watched her ass while she walked away. She knew I was looking, and I knew she knew. I was shaky from adrenaline and fatigue and lust. I wanted very badly to go home and make love to Anne. Make love to Anne and think about this Tina who was as different from Anne as a wild tiger cub is from a kitten with a ribbon around its neck.

Kraut came over, a smirk twisting his hard mouth into an awkward bow. "I hope you at least got her phone number."

"You know I got a girlfriend."

He shook out his punching hand, flexed it. "That don't mean shit." There was a bottle of Jameson at his feet, and he picked it up and looked at it speculatively.

"It does to me. I'm in love with her."

"That's nice."

"Up yours."

We sat in weary silence for a while. We were supposed to be cleaning up, but no one was. "Look at this fucking place," he said. "You know he's gonna take the damage out of my end, too."

"No doubt. Now give me some of that."

He found two tumblers and splashed a bit of whiskey into each of them. We were in the middle of a small, ironic toast to our good fortune when Clean appeared. His hair had fallen down over one eye, there was a smudge of white powder on his upper lip, and his shirt was unbuttoned to mid-chest. The way he strode in you would have thought he expected to find the brawl still in progress and was ready to put a stop to it singlehandedly. I had a mental image of Custer's relief thundering into Little Big Horn a day or so after the battle.

"Hey, cuz," I said. "Long time no see."

"What the Christ happened in here?"

"A fight." Kraut said.

"No shit, a fight! Place looks like a fuckin' bomb hit it!"

"We took care of it," I said.

"Oh, you took care of it?" He kicked playing cards and broken glass and cigarette butts toward us with his shoe like an enraged manager kicking dirt on an umpire. "Is this what you call taking care of it?"

"It's not as bad as it looks," Kraut said. "It's no big deal."

"Oh?" Clean said, his lip curling. "Then you won't mind if it comes out of your end."

Kraut's jaw tightened but his expression did not change. "You're the boss."

"And you're the fucking muscle, Kraut. You're supposed to keep the lid on, remember? *Both* of you."

"Clean, the fight was already started," I said. "We just finished it."

"I don't give a fuck! You don't fight *in* the Joint. You get them outside. Then you can kill the motherfucker for all I care. But you don't fight in the goddamn Joint! Now in addition to all this shit, we lost the rest of the night. We're gonna have a light bag this week. Gino don't wanna see a fucking light bag. He sees that, I'm gonna get heat. And I promise you every fuckin' ounce of heat I get on my head I'm gonna bring down on somebody else's ass. We clear?"

"Yeah," I said, because Kraut wasn't saying anything. He was looking into his glass, mouth clamped.

"Good," said Clean. "Now get this shit cleaned up. Nobody goes home 'til that happens. Then, Kraut, you and me are going over the take. What there *is* of the take. And then we're gonna have a little chat about tightening things up around here. Shit is getting sloppy, and I ain't gonna have that. You understand what I'm laying out?"

Kraut drained his glass and rubbed his face. He had carpenter's hands – big-fingered and broad-palmed, with thick, muscular wrists and brutally short nails. The callousness on his hands rasped on his blond stubble. Kraut had told me that when you worked a shift this long, twelve, sixteen hours, you could accurately tell the time by how far your beard had grown out from your previous morning's shave. He looked at Clean with weary defeatist calm. "Yeah."

Clean stared coldly at him for several seconds and then turned to me. I dropped my eyes to the rim of my glass. I was drinking too much lately. You weren't supposed to drink on the job, but everyone did, and now I was. I could taste Tina's lipstick. You weren't supposed to kiss other women but everyone did that, too, and now I had.

"Your job ain't to 'finish trouble,'" he told me. "It's to stop it from happening in the first place. Next time you fuck up, the whip comes down. *Capice?*"

He turned on his heel and stalked out, leaving us in humiliated silence. With the lights up and the patrons gone, the Joint looked small and shabby. The staff was sullen with fatigue. We swept up broken glass and cigarette butts and the rungs of broken chairs and jagged chunks of ashtrays, righted the tables and stools, stacked the poker chips, collected the loose cash, and made an inventory of everything that would have to be replaced. The damage was actually minor, but by the time we finished, we were too tired to care.

Chapter Eight

It was still dark when I left. The air was cold and damp. It felt good, scouring my lungs, purifying them of another night's cigarette smoke and cheap perfume. Around me, Queens was still and early-morning silent: no dogs barking, no sirens, no traffic save for Gavin's midnight-blue Impala whispering up the street in a brief blaze of taillights before disappearing into the night. I was exhausted and my hands hurt and it was a long walk to my car and a long drive home. I never parked near the club in case the vice squad had it under surveillance. If they wanted to get my name in an OCCB file, I was going to make them work for it.

I thought about Anne. Being married to Anne. In the summer, we could have dinner on the patio overlooking the lake. We could drink chilled white wine as the sun went down and listen to Vivaldi while we ate duck l'orange. We could talk about the night I won the championship or the day she'd gotten her Ph.D. or where we were going to spend Labor Day weekend. We would never discuss points, or vig, or ends, or light bags, or goulash houses, or the tables of probability and how they applied to side-bets. And I would never come home at dawn nursing broken knuckles, to fall into an empty bed.

There was my car, sitting low on its springs under the streetlamp. Even the mist couldn't make it gleam. Anne drove a white BMW convertible that still had its showroom shine. Anne had twenty pairs of shoes in her closet and all the music the Three Tenors and Dave Matthews ever sang. She read *The Wall Street Journal* and actually understood it. She talked fine art like a baseball enthusiast talks box scores. Her fascination with me was an inexplicable gift. Please, God, let her be there when I get home.

I heard a scuffling sound behind me, and as I turned, something exploded off the side of my skull. Red agony poured into me, and I was down on the ice-cold pavement with someone standing over me, kicking me, hard steel-toed shoes drilling into my ribs, my arm. I rolled over and took a shot in the base of the spine, another in the kidneys. I rolled over the other way and got kicked in the forehead for my trouble, kicked three times in the face in quick succession, every shot filling my head with a great silvery-white flash of light, and my fear melted into a dreamy sort of calm. I heard quick breathing above me, the scuffing sounds of his shoes as they worked on the pavement, the grunts my attacker made when his feet hit home. My last coherent thought was, *If this doesn't stop soon, I'm going to die.*

I don't remember passing out. I don't remember coming to. At some point I became aware of certain physical sensations reputedly beyond the ability of a dead man. I was in pain, and the pain was coming from several different directions at once, like a traffic jam in my central nervous system. The pain had a surreal quality, as if it were emanating through a morphine haze. After a moment I understood why. I was lying face-up in the rain, and the temperature was not far above freezing. Something hard and wet was shoving against one side of my back, and I had a sensation of something else, large and solid, looming over me.

I opened the eye that would open, my right, and felt an immediate vertigo so powerful I had to close it or vomit. I lay still for perhaps a minute, listening to myself breathing, before I tried again. A light rain fell through the feeble yellow glow of the streetlamp, prickling coldly against my swollen face. I did not know how long I had been out, but any time spent lying unconscious in the freezing rain is probably too long. I now realized I was lying in the gutter beside my car. It was hard to climb free, because with the pain and cold and swelling, my body answered every command a few seconds late, the way a boat responds in a bowing sea. I heard cars pass by me on the street, drivers completely oblivious to my plight. The sidewalk was empty, the little houses of this anonymous neighborhood dark. Rain pattered on their corrugated steel awnings.

Someone had left wind chimes out despite the season, and the breeze manipulated them mournfully with its cold, skeletal fingers.

Several minutes of effort left me face-down on the rain-soaked sidewalk. I pushed myself upright, watched blood drip down between my hands. There was a lot of blood. I got a foot under me, staggered, and came to rest on the side of my car, gasping as if I had just done ten hard rounds. Now for the keys. I could feel them in my pocket, but my fingers were half-paralyzed with cold and it seemed to take a very long time to get them free. Inside the car, my breath fogged the windows. I was bleeding into my good eye and it was hard to see the dash because I could not get anything to focus. I drove on instinct, remembering in stages to turn on the headlights, defroster, windshield wipers. There was almost no traffic, and the stoplights passed over me blinking red or yellow. I found an old White Castle napkin between the seat and the console and pressed it to the cut on my temple. It stuck there like a post-it note.

It was getting light – as light as a day like this could get – and I could see the blood gleaming stickily on the wheel and on the dashboard. Unconsciousness pressed up against me with an insidious, seductive grace, promising refuge from the pain if I would let it take me. I gritted my teeth until I could taste blood on my tongue and breathed in slow and deep, the way you breathe on a stool between rounds. The turn signal was on, for how long I did not know. I flipped it off, tried to stay in one lane, to drive the speed limit, to look as normal as possible slumped over the wheel with a bloody napkin jammed to the side of my head and one eye swollen shut.

Exits slid past, blurry in the rain or because I could not focus. I knew I should go to the hospital. I certainly had a concussion, and you can't play with concussions. But I did not want to go to the hospital. I wanted to go home. To see Anne. Somehow seeing Anne would make it right, would make it all better. She could take me to the ER and hold my hand in the waiting room. Somehow that seemed terribly important, more important than anything in the world.

The trip seemed endless and then, without me noticing it, it was over. I seemed to have made the last mile or so on pure instinct. Now I was pushing myself out of the car and staggering toward my building. The cold and the rain made it easier to keep my head clear, to keep from falling down. I keyed into the building and dragged myself up the steps. Almost there. The door – open *up,* damn you. Familiar smells, radiator heat on my face. The lock clicked in place behind me. It was very quiet. Too quiet. Empty.

I stumbled into the bedroom. Weak gray sunlight diffused through the blinds, revealing rumpled sheets. Anne always made the bed when she left. My frayed navy blue slippers were in their usual place by the foot of the bed. Anne liked to pad around in them when she stayed over and invariably left them in the bathroom. She also smoked a cigarette with her morning coffee. There was no cigarette in the glass ashtray on the nightstand. There was no Anne-smell. There was no Anne.

I sank to the floor, back braced against the foot of the bed, and dripped blood and water onto the carpet. It was a cheap green commercial, bought by the yard, and it had started to ravel at the corners. Anne detested my carpet. One of the first gifts she had ever given me was a Dirt Devil. She gave it to me with a sly smile and a silk ribbon. It made a hell of a racket but took care of the gray-green dust bunnies that collected in corners. Now the silence was ringing in my ears. I was shaking and nauseous, and the pain was very bad, getting worse now that I was warming up. I had to get to a hospital. But I needed something else more. Something else that I thought I might be losing, might have already lost.

I pulled the phone off the nightstand and called Alton. He had been a combat medic in Vietnam and had spent years as a cutman. He had also done five years' hard time. He didn't ask any questions, just said he was on his way. Then I called Anne. She was a late sleeper on weekends. On a day like this she would be under the covers until noon. Her phone rang and rang. She did not answer. The answering machine did not pick up. I felt sick. The ringing filled my head. I laid down on the carpet with the phone next to me. Please pick up. Please please please.

I don't remember anything more. I woke up in the hospital many hours later. My vision was still fuzzy. There was a splint on the index finger of my left hand and tape on my ribs. I could not open my jaws, but the pain was very far away. I was tired, could not seem to stay awake for any length of time. When I was awake, I noticed that the call buzzer was fastened to the rail near my good hand. Several times I closed my fingers around it, but I never pressed the button. I was afraid that the nurse would tell me that Anne was not in the waiting room. It was better not to call, and not to know.

I slept again and dreamed. I was sitting in the card room at the goulash house, sitting with Gavin under the yellow glow of the glass-hooded lamp. Gavin had his head in his hands. He was saying, "You think you're stuck? Talk to me in thirty years." He mumbled it again and again. The air in the room was used up and stale, and the cigarette smoke loitered sullenly in the cone of yellow light. I was thinking that it would have been good to let in some of the rain. But of course there were no windows.

Chapter Nine

Kraut came to visit me one night not long after I was moved to Recovery. It was way past visiting hours, and his engineer boots were very loud on the hospital linoleum. He pulled out a folding metal chair from the opposite wall and sat next to me, as if he were going to read me a bedtime story. Instead, he produced a flask.

"Good for what ails ya," he said.

I shook my head slowly.

"Sure?"

"Got me doped up enough as it is," I said through my teeth. The wire holding my jaws together grated with every syllable.

"You look like a fucking truck ran over you. Know how much longer you're gonna be here?"

I shook my head.

"You're a strong kid. I bet you'll be out soon." Kraut unscrewed the cap, took a long swallow, smiled with pain and pleasure. "That puts a little pink in the day. Sure you don't wanna?"

I said nothing.

"More for me," he said. But he didn't drink any more.

"So," he continued after about thirty seconds of silence. "How you doin'?"

I stared at him with the eye that was not swollen shut.

"Okay," he said. "Stupid question. No more chitchat. You know why I'm here."

I nodded.

"This is a delicate situation," he said.

I shrugged.

"It would help a lot if you had seen who did it."

I shrugged again. Angrily. It hurt.

"I know it's not your fault," he said. "You got blindsided. But that don't change the fact that it's a delicate situation."

"I don't give a shit," I mumbled. "Look at me."

He looked for a long time and then sighed. I could smell the whiskey and felt a pulse of nausea. In the light of the bedside lamp, Kraut looked much older. The lines on his forehead were graven, his blue-gray eyes dull and blood-hooded. White flecked the bristly stubble on his chin. "You *sure* it was Red that beat you up?"

With my good hand I pointed to the bedside table, where a dozen long-stemmed roses drowsed in a vase. Kraut picked up the card lying beneath the vase and opened it. His eyes widened momentarily, then narrowed, before he tossed it back on the table in disgust. "Christ."

The card landed open. The original sentiment had been obliterated with angry strokes of a red pen, and scrawled over the blank white space beneath a new one had been substituted in crude block lettering: DONT GET WELL TO SOON BECAUSE NEXT TIME I SEE YOU IM GUNNA FINNISH WHAT I STARTED SCUMBAG

"He may as well have signed it," I said.

"But he didn't," Kraut said stubbornly. "And you didn't see his face."

"No."

"You can see how it's a delicate situation then. I mean, it coulda been anybody in the Joint. They all had cause. Hell, it could been somebody you threw out or had a beef with two weeks ago. It coulda been Tommy Battaglia, all you know."

"You think it was?"

He sighed again. "No. He woulda killed you. Besides, that beef was settled. Bruno swore to Gino they'd leave you alone, and he can't go back on that." He scratched his jaw in an irritated manner. "But just because it wasn't Tommy don't mean it had to be Red."

"Who, then?"

"Okay, dammit. I think it was Red too. But so what? We got opinions and no proof."

"You mean nothing's gonna happen."

"I mean nothing's gonna happen that's gonna make you feel any better. Look, Mick, you're a good guy. I like you. I think you could go places if you want. But the fact is you're just an associate, a new one at that. You think Gino is lying awake right now trying to figure out who did this to you? You see him here visiting? Hell, no. You're a piece of fucking equipment to the guy. One of many. If you could say for sure that Red did it, then that would be different. But you can't. So what can anybody do?"

"I can beat the shit out of him," I said as deliberately as I could through clenched teeth. "That's what I can do."

"Don't talk stupid."

"Stupid? Kraut, look at me. I could have died."

"Mick, Dago Red is not the kind of guy you can slap around."

"Why? He's not with anybody. He's not connected. He's just a hood. He doesn't have anybody to run to."

"I'm not talking about that. I'm talking about that he's a fucking psycho. He beat you half to death over some words at a card game. What do you think he would do if you beat the shit out of *him?* You gotta think these things through, kid."

"You're saying I should just take it, then?"

"No. I'm saying, if you go after Red you have to go all the way."

We stared at each other in the feeble wattage of the bedside lamp.

"You're saying I should—"

"I'm saying it's an all-or-nothing deal. You go all the way or you don't go at all. You gotta stop thinking like a fuckin' civilian, like this is some kind of boxing match where you touch gloves when it's over. He ain't gonna take a beating and then say, okay now, we're even. He'll come after you. Do you understand what that means?"

Silence. I had trouble meeting Kraut's gaze. When I did, I saw eyes as lifeless as those of a wolf in a taxidermist's shop. "What would you do?"

"What I'd do don't matter. For me, it's not even a question. But you're not in this Life so deep you can't get out. You do something like that, there's no going back. Not ever."

More silence. He tipped up the flask and drank. The grimace afterward showed all of his teeth.

"Do you think," I said. "If I let it go, that Red will drop it too? Leave well enough alone?"

He shrugged leather-clad shoulders. "That ain't the question. The question is – can you?"

The silence came a final time and neither one of us broke it. At some length he put the flask away, stood up, and squeezed me once, firmly, on the shoulder. Then he left me alone with my thoughts and my pain in the yellow-lit gloom.

Chapter Ten

I should have known. When she didn't take her coat off, I should have known. But I was feeling so good that morning, feeling really good for the first time since I had gotten out of the hospital. The day had dawned bright and cold, and I had done a hard five miles on the concrete and left the shower feeling born again. When you spend weeks with your jaw wired shut and your ribs taped, you learn to appreciate the simple things. Standing up. Breathing deeply. Eating solid food. Sitting down to a meal with the woman you love.

We'd agreed to meet at the luncheonette near my apartment. It was a favorite of ours, the scene of our first date, but it seemed a very long time since we had been there together. The bell over the door jingled merrily into the heavy silence that preceded the lunch rush. I saw Anne sitting at a small table by the window. The tables around her were empty. She was wearing her heavy black peacoat, and her gloves lay on the table. This seemed strange, because there were two cigarette butts in the ashtray. Anne generally liked to settle in no matter where she was. I had once picked her up at a doctor's office and found her in the waiting room with her shoes off and her feet on the coffee table, reading *Vogue* and singing lyrics over the Muzak.

"Hey, kiddo," I said, pulling out my chair. "You cold or something?"

She shook her head slightly, lips pursed. Anne had a very full lower lip, and she had a habit of chewing on it. I told her this was a bad habit. She countered by saying she would chew it less if I would chew it more. I found this logic agreeable. She looked like she wanted to bite down and was resisting with some effort.

I sat down. A waitress appeared. She smiled at us vaguely and asked us what we wanted to drink.

"Black coffee," I said.

"I'm fine," Anne said.

We sat in silence. The only sounds were muffled clatterings from the kitchen. The waitress came back with my coffee. It was too hot. I pushed it away and watched the steam rise up between us. The morning sunshine flooded boldly through the window without making it any warmer.

"I went for a run this morning," I said.

She said nothing.

"First time in a long time," I said. "I think maybe I'll be ready to start training again soon."

A nod.

"Alton says Mikhailis is pretty pissed off about me withdrawing from the April card, but he's agreed to give me a spot on a show he's putting together this summer in Atlantic City. Same deal as before. If I win, I get a contract."

Anne lowered the menu. She had good posture; even sitting down you could see it. Tall and slim, hair a wavy torrent of melted gold leveed behind her ears, the eyes impossibly green. She was wearing a black turtleneck sweater to match the topcoat, and her chiseled face with its familiar hollows seemed to hang suspended in space opposite me; bodiless, unsmiling, and beautiful.

"Mickey," she said. "We need to talk."

Her face was motionless. The sunlight seemed to gleam on her cheek as if it were polished marble.

"I don't want to see you anymore," she said.

Sensation of falling suddenly.

"It's over," she said. "I'm sorry."

I stared at her.

"I'm sorry," she repeated. "I didn't want to do this. All week long I've been trying to think of reasons not to do this."

My voice was somewhere inside of me. It was just a matter of finding it. At last I did.

"I have a reason. I love you."

This seemed to pierce the marble exterior, if only for an instant. She turned away, spoke to the window. Her breath fogged it faintly when she spoke. "I love you too. At least I think I do."

"Then why—?"

The waitress padded towards us, sensed something wrong, backed away.

"When I met you," she said at last, "you were different from anybody I had ever known. You didn't have anything, but you were hungry. You were so damned determined to make something of yourself. Something special, something good. And you worked at it like nothing I've ever seen. Job, school, those books you were always reading, and the fighting thing…I'd never met anybody who made less sense to me. It seemed like you were trying to take on the whole world by yourself, six different ways at once. But you were going to be something, by God. And you made *me* want to be with *you.*"

"I still want that," I said. "I don't see—"

"Let me finish." But then she was silent for a time. Listless Saturday-morning traffic passed us on Flatbush Avenue, heading toward the Manhattan Bridge. At last she went on. "I grew up – you know how I grew up. Aspen and the Hamptons. The Hamptons and Aspen. It was all so goddamn boring. I thought if I didn't get out of there, I'd die. Every summer, coming back from school, it was like I was suffocating. And then, finally, I was done. I could do what *I* wanted to do. I could have gone to Paris for a year, or gone skiing, or found some a trust-fund jockey and gotten engaged like all my friends did. But I came here." She looked at me again in remote beauty. "I came here because I wanted that edge, I wanted that excitement, I wanted to know what it was like to get up in the morning and face the day, really face it, not knowing what was going to happen, not being in control of it. Not being *safe*. I wanted to live that life. A real life. And I did."

She picked up her purse from the floor and placed it on the table. A bulky tan envelope was sticking out of the top. She reached around it and withdrew her cigarettes, quickly lit one. She smoked urgently, but without passion, as if it were need and not desire that drove her. "I thought, when I met you, that you could… teach me something about life. About real life. About what it was like to struggle for what you wanted, to earn it. And you did, Mickey, you really did. But this, this thing you're involved with—"

"Anne—"

"You've changed. You don't go to school anymore. You don't go to the gym."

"I was in the fucking hospital—"

"You don't care," she continued, as if I had not spoken. "You've lost it. You were gritty, when I met you. Tough. But you were harnessing it. You were making it work for you. I loved that. You were trying to rise up, and I was – hell, I don't know. Trying to stoop down, I guess. And we met in the middle. It worked. It clicked. But you're not the same person anymore. You're going down. And I'm not going with you. Not that far. I can't. I won't."

"You're making a big deal out of a temporary situation. A very temporary situation. I got myself jammed up—"

"You've made a habit of it lately."

"—but that doesn't mean forever. This is nothing, Anne. Nothing. It's a bump in the road."

"You were in the hospital for two weeks. You could hardly stand up for a month. I had to help you pee, for God' sake. Was that a bump in the road?"

"I got mugged walking to my car."

"You got mugged, but they didn't take your wallet. You had your car keys in your hand, and they didn't take your car. Do I look stupid, Mickey? Is that what you think? That because little Annie ain't from Brooklyn she can't put two and two together?"

"I haven't set foot in the Joint since it happened."

"Only because you could barely get out of bed. The minute your friend Clean finds out you're ambulatory, he'll have you back there before you can hum *The Godfather Waltz*. Am I wrong?"

I knew I should have said something. I didn't. I was frozen with the fear of losing her and with something else, something I had not known was there: the sudden, awful suspicion that she was already gone.

"See?" she said.

"Anne." Desperation had crept into my tone. "It won't last forever. If you could just wait awhile, get out of the moment, you'd see – we'll look back on this five years from now and laugh about it."

"Could we? Tell me this, Mickey: if it won't last forever, how long will it last? Do you know? Do you even have an idea? It's been months, and you don't know. They won't tell you. Did you wonder why they won't tell you? Because they have you. Why should they let you go? And if they do, a year from now, two years, do you think you'll just pick up where you left off? You're changing just being around them. The way you walk. The way you talk. You hardly ever used to curse in front of me. Now every other word out of your mouth is 'fuck.' What happens when you get arrested? What if you go to jail? What will you do then? Did you even think about that?"

"Anne, for God's sake, I'm not dealing drugs on a street corner. I'm not out there clipping guys. This is gambling we're talking about, liquor law violations, bullshit beefs. You get a fine and a lecture – that's all."

Anne snorted dry laughter that had no humor in it. "Listen to yourself. My God. You even *sound* like a gangster. Do I look like the kind of woman who's going to bail you out at three in the morning? Do you think I'd hock my engagement ring for you? That's Lorraine Bracco you're thinking of, Michael, not me. I went to Vassar, for God's sake. You think I'm going to live that kind of life?"

"I'm not asking you to—"

"The hell you're not."

"Fine. I'll go to Clean's today, right now, and I'll tell him I'm out."

"Oh, that's brilliant," she said. "You just got out of the hospital. You want to go back?"

"Clean wouldn't do that to me."

Anne just stared. The contempt on her face was worse than any expression of anger.

"It wouldn't come to that, Anne, believe me," I said. "We could work something out."

"It's bad enough you're lying to me. Don't lie to yourself, too."

"I'm not lying."

"What, then? What would you have to do to get yourself free and clear? We both know you don't have money."

"I *do* have money."

"Enough to buy you out of this?"

I said nothing.

"What, then?"

"Anne—"

"Don't. Don't tell me. I can just imagine you sitting in a goddamn getaway car somewhere, trying to pay off this debt. And then in court: 'You don't understand, Judge, I grew up with this guy! I had to do it!'"

"Now you're just being ridiculous."

"Am I? That's how these people think. You told me that yourself. You owe, you pay. Well, *I'm* not paying for your mistake. Not any longer."

"Don't you think I regret it?" I demanded. "Don't you think I wish every goddamn day I hadn't hit that idiot? But I couldn't just stand there and let Clean get his head bashed in!"

"Why not?" She said. "Why the hell not, after all the trouble he's caused you?"

"Because –" But there I stopped. How could I explain to Anne when you live an almost friendless adolescence, when you see both your parents buried before you're old enough to drink, that every bond you have is precious, no matter how impractical it might be?

"Forget it," she said. "I already know the answer. Because he's more important to you than I am. Than *we* were."

"He's not – he's never been more important." I was literally stammering. Her use of the past tense had hit me harder than Wilson Kreese. "He was my friend and I stepped in for him, yeah, but I would have done the same for anyone else."

"Don't give me that crap. You've been doing Aikido with Alton since you were a little kid. You know how to put a guy down without hurting him. But you sent this Tommy to ICU. Why? Because he insulted you? You get insulted every time you go to work! No, you broke his jaw because you wanted to show off for your gangster pal. I think you were *auditioning* for him."

"Forget ridiculous." I was struggling to keep my voice under control. "That's insane. If I wanted that kind of life, I'd have taken it up years ago."

"Years ago when your father was still around to stop you? I don't think so."

"Jesus Christ, Anne, you're taking this graduate psychology too far. I've never wanted to be a wiseguy. Not now, not when I was a kid."

"But you chose one for your best pal, when you knew he was nothing but trouble." Angry color crept into her face now, and her voice had taken on the tone of someone who has been rehearsing their words for a long time. "Ever since you and I met, you've tried to make it sound like he was this millstone around your neck, your mobbed-up friend, this guy from your past you couldn't cut loose. But now I think you like being around him because he *is* a crook. That he's this up-and-coming wiseguy. You like that when you go someplace with him you never have to wait in line, everybody gets out of your way and smiles at you and kisses your ass. All that makes you feel like a big shot, doesn't it?"

"Maybe it does," I said. My own face was growing hot. "But who the hell are you to judge? You grew up with the good life. You had a choice to try to make it on your own. It was a big fucking adventure to you – can I make it in the Big City? Let me ask you something, Anne. Did your father soak his face in brine every morning to toughen it up so he wouldn't cut in the ring? Did you ever see him come home at night with an eye swollen shut and get up the next morning at six and go to work like it was nothing?

Did you ever cry at night because you thought he might drop dead from exhaustion? How many funerals did you go to as a kid because some friend of your family fell forty stories off an I-beam? How many people you grew up with are dead? Or in jail? Or punch a clock at some dead-end job with a three percent raise every year, and feel lucky that they have it? You talk about grit, about having an edge. What you're really talking about is slumming. And it was fine as long as you didn't get too dirty yourself. You talk about reality. What the hell do you know about it? For you, reality is an *option.*"

She stared at me. Swallowed. Her mouth quivered for a moment. She crushed out the cigarette. Slowly. Deliberately. "I know that this is too much reality for me. You want to wallow like a pig in shit with your gangster friends, fine. Do it alone. I'm through with you. And you know what? I think maybe I'm glad about it." She pulled the envelope from her purse and slid it toward me. "Your keys are in there. And some other things. I boxed up the stuff you had at my place and left it with my doorman. You can pick it up whenever you want."

I stared at the envelope. At her hands. Anne had neat, pale hands with short, immaculate nails. Unpainted today. No rings. No makeup on her face. No perfume. She was neat, scrubbed, neutral, as if she were going into surgery. In a way I suppose she was.

"Anne," I said. My voice had become small and weak. "Please."

"Don't do that," she said, averting her gaze. "Don't."

"What do you want me to say?"

"Nothing." She stood, picked up her gloves, her purse. "I hope," she said, and now, at last, too late, there was emotion in her voice, grief, loss. "I hope everything turns out all right for you, Mickey." Her lips quivered again. The lips I had kissed so many times. Her eyes were shining. "Goodbye."

The bell jingled merrily when the door swung shut behind her. Where she had been there was a hole in the air, a feeling of lost space. I sat, motionless. I could not move. The envelope sat on the table by the ashtray. I opened it. The spare keys I had given her slid out onto the white tablecloth, along with the silver ankle bracelet I had bought her at an antique shop in Greenwich Village. There was more, but I didn't look at it, couldn't. Eventually, the waitress approached. Her voice was tentative.

"Are you all right?" I heard her say. "Can I…get you anything?"

"Just the check."

"Honey, it's on the house."

I stood up. My thigh muscles fluttered. I felt weak. Hollow and sick inside. I could feel the woman's stare on my back. The bell tolled, and I was out in the bright cold. Traffic passed me, headed into Manhattan. For a moment I did not know where I was going. Then it came to me. I walked back home and got into my car. My hands shook on the wheel, but I drove slowly and carefully and arrived at Clean's apartment by noon, with grief in my heart and murder in my mind.

Chapter Eleven

Clean lived alone on a cul-de-sac in the Forest Hill section of Queens, in a neat two-story brownstone inherited from his grandmother. The location was quiet, tree-lined, and convenient to the Grind Joint and his various sundry business interests and *goumadas*. I parked behind the house and pressed the buzzer for two minutes until he answered.

"Who the fuck is it?"

"Mickey."

Long pause. Then the door unlocked itself. The front hallway was narrow with parquet floors. Framed family pictures hung at eye-level on cream-colored walls: his father Dominic, his uncle Vincent, and the grandmother we shared. The last one was a glamour shot of Clean in a tuxedo with a red carnation in his boutonnière and a cat in his arms, doing his very best to look like Marlon Brando. I clanged up the wrought-iron staircase and found him, corkscrew-haired and unshaven, wearing a thick white bathrobe with a gold monogram.

"What the hell is it?" he said, blinking bloodshot eyes. "I just went to bed."

I hit him once, fast and very hard, on the lower edge of his sternum. He doubled over my fist and fell to the floor, gagging.

"Jesus Christ," he groaned at last. "What the hell was that for?"

"Anne fucking left me."

"So you hit *me?* What the hell's the matter with you?"

"It's your goddamn fault."

He started to rise. "Are you *ubatz?* How is that my fault?"

"If I had been there any time in the last four fucking months, this wouldn't have happened, that's how it's your fault. Now get your ass up."

He sat back down, grimacing. His robe had fallen open and I got a much better view of him than I wanted. "Why, so you can hit me again? Get the fuck away from me."

"Goddamn it, Clean, you get up or I'll kill you."

"Mickey, you fucking idiot, you can't just hit me. Who the hell do you think you're dealing with? My uncle knew you hit me he'd have you whacked!"

"Fuck your uncle and fuck you, too."

Clean sat up and crab-walked away from me until his back came to rest on a leather couch. He was breathing hard, one hand splayed on his belly. "You don't really mean that."

"Yes, I do."

"You're just upset."

"Stand up and find out how upset I am."

"Stop it with that shit. Do you want to die? Is that your thing? Because if you keep acting like this, you're going to."

"I'm not afraid of you or your fucking uncle, you gutless sack of shit."

"Oh, that's good. Call me names now, too."

"I'm through with both of you."

"Fine."

"I don't ever want to see you again." My fists were clenched so tight I could feel the strain all the way to my elbows. "And if somebody has a problem with me walking away, then they can just try me. Just fucking *try* me."

"You want me to pass that along to Gino?"

"Yes."

"No, you don't. Now listen to me carefully – wait a minute." He pulled himself onto the couch, closing his robe over his knees in a dignified manner, his free hand still clutching his belly. "You're upset. I understand that. You loved her a lot."

"You *don't* understand. You never gave a fuck about any woman."

He looked at me for a moment and then shrugged. "I can't play basketball either, but I know how the game works. Look, Mick, I'm sorry for what's happened to you. But you can't just barge in here and hit me. If you had done this in the club, you would be dead. Do you understand?"

"Fuck all that bullshit. This is between you and me."

"Mick, nothing is between you and me if other people see it. I'm almost a made guy. My uncle *is* a made guy. So is my dad. You can't do what you just did."

"I did do it."

"Don't I fuckin' know it. That was a cheap shot. You never hit me before."

"You never ruined my life before."

He sighed slowly, probing his stomach through the terrycloth. "I'm gonna stand up now. Are you gonna do something stupid?" I didn't answer. He got up and went to his kitchenette bar, produced two tumblers, and slopped brandy from a glass decanter. "I need a drink. Here, take this."
"I don't want a goddamn drink."

"Yeah, well, you need one."

I took it and sent it down the hatch with a single flick of the wrist. His eyebrows rose briefly, then he shrugged and did the same. "There," he said, grimacing. "Now maybe we can talk like two rational human beings."

I said nothing.

"You don't wanna talk, then listen." He took another deep breath, as if choosing his words. It was a feature of Clean's personality that when he was not drunk or coked-up and not talking about money, he could be quite reasonable and understanding. "You had something bad happen to you, and you want to take it out on me. Okay – maybe I deserve it. I mean, I was the guy who talked you *out* of this Life all those years ago, and here I go and pull you in just when you were about to make something of yourself. Don't think that ain't kept me up nights, because it has. Damn it, Mick, I never wanted this shit for you – and not because I didn't think you'd be good at it, but because I figured your goddamn temper would get you killed." He rubbed his chest. "Case in point! But I'm not gonna lie; guilt or no guilt, I've enjoyed having you around these last months."

"Coulda fooled me."

"I admit I ain't the easiest person to work for, but you gotta admit, *you* ain't the easiest person to work *with,* either. You got a big mouth on top of that short temper." He found a pack of English Ovals on the counter, shot a cigarette loose, and lit it with a solid-gold lighter the size of a Spanish onion. "And I gotta say, it cut me some to see how fast you got buddy-buddy with Kraut. I been working with that cocksucker for years, and he won't give me the time of day. But he cozied right up to *you.* Knows one of his own kind, I guess."

"His own—?"

"A tough guy. Something you been since birth and I never come within screaming distance of my whole goddamned life."

"Clean…"

"Don't bother denying it." He blew a dispirited smoke ring at the ceiling. "I know what they say about me in the Joint. I know what Gino and Nicky Cowboy say about me, too. And since we're baring our asses as well as our fuckin' souls this morning, I may as well tell you I been kind of jealous."

"Of what?"

"Of you. I'm at where I'm at, I'm going where I'm going, because of my dad and my uncle. Without them, I'm slopping puke off the Grind Joint floor or doing the sandwich hustle for the wiseguys playing craps; at best I'm somebody's driver. I know it and you know it. They'll make me soon, and that'll be great, but I got no illusions as to *why.* But you…you're a natural, Mick. The guys who come to the Joint, they respect you. Hell, you've made a little name for yourself already, and you weren't even trying. So yeah, there's been part of me that wanted to step on you a little, because, goddamn it, people look at you in a way they've never looked at me. But if I look past my ego, if I think of you as my brother and not some thunder-stealing motherfucker, I got to ask myself this: What if you *were* trying? What the hell could the two of us accomplish then?"

We stared at each other. His bleary-eyed, handsome face was as unguarded as I'd ever seen it. I realized he was speaking the absolute truth – for the first time in who knew how long?

"I don't understand," I said at last. "All these years, I've looked at you as the guy who pulled me back from the brink. Saved me from a bad choice. And now you're telling me—"

"I'm telling you that you're not eighteen anymore." He cut in harshly, jabbing the cigarette at me like an accusatory finger. "You had a choice back then – in or out. Now the only choice you got is whether or not you're gonna acknowledge the situation you're in or keep kicking against the fuckin' tide like you been doing these last months. *You're in the Life, Mick*. Whether you want to be or not. So decide. Half a wiseguy…or all the way."

I said nothing. It was so silent I could hear the ticking of the kitchen clock. Clean ran a hand through his hair, over his beard, and sighed. His breath smelled morning-sour beneath the smoke. "It's too early for this shit. Look, man, I'm sorry about your girl. Really, I am. But it's better it happened now than a year from now, or two, or God forbid after you got married – that she find out what you are."

"And what's that?"

"One of us," he said simply, as if it were obvious. He pulled up a leather-covered stool and sat on it. "Goddamn it, I think you broke my fucking – what's this part here?"

"Sternum."

"I think you broke my sternum."

"No," I said. "It just feels that way."

"Did you pull the punch at least?"

"Not really."

"Well, fuck you then," he said, and belched. With his bed-matted hair, red-smeared eyes, and rumpled white robe, he looked like a debauched Roman prince. "Okay, we got to look at the situation as it is. You're single. You flunked outta school. You got bills you can't pay and no money coming in. You see where I'm going with this."

"Yeah."

"Figure you'll come in with me now. Take a piece of the club." He yawned. "It's all you really got."

"I can still fight."

"Don't I fuckin' know it. But there's no law says you can't do both, is there? And even if there was, you wouldn't have to follow it. That's the joy of being in the *brugad,* Mick. You don't gotta follow nobody's rules but our own."

I said nothing for a long time. The details of Clean's apartment pressed unwillingly onto my senses. His taste was *mafioso* but not without a certain charm; everything from the lamps to the lampstands, the ceiling fan to the carpet, the furniture to the nudes on the walls, was enormously expensive and looked showroom-new. Even the bottles on the bar gleamed as if they'd been hand polished that very morning. I wondered what it was like not to wake up every morning and be greeted by the water damage on your ceiling. At long last I nodded.

"All right," he said. "Scrape whatever dough you got together, and we'll go to Gino and put it all on the record."

I nodded again.

"All right." His voice had a note of relief in it. "Go home. And stop looking so fucking down in the mouth. She's not worth it, bro."

"You wouldn't know."

"And I'm better off for it. You don't see *me* crying over some cooze. You know why? They come and they go, that's why. And as long as I come, I don't care where they go."

"Maybe you can teach me that one day."

"I can teach you a lot," he said. "If you're willing to learn. Now get out of here. I need to sleep. If I *can* sleep. I can't believe you hit me over a broad."

I went back outside. It was still bright and very cold despite the sun. As I drove home, I looked down and saw the envelope on the front seat. I could not stand the sight of it. I could not have it sitting next to me like a conscience and do what I was going to do. I pulled the car over next to a park off Queens Boulevard and climbed out, envelope in hand. It felt unreasonably heavy, as if the dreams inside had a physical presence, a weight. There was a trash can nearby. It seemed a simple matter to drop the envelope inside, but my muscles simply would not obey the signals from my brain. Perhaps they remembered too well what it meant to be within Anne's embrace. I don't know how long I stood there struggling with myself, the envelope half-crushed in my fist, pleading with my fingers to open, to acknowledge what had just happened, to face up to the nightmare reality; but at long last I gave up and went back to my car, stuffing the envelope in the glove box and locking it there. It was absurd, of course, like holding onto the rose one is supposed to throw upon the casket – but it occurred to me, as I drove dry-eyed toward my empty apartment, that I had in fact kept the roses intended for both my parents' graves. Still had the petals, too.

What can I say?

Love makes cowards of us all.

Chapter Twelve

Falling in with the mob, even when one is only doing so as a low-level associate, is so easy as to be almost without dramatics. There is no ceremony, no sinister background music, not even any appreciable tension. I was simply told to appear at a social club in Brooklyn called the Friends of the Friends, and to bring the twenty thousand dollars which represented the whole of my life savings. When I saw the place, a nondescript one-story building with smoked-glass windows, almost indistinguishable from the storefronts on either side, my main feeling was one of disappointment. Don Corleone lived in a palatial estate on Long Island; Gino Stillitano flew his flag between a bakery and a frowsy little tailor's shop that looked as if it had seen its last customer in the era of snap-brim fedoras and spat shoes.

The interior was equally disappointing. The only electric lights running in the place were the orange and red flashers on the old Rock-Ola juke box in the corner, and it took me a moment before my eyes adjusted to see the Italian and American flags hanging on the wall. There was a small bar, atop of which sat an enormous espresso machine of beaten copper, and a row of stools with mismatched leather covers. The rest of the décor was no different than a bingo hall: card tables with dirty brass ashtrays, folding metal chairs. The most interesting thing in the entire place was an ancient-looking payphone mounted on the wall, above which was taped a sign that read: **WATCH WHAT YOU SAY, THIS PLACE IS BUGGED.**

At one of the tables sat Nicky, the urban-cowboy mobster who had threatened me at Presto Repairs. He was wearing his tinted sunglasses, despite the gloom, and sitting in such a manner as to convey an extreme disinterest in the matter at hand. His only acknowledgement of my presence was a slight twitch of his chin in the direction of an empty seat, the sort of gesture you'd make at a dog or a slave. As I sat, I nodded at Clean, who was wearing what was known on the streets as "the uniform" – a custom-made Armani suit of steely gray, a mock turtleneck sweater, and a gold pinky ring upon which dazzled a blue-white diamond of at least two flawless carats; and at the plainly-dressed Kraut, who was crushing out an unfiltered Camel and was, as always, completely unreadable.

"All right, Punchy," the Cowboy said, getting right down to business. "Understand what I'm layin' out. The Grind Joint's owned by Don Cheech, Gino, and Kraut here. You wanna buy a piece of it, you got to have permission from all three. But Cheech is upstate, so Clean is speaking for him. And since Gene can't be bothered with this petty bullshit, he sent me here for the same fuckin' purpose. About which I am over-fuckin'-joyed. So, first order of business. Does anybody object to this guy buying into the Joint to the tune of – how much money you got in that bag, Punchy?"

"Twenty thousand dollars," I said.

"'Twenty thousand dollars,'" Nicky piped, in a singsong falsetto that was apparently meant as an imitation of my voice. "It's twenty *grand,* moron. Learn the lingo or somebody may whack you for a cop. Anyway, Punchy wants in to the tune of twenty balloons. Anybody got a beef with that?"

The other two men shook their heads.

"Truth is Gene don't much give a shit either way. He says he's willing to take a five percent hit of his weekly gross from the Joint in return for seven Gs up front, with the understanding that Punchy here keeps the lid on tight." The Cowboy turned to me. "You see, Punchy, Gene figures with a real *tough guy* in the house, they'll be less problems, which means more business, which means what he loses by paying you out as a junior partner he gets back with interest by having more people come through the doors. Follow?"

"Yeah."

"Hallelujah." Nicky produced a pack of Lucky Strikes, accepted a light from Kraut, and blew an astonishing quantity of smoke at the ceiling fan turning slowly overhead. "Mind you, I find the whole fucking arrangement *ubatz*. You're so fucking tough, how'd you end up on the sidewalk looking like a fuckin' steamroller backed over your nuts?"

"I got jumped."

"Of *course* you got jumped! You work the door at a goulash house, moron. Half the guys come in there want to see you dead as a matter of course. Why weren't you ready for it? The answer is, asides from being a moron, you're a *fugazy* tough guy. You don't know nothing about street fighting. What you do, you put on those faggot gloves and faggot tights and dance around that cage, grinding your hips on some other guy and singing 'Kung-Fu Fighting,' and it's just faggotry is what it is. Pure and simple faggotry."

I ventured a glance at Kraut. He moved his head a sixteenth of an inch to either side. So with considerable difficulty I swallowed what I was going to say and instead muttered, "I wear trunks."

"Trunks, tights, thongs – let me tell you something, Punchy. I've had food poisoning and shit tougher than you'll ever be. Jesus, if Gino had any brains, he'd hire the guy that beat *you* up and send you back to Frisco, or wherever it is you're from."

"Hell's Kitchen," I said.

"You're from Frisco if I say it's Frisco," Nicky said, and took a long, meditative drag on his cigarette. After a few moments, he looked at me as if surprised. "Well? What the fuck you still doing here?"

"That's it?"

"What did you want? A needle in your finger? Leave the bread on the table and get the fuck out."

And that was it. Clean winked at me as I stood up, managing to look proud and pompous simultaneously, though behind Kraut's cold blue-gray eyes I thought I saw something else. Just the faintest glimmer of regret. But then again, it may have merely been a trick of the light.

I got in my car and drove home, noting by the dashboard clock that I had been in the Friends of the Friends for less than ten minutes. And yet with the exception of a slightly sickly feeling in my guts, caused only partially by the fact I was leaving all the money I had in the world in the possession of three professional criminals, my only sensation was one of disappointment. Talk about anticlimax. We hadn't even had a drink on it.

But much later, as I tried to sleep, something my grandmother had told me long ago resounded in my head as if spoken aloud: *Trouble's like quicksand, Mickey. It's only the getting out that's hard.*

Chapter Thirteen

Time flies when you're having fun. It flies faster when you're getting your ass kicked.

The mornings were the worst. At six o'clock, with darkness still dead weight on the windowpane, the brass alarm clock on my nightstand jangled me out of exhausted sleep and into a shower so cold it sent my heart galloping like a spooked horse. Then it was down to the streets for my roadwork – five miles on rain-puddled concrete as the sun slowly lit Brooklyn around me. At last my apartment would appear, jolting in my sweat-stung vision through the screen of willows that shielded it from the street, and with lungs bursting, I'd knock open the lacquered iron gate and pound up the steps to my door. An hour later, my ancient bottle-green Ford Maverick would rumble into the wind-whipped parking lot of the Hard Knox. As I climbed out of the car, three stories of weather-pitted brick, tape-mended windows, and steel door towered over me, and every day I had the same mild feeling of surprise that even a spring sunrise could not soften its ugliness.

Inside, pain lay in wait like a spider, though the spider had different faces and different fangs containing different poisons. Some days the spider looked like Massimo Raia, who in the execution of a jiu-jitsu movement recognized only two categories: exactly right or entirely wrong. I often discovered that I had committed wrongdoing when I woke up on the wrestling mat with a feeling as if my windpipe had been crushed under a boot heel and was only slowly resuming its normal shape. Other days the spider resembled Alton, who knew me too well and could instantly detect when I was giving a half-percent less than my best effort. His poison was what he called The Conveyor, a term borrowed from a method of continuous interrogation pioneered by the KGB. He'd send me into the cage and make me spar five five-minute rounds, each round against a different partner, each partner stepping in completely fresh while my own energy guttered and dwindled. The end of these sessions often saw me gagging vomit into a bucket while Alton barked abuse at me, saying my *father* didn't need no muthafuckin' bucket after no sparring session, and to get my ass up up *up*, 'cause he wasn't finished with me yet, not by a damn sight. The spider's third face was Old Sam. A hundred fights in the prize ring, against the likes of Sugar Ray Robinson and Tony Zale, Kid Gavilan and Rocky Graziano, had set his bar at stratospheric heights. I dreaded his conditioning drills more than the surgeon's knife, because at least the surgeon showed up with anesthetic. Sam's black bag contained only the medicine ball, the jump rope, the speed bag, and other archaic devices that would have done the Inquisition proud.

After these sessions, I sometimes had to sit in my car for as long as fifteen minutes before I could find the energy to turn the key. What throbbed worse than the pain of fatigue was the sensation of disappointment that lingered on me like sweat: the knowledge that I was too tired, too drained, too stressed-out by the ceaseless pace of the Grind Joint to bring the full measure of my devotion into the gym. Arriving home just before noon, I'd eat whatever was handy and then fall face-first into bed. I craved oblivion, but my slumber was punctuated by memory dreams of Anne. Of watching her play in the surf by the East Chop lighthouse the previous summer in her trademark electric-blue bikini, a sight more dazzling than the sun. Of candle-lit dinners in little Manhattan bistros that stayed open into the watches of the night, and whose wood-fired ovens scented the air with fragrances more lovely than any perfume. Of the lovemaking afterwards, the fusion of bodies, of the particular sheen of her gold curls as they lay against the pillow in the moonlight. I'd awake with the taste of her on my lips and reach over to her side of the bed, and the pain of finding it empty would sting my eyes until they brimmed with tears I told myself I was too tough to shed.

Evening saw me descend into my other life. Unshaven and still groggy with the sleep of bone-deep fatigue, I'd slug down a shot of whiskey to chase away the cobwebs, then shrug into my black leather jacket and in a jingle of keys descend the steps to my waiting Maverick. Half an hour later, the Grind Joint would loom in the soft blue twilight of spring, its bricked-over windows staring like sightless eyes. Looking at it, sometimes the reality of my situation hit me over the head like a hammerfist. What the fuck had I gotten myself into? How the fuck was I ever going to get out of it? But these thoughts were fleeting. The pain of losing Anne was always there, ready to break over me like a storm in any moment of calm, and so I pushed open the scuffed steel door and entered the place where chaos took the throne.

The Joint had no fixed hours. Sometimes the games wound down of their own accord by one or two in the morning; sometimes they were still going strong when the first muted rays of dawn shone dusty yellow on the railings of the Clearview Expressway. Either way, I was bound to stay until the last spin of the roulette wheel. On the nights when my head hit the pillow by three in the morning, I was a lucky man indeed. But always the hateful alarm clock by my bedside waited patiently, yet another spider in the endless web that my life had become. I didn't know precisely how much sleep a man needed to live, but I did know how much I needed to function properly, and I was many hours short of that minimum.

Meanwhile, the day of the fight was fast approaching. I did a little promotional work, mainly telephone interviews conducted in my car on the way home from the gym or on my way to the Joint, but I didn't have a lot to tell the reporters. I knew very little about my opponent, a Russian who had spent his whole career fighting overseas, except that he was undefeated. Alton was distressed at this lack of intelligence, which made it very hard to draft a strategy of the sort we'd used to get the best of Wilson Kreese, and was reduced to trolling the Internet for fragments of information. I, however, couldn't afford to brood. Early in my career, I'd often heard the bolt on the cage door slide home with scarcely any more knowledge of my adversary than his name, and while there was considerably more at stake now than there had been back then, nothing else had changed. When the buzzer sounded, this Dem'yen Draganovich Suba would try to take my head off the same as the twenty-seven fighters who had preceded him, and if past was prologue, end up face-down on the mat for his trouble.

Yeah, I'd beat this Russian – or Ukrainian, or Hungarian, or whatever the hell he was – and send him back behind the rusty-ass Iron Curtain to lick his wounds and wonder what the hell went wrong. Mikhailis Morganstern would appear, holding the contract and a Cross pen, and I'd scratch my name upon it and for the first time in my life, know the pipe-wielding landlord was at bay – not just this month or next month, but forever. And Anne? She'd realize she'd been wrong about me, that what went on at the Grind Joint didn't define who I was, didn't even matter, because it was temporary and we were still young and had the whole rest of our lives ahead of us.

A week before the fight, one of Morganstern's people invited me, or perhaps I should say *instructed* me, to appear at a press conference conducted at a steak house in Manhattan called Sperazza's. When I arrived, during a spectacular summer thunderstorm that saw torrents of rain falling through columns of steamy gold sunlight, I reflected briefly on a series of ironies. In my early childhood, Sperazza's had been the scene of an infamous triple murder which had wiped out the "Administration" of a certain New York Mafia Family – boss, underboss, and *consiglieri.* One of the men who had reputedly engineered that massacre was Clean's uncle, Dominic "Don Cheech" Immaculata, who had controlling interest in the Grind Joint and was therefore not merely my business partner, but, in the grandiose pyramid scheme that was the *brugad,* my boss. It was true that I was only a low-level associate, on the fringe of the fringe, and about as much an actual part of the mob as the guy who catered Sonny Corleone's wedding; but that would make little difference if my involvement ever hit the sports papers. Morganstern, ever sensitive to public ridicule, would have my contract in the shredder before he finished the article. Assuming I had one to shred. If I didn't…well, that's what blacklists were for.

Dem'yan Suba wasn't there. Apparently some hang-up with his visa had delayed his entry into the country until a day or so before the show. I was disappointed; staredowns are silly and discomfiting, especially when a blaze of igniting flashbulbs makes it virtually impossible not to blink, but they have the benefit of letting you see the enemy up close. See how he carries himself, how he moves, whether he's cool or pugnacious, whether there is fear or doubt shallowing in his eyes. I'd have none of that information, which added a dollop of fuck-all to the six-course serving of jack-shit that I knew about the man.

I spoke briefly with Mikhailis. The heavy-boned features of his face were as closed as a poker player's, his manners languid and leonine as ever, but something in his gaze made me uneasy. It was not hostile; rather it seemed amused somehow, as if its owner were in on a private joke. Several times during the press conference I caught him glimpsing at me with that same self-satisfied sparkle in his eyes. What was it that he knew that I didn't?

Driving home, I told myself that it didn't matter. Eating my solitary dinner, washing down boiled broccoli and boiled chicken with distilled water, I told myself that it didn't matter. Lying in bed that night, listening to the breeze shake rain from the willows outside, I told myself that it didn't matter. And it went on not mattering even when I rose, even when I hastened into my clothes and snatched my car keys from the hall stand and bounced into my Maverick. Its not-mattering was unbroken all through the drive over the Manhattan Bridge into the City, and remained intact and solid as I climbed the FDR parkway north to the Upper East Side. For a long time, Manhattan was a solid wall of light to my left, the Con-Ed building a towering brickwork under huge stovepipe chimneys; then at last, the architecture began to change, become heavier, more baroque, more imposing. By the time I hit the 60s, it was as if I could smell money in the air, blowing through my half-opened windows along with the more-familiar scent of the East River. I had arrived in Anne-country.

She lived in a historicist building on East Sixty-Third Street, one of those places where the doorman wore a peaked cap and gold braid and aiguillettes that swung imperiously when he lifted his white-gloved hand to hail a taxi, and he guarded his marble-floored lobby like a dragon. If I'd paused my car within sight of the awning, he'd undoubtedly have been on the phone to the NYPD within seconds, so I passed it and parked illegally in a construction zone two blocks to the south. It was a warm night, and extremely quiet; the light of the streetlamps reflected in still-watered puddles along the street. I felt as if I were acting out a part in a bad movie; all that was missing was the obligatory cigarette. And yet I was exhausted enough, mentally and physically, not to question the silliness of what I was doing; events seemed to be unfolding with the peculiar but unarguable logic of a dream.

I waited for what seemed like ages. The grimy clock on the dashboard ticked off the hours; the radio murmured indistinct blues. Sometimes a deejay with a deep, slightly rusty voice came on to speak in the intimate way of late-night deejays, who know they are preaching to an audience of lovelorn insomniacs and sticky-eyed security guards and cab drivers with aching backs. I fell asleep once and awoke to the sound of rain hitting the corrugated metal covering the walkway beside me. It was five o'clock in the morning, and I felt that if I climbed out of the car and stretched, the sound of my vertebrae cracking would shatter every window on the block. I wanted my bed like a prisoner wants parole, and yet something rooted me in place. I felt that whatever I had come here to see was going to happen soon.

And it did. As the darkness began to soften into something that was not light but the anticipation of it, headlights glared to a stop beneath the portico of Anne's building. After a few seconds of blinking, I made out the shape of an enormous limousine, its black metal skin polished to such a gloss that it looked to have been carved out of a single piece of dark radium. The driver got out, clutching a swift hand to his cap as a sudden gust howled down the canyoned street. He wore the traditional black suit of the limo driver, but his movements had a hard purpose I had come to recognize after years in the fight game and months in the Grind Joint. If he hadn't served years in the military or in law enforcement, or come up on streets hard enough to shatter the ordinary man, then I was Frank Sinatra's ghost.

As he came around the vehicle to open the passenger door, the entrance to Anne's building swung open, and the doorman emerged, his coattails flapping in the wind. His manner was so servile that he appeared to be resisting an urge to genuflect. There was a small pause, and a tall, powerfully-built figure stepped out of the building and onto the sidewalk. He wore a rumpled-looking suit and his white shirt was open at the collar as if only partially buttoned. He took a deep breath, as if relishing the damp and the early-morning air, and then he climbed inside the limousine. In a few moments it was gliding up the street and gone.

I sat there unmoving, watching individual drops of rain crawl down my windshield, for only God knew how long. Pain filled my jaws where my teeth clenched against one-another hard enough to crack the enamel. Pain filled my hands where they clenched on the steering wheel as if to tear it from its moorings. Pain filled my heart like the blood that was pumping madly, furiously into every chamber, threatening to explode it within my chest, because I had just seen Mikhailis Morganstern leaving Anne's apartment, and I had discovered something else:

It mattered.

It mattered a whole hell of a lot.

Chapter Fourteen

"I don't know what your problem is, boy, but you better get your shit together," Alton shouted. "There's a man out there who wants to take your muthafuckin' head off!"

"I'm fine," I said.

"You don't *look* fine," Old Sam chimed in. He was leaning against the doorway with his arms folded, disapproval etched into each of the innumerable lines that composed his ancient face. "You *look* like something fell out o' my ass."

"I'm fine," I repeated dully. "Let's go out and do this."

We were in the dressing room in Atlantic City – myself, Alton, Old Sam, and Massimo. On the surface, it all looked normal. Alton had his post-fight victory cigars in a zippered pouch on his hip, Massimo had followed his good-luck ritual of avoiding a razor blade for a week before the fight, and Sam was wearing his old-school silk cornerman's jacket, billiard white with red trim. I was dripping with sweat from the warm-up, my fists enclosed in their four-ounce gloves, the tape on the wrists bearing the signature of the rep from the Athletic Commission. When I looked in the long mirror on the wall, I saw the same two hundred and five pounds of Irish-Italian badass I had always seen staring back at me. Nothing had changed.

But nothing was the same, either.

We went out into the hallway. All at once I could hear the crowd roaring, a muted but savage sound, like a dog growling through a muzzle. I put my head down against the glare of the cameras waiting for me and made my way towards the noise. The hallway seemed very crowded. There were security people from the venue in sober-looking maroon blazers, police officers who had polished their badges and boots just for the occasion, officious-looking men from the State Athletic Commission who wore laminated identification tags over their neckties, and some beautiful young women of the backstage-pass variety who cheered and whistled when I passed by, even though it was dollars to donuts they didn't know who the fuck I was and couldn't have cared less. Reflected glory is still glory.

The roar was getting louder. The chilly concrete hallway was an echo-chamber en route to a slaughterhouse, and I was about to hit the killing floor.

I entered the stadium. The arena. The asylum. The crowd pressed close on either side, faces frantic, hands waving, overfilled cups spilling overpriced beers on the bleacher seats. Ten thousand of them. Screaming. Spotlights, blinding bright and scalding hot, fell upon me with an animatronic *snap*. My entrance music began to blast over the stadium speakers, and I waited for the adrenaline. There had been times when the music, the roar of the audience, the blaze of light and the hot surge in my guts seemed to lift me clear of the earth and into the cage. And why not? This was *my* time. The fuse that had been smoldering so maddeningly for months, all through the torture of training, had burned down to the critical point, the last eighth of an inch before fire hit powder. I'd earned that moment of release, of complete abandon, where the weight of my world slipped from my shoulders, and I was free to be what I truly was. Fighter. Warrior. Gladiator.

But nothing happened. I wasn't Rocky Marciano or Shaka Zulu or Spartacus, just plain ol' Mickey Watts, eyes stung from lack of sleep, cheeks hollowed by resolute starving, T-shirt plastered to my chest by dressing-room calisthenics. My brain brimmed with dangerous knowledge and my reflexes were honed to a killing edge, but the heart that moved them beat at a pedestrian rhythm. I wasn't exhilarated. I wasn't scared. Near as I could tell, I wasn't anything at all.

Down the ramp I went, the security people like a guard of honor, the outstretched hands of fans thrusting over their shoulders, hoping for a high-five from yours truly. Not tonight. Tonight the faces attached to those hands repulsed me. Goddamn bloodthirsty freaks, inflamed by beer and bloodlust, delirious almost to the point of orgasm. They might as well have been wearing laurels in their hair and screaming in Latin to bring out the lions. Instead, I focused on the cage. A septagon shape, thirty feet across, at the center of a great web of glaring vary-colored light. The cages of the Cage Combat League were of the very best quality: the padding was durable and thick, the chain-link coated in plastic, the mats clean and without pucker or fold. Not like the venues I'd come up in: old boxing rings with tape-shod turnbuckles, sagging ropes, and canvas soaked with blood. Such things would never happen while Mikhailis Morganstern was in charge. He was a fanatic about quality. Everything had to be the best. The fighters in his League. The shirts on his back. The jewelry on his fingers.

The women in his bed.

A cage always looks vastly larger from within than it does from without; at least until they lock the door. I took a quick jog around the perimeter, not so much to conduct reconnaissance as to lay claim to the space, to mark the whole fighting surface as my own. My turf, my territory, my house. My team surrounded me like a wolf pack grooming their baron before the hunt, murmuring encouragement, examining the thickness of the grease on my face, making needless little adjustments to my gloves. Normally it was comforting, but not tonight. Insincerity shallowed in their eyes. They knew my preparation had been weak, undercut by the endless hours I'd put into the Grind Joint and by the far more devastating blow of Anne's departure. They knew as well that Dem'yan Suba was a ringer, specially imported by Morganstern to defeat me. This was nothing we'd been told in so many words; it was simply the conclusion Alton had reached after pressing his vast network of connections in the fight game for information: *This Ruski -- he ain't a fighter, he's an assassin. And you're the target.*

I searched the front rows surrounding the cage, quickly spotted Mikhailis, his shaven head agleam in the overhead lights. Wondered if he kept a pocket version of *The Prince* on Anne's nightstand. Wondered if he was writing his own companion volume, *The Methodology of Machination.* Wondered if he'd still give me a contract if, after winning this fight, I elected to knock out the majority of his front teeth.

My music died away. There was a short pause, during which the crowd grew restless with anticipation, and then a fresh song broke out over the speakers. The lyrics were in Russian, and they had a harsh resonance that set my eardrums ringing. Across the stadium floor I saw a ripple of commotion at the opposing entrance, a cluster of heads bobbing slowly toward me. I couldn't make out Suba from his entourage, and didn't try very hard. Whatever he looked like, he'd be unrecognizable when I introduced my fists to his face.

The announcer was making the introductions, but I made a show of turning away and staring resolutely into the audience as I shook out my fists. Normally I was all in favor of sportsmanship, but this had ceased to be an athletic event a long time ago. There was too much at stake, and dear old Mikhailis kept upping the ante. This chip here was the contract. That one was a title shot. Over here was six figures' worth of endorsement money. And this? Why, that was nothing less than the woman I loved.

Was she watching now? The thought smoldered in my brain, refusing to extinguish itself. I'd first met Anne when I was fighting under bare bulbs in meatpacking halls for less money than I needed to get stitched up afterward. She'd been with me almost my whole professional career. How many times had we talked about what we'd do, where we'd go to celebrate, when I finally had the title belt cinched around my waist?

Sam barked something at me, hard enough to nearly dislodge his upper plate; he settled it back in place with a look of reproach in his rheumy old eyes. I realized that the crowd was cheering for me and belatedly lifted a fist in acknowledgement. Daydreaming now, of all goddamn times. Got to get my heart pumping, put mind and nerve and muscle together. Because everything I worked for, slaved for, fought for, bled for, is on the pass line *now,* and the dice are in my hand.

I turned around and saw the Russian for the first time. He was several inches taller than myself, clad in the abbreviated fighting shorts the Europeans seemed to prefer, the sort that look like 40s-era swim trunks. He was staring at his gloved hands with a cold, somewhat disinterested expression, and as he examined them I examined him.

Thick blond hair, darkened by warm-up sweat. Boyish features with a dimpled chin. An oddly functional build, not unlike my own – muscle-heavy in the shoulders, thighs like a hockey player, nothing on that frame that didn't need to be. Skin pinkish, hairless, tattooed on the elbows, the insides of the forearms, the backs of his triceps, on both knees, full of arcane symbols, glyphs, runes, words in Cyrillic and Latin, a growling tiger on his shin.

The referee called seconds out, motioned us to the center of the cage. For the first time, my gaze met that of my opponent. His eyes were heavy-lidded and gray and held about as much warmth as an Antarctic landscape, but there was no hostility in them. He seemed calm almost to the point of boredom, and his expression kindled the first real emotion I'd felt all day: anger. You're in the cage with Mickey *Watts,* motherfucker, and you look like a jock listening to a lecture on Keynesian economics. We'll see how bored you are when I plug the dimple on that chin with my fist.

We touched gloves, the first contact, and then I was backing up against my side of the cage and he to his. My perceptions were closing down; I could no longer feel the heat of the lights or hear the crowd or see the glare of the Jumbotrons mounted throughout the stadium. The world was contracting, falling in on itself like black hole, until nothing remained but the white-floored cage and the two men who stood upon it, waiting.

We didn't wait long.

The referee, standing center-cage, brought his palms together, and I was moving forward, chin down, fists up. I had no special stratagem for dealing with Suba, no elaborate ruse to fatten his confidence or short circuit his fighting style. I hardly knew what his fighting style was. Ah, well. Sometimes *gladiator in arena consilium capit!*

I was gonna have to wing it.

Suba came out in an odd stance, right hand cocked, left down by his hip, and advanced with his body half-turned, like a giant crab. His face was still composed, but the eyes within it burned with unnatural intensity as he circled around to my left – away from my power hand. Curse of having half your fights on the World Wide Web; *he* knew precisely who he was dealing with.

I decided to set the tone of the fight right then and there. I took a couple of running steps and sprang off the mat, directing my knee at his chin as if it were a battering ram. It was a beautiful move, perfectly executed with almost no warning, and I was still admiring my technique when I realized that his chin was no longer where I wanted it to be. I hit the fence with the shivery metallic clang and spun around to find Suba blurring towards me, fist whistling at my head, and it was only muscle memory, years and years in the same boxing gyms that had stamped out my father and grandfather, that allowed me to take it on the ear and not the cheekbone. The impact was a painless explosion, like a balloon filled with warm water, and I stumbled sideways, turned the stumble into a summersault, came up on my heels and whirled, fists clenched and a grin on my face. Takes more than *that,* comrade.

He resumed his circle to my left, and now I circled the other way, ear throbbing, looking hard for an opening. He kept his left hand very low; as bait, or because he thought his reflexes were too fast for anyone to exploit the position. I decided to test that theory with a Superman punch and grinned again when I felt the sweet jolt of his jaw against my knuckles. But no sooner had my feet hit the mat with a thud than his right hand blurred in an uppercut that caught me flush. My knees buckled, and to my horror, I felt his hands close around my neck in a Muay Thai clinch. Instinctively, I crossed my arms tightly across my chest, just in time to block the left knee, right knee combination he'd launched. But there was no time for self-congratulation; before I knew it, he'd changed his grip and suddenly my feet jerked clean off the canvas as if someone had kicked out the bucket upon which they stood, and I was sailing clean over his hip and hitting the mat with a thud that must have rippled the water in Hudson Bay.

I was grateful, as I turned the momentum into a roll, that the first thing they teach in you in martial arts is how to fall and that Suba seemed to have no desire to follow up on his attack. But that gratitude occupied only ten percent of my mind; the rest was blazing with humiliated fury that I'd been caught by a throw any first year judoka could have avoided.

I sprang to my feet and came at him, firing a series of hard left jabs at his mouth. He slapped them aside as I expected him to, his eyes narrowing at my cocked right, and as they did, I turned the fifth jab into lead left hook that caught him flush on the ribs. His grunt of pain and surprise filled me with malicious joy. I came forward again, looking to follow up, but his long right leg lashed out, trident against my dagger, and caught me low on the thigh. Pain extended from the impact point like the rays of a comet, and I had to bite down hard against my mouthpiece to keep my face from showing it. I jumped in and swung a wild right at his jaw, saw it crash instead on the rolling muscles of his left shoulder. Classic boxing technique. He countered with a short right that found a home on my lips, and now for the first time, I tasted blood along with molded plastic in my mouth.

The next few minutes were more of the same, a Möbius loop of frustration and pain. He was the tallest man I'd ever fought, and his footwork was excellent; no matter how quickly I moved, he always seemed to lay just outside my shooting range and just within his own. Again and again I pressed in, my fists aching with unsatisfied lust; again and again he flung his foot or shin at the muscles of my thigh. Sometimes the kicks landed; sometimes they crashed against my guard, but the effect seemed to be cumulative. When at last I timed him, checked the kick with the edge of my shin and then tried to counter by driving the ball of my foot into his guts, I discovered that my left leg would no longer take my whole weight. I stumbled forward and nearly ate a knee for my trouble. Backing away, I stomped my heel repeatedly into the mat, trying to restore function to the nerve-endings, and then abruptly decided I'd had enough of playing catch for one evening. If I couldn't find my striking rhythm, then I'd take the fight to the mat, where all his height advantage did was give me a bigger target.

In a single motion, rendered unconscious by countless hours of practice, I fell into a predatory crouch and, driving off my heels, smashed my shoulder into his waist, my arms hooking around the backs of his thighs in a classic double-leg takedown. For the first time in the fight he was taken completely by surprise; equilibrium smashed, he fell like a ninepin.

Fighting is a lot like making love. Timing is everything. Suba was an experienced grappler, and I knew I had perhaps a second and a half to get into full mount before he recovered and clamped me in his guard. A simple-enough calculation, but as Clausewitz once observed, there was a fair country distance between simple and easy.

It was an ugly, vicious brawl, conducted at the closest of quarters between two men who knew a thousand ways to hurt each other. With rhythmic surges of brute force, I was sliding his body toward the fence, hoping to screw his head into the chain link where it couldn't move, and then smash it into so much raspberry jam. He was punching my ribs, smashing his heels into the backs of my calves, even head-butting my sternum, and all the while thrashing, writhing, bucking his hips – anything to prevent me from obtaining position. But he was only prolonging the inevitable. Because guess what, friends and neighbors? A tiger is only an apex predator until the dude with the hunting rifle shows up. Then he's a fucking throw-rug.

Clang. The crown of Suba's head hit the fence, and it was worth every calorie I'd just burned to get it there. I peeled myself off his chest and, slapping one hand on the mat for balance, drew back my opposing fist and buried it in his cheekbone. A good shot. I withdrew it and dropped another, harder blow that landed on the edge of his jaw. The sonofabitch was still bucking like a bronco, trying to spoil my aim. I struck him hard on the forehead with the edge of my left – what Alton called a Fuck You punch – then switched hands and threw a hard elbow at his brow. Bone met bone, and I felt a burst of savage pleasure despite the obstinate calm on my opponent's face. Sure he was tough – tough *and* slippery – but I had the angle now. I pulled back my arm, tensing bicep and tricep and fist, squinting against the sweat that burned in my eyes as I locked on target, and—

Eeeeeeeeeeeeeeehhhh. An air horn blew, and the referee's hand closed on the crook of my arm, staying the shot before I could throw it. The round had ended. In my close-minded determination to finish Suba, I hadn't even heard the ten-second warning. For a long moment I sat there, panting, fist clenched and trembling, a kind of horror rushing in to replace the schadenfreude that had suffused me seconds before. I felt like a starving wolf being dragged away from its own fresh kill.

Suba climbed easily to his feet. His eyes gleamed like ice in sunlight, but the features around them remained composed, as if the furious hand-to-hand struggle of the last two minutes were just an adjunct to his warm-up. If there was an expression on his face it seemed to be saying, *Not bad – for an American.* And now the American was in extremis, walking stiltedly back to his corner. There were my guys, my *compares,* crowding into the cage. A flat surface pressed against my bottom. Something cold sat on the back of my neck and something else, just as cold, pressed against my cheekbone. There was Sam, good old Sam, washing the blood out of the mouthpiece, water from the squeeze bottle sluicing over the plastic crescent, turning pink, drops falling into the bucket between my feet. Sam was talking, lips moving over the sunken mouth, but I could not hear the words, just nodded, nodded. Alton was yelling something I could almost hear, something like *Stop fuckin' about and fight your fight!* Okay, okay, big nods, mouthpiece cold and wet against my teeth, standing up, Massimo last out the cage, the cage door swinging shut behind him, the arena back in business.

The horn sounded – *Ave, Caesar!* – and Suba was screwing toward me like an auger. I needed to breathe and got on my bicycle, circling away from his power hand just as he had circled away from mine minutes before, but it was no easy task. No matter how hard I tried to maintain distance from him, he kept stepping into the chord of my arc, cutting me off, forcing me to switch direction. You didn't see footwork like that in the cage very often; guys who went into mixed martial arts usually came from wrestling, kickboxing or jiu-jitsu backgrounds; sometimes from judo or karate. Boxers were rare, but nobody moves the way they do. Nobody else has that sweet fluidic rhythm, the rhythm of a perfectly-tuned machine whose business was destruction. At last I realized it was costing me more energy to run than it would to fight, and I stopped in my tracks and swung a hard right hand lead at his chin.

The punch landed, turning his head on a spray of sweat. Hope kindled briefly within my breast once again; Suba wasn't the only boxer in the house tonight. My follow-up left to the ribs bounced off his elbow, and he ducked and whipped a right of his own at my cheek. I slipped it and crashed another hook off his guard, and suddenly we were going toe-to-toe at the center of the cage, all strategy forgotten, all defense abandoned. Pain exploded against my forehead, the side of my jaw, my arm, where my trunks covered my hip, but pain was my medium and sometimes you had to take it to give it. So I gave. And gave. And gave. But something was wrong. The blows were landing, the almost sexual pleasure of impact was jolting my knuckles beneath their padding, but the Russian wasn't going anywhere. With a horrible sort of agility, a continuous bob-and-weave of the head and upward-downward movement of his torso, he was taking the shots on his shoulders, elbows, forearms, gloves, all the while delivering pinpoint counters on my face, chest, and ribs like a sniper switching foxholes between each shot, and now he fired again, catching me clean on the liver with a hook that nearly dislodged my mouthpiece on a glittering rope of spit and blood and bile.

My legs betrayed me, sent me reeling away from the source of my torment until at last the cage itself checked my momentum, the chain link cutting a pattern into my quivering back. Suba was on me in an instant, fists crashing into me with merciless fury, knocking aside my arms and landing again and again on my body. He was like a demented biologist trying to demonstrate the dangers of alcoholism. This, Mr. Watts, is what happens when you drink. First goes your *liver,* then your *kidneys*, and even your *stomach,* bang bang bang. Maybe you'd like to quit. No? Perhaps I'm not demonstrating correctly. Allow me to start over again. From the top.

I shoved my way out of the trap and clipped him across the jaw with an overhand right, but no sooner had he recoiled from the blow than he was coming in again, squinting a bit as he searched for an opening. He carried his left so low he was all but begging for a straight right to the chin, but I seemed to have no strength in my arms, no strength anywhere. I had to use my own footwork, stay out of range until I caught my second wind. But it seemed his range was very long; his shin cracked off my thigh like a meat mallet, and as I straightened my buckling knee he landed again, harder this time, a raw kind of pain amidst spreading warmth as the capillaries broke. I tried to retaliate with a kick of my own, but my leg quailed at the additional weight, and I stumbled again, this time into a lead left hook that landed on the rim of my eye socket. I swung wildly and felt my left slap into his shoulder, then ate a hard uppercut that nearly wrenched my head free of my shoulders. I knew I'd fallen when my knees jolted against the mat, but with a clench of teeth that nearly split my mouthpiece in two, I managed to take my feet again. Suba's foot smashed into the inside of my right thigh, so high it brushed against the edge of my cup, and fresh agony thrilled down my inseam. I could hear the commentators shouting through the fence, their voices somehow piercing the ocean-like roar of the crowd, something about why wasn't Suba going for the takedown, but I didn't have time to wonder. I'd only just avoided a haymaker that puffed the sweat-tangled hair off my forehead, and nearly fell on my ass for my trouble. My body was no longer responding smoothly to the commands of my brain; everything seemed to come a second too late, and jerkily, as if I were a dummy being manipulated by a drunk.

He went for my legs again and again, every clean shot echoing about the stadium. There were no more individual shouts of pain but a sort of chorus that sang from my thighs, from my knees, from my calves and the sides of my shins, so that the very act of remaining upright became a torment. He was corking my legs, busting the vessels within them, bloating them with blood. And still I stood there, fists clenched, waiting for him to step inside punching range waiting for the miracle mistake that would let me turn it around. I wasn't a praying man, but I prayed now, prayed to God, to the Devil, to Whoever or Whatever would grant me my wish. Come on, man, take the step. Come on, come on, come *on*...

Suba took the step. I swung for his jaw, swung with every watt of power my body could muster, swung for the fences, putting God and Mother and Country into my fist as it described an arc toward the point of his chin.

And missed.

The power of my swing turned me a hundred and eighty degrees, exhilaration turning to horror when I realized I'd given up my back while still standing, and before I could react, his arm was sliding around my neck, the crook of his elbow seeking my throat, the flat of his free hand jamming itself against the back of my head, his knee prodding the back of my knee so that my weakened legs folded and I fell into his choke hold. In desperation, I forced my chin down, down between the points of my collarbone, began to screw it hard to the side, trying to keep my windpipe open. My hands fought frantically of their own accord, trying to find purchase on his sweat-slick flesh even as the pressure on my throat increased. I found myself praying again, this time in cowardly panic. Please, God, not a rear naked choke. I can't lose to a rear naked choke, any first-year jiu-jitsu student can defend against this move, and I could slip it if I had any strength left at all. Let him knock me out, break my arm, bash my head into the post until my brains scatter over the mat like oatmeal – anything but this…

The world was darkening, disappearing in a black fog that blew in from the edges. I couldn't hear anything except the increasingly frantic pounding of my heart, couldn't feel anything except that horrible constricting pressure on my windpipe, couldn't form any other thoughts than that I must not submit, must not, *must not,* that it was better to black out, better to die than surrender to this man…when my lowering gaze fell upon the face of Mikhailis Morganstern. He was sitting cageside, dressed in his trademark Savile Row, staring up at me out of those dark deep-set eyes with just the faintest trace of a smile on his lips. And in the moment before I blacked out, those lips formed a single, silent word.

Gotcha.

Chapter Fifteen

"Excuse me," I said, and then belched. "I'm looking for my *oh*. Have you seen it anywhere?"

"What the fuck is he talking about?" Baby Joe demanded, hanging his coat over the back of his chair.

"Nothing," Kraut sighed. "Literally."

"I am looking for my *oh*." I repeated, and slopped more whiskey into my water glass. "I last saw it in a cage in Atlantic City."

Baby Joe sat. It was a hot night, and his brute-jawed face was already crimson-cheeked and sweating. He produced a cigar from his shirt pocket and began to unwrap it, glaring at me with his fat-enfolded eyes of storybook blue.

"My *oh,* known to science as a zero, was a representation of what is referred to by mathematicians as a null value," I said, and burped a second time. It is no fun to burp when you've been drinking Jim Beam since you woke up.

"I got a null value for you," Gavin said, shuffling the deck. "It's what's between your fucking ears."

I slugged down a mouthful of whiskey, grimacing as it described a fiery streak into my guts. "No. In this instance, the *oh* indicated the number of defeats I had suffered in the cage. It was a representation–" I stammered over the word. "—of my undefeated status. But now I can't find it. It's gone."

"You mean you *lost* it?" Baby Joe said, touching a flaring kitchen match to his stogie.

"No," I said. I had learned in recent minutes not to shake my head, as it started a spinning process that was difficult to stop. "You can lose car keys, or virginity, or your mind. You can't *lose* your *oh*. It must be taken from you. Mine was pickpocketed from me in A.C., and I want it back."

A guy who was still known as Johnny Wheels, despite the fact that he had retired from the getaway-driving business to run a policy game in Brooklyn, swaggered in and sat down. He looked like a member of the Rat Pack with his plastered hair, e'er-burning cigarette and tumbler of bourbon, except that I'm pretty sure neither Deano nor Frank nor Sammy wore a shoulder holster beneath their suit jacket. "Somebody picked your pocket?"

"Oh, Jesus," Kraut muttered.

"You're damned right they did," I said. "Goddamn Russian sonofabitch."

"I fuckin' *hate* pickpockets," Johnny said. He had a scar that ran beneath one eye, over the bridge of his nose, and onto the other cheek like a road cut into a mountainside; probably the impress of a steering wheel. "Goddamn sneaky, dishonest way to make a living."

Baby Joe puffed pepper-scented smoke at him. "Says the bank robber."

"Banks is federally insured," Johnny said. "Wallets ain't."

"I guess I should have paid attention to the announcer before the fight," I said. I wanted to pace up and down the room, ticking off points on my fingers, but I found I was too drunk to move. "He told the crowd, 'Somebody's *oh* must go!' Because, you see, we were both undefeated. Me and Suba. But I never thought my *oh* would be the one to go, and I want it back."

Johnny looked at me for a few moments. "What the fuck are you talking about?"

"Here we go again," Kraut sighed.

"I am offering a reward for the immediate return of my *oh*. It was last seen in the company of my self-respect, which is also missing."

"Oh, for Christ's sweet sake," Gavin said, reshuffling the cards. "Mick, if Clean comes in here and sees you like this, he'll pitch a fit. You're supposed to be working."

"I am working," I said. "I'm prepared for trouble at a half-second's notice. Ready to spring – like a tiger!"

I tried to spring like a tiger and managed to fall off the couch. The floor was warped and thick with dust and cigarette ash and the ring-tabs of innumerable cans of beer, yet oddly comfortable.

"Here I am on the ground," I said to the floorboards. "A strangely familiar pose."

"You make me sick," Baby Joe said. "Goddamn rummy."

"He's no rummy," Kraut told him. "He just never lost before."

"He ain't taking it so good," Baby Joe said. The point of his shoe spurned my forearm. "I seen vags in the gutter that look better."

Gavin continued to shuffle the cards, a smooth unconscious motion like worrying rosary beads. Evidently he was waiting on someone. "You don't look so hot when you lose either, Joey my lad."

"I only lose when I'm cheated," Joe said.

"Exactly!" I shouted.

"I'm confused," said Johnny Wheels. "This isn't about a wallet?"

"How could it be?" Joe dabbed sweat off his brow with a handkerchief of monogrammed silk. "No self-respecting wiseguy even carries one."

"*I* carry one," Wheels said. "My *goumada* bought it for me for my birthday. The finest fuckin' Italian leather."

"Oh, come on," Gavin said. "Am I s'posed to believe an Italian cow is better than an American cow?"

"Yes," Baby Joe said. "Everything's better in Italy."

Kraut's engineer boots thumped into view. With a grunt, he hauled me to my feet and shoved me back on the couch. "Gavin's right about Clean," he told me, the worry-lines on his forehead deepening. "He comes by and sees you like this, he'll shit himself."

"Oh, let him," I said. I was now staring at the ceiling, which was so blackened by generations of tobacco smoke it looked like the inside of a chimney. "You know what he said to me after the fight? 'I had eight *grand* on you, Mick.' Some fucking pal."

I was not quite plastered enough to miss the uncomfortable silence this remark produced. On the one hand, everyone in the Grind Joint, including the patrons, despised Clean; on the other, he was kin to Don Cheech and very nearly a made guy, and people can get killed for running their mouths in that direction. At that moment, however, Philly Guido swung into the room with a rustle of acrylic fabric – he was, as usual, clad in a designer warm-up outfit and sneakers that looked as if they'd never touched the sidewalk. Taking a seat, the gold chains around his neck swung forward and caught the light in such a way as to brand a crucifix-shape on my retinas. He glanced over at me and said, "Fuck's the matter with him?"

"Don't ask," Kraut said. "Mick, let's you and me take a walk."

"Don't wanna walk," I said. "Wanna watch the game. Also, continue my search for the missing *oh.*"

"Come on, get up. *Aufstehen.*"

"It's my job to guard against trouble," I said, waggling a finger in his general direction. "This room is filled with dangerous people."

"Yeah," Kraut said. "And I'm one of 'em, so do as I tell you."

I ignored him. "Take Baby Joe over there. In addition to being, uh, touchy about losing–"

"You should fuckin' talk," Baby Joe mumbled.

"—he also carries that blackjack on his left wrist, tucked inside his cuff. Don't think I don't know, Joe. Then there's Johnny Wheels here, who is packing serious heat under his Brioni. What you got under that hood, Johnny Wheels? A three-five-seven?"

"Wouldn't you like to know," he said, crushing out his cigarette. "Come on, Gavin, let's get started."

"And then there's Philly Guido," I said, though at that exact moment there were, in fact, three Philly Guidos, blurrily superimposed over each other in my vision. "He's a thief, so he may have stolen my *oh.*"

"Stolen your *what?*" Philly said, each of his deeply tanned faces showing umbrage, though perhaps not as much as they might have, since Gavin had begun to deal out the cards.

"Never you mind," Kraut said. "Mick, get up. Now."

"Make me," I said.

He made me, and without any particular difficulty, either. A fireman's carry. For a moment I regarded the upside-down faces of Gavin, Baby Joe, Johnny Wheels, and Philly Guido; then my head struck the doorframe hard enough to remind me of Suba's left hook, and I was being hauled like an old straw dummy down the hallway, through the roulette tables, and down the back steps. I heard a curse in German, the clack of a bolt being driven back, and clanging footsteps. The glare of lights faded into darkness, and the quality of the air changed; we were outside. Without any ceremony at all, I was dumped on the ground. I lay there bonelessly, head reeling, the scent of the dirt heavy in my nostrils. Of their own accord, my hands clutched at the wet grass, as if by doing so I could prevent myself from being hurled off the face of the earth. My sole wish at that moment was not to puke. *Don't puke*, I thought, *don't puke. Cling to the last shred of dignity you've got, and hold it in. Don't puke don't puke don't puke—*

I puked. An eruption of whiskey and beer and whatever it was I'd had in lieu of lunch, forcing my jaws apart, spraying out in a vindictive gush. Amazing, isn't it, what the human body can hold? You can paint a room with a man's blood, and you can cover a good-sized floor with the contents of his belly. It's not feng shui, but it gets the job done.

When at last my guts had emptied themselves, I thrust my face into the grass and cooled my burning cheeks on the evening dew, listening with a sort of academic shame to the wretched sounds emanating from my throat: gagging, retching, sobbing. At some length, these trickled away and now I heard only the night sounds of Queens: a dog barking, the reedy hum of crickets, the whisper of traffic on the Clearview Expressway

Kraut said, "You wanna tell me what the fuck is the matter with you?"

"Ask Damien Suba."

"Don't feed me that bullshit. There's more to this than losing a fucking fight."

"Maybe I just can't take defeat."

"If I thought you were that big of a pussy I wouldn't have gone partners with you."

"Maybe you misjudged me."

"I better not have, because this–" He jerked a thumb at the dark mass of the Grind Joint, rising up behind him like an enormous curtain. "—isn't a fuckin' game."

"No, it's a joke. This whole life is a joke. *My* whole life is a joke."

"Then maybe you should try laughing. It's healthier than buckets of Jim Beam."

"Good old Kraut. Nothing rattles you, does it?"

"There's not much worth getting rattled over."

"Maybe when I'm your age I'll have perspective."

"You won't live that long, the way you're going."

"What a fucking tragedy that would be."

"I don't get you. I lost fights before. I never crawled into a bottle afterwards."

"You should try it sometime. It's cozy."

I can't swear I heard steam coming out of his ears, but that's my sincere belief. "I'm gonna ask you one more time to tell me what's going on."

"Ask Mikhailis Morganstern," I said.

"I don't truck with Jews."

"I forgot, your father was in the SS, wasn't he? Shit, you must have had a fun childhood."

"I guess I didn't get my point across." Kraut's voice sounded funny, as if he were speaking through clenched teeth. "I want answers and if I have to give you another beating to get 'em, then a beating you will take."

I climbed painfully to my knees. The world was no longer spinning, but it was doing a pretty good impression of a boat buffeted by thirty-foot waves. "You ain't got the equipment, old man."

The dew-dampened sole of Kraut's engineer boot clumped on my shoulder. The next thing I knew I was lying flat on my back, looking at the blank night-rusted sky. You seldom see stars in Queens. The moon, sure;

and good old Venus in the morning. The running lights of aircraft and police helicopters. But no stars.

"That was uncalled for," I said at last.

"It was kisses from a broad compared to what I did to the last fuck who called me 'old man.'"

We were silent for a time. I heard the distinctive crumple of a cigarette pack, the metallic *flink* of a Zippo, the sound of rolling papers burning. A flare of orange light lived and died.

"Anne smokes, you know," I said at last. "Not the unfiltered death-sticks you suck down. Some menthol ultralight shit. She kept a pack by my bedside. They're still sitting there. Every morning I wake up and say, 'I should throw those out.' But I don't. Why don't I throw 'em away, Kraut?"

Kraut dragged on his Camel in an *ah-ha!* sort of way.

"And don't you fucking tell me to just deal with it," I said. "Don't tell me to man up. I got enough of that from Clean."

"Don't ever imply that I'd say the same thing that Clean would say about anything. If there was a bucket of blue paint on the floor and he said, 'That's blue,' I would say it was green on general fucking principles."

"All right."

"Tell me what happened."

I told him. It was strange, lying there on the wet grass with him standing over me, smoking – almost like being in a psychiatrist's office, if your psychiatrist was a nature-lover who got most of his education in prison.

"You think she was balling Morganstern when she was with you?" He said when I'd finished.

I shut my eyes and immediately regretted it; not because of the riptide of nausea that tugged at my guts, but because of the images that writhed with horrible eagerness before my mind's eye. "I don't know."

"But you got your suspicions."

"The door was open for it. At the end, I mean. They had a history, he never stopped loving her…and I wasn't *there.*"

"You blame yourself?"

"You leave a beautiful woman alone, somebody else is bound to move in."

"True, but that don't mean you got to forgive the bitch."

"Forgiveness doesn't have anything to do with it. I could hate Anne's guts for the rest of my life and still love her."

I waited for the storm of ridicule which was certainly coming. If there is one thing wiseguys cannot stand, it's a man who allows a woman to make a fool of him. But Kraut said nothing, so I just lay there in silence. The taste in my mouth was unspeakable, and I could feel the dew soaking into my jeans in a very unpleasant sort of way. The smell of regurgitated whiskey mingled with Kraut's cigarette smoke made me want to dry-heave, but I said nothing, did nothing, just lay there listening to the sound of my own ragged breathing.

"You know I never hitched," Kraut said at last. The tone of his voice had changed ever so slightly. It had become an imitation of itself, as if the very casualness of the tone existed as a mask, a cover for something else he would not, could not reveal. "You ever wondered why? And think three times about saying it's cause I'm queer."

"I never thought you were queer," I said. "Bisexual maybe, but not queer."

"You're lucky you're on your back already." Kraut put the cigarette between his lips and unbuttoned the black Henley he was wearing. The lighted Camel gleamed feebly on a thread of gold chain, upon which hung a circle of gold crowned by a small diamond. He let the ring dangle for a few moments, not looking at it, then tucked it away again. "I bought this for a girl before you were born. But I never got it on her finger."

"Who was she?"

"Nurse. Met her in the ER. Somebody busted my forearm with a tire iron outside a bar in Brooklyn."

"Romantic."

"Yeah. In those days the girls still wore whites, and boy, did she fill 'em out. When I saw her, I forgot all about the bones sticking out of my arm."

"What happened?"

"We had a thing. For years. She kept walking on me, but she always came back. Until she didn't."

"Because of what you do?"

"Some chicks can handle it and some can't. She couldn't."

"I know the feeling."

"Point is, Mick, when she walked for the last time, I was two seconds away from eating my gun. And I don't just mean one time. On a daily fuckin' basis."

"But you got over it."

"Don't be a sap. You never get over The One. Especially when she tosses your heart into a fuckin' wood chipper. You just…go on. And try not to think about it too much."

"But you never married," I said. "And you still got that ring around your neck after all these years."

"Yeah."

I burst into laughter. It was the giddy, slightly hysterical sound a man makes when what he really wants to do is scream. "Jesus Christ! Was that supposed to make me feel better?"

"What am I, a fuckin' Hallmark Card?"

He extended a hand. I took it and was pulled roughly to my feet. We stood there for a moment, hands clasped. The glow of the cigarette deepened the shadows on Kraut's face and accentuated the fine wrinkles around his eyes and mouth. I wondered, in the odd, philosophical manner of the drunk, about the life that had shaped that face. Every crease told a story, and not many of them had happy endings. We all want to believe our pain is somehow different, somehow more profound or refined, than the pain of others, and I was still drunk enough to want to cling to that illusion…but not quite drunk enough to forget that it *was* an illusion.

"You have to understand," I said. "It's not just losing the girl. It's thinking that maybe I never had her to begin with."

"I ain't saying you ain't got a right to be pissed," Kraut said. "I'm just saying there's ways of dealing with it and ways of dealing with it."

I took a deep breath, the night air cool against the burning interior of my mouth. I had that feeling which isn't shame exactly, but awareness of the shame which I would feel tomorrow when I remembered this night and the nights before it. "And how would you deal with it?"

Kraut watched his cigarette smoke curl away on the breeze. One corner of his mouth raveled into that rarest of all facial expressions: a smile. "That's for me to know and you to find out."

Chapter Sixteen

"So," I said. "Can you tell me what all this is about *now?*"

Kraut, smooth-shaven and dressed in his Sunday best, paused to button his suit jacket. "No."

It was a balmy evening in July. The three of us – Gavin, Kraut, and myself – were approaching the stoop of a large, rather nondescript townhouse in the Murray Hill section of Brooklyn. Gavin's freshly buffed 1968 Impala, gilded by the lingering sunset, was parked behind us. I could hear its engine ticking as it cooled.

"If I were a suspicious person," I said. "I'd be a bit nervous about going through a door with you two when I don't know what's on the other side."

"Yeah," Gavin replied. "Good thing you're so naïve."

"I'm not gonna get the Joe Pesci treatment, am I?" I made a pistol with my forefinger and thumb, pointed behind my ear. "Because I gotta tell you, I'm not really comfortable with being shot in the head."

"Wiseguys get shot in the back of the head," Kraut said. "You're no wiseguy."

"I'm not?"

"Hell, no," he said, laughing gruffly. "Didja think you were?"

"I wasn't sure," I said.

"Wiseguy." He shook his head ruefully. "That's a fucking laugh."

I didn't know whether to be offended or relieved. "What am I, then?"

Kraut hesitated, then showed his crooked-toothed smile. "You're an entrepreneur. Just leave it at that."

We mounted the steps toward an oak-paneled door lit by a shaded glass bulb. Ignoring the heavy brass knocker, Kraut pressed a doorbell recessed into the brick facing. He smiled at me the way a man smiles when he's in on a wondrous secret. Gavin straightened his tie's knot with dexterous fingers. No one spoke.

The door opened. A woman stood there – a beautiful young woman in a very short cocktail dress. She was a silken five-nine in three-inch heels, with the impossibly high cheekbones and bee-stung lips of a model. Her makeup was flawless, her hair professionally bound atop her head save for two elegantly curled strands framing her face. Her neck and shoulders, bare except for spaghetti straps, were as smoothly alluring as fresh satin sheets. "Why hello there, Kurt, Gavin. You're as handsome as ever. And who–?" Her eyes turned to me. A clear, deep brown, crowned by long lashes. "Who do we have here?"

"Deanna, this is my friend Mickey," Kraut announced proudly, and clapped a hand on my shoulder. "He's with me."

"Really?" Her voice was dulcet, her stare unblinking. "Well, we'll do *everything* we can to make sure he has a good time."

She ushered us into the vestibule. Still staring at her legs, I made vague note of my surroundings: inlaid marble floor, oak-paneled walls, vaulted ceiling with a brass chandelier from which flame-shaped bulbs emitted a mellow glow. It was like a foyer of a good country club.

"If you'll follow me," she said, in a charming hostess voice, leading us through French doors and up a red-carpeted marble staircase balustraded in polished oak. A huge oil painting of Venus on the half-shell in a grossly ornate gilt frame, lit by tiny recessed lights, dominated the landing. A white Victorian fainting couch trimmed in gold brocade sat underneath. The floor was parquet, the lighting subdued. I heard the low murmur of chamber music from somewhere up ahead.

"What the hell *is* this place?" I said to Gavin as we moved down the hallway to another door.

"See for yourself."

Deanna opened the door to a cavernous wood-paneled drawing room featuring a large baroque fireplace. The furniture was leather; opulent Oriental rugs covered the floor. Tapestries and gilt-framed portraits of frolicking nymphs and Renaissance nudes hung from the walls. I had not been mistaken about the chamber music; it was Mozart, playing softly from cleverly hidden speakers. But all of this was merely backdrop. Arrayed about the room like a scattering of bright flowers – on sofas, elegantly perched on overstuffed chairs, standing with the exquisite hauteur of professional models – were about a dozen of the most beautiful women I had ever seen. They were dressed in such a striking variety of costumes that my eyes simply could not process it all at once. It was as if someone had shuffled the deck of erotic fantasies and dealt out a large and random hand.

A Dallas Cowboys cheerleader – complete with blue-and-silver pompoms. A blonde stewardess in form-fitting jacket and pencil skirt slit halfway up the hip. A pouty-lipped brunette costumed as a French maid. A tall, willowy Latina with windblown hair, dressed for mambo. A voluptuous, porcelain-skinned redhead in skimpy tennis whites. Every color in the spectrum was represented, every body type displayed. Some were engaged in conversation with the half-dozen or so men in the room; others chatted pleasantly with each other, sipping from fluted glasses. A few sat alone. No one seemed even the slightest bit self-conscious.

"Put your jaw back in," Kraut muttered.

I had indeed been staring slack-mouthed and shut it with a snap.

"All of your favorites are here tonight," Deanna said from behind me. "But we also have some new talent if you feel like experimenting."

"I like to try something new every day," Gavin said.

"Oh, you," Deanna waggled her fingers at him playfully. She turned to me, then glanced at Kraut. "Would now be a good time to go over our rates with your friend?"

"Just see me about it later, dear." Kraut said. "I'll take care of it."

Deanna beamed. "In that case…I'll leave you to your fun. Mickey, I hope you enjoy yourself this evening."

"Oh, he will," Kraut said, clapping me on the shoulder. "Believe me."

She left, closing the door behind her.

"Mother of God," I whispered.

"Look around," Gavin said. "She's probably in here somewhere."

He moved off. A tall, light-skinned black girl with elaborately braided hair greeted him with outstretched arms and a familiar smile. Her peach silk pajamas shimmered as she moved.

I turned to Kraut, my voice an indignant hiss. "You took me to a whorehouse?"

He gave me a pained glance. "This is a gentleman's club. Protected and very exclusive. You are here on my watch. So behave yourself."

"How can I behave myself in a whorehouse?"

"Oh, take the rod out for a night, won't ya?" A table in the corner, covered in white linen, played host to a generous assortment of liquor bottles and beer on ice in a steel tub. A blonde who was a dead ringer for the St. Pauli Girl tended the drinks. Kraut strolled over.

"Guten Abend, meine gnädige Dame," he said formally.

"I don't actually speak German," she said after a short silence. Her accent was pure Boston. "It's just a getup."

"That's quite all right," Kraut said, with that odd gentlemanly courtesy that was so unlike the man I knew from the Grind Joint. "I'd like a Beck's. And one for my friend."

"Kraut," I whispered. "I'm not doing this."

"Mickey, what are you worried about? I told you this place is protected. And these girls…shit, you think you can do better going to a bar? Go try it. You're good looking, but you ain't *that* good looking."

"That's not the point—"

"It's precisely the fucking point. You got to get past that rich broad, and this is how you start."

He walked off. I stood alone by the bar holding a cold bottle of Beck's, feeling foolish. The St. Pauli girl was diligently replacing the beers from a case under the table. Her pale, freckled cleavage, exposed by the white peasant blouse, quivered slightly with every movement. I stared in spite of myself – you don't see many natural breasts in the Grind Joint. Indeed, there were none of the subtle signs of wear or cosmetic tampering that I'd grown so used to. This girl looked as wholesome and fresh as a pail of milk. She caught me looking and smiled a helpful, faux-flirtatious sort of smile. I was embarrassed, but it seemed I was alone in that regard. The confidence of the cheerleader, as she rustled her pompoms and flashed a million-watt smile, was matched by the ease of the thin, balding, conservatively dressed man opposite her. His flow of eager words was interrupted only by an occasional pull at his tumbler of Scotch. It made no sense to me. Protected or not, only three doors separated this bizarre scene from the outside world. I had seen no security camera outside, no doorman, no bouncers, not even a hefty bartender to make the drunks think twice before they hurled a chair into the gilt-framed mirror over the mantle. Except for customers, there were in fact no men at all. The pattern of dress seemed to be evenly divided between mob chic and Wall Street. If there were specific criteria for admission to this place, I couldn't see it.

Protected. The word sounded in my head with new force. The after-hours joint was protected too – with a security door, bouncers, bodyguards to escort the winners home. But even with that, there was still a faint undercurrent of menace, brought on by the threat of a sudden explosion of violence or a raid by the gambling squad, or by a renegade stick-up crew that didn't know or care who actually owned the place. You could never relax completely there, and it showed in the tense, cat-footed way everyone carried themselves. There was no trace of that tension here. We might have been at a costume ball at the Playboy Mansion instead of a Brooklyn whorehouse tucked between an architectural firm and a vacant townhouse. Whoever was protecting this place must be very powerful indeed.

"You look lonely." A honeyed voice in my ear. "Mind if I join you?"

I turned. The voice belonged to a young woman of about twenty-five. Her hair, black as a crow's wing, fell over and around her face in a style strongly reminiscent of Cleopatra. From within the caramel gleam of a good spray tan, her eyes shone like two brilliant emeralds, and the fact that they were obviously colored contact lenses did nothing to reduce their impact. Her dress was a modern take on the Flapper style, fitting her curves like paint before ending abruptly at mid-thigh; it showed just enough of the body beneath to make you desperate to see more. In that deck of lurid schoolboy fantasy, her dark, exotic beauty stood out like a wild card.

"Sure," I said. "Do you – uh, want something to drink?"

"I wouldn't say no to a beer – a light beer. Girl's gotta watch her figure."

Her grin was mischievous. It made her beauty accessible in a way it had not been a moment before. I got a beer from the Saint Pauli Girl and handed it over to her.

"This is your first time here," she said.

"Is it that obvious?"

"First-timers always just sort of stare. What do you think of it?"

"I think I died and woke up in Hugh Hefner's heaven."

Her laughter was musical, like a single stroke of fingers over a harp. Her teeth were perfectly white and even. "I'm Rainn – with two *N*'s."

"Mickey. With one *C*."

"Is that short for Matthew?"

"Michael," I said.

"Michael. That means 'who is as God.' Didja know that?"

"I think my mother told me once," I said stupidly. One should probably not mention one's mother in a whorehouse. "Are you Catholic?"

"No," she said. She seemed to be suppressing laughter, though whether it was caused by the stupidity of my conversation or something else I wasn't sure. "They don't have them where I come from."

"New Yorkers or Catholics?"

"Either."

"We're a strange breed."

"New Yorkers or Catholics?"

"Both."

"You're funny," she replied, narrowing long-lashed eyes whose lids were dusted with charcoal eye shadow. "Do you need a sense of humor to do what you do?"

"You don't know what I do."

The mischievous smile resurfaced "Are you going to tell me?"

I opened my mouth to reply that I was a cage fighter – I usually use that description, even though Morganstern prefers us to say 'mixed martial artist' – and then, without knowing why, said: "I'm an entrepreneur."

She returned my gaze and then burst out laughing. "That's a new one."

"You don't believe me?"

"I've just never heard it described that way before."

"Never heard *what* described that way before?"

"Oh, you know." She said, tapping her index finger to the side of her nose and winking. "Don't make me say it."

"If you think I'm a wiseguy, Rainn, you're barking up the wrong tree."

She patted me on the arm. "Hey, I believe you."

"No, you don't."

"No, I don't. You came in with *Kurt,* for God's sake."

"Kraut? So what if I did? So did Gavin."

"Yeah? Well, that proves my point."

"Gavin isn't a wiseguy. He's dealer." Her smile was widening. "A *card* dealer, smarty. That's it."

"And you're an entrepreneur. Should I ask how you make your money?"

"Why don't we talk about your job for a while," I said with a sigh.

"Sure." Her tone turned brisk. "It pays good, it's fun, and I get to meet interesting people like you." She touched my arm and squeezed gently. "Plus, I don't have to go to bed with anyone I don't want to."

I had felt a number of emotions that evening – anticipation, surprise, discomfort. Galloping right up behind them was lust. "Is that, uh...standard?"

"Oh no, God, no," she smiled. "It's sort of a pay-for-performance thing, if you get my meaning."

"I think so."

"Why don't you come with me, then?"

Rainn took my hand and led me gently, as you would lead a puppy on its first leash. Her hand was warm and dry. I was embarrassed that mine was wet. As we exited the drawing room, Kraut, standing with the redhead in the tennis outfit, turned and gave me a smartass grin and a wink. The hallway was lined with numbered oak doors: Rainn opened one and ushered me in. The room was small and functional: queen-sized bed with a plain wooden headboard, mirrored ceiling, deep-pile carpeting. There was no other furniture except for a dressing table that held a CD player, a wood-and-bronze incense burner, and a bedside lamp. A second mirror was mounted over the dressing table and a third faced it, off the tiny bathroom. The bedspread appeared to be lavender silk, and the room smelled lightly of incense and perfume.

"Do you like jazz?" She asked, switching on the player. "Jazz is better for making it, I think."

I heard the tinkling notes of a jazz piano. Rainn inspected her reflection briefly in the mirror and turned back to me with a grin.

"Jazz is fine," I said. "Jazz is great."

She removed a small tin box from a drawer. "Do you get high, Mickey?"

"When I was a kid. My friend Clean – do you know Clean? – he would show up at school with a joint sometimes, and we'd go behind the bandstand and smoke. Tell you the truth, it just sort of made me cough a lot."

"Well, this is the real stuff. I'm going to smoke a little before we get started, if that's okay with you."

"Sure. Knock yourself out."

I slipped off my shoes and was surprised to find my hands trembling ever so slightly. I heard the flare of a match and smelled the sweet odor of marijuana as it mingled with the incense and perfume.

"Sweetie," Rainn said huskily, after blowing an astounding quantity of smoke across the room. "There's no reason to be nervous. We're gonna have a lot of fun."

"Okay."

"All right then." She placed the joint in the incense burner. The piano rippled out silvery notes; a drummer evoked a sexy whisper from his cymbals. Rainn looked at me with slightly glazed eyes, her backside resting against the edge of the dresser. "Come here, Shy Boy."

I did as I was told, and as soon as I came within striking distance she had me by the tie and pulled me toward her with astonishing strength. Her mouth clamped on mine, and bewildered shock coursed through me when I felt her tongue thrust impudently against mine. I had just enough time to think, *Hookers don't kiss their clients!* She shoved me onto the bed with a two handed-push, then stripped out of her clothes as if they were on fire. I hardly had time to take in that flawless, magnificent body before it was on top of me.

The sex was quick and brutally efficient. After a few seconds, I gave up any pretense of control and simply let her work her will. In minutes, I understood why she was allowed to choose her own clients, and then I was groaning out a name that was not hers as an orgasm ripped through me with the vicious intensity of a gunshot blast. Afterwards, I lay flat on my back, gasping for breath, staring at my reflection in the mirror above. Rainn rolled off and propped her hands behind her head, grinning as if at some private joke. My gaze moved languidly over her, taking in what I had not had time to examine before: the gentle rise and fall of her heavy breasts, the concave smoothness of her belly broken by the slim circle of her navel, and finally the smooth-shaven V between her thighs.

"I'm lucky I don't get paid by the hour," she said at last.

"I'm sorry."

"Did you enjoy it?"

"Hell, yes."

"Then don't be sorry. Just…pace yourself next time. We're here for your benefit, remember? Well – mostly." She poked me in the ribs. "You know, I don't think anyone's ever apologized to me in this room before. I think you might be too polite for the line of work you're in."

"Here we go again. I'm not a damn gangster."

"Come on. You can tell me."

"There's nothing to tell."

"Nothing to tell or nothing to hide?"

"Rainn," I said with a sigh that might have been exasperated under different circumstances. "I have a piece – a *small* piece – of a little gambling joint in Queens. What they call a goulash house. Nothing goes on inside that doesn't go on in any casino in this country."

"But it's *illegal,*" she said, and for a moment managed to summon up a look of great moral anguish. "It's *against the law.*"

"In Queens, it's illegal. In Atlantic City, it's hospitality."

"Now you sound like Robert De Niro."

"Maybe he was right."

"Tell me this," Rainn rolled onto her side and slid a hand across my chest. "Have you ever killed anyone?"

"What?"

"You come in here with Kurt Kroos, I have to wonder. Or are you gonna tell me he's a legitimate businessman, too?"

"He is what he is, I am what I am. Anyway, who are you to judge?"

"I'm not judging. I just have this *weird feeling* about you. Like maybe you're this really dangerous type of a guy."

"And you like dangerous types of guys."

Her fingertips marched down my hip, came to rest on my thigh, drew patterns on the flesh there. "Maybe," she said.

We were silent. It was very pleasant to lie there with the silk of the sheets against my back and the silk of her body on my side, breathing the gentle lilac scent of the incense while the music played. I felt myself drowsing, and then her toe digging at one of my socks. "Are you gonna take these off, champ?"

"Rainn, I don't mean to offend you, but I think I'm retired for the night."

"Like hell you are."

She got up and went to the dresser, moving with the complete unselfconsciousness of one who knows her body to be flawless from any angle. "You're paying for this, and you're not leaving 'til you get your money's worth." She lay back down next to me with the joint in one hand and a fresh condom in the other. "Plus, to be honest, you're one up in the orgasm department, and that's just not gonna do."

I was about to say she was one damned unusual hooker when I realized this was not exactly a compliment and took a drag on the cigarette instead.

"Well?" Said Rainn.

"To be honest," I said, coughing. "It pretty much tastes like the air in the Grind Joint on a Saturday night."

She smiled and leaned over me so that her hair tickled the muscles of my belly. I felt hot breath, and looked down to see her tongue, pink as a serpent's, tracing a slow circle around my navel. "How about now?"

"Uh-huh," I said thickly. "But I'm not sure it's from the dope."

The tongue completed its circle and began to descend my abdomen. "Try it again."

I did as I was told, filling my lungs with hot smoke. The blood throbbed in my temples and lips and balls, and when I spoke again my voice was shivery, breathless. "I feel warm and stupid and happy and tingly all over."

"That's a good way to feel," Rainn murmured. "But I can do you one better."

Pillowed lips engulfed me, and the thing I had declared to be retired came out of retirement with astonishing speed. When the lips could coax forth no more length or girth they came away with a gasp; in an instant, lubricated plastic unfurled in their place. I rolled her roughly beneath me and with a violence needless of my purpose, rammed myself inside of her.

What followed wasn't lovemaking, or sex, or even the most frantic fucking. It was a literal and naked savagery, a slapping, pummeling, gasping act of violence that went on and on, jolting Rainn's great breasts, then the bed beneath us, and finally the mirrors on the wall, so that we seemed to be at the epicenter of an earthquake of pure lust. Rainn's eyes hardly closed, but stared up in a look half-defiant, half-gloating, as her emerald fingernails draggled painfully up and down my back. And yet it was not enough; the pent-up frustration of the last months demanded still greater exertions. I pulled myself free, wrenched her body around and plunged into it from behind, my hands slipping against the sweat-slick hourglass of her waist.

She bucked against me, challenging. My hips worked awkwardly at first, clumsily, then up to a slow clapping rhythm, then faster and faster still, pounding into the eager curve of her ass as if trying to flatten it. She was screaming my name. I was screaming hers. My eyes stung with sweat; my belly muscles cramped with fatigue. I kept on, felt my orgasm coming as if from some inconceivable distance, a tiny spark of light growing into a match head, a flame, then suddenly exploding, blotting out everything in my head, threading itself instantaneously through every nerve ending in my body. And as I slumped down on the sheets, stars twinkling before my eyes, I realized that Kraut had been right – half-right, anyway. If pleasure for its own sake couldn't actually destroy pain, it could sure as hell knock it into the background for a spell.

"Much better," Rainn said contentedly some time later, watching me get dressed. "You make a great case for the legalization of marijuana, my friend."

"I'll pass that on to my congressman. Do I put my tie back on?"

"Nah. Open your collar. Gives you more of a badass look. There. Now you're right out of *The Usual Suspects*. Did you enjoy your evening?"

"Yes, ma'am."

"Me too. Tell you what," she said, and once again seemed to be suppressing laughter. "Come by my work some time – my real work – and we'll have a drink." She reeled off an address in Manhattan. "Think you can remember that?"

"I'm absolutely sure."

"Well, good night, Mickey with a *C*."

"Good night, Rainn with two *N*'s.

I closed the door and made my way through the drawing room into the hallway, heading for the stairs. One of the club chairs in the lobby was calling my name; it was as good a place as any to see whether masculine pride at being asked on a date by a gorgeous hooker would triumph over shame that the first woman I'd shared a bed with since Anne had *been* a damned hooker. I had just rounded the corner when someone clipped me hard on the shoulder as he moved past, half-spinning me around. He did not stop.

"S'cuse you," he said, walking swiftly away. He was short but moved with a jaunty, confident, somehow familiar step, his arms swinging.

"Hey. *Hey!*"

"Hey what?" He said over his shoulder.

"You wanna watch where you're going?"

He turned around so abruptly I took a step back. "Not really."

It was Dago Red. His hair had worked free of its gel and strands hung over his forehead like loose copper wire. His gunmetal suit was rumpled, the black silk shirt beneath it opened to the middle of his chest. He was grinning. "Ain't seen you in a coon's age, buddy boy. Hurt yourself or something?"

"Or something."

"Actually, I heard you got your ass kicked," Red said. His grin that of a jack o'lantern, fixed and toothy. His eyes were very bright. "Big tough Mickey Watts got his ass kicked real bad."

"I got jumped," I said, and for the second time that night I could feel my pulse in my lips. "From behind."

"People always say that when they get their ass kicked. 'Five or six guys' they say."

"I think it was just one."

"Even worse. Tough guy like you, big badass fighter, getting the shit kicked out of you *mano e mano.* I bet you were pretty fuckin' humiliated, huh? All that time in the gym, hitting the bags, jumping rope, eating egg yolks and shit, and what happens? You get beat down right in the street like some fuckin' punk. I bet that hurt even worse than the ass-whipping you took."

My face was hot and my hands were tingling the way they do when they want to be fists. "I think you need to leave, Red."

"Oh, I'm goin'," he said cheerfully. "But I'll see you around, buddy boy." He turned for the stairs and then looked back, one hand on the oak railing. "Be real careful walking to your car, Mickey. This city can be dangerous." He started for the steps, whistling.

Something burst in my head, burst like an overloaded artery, splattering crimson memories of pain and humiliation every which way, and my body was leaping at him, my left hand snagging in his sweat-dampened hair, the edge of my right hand whipping downward at his neck in a chop that had once shattered four inches of pine board. He went down to his knees in a heap, uttering a bark of pain and surprise, and no sooner had he landed than I followed up with two, three, four more blows, as if I were trying to cleave his head from his shoulders. He flung up an arm to protect himself and I drove my knee into the back of his skull, smashing it into the marble so hard I actually heard the cartilage in his nose give away.

He was finished, but I wasn't finished with him. My heart pumped fury into my veins, and thus suffused, they filled my muscles with a demonic purpose quite distinct from the pleadings of my rational mind. All the pent-up rage of the last few months exploded into his hapless body in a kind of ghastly orgasm of violence. Slobbering out of a grinning mouth, I kicked Red, stomped him, punched him and elbowed and hammerfisted him, picked up his groaning, feebly struggling body and slammed it against a hallstand, smashing its display of erotic ivory figurines, until in a last spasm of rage, I lifted him to my collarbone and hurled him over the balcony, twenty feet to the floor below. And as he cleared the railing, one shoe coming clear of its foot like a hubcap shed on a racetrack turn, I heard a terrible scream – a single word, distorted by terror and disbelief.

"No!"

But it wasn't Red screaming.

It was me.

Chapter Seventeen

The rational mind is a lot like the cops. Never around when you need it. No sooner had the fabric of his jacket and trousers left my grip than the jammed-up gear-wheel of my sanity sprung itself free and turned once, frantically in the direction of mercy. I surged against the balustrade as if to catch the body in mid-air, and was rewarded instead with a God's-eye view of the fall and the impact. One hundred and forty pounds of Italian-American hoodlum hit unyielding marble with a sound like a bomb going off in St. Peter's Cathedral.

The sound faded quickly. I stood at the top of the steps, staring down at what I'd done in horrified disbelief, then at my throbbing hands as if for an explanation. None came.

Heels clicked abruptly on marble, and there was Deanna at the bottom of the stairs, hand pressed to her open mouth, eyes wide.

"What the hell happened?" she gasped, sounding not at all like the charming hostess. "What did you do?"

I said nothing. Just stood there, panting. She knelt down beside Red's body, face twisted with revulsion, the helm of her black dress hiking up over shapely thighs, "Jesus Christ," she said. "J-e-s-u-s…*Christ!*"

I turned my hands over. There was a tiny jewel of blood on the heel of my left. Red blood. Red's Blood. Don't think about that. Think about what you're going to do. *Think!*

"Get Kraut," I heard myself say.

"What?"

"He's with the redhead, the one in the tennis outfit. Get him *now.*"

"I don't know which room—"

"Find him. *Move!*"

She stood up, dazed and horrified, then started up the stairs. She passed me, stopping only to curse, kick off her heels, and she was gone. And I was alone with Red.

His nose was gone, crushed. One brown eye stared through the glistening red mess with an expression of idiot surprise; the other was submerged in a welter of blood like a rain-flooded crater. Blood was still trickling down over the sides of his face; some of it touched the sole of my shoe, and I drew back quickly, as if it were acid.

A surprised grunt at the top of the steps, and there was Kraut, shirt unbuttoned, fly open, eyes incredulous. "Holy shit!"

In bare feet, he and Deanna made very little noise coming down the stairs. Kraut knelt by the body like a battle surgeon, his mouth hard and grim. He took Red by the jaw and swiveled his head. It moved with disgusting ease. "Dago Red. Thought I saw him when we came in. You did this?"

"I didn't mean to," I said desperately. "It was an accident."

"Well, I'd hate to see what you'd do if you were trying, 'cause he's fuckin' dead." His voice was harsh but controlled. "We gotta get him outta here."

"What do you mean?"

"What do I mean? You wanna call an ambulance? He's gotta disappear." He stood up and kicked the body like a tire. "The trade won't talk, but we got civilians upstairs. They can't see this. Shit, Mickey, you can't do something like this here." He shook his head and ran his hands through his thick blond bristles. "All right. All right. Okay – Deanna, go round up Gavin. Don't tell him what happened, just get him down here. Mickey 'n me'll get this outta sight. You got a mop, cleaning rags, anything like that? Good. Get Ernie and get this fuckin' mess cleaned up. Nobody else but them. Tell Gavin to meet us in the storage room. Understand?"

Deanna was staring at him dully, one spiral of brown hair falling over her exquisitely molded cheekbone. Kraut snapped his fingers in her face, and she blinked as if coming out of a daze. "Right. Okay."

"Get his feet," Kraut said, lifting Red by the armpits. I just stared. Red's shoe was lizard skin with a two-inch heel. His socks were sheer. I could see his toes through the ribbed cotton.

"Hey!" Kraut's voice was sharp and angry. "I said get his fuckin' feet!"

I took Red by the ankles and we lifted him, leaving behind a great lake of blood. I was careful to step around it as we carried him into the darkened hallway under the stairs. His head lolled grotesquely; I could hear the blood pitter-pattering on floor beneath our feet.

"In here," Kraut said. Evidently he knew where he was going. He kicked a swinging door open with his heel, and we staggered into a storage room lit by a pair of naked hundred-watt bulbs. I saw a pair of industrial sinks, a sandwich table, and a walk-in refrigerator with a duct-taped handle. Cases of beer and liquor stacked floor to ceiling. As soon as the door swung shut, Kraut dropped his half of Red's body – *thud* – and stepped back to glare at me. "What the fuck happened?"

I stared at him, still holding Red by the ankles. I dropped his feet to the floor. "I don't know. I just, I mean, I came out of the room, Rainn's room, and he hit me—"

"He hit you?"

"He bumped into me."

"So you threw him off the top deck?"

"No – I mean, we got into it a bit, about, you know, about what happened, and – oh shit!" I pressed my palms against my cheeks. "I can't fucking believe this!"

"He's dead," Kraut said harshly. "Believe that. Now we got a whole new set of problems. Gino Stillitano owns this place, and he don't permit no violence here. We don't play this right, you'll be bobbing up in the fucking East River before the end of the week. Jesus, what is it with you bashing people anyway?"

The door banged open, admitting an indignant-looking Gavin. "What the fuck—"

He saw Red's body and stopped. The scowl melted away, leaving a look of bafflement that, despite the elegance of his features, was somehow Neanderthal in its stupidity.

"Don't just stand there, dumbass!" Kraut said. "Get the fuck in here and help us."

"Who is it?" Gavin whispered, stepping into the room. His eyes searched the ruined face dispassionately. Then he saw the hair – dull red copper, matted with blood – and his eyes widened again: "Son of a bitch."

Kraut found his cigarettes in his pocket and had stuck one of them into the corner of his mouth. "Congrats. You win the door prize. Anybody got a light?"

We stared at him. He stared back. It was very quiet. The refrigerator hummed gently; the faucet dripped. Kraut threw the cigarette on the floor. "Shit."

Gavin squatted down to get a better look. The scowl had come back to his face as if it were made out of some resilient rubber, but now there was a certain element of disgust in it as well. "His fuckin' head is bashed in," he said in an authoritative voice, as if announcing some great forensic discovery. "What the hell'd you whack him for?"

"'Cause he's a Giants fan." Kraut snapped. "Fuck you think? 'Cause of what happened outside the Grind Joint with Mickey!"

Gavin looked back and forth between us, his eyes narrowed slightly, as if he were trying to determine whether we were playing a joke on him. "You guys thought *Red* did that?"

Kraut and I looked at each other.

Gavin shook his head as he straightened. "He couldn't have."

"How the fuck do you know that?" Kraut said.

"Because I left the Joint same time as you that night, remember? And when I got to my car, the little fucker was waiting there for *me*. See…" His face began to pink in the naked light, and he rolled his tongue against the inside of his cheek before he spoke again, a habit of his when deeply embarrassed. "The truth is…Baby Joe wasn't *entirely* wrong about me dealing off the bottom of the deck that night. Fact is, I threw the game for Red."

"What?" The word ejected from Kraut like gristle out of a windpipe.

"Hear me out," Gavin said hastily, showing us spread fingers and open palms. "It ain't a habit or anything. I ain't looking to get clipped. It's just that it was Red's birthday, and he wanted to put one over on Baby Joe for a change. He offered me a fifty-fifty split if I stacked the deck for him, just that one time. So when I left the Joint, I met Red at my car, he handed over my end and we went off to Hard-Luck Harry's to have a drink on it. Shit, Mick, we drove right past you while you were walking to your car, and you were just fine."

In spite of everything – the adrenaline, the lingering sense of fury, the dwindling sense of hope that this was all a nightmare – I somehow had room for a new sensation: horror. Because in that instant I remembered it. Remembered the backend of Gavin's Impala as it glided swiftly past me up the street and into the darkness. But if it wasn't Red–

"Doesn't matter now," Kraut said, as if I'd spoken aloud, and turned to Gavin. "We've gotta ditch this body. Follow?"

Gavin's eyes widened suddenly as he contemplated a horror far greater than the still-warm corpse at his feet. "Not in my car!"

"You want I should call Rent-A-Hearse?"

"You're not putting this piece of shit in my car! Look at him! He's oozing all over the fuckin' place!"

"We'll wrap him up," Kraut said.

"I don't give a damn if you wrap him like King-fuckin'-Tut! You're not putting him in my car. *I* didn't fuckin' whack him. *You* whacked him. You want to put him a car, put him in *your* car."

Kraut stared at him for a good ten seconds. Red continued to leak slowly onto the concrete floor. I contemplated the extremely long odds of me successfully breaking up a fight between the two of them before we had a second body to deal with. At last, Kraut said: "Mickey, go give Deanna a hand. Get the fuckin' mess cleaned up. And keep everybody out of the lobby. Enough people already seen this."

I found Deanna on her knees, wearing bright yellow kitchen gloves, mopping up the blood along with what could have only been Ernie, who I had figured for house muscle. The qualifications for house muscle seemed to have slipped, because Ernie looked to be a hard seventy and was wearing a plaid bathrobe and shower shoes. He was square-headed and stubby, his face sun-seared leather, his eyes glittering slits below a salt-and-pepper crew cut that was awful short on pepper. He glanced over at me without any visible interest, squatted with a grunt, and set a bucket of soapy water down by Deanna's knee.

I said: "Kraut said to keep the lobby clear."

"No shit!" Deanna said viciously. Tears gleamed over her model's cheekbones, and the lovely cupid's-bow of her mouth was drawn down in a tremulous frown of revulsion. As I watched, she slopped an oversized sponge over the bloody mess on the floor and then squeezed it over the bucket. "Wouldn't want anyone to see your handiwork, would you?"

"I'm sorry."

"Sorry?" The sponge slapped wetly on the marble; the water from the bucket had misted pink. "Your first time here and you have to *kill* somebody? Can't you people give it a rest when you're getting laid, for God's sake?"

"Honey," the old man said gently, in a gravelly rasp that so abrasive it made my eyes water. "No need for that now."

"No need? No need? There's a dead man in the storage room, Ernie!" She wrung the sponge out over the bucket so fiercely sure she was picturing my neck.

"It'll be all right," Ernie said, glancing at me and back at her. "Kraut will take care of it. He's a good fella."

"He better take care of it," Deanna said. "He damn well better. People are supposed to feel safe here. They don't feel safe, they won't come. And then *you* will be in some very deep shit." She glared at me again, then plunked the sponge down in the bucket and stripped off the gloves off angrily. "Here. You finish it. I've got to get upstairs and run interference."

She stood up and tossed the gloves at my feet. Bloody water ran down one smooth-shaven calf, and she made a deep glottal noise of disgust and anguish. "You… *bastard!*" Then she was gone in a flash up the stairs. I looked at the old man; he looked up at me.

"Uppity little cunt, isn't she?" He shook his head ruefully. "You think she'd never had it run down her legs before."

"I'm really sorry about this," I said after a moment, picking up the gloves. "I don't know what happened."

"Happened is, you kilt yourself a guinea. Was he askin' for it?"

There was something unreal about his calm. We might have been discussing whether it had been appropriate or not to flip a fellow motorist the bird for cutting me off in traffic. "Yeah. He really was."

"Then don't fuss about it." He made a hurry-up gesture at the sponge. "Help me with this, Sonny. I'm not as quick as I used to be."

We worked hurriedly, not speaking. I heard voices near the top of the stairs, but they were all female. When we were finished, Ernie pointed a blunt finger at the bucket. "Better go dump this. I'll finish with the stairs."

I lugged the bucket back into the storage room, trying not to slosh the pinkish mess as I did so.

"'Bout fuckin' time," Kraut snapped at me. He had draped a bar towel over Red's face and it had molded over his features like a mask of red clay. "Here's what we're gonna do. Gavin and I have to go upstairs and get our shit. I'll be right back with a sheet. You and me are gonna wrap this fucker up, and Gavin's gonna bring the car around back." He threw Gavin a frigid glare, as if daring him to disagree, but the dealer said nothing, just looked at his feet. I wondered fleetingly what had been promised – or threatened – while I was gone. "We load him in the trunk and get the fuck out of here."

They left me alone with Red in the storage room. The refrigerator had kicked off. There was no sound at all except the drip-drip-drip of the faucet. I tried not to look at Red, but a dead body is always the center of attention.

Ernie came back into the room. He was holding something in his free hand and tossed it at me. "It's all clean out there. Don't know what you want to do with that."

It was a shoe. Red's lizard skin loafer. It felt warm; there was a smudge of foot powder on the red lining.

"Only a wop would wear lizard skin shoes," Ernie said with certainty.

The door banged open again. Kraut came in looking very much like a man who had dressed in the dark.

"Hey there, Kraut." Ernie said casually. "Looks like we had some trouble here."

"Yeah," Kraut said. He was carrying a bedsheet. "Sorry about this, Ern. You know we wouldn't disrespect the joint on purpose."

"No bother really. Just so's you boys get him out of here discreet. You know Gino wouldn't want no trouble in his place."

Kraut laid out the sheet beside Red's body. "We don't want no trouble, either. Mickey, roll his ass into the sheet and wrap him up good. Roll up the ends like a joint. And put his shoe back on. Ern, you got some rope around here? How 'bout an extension cord? Perfect." He turned to me. "What the fuck are you waiting for? Roll him up! And put his fuckin' shoe back on, less you want a souvenir."

Red's body was as loose as a half-filled sack of grain and would not roll. We had to turn it onto the sheet and rotate him until the sheet wrapped around him like a tortilla. Blood welled redly through the layers of cotton like flowers blossoming in fast motion. "That oughta hold him," Ernie pronounced, cigarette bobbing in his mouth as he knotted the extension cord. He sounded like a veteran fisherman weighing in on some tackle. "He won't go nowhere." He straightened up, vertebrae and knees popping like a string of cheap firecrackers. "I've had enough excitement for tonight, fellas. I'm goin' back to bed."

"Ernie, you're cool as a fuckin' cucumber," Kraut said.

"You seen one dead wop, you seen 'em all," Ernie replied with a shrug. He stubbed out his cigarette in a black plastic ashtray and left, whistling an old man's tuneless whistle.

“Who the fuck *is* that guy?” I said.

“Ernie the Coffee Boy,” Kraut said. “Retired wiseguy. He lives here. Now, let’s get this outta here.”

The back of the townhouse had not been renovated. The floors here were linoleum, bare walls cracked and peeling. The back door was high-security steel augmented by deadbolts the width of railroad spikes, and the window overlooking the alley barred and wire-meshed. I could see nothing except the fragmented glare of a single streetlight. Kraut slammed the bolts aside like a U-boat commander popping the conning tower hatch and kicked the door open. I felt a rush of summer-fragrant air, heard the sounds of traffic on the street nearby, but the small yard was hemmed in on either side by a high wooden fence overgrown with ivy. The alley itself was shadowed and empty.

The Impala appeared, looking funeral and sinister with its lights off. Gavin backed carefully into the grass-and-gravel yard and stopped a third of the way to the rear stoop. We heard the trunk pop.

“Son of a bitch doesn’t want to get it dirty,” Kraut said, managing to convey enormous rage in a voice barely above a whisper. “Come on, let’s do this.”

We picked Red up again. He swung easily, if awkwardly, between us, and again my mind struggled irrelevantly for the right description: a half-filled sandbag, a broken doll, an old fireman’s dummy, a roll of worn-out carpeting. None of them quite fit. Carrying a body is carrying a body and like nothing else.

We crossed the yard to the Impala. Kraut swung the trunk open. It was empty save for a folding jack in a black vinyl sheath, and it smelled of carpet shampoo. We hoisted the body inside. For just a moment Kraut stared down at it, his face red-lit by the brake lights. Then the lid came down with a slam, and he was moving toward the passenger door.

I went around the other side and pulled at the rear door handle. It was locked. I rapped angrily on the glass and the lock popped. I opened the door and was halfway into the rear seat when I saw movement at the top of the steps behind us, two figures lit by the overhead yellow bulb in its wire-mesh hood. I recognized Deanna instantly. She stepped out on the stoop and pulled the heavy handle of the security door with both hands. As she did, I saw Rainn just behind her. Except that it couldn't have been Rainn – Rainn had lustrous jet-black hair that covered her forehead and ears, and this girl's, glinting auburn in the bulb light, was pinned flat against her scalp, tamped down as if to accommodate a wig, thus exposing the whole of her face. A face that now revealed was oddly familiar beneath its spray-on tan, a face I now recognized belonged not to Rainn but to Tina, Tina of the nightclub and the Grind Joint, Tina whose irresistible chameleon beauty had set in motion the chain of events whose latest link was a corpse in the trunk behind me. I had just enough time to see the almost orgasmic expression of excitement on her face, see her hand raise in a small, ironical wave, and then the car was lurching forward, tires spinning on the gravel. I fell into the backseat and slammed the door shut behind me.

"Who was that?" Gavin demanded, squinting into the rearview mirror.

"Nobody," I said, sinking down into the seat. "Just drive."

Chapter Eighteen

Life is full of dividing lines: some subtle, some gross. At any one of a hundred points it started for me, and at any one of a thousand moments afterward it became too late to stop. It would be easy to say that killing Dago Red was the point of no return. But the point of no return is most likely something you invent for yourself long after the fact, when you are grasping for an alibi, an excuse to show that everything you did was inevitable and beyond your power to control. That I had killed Red was undeniable. Its effect on me afterward was an open question.

I had become a murderer, but the world had not stopped turning. The morning after we had dumped Dago Red's body in a deserted lot in Jamaica, the sun shone through the blinds in my bedroom just as it always had. The bathroom mirror held its usual reflection. I was a trifle pale under the stubble but otherwise looked normal. My eyes were not haunted, and there was no blood on my hands. The events of the previous evening were vivid but fantastical, like fever dreams.

Outside, it was the same. Slanting sunshine in a blue sky, a lazy breeze, just a hint of the humidity forecasters had been warning about for days. Familiar early-morning whisper of traffic down the Avenue toward the City. Self-absorbed faces passing on the sidewalk. None of them paid me any mind. No one stopped to stare. No muttering, no pointing, no hurried steps out of my path as I bought my coffee and newspaper. I was a murderer. Nothing else had changed.

A small bribe to the building super had permitted me to install a weight bench and heavy bag in the boiler room. In the heavy odor of must and burnt fuel oil, I proceeded through my normal workout under the bare sixty-watt bulbs. The New York State Athletic Commission had whacked me with a three-month medical suspension following the Suba fight, and it would be at least half that time again before I could stomach the thought of returning to the Hard Knox, but bruises or not, I had to keep fit. I pounded on the bag, clanked the weights, and skipped rope until my calves quivered with exhaustion. The whisper and slap of the rope was soothing, the sweat coursing down my body a steady release. In my mind, the thought that Red had been killed for a crime he had not committed kept reasserting itself, but it seemed to have no power, impact, no resonance. I was aware of it, but I did not care.

I went upstairs and took a long shower. The sun was strong through the windowpanes, and it was getting uncomfortably warm in the apartment. Toweling off, I shut the windows, drew the blinds, flipped on the air conditioning unit in the window. A baseball game flickered on television. The Mets were a sorry eight games back, which was a disgrace in light of their payroll. Wars had been financed for less.

Cool, cool in the apartment. The ice clicked in my glass. The air conditioner droned. I was conscious of feeling very good in a physical way: slept out, sweated out. It didn't seem right that I should feel good when Dago Red could no longer feel anything, but that was the way it was. The game progressed, the first of a doubleheader. Baseball was the only sport played at the pace where you could have a doubleheader. At that pace it was a wonder more of the players weren't built like Babe Ruth rather than Mark McGwire.

I was dozing. The organs of the seventh inning stretch sang like a lullaby in my ears. I kept waiting to feel remorse, but it simply would not come. Buy me some peanuts and Cracker Jack, I don't care if Red never comes back. I slept until the third inning of the second game. When I woke, the quality of the light had changed through the slits of the blinds. I knew without seeing that outside lay another dog day afternoon. You wait all damn winter for the sun, and when it arrives it thanks you by turning the sidewalk into a pizza oven.

I dressed, drove over the bridge into the City, and found what I was looking for without too much difficulty. The thing about strip joints, even high-end strip joints, is that they all possess the same furtive air, regardless of the architecture. Maybe it was the lack of windows, or the tassels on the marquee, or the way the men entering and leaving moved swiftly without looking around, as if afraid to make eye contact: but Juggernauts was unmistakably a place where women got paid to take off their clothes.

During daylight hours there was no cover charge. After the humidity and glare of the streets, it was lovely to be inside. The club was spacious, high-ceilinged, dark, and cool. The tables looked clean and the bouncers formidable but civilized, like well-kept guard dogs. There was no lighting over the tables, and the few patrons were indistinct shadows nursing their beers. The spotlights illuminating the stages ticked off one color after the other: pink, blue, yellow-gold. I took a table just outside the shifting cone of light and watched the bubbles stream up through the ten-dollar beer I had ordered. The music was too loud considering how empty the place was. Three girls came and went like an inning. Between the girls' sets, disco balls flashed and glittered against the full-length mirrors behind the stage. A waitress in hot pants asked me four times if I wanted another drink. On her fifth try I agreed, thinking idly that I could have bought a case of beer for what I had already paid. Then Tina came on stage, and I had no more idle thoughts.

I recognized her at once, despite the shimmering platinum blonde wig – fool me twice and all that. Her body was a triumph of isometric exercise and breast augmentation surgery: silken, pliant, firm, but white now, the spray tan scrubbed off without leaving a trace. She had no hair at all below her eyelashes. There was a small tattoo of a chameleon on her left ankle. She was down to her G-string, garter, and white heels before she made out my face in the shadows. Her mouth softened briefly into a sly smile and then resumed its coolly indifferent cast. Three Japanese men in blue suits fed her five-dollar bills in a sort of relay while she rolled her bare hips inches from their upturned faces, her hands on the brass pole, her eyes never leaving mine.

I was aroused. It was not merely that her milk-pale skin shone to a high gloss over the delicious curves of her body, or the way her breasts thrust out so aggressively they seemed intent on crossing the distance between us. It was not the length and shape of those legs or the way her spiked heels brought out the muscles in her calves. It was not even the hypnotic movements of her hips – liquid, rhythmic, promising ecstasy almost beyond imagination. It was that stare. A man can go his whole life and never be stared at like *that* by a woman who looked the way she did. And it was not part of the act. Unlike everything else being offered, it was strictly for me.

When her set was over, she dressed and sat down with me at the bar. She had glitter in her hair and on her skin. Even in dim light it had the delicious sheen that is partly youth and partly the result of a good moisturizing cream. I bought her a drink and her lipstick formed a perfect, silvery-white crescent on the rim of the glass. As we drank, we shared one of her cigarettes. It was part of the dance to share it, just as it was part of the dance for me to carry cigarettes although I rarely smoked them. I had not danced with Anne this way. The first conversation I had with Anne was about poetry. She was sitting at a Manhattan café on a bright spring day, drinking coffee and reading *The Collected Works of Robert Frost.* I was at the next table, drinking beer and reading a dog-eared old Captain America novel called *Holocaust for Hire.* We caught each other looking at the titles of the other's books and started laughing. She'd asked, with a friendly sort of contempt, if it was a good book. I replied that it was no "Stopping by Woods on a Snowy Evening" but would do in a pinch. The way her eyebrows rose I knew I had scored a point. I knew I had scored a point with Tina when she put her hand on my knee and thrust her tongue into my mouth.

"I'm getting off at midnight," she murmured. "Whether I'm getting off again after that is up to you."

"Just one question," I said, though it was difficult to speak with my lower lip caught between her teeth. "Is Tina your real name?"

"I'll answer that," she replied. "If you tell me what you really do for a living."

"You tell me. Then we'll both know."

I was a bit tipsy when I went back out into the sunlight. Too much beer and no lunch, and it was too hot for my black leather jacket and designer jeans. I had never dressed this way with Anne. Anne liked me civilized: clean-shaven and khaki. I liked it too, though sometimes I felt soft in those clothes. I never felt soft now. I felt a lot of things but soft was most definitely not one of them.

I did not go home but stopped in a pub that I favored sometimes because no trade ever went there. It was one of those places where you have to walk down a flight of steps to get in, and it's always dark and cool. The few lights are shaded in yellow glass and everyone talks in a murmur and minds their own business. They had Boddington's Ale on tap. I ordered a pint and sat at the bar and drank it slowly, seated among the ferns and rich, dark wood and polished brass. Then I decided I was not going to be much good to Tina if I kept drinking on an empty stomach. I ordered the sliced steak, medium rare, with fries and a side of sautéed mushrooms and onions. It took a while to appear, but I was in no hurry. Midnight was a way off.

My food arrived and I dug in eagerly. My, this steak was good – melt in your mouth good, the way steak is supposed to be. And the onions! Sautéed to perfection. Mushrooms were easy, but onions took some doing. They were always served raw or looked like burnt shoestring, but not here. This was the kind of meal I fantasized about when I was trying to make weight. When Sam was feeding me watery fish soup, raw vegetables, egg whites – all the stuff that is so good for you and tastes like shit. I'd look at my plate and think, goddamn it, I want something that bleeds. A cheeseburger on a sesame-seed Kaiser, half-buried in melted cheddar, Bibb lettuce, and freshly sliced tomatoes, heavy on the catsup and mayo. Pork chops. Barbecued beef ribs. Buffalo wings served in Anchor Steam hot sauce with bleu cheese dressing on the side. A lovely, tasty steak with all the trimmings, served with a beer so cold, slivers of ice ran down the sides of the glass. God, yes. That was what you gave up. All the things you really liked. Food. Beer. Sleep. And women.

When I finished my meal, I declined the barkeep's offer of another ale, tipped him with a twenty tucked under my empty glass, and walked back out into what was now early evening. I was at the stage where you have to keep drinking or stop cold and walk it off, and I knew if I kept drinking I would be dead drunk by the time Tina had collected her last dollar bill. It was very warm, and here by the East River, the breeze blew away most of the humidity. I strolled aimlessly up and down the quiet waterfront streets, which as always made me long for the artistic talent to describe them: the pen of a Proust, the brush of a Basquiat. The neon-lit bodegas that never seemed to sleep, battered cars parked bumper to bumper in long ranks almost military in their precision, splatters of graffiti on sliding metal shutters, grimed-over street signs, potted plants teetering on windowsills, rust-encrusted fire escapes. All of which, viewed through my lover's eye, seemed not squalid and disagreeable but homey and charming. New York, I thought, was a city defined by its flaws. In every possible way, its virtues were overwhelmed by its vices, as Jekyll was by Hyde. Yet it was these very vices that gave the city its character – like tar in an oak barrel lending its flavor to Scotch. Dago Red lying amid this gritty residue of urban supremacy seemed to me not pathetic but fitting. Live by the streets, die in them. And was it so bad, really? We all have to die, and none of us but suicides choose the when of it. Wasn't it better, in the long run, to go out as he did, as close to his criminal prime as he would ever be, the full bloom of health still upon him and fresh from a woman's bed?

At midnight, I met Tina in the Juggernauts parking lot and followed her pink Jeep back to her high-rise apartment on East Seventy-Eighth Street. Her rooms were larger than mine and decorated in surprisingly good taste, but also somewhat sterile. The furniture was new. The color scheme was neutral. No photo album on the coffee table, no magnets on the fridge, no dishes in the sink, and no dust anywhere. Clean and impersonal, like a hotel room just after housekeeping. She offered me a glass of mineral water, seated me on the sofa, and excused herself. The shower ran on and on. Her apartment was on the twelfth floor, and the windows were closed; it was surprisingly quiet. Only the soothing hush of central air conditioning.

When she came back out, she wore a man's terrycloth bathrobe drawn up to her throat and belted around the waist like a fuzzy blue *gi*. I realized at that moment I had never possessed a clear idea of what she actually looked like. Her hair, sans wig, was a nondescript reddish-brown, and in bare feet she barely rose to the level of my chin. Scrubbed free of makeup and glitter, she was considerably less intimidating. The effect was of an Amazonian stripped of her armor. But seeing her so vulnerable did not make her less attractive to me. Scrape off all the icing and a cake is still a cake.

She led me into the bedroom. It smelled of vanilla and was so dark she had to lead me by the hand. Her robe slipped to the floor in a rustle, and she turned down the bed as I undressed. Even in near-total darkness her white skin gave off a feeble luminescence; I reached out and slid my hands across it, fascinated. Took in the silken feel of her shoulders, her heavy breasts, the smooth play of her back muscles, the equally smooth curve of her backside. Then we were naked between the sheets, the sound of the air conditioning soon muffled by the sound of bodies in motion. Slowly at first, almost tenderly, then with urgency, the bedsprings groaning slightly under the steady rhythm, her soft-lipped mouth reaching up to meet mine. I thought fleetingly of Anne, how the faces changed but the act was always the same, the need was always the same, no one drew a line between the sex you bought and the love you made, and your body could not tell the difference.

I woke in the middle of the night. Tina was sleeping soundly beside me. It was perfectly black; not even a glimmer of streetlight shone through the blinds. All needs satisfied, all lusts spent, I lay with my hands laced behind my head and stared at the ceiling, listening to a silence barely stirred by her breathing. It struck me then, as I was drifting gently back toward sleep, that my first day as a murderer had been one of the finest of my life. But the thought did not disturb me, and at some point I slipped off into a deep, restful sleep, and did not dream.

Chapter Nineteen

When I went back to work, I found that very little had changed. Those who knew treated me with a curious lightness or otherwise stiffly, as if we had taken opposing sides in a minor family feud. No one spoke of what had happened, and after a few days, their expressions softened. Life at the goulash house returned to its normal, jolting rhythm. When the police finally discovered Dago Red's body, there were a few discreet glances from some of the patrons; I discovered to my surprise that they were directed at Baby Joe and not at me. The fat man had it in for the little prick, I heard more than once in muttered conversations, and had probably whacked him. The consensus was that it was no big loss, and a few expressed undisguised glee. If Red were missed, it was only at the blackjack table, where he had been an inveterate loser.

The Grind Joint was a very demanding mistress. Aside from the brutal hours, the need to be constantly on guard, to work yourself up to that taut-spring pitch of concentration and readiness every time you stepped over the threshold, was incredibly taxing. I'd hoped I would become accustomed to it in time, but it was impossible. As Kraut liked to say, even world-champion bull riders get butterflies in the stall. But rodeo riders don't ride every day, and it seemed that every time we opened our doors, another crazed beast came charging in, looking to gore someone. With our clientele, it was impossible to avoid. For some of our patrons, fighting was as much a part of the experience as drinking, gambling, and copping a feel from that coked-out hooker on the dance floor. In the beginning, I'd thrown myself into the midst of these battles no matter how large the participants, and in doing so, I learned a lesson for the street I had already learned in the cage: no matter how hard you hit, there is always someone out there who hits harder. I came home some mornings with cuts, contusions, black eyes, bruised ribs, and once with an ear so red and swollen it looked as if it had been bitten by a rattlesnake. The worst came when a drunken second-story man with a bad coke habit and a literal ace up his sleeve came at me with a switchblade. In one blurred motion, he flashed the tip from my ribs to my hip-bone, and scampered over the card table like the ape in the Rue Morgue, looking to add some thrust to his slashing foreplay. At that moment, Kraut connected a flush, brass-knuckled right hand to his cheekbone. The ape's face came apart in a spray of blood and broken teeth, and the knife, sliding free of his nerveless fingers, landed point-down on my stomach, adding another four stitches to the forty he'd just required of me. But when you run your own business, you don't take medical leave, and when you run your own criminal business, you don't go to the E.R. I was stitched up by a man jokingly referred to as The Family Doctor, a defrocked G.P. from the Bronx who owed the house a fortune and could be counted on to discreetly clean stab wounds, probe bullet holes, and set the occasional bone. In a basement "office" that looked like the set of a B-grade horror film, he gave me a slug of rye and a tetanus shot and sent me on my way. Three days later I was back at work, fingering my own new pair of brass knuckles and wondering how I had managed to take a vacation from the cage without increasing my life expectancy.

Time went by: days, weeks. I grew accustomed to sleeping late and staying up later, to breathing more cigarette smoke than oxygen, to sneaking the occasional butt myself. I grew accustomed to living in a world of hard cash – to the feel and texture of it, to the peculiar weight of it when it was rolled up and bound with a rubber band and resting in my pocket where my wallet had once been. It seemed I always had a lot of cash, and the scent was intoxicating. When the take was good, sometimes Tina and I would spread it over the bed and make love amongst the crumpled Hamiltons and Adams and Benjamin Franklins. When we were finished, we'd peel the sweat-dampened bills off our bodies and go out on the town, not loving each other and completely content in it.

We had a good, safe time, Tina and I. Good because we had no common cause but pleasure, safe because we did not allow our pleasure to be confused by inconvenient emotion. We did things together and drew different satisfactions from them. She had an eye for fine things and enjoyed spending my money for me, picking out leather jackets and heavy silver jewelry and expensive bottles of cologne. When I took her to fights at the Garden, I was pleased to have a beautiful woman on my arm, and she was pleased at the attention she always got in a crowd. Sometimes, of course, we went weeks without seeing each other, and I knew she was in the arms of another, wealthier man. I didn't care and was pleased with the not caring. She would come back eventually, and while she was gone, there were other fish in the sea. I caught some of them and was not lonely.

My relationship with Clean continued to change. He had become more of a boss than a friend, and he was a bad boss to work for. He alternated absenteeism with periods of unbearable micromanagement. It is no small act of humiliation for a man who has been dealing cards for thirty years to be lectured on exactly when he should or should not allow a customer to double-down on a bet, and Clean did not confine himself to telling his dealers, stickmen, and pit bosses how to do their jobs. He had an on-again, off-again obsession with cutting costs, and this manifested in bizarre ways. The fellow who ran the kitchen was subjected to screaming fits over his lavish use of condiments and such precious sandwich-making materials as bread, lettuce, cold cuts, and Swiss cheese. It was easy to forget, watching these displays of frugality, that most of our foodstuffs had been bought at twenty cents on the dollar out of the back of a truck, if they had not simply been hijacked at gunpoint off the Nassau Expressway. But it was over booze – for which we often paid nothing at all, since it was Don Cheech's policy to supply us with hard liquor, wine, and sometimes beer from the stockrooms of restaurants he had muscled into, busted out, and then burned down for profit – that Clean achieved his apotheosis. Linda, who was *de facto* head barkeep for the back room, and who was probably the toughest and meanest-spirited bitch I'd ever met, was reduced to tears of frustration more than once over Clean's meddling. He wanted to water down the drinks, and when she steadfastly refused to do this –

admittedly more out of a fear of what it would do to her tips than over any ethical considerations – he made her life a misery by hovering behind the bar to insure that she did not pour so much as an extra milliliter. After several violent arguments, he agreed to abandon this practice, and then promptly installed a machine that dispensed liquor to pre-programmed specifications and made Linda's job largely irrelevant. And just when his cocaine-fueled mood swings from solicitous geniality to hostile suspicion had us all on the verge of open rebellion, he would vanish, like a banshee in mid-scream.

It was Kraut who really ran the club – openly when Clean was gone, in spite of him when he was around – and he treated me now the way Old Sam had behaved toward me after my first professional fight: as a father who had been through the wars might treat a son returning from his first battle. He knew a lot and taught it to me casually and without obligation, and I found that I wanted to learn. I learned too that it was he who had spread the rumors that Baby Joe killed Dago Red. A cynic – and I was in a business where cynicism was considered part of your kit, like brass knuckles or the bail bondsman's phone number – might have observed this as mere self-protection, since he had been party to what had happened in Murray Hill. But I knew better. Kraut was a stand-up guy in the old tradition, in a strange way reminiscent of my father in his steadfast refusal to abandon a position once he had taken it. It was a quality I lacked, and so admired in others when they were not using it to beat me to the canvas or break my heart.

It was, all told, a strange life. In many ways disagreeable and always dangerous, but never dull. In the few quiet moments when I was alone and had the energy for introspection, I could not say I was unhappy. A rollercoaster ride doesn't actually go anywhere, but that doesn't make the ride any less exhilarating. And this exhilaration was bound up in pleasures I had forgotten during my years with Anne: the very real high that physical lust brings when it is raised to its highest peak and then satisfied; the cheap thrill of breaking rules and getting away with it; the feeling that my heart was beholden to no one but myself and therefore secure.

I thought a lot about Anne. It was impossible not to. The city was littered with our old places, from the luncheonette down the street from my apartment where she had broken up with me, to the open-air market on Queens Boulevard where I had bought her an ankle bracelet on a whim, to that particular swath of grass off the Bridle Path in Central Park where we had once picnicked on roast duck and cold white wine and only narrowly talked each other out of making love in public. It was not her city, but it seemed to belong to her memory, and the hardest part was accepting that she was still here, still going about her daily routine with nothing changed except that I was no longer a part of it. There were times, usually late at night when I had taken one too many sips of whiskey and had no one sharing my bed, when I resolved with the bitterness of the scorned never to speak her name aloud, or wished her stricken with illness or ugliness, or plotted petty acts of revenge. It was all meaningless. I loved Anne and knew I always would. If there was a fantasy, it was of apology, reconciliation, marriage, children, a peaceable middle age behind a white picket fence in Parsippany, memories of the Grind Joint and everything that had gone with it sealed off forever, as if in scar tissue.

Someday, I thought – on the good, sunny mornings when you feel the full power of your own life and everything seems possible – I would make it happen. I would quit the club, finish school, buy a suit and take the train to work. I would show Anne I was the man she had always believed me to be, and she would love me again. It was true I was now a murderer, but this was nothing *she* had to know. In any case, what had happened in an old life should not matter in the new. And I would have that new life. I swore to God I would.

Just not today.

Chapter Twenty

We were standing around the espresso machine at the Friends of the Friends, dressed in our Sunday best, making nervous chitchat over the clink of glazed china. It was just shy of noon on a jewel-bright summer morning. The sunlight diffusing through the storefront windows filled the room with a strangely ethereal glow. The tables were empty, the greasy decks of Bicycle playing cards neatly stacked by freshly emptied ashtrays. The television mounted over the bar was dark. Even the flashers on the muted Rock-Ola jukebox seemed strangely subdued. Occasionally the muffled whiff of a passing car filtered in through the glass; otherwise the two of us might have been alone, like fish in a smoked glass bowl.

"How do I look?" I asked Kraut.

"Same as five minutes ago. Stop asking."

"I'm nervous," I said.

"You hide it real good."

"You're not nervous?"

He sipped coffee and returned the cup back to its saucer. We were drinking it the Brooklyn-Italian way, holding the saucers in the palms of our left hands and the cups in our rights. When in Rome and all that. "I respectfully decline to answer that question on the grounds that my answer may tend to incriminate me."

"Well, you don't show it."

"I got a good game-face," he shrugged, sipping carefully. "Come to think of it, you should have one too, bein' a fighter and all."

"My game-face is threatening. I don't think I want to scare Don Cheech."

When a made guy gets out of prison, it has roughly the same effect on the *brugad* that the arrival of a new planet would have on an existing solar system. All the old orbits are disrupted. Of course, the size of the disruption is determined by the strength of the gravitational field exerted by the newcomer – in other words, by how big the fucking thing is. A rinky-dink planetoid the size of Mercury might cause only a small wobble in the existing constellation, quickly accommodated and then forgotten. On the other hand, the appearance of a gas giant as big as Saturn would throw everything into the most profound chaos, and re-write not only the total number of planets but the relationship they have with each other.

The FBI likes to display charts which explain the hierarchical structure of the American Mafia. These charts always take on a hard and easily definable shape, like an Aztec pyramid. It's satisfying to look at and simple to understand. But I like my analogy better. A pyramid is hard and unyielding; a solar system is in a constant state of movement, flux, and dynamic tension. For your convenience, though, I'm going to blend the two. At the top is the boss. Immediately beneath him on either side are the underboss and *consigliere,* who together form that entity known on the street as "the Administration." Consider them collectively the Sun. Spreading out beneath this starry apex are the captains. These are the planets. Within the gravity well of each planet are the made men – moons, if you like – and within the pull exerted by each made man a huge number of smaller objects, asteroids and comets and such, known as associates. The arrival of a new associate, such as myself, effects the constellation not at all. Just one more grain of dust in a glittering cloud surrounding the fist-sized chunk of iron known as Kraut, who in turn orbited the building-sized Immaculata Comet, which in turn was tugged along by the gravitational field of the Stillitano Moon, which encircled the Planet Immaculata – et cetera and so on. But here comes the tricky part, the part the FBI never quite understands. Just as nature abhors a vacuum, so does the mob. When the Planet Immaculata was sucked into the black hole known as Lewisburg Penitentiary, Gino Stillitano became a planet by default – an "acting captain." He was the next-most-dominating force in the vicinity, and so the gravitational field shifted in his direction. All that had been Immaculata's became Stillitano's, swirling about him, adding to his mass, increasing the strength of his influence, until, for all intents and purposes, he really *was* a planet. Sure, he was only *acting*, but on the street, proximity's everything, memories are short…and gravity kills. As far as I was concerned, Don Cheech was just a name; Gino was the boss.

Then the parole board intervened.

I honestly don't know how a criminal of Dominic Immaculata's stature wangled an early release. The guy's rap sheet looked like the Yellow Pages. I suppose some enormous bribes were involved. Failing that, blackmail. At any rate, eighteen months before he was due to max out on his sentence, he was given his walking papers by the Bureau of Prisons, and his release created gravity waves that were felt as far as the Grind Joint. Clean, whose impatience to receive his button had been making him almost as miserable as he was making everyone around him, now sauntered about like some Dean Martin, a cigarette in one hand, a tumbler of Scotch in the other, humming "Hey, Goombati" and not troubling to wipe the lipstick from his grin. Things, he was fond of repeating in a slightly slurred voice, were about to change Big Time. At last, Gino Stillitano and his *fascina* friend, Nicky Cowboy, were going to be shoved back in their proper places. At last he, Clean, would be able to stand among them as an equal. No more cheek kissing, no more *fugazy* respect. *In fact,* he told me one night, whispering drunkenly in my ear, *If things go the way I 'spect, it won't be long before those two* figli di puttana *are puckering up when* I *come in the room. How 'bout that, huh? My uncle in the Administration, and me skipper of his old crew!*

Gino, of course, had other ideas. He'd been running Dominic's gang with brutal efficiency for years; he now considered it his own and wasn't about to hand over the reins without an argument. But you'll notice I said *argument.* A fight was out of the question. No way Gino would shoot it out; without the backing of the bosses, he'd have had about as much chance of overthrowing Don Cheech as Satan had of deposing God. According to Kraut, who was a very reliable source of mob gossip, Gino had simply put up a beef with the Administration. This was his right, but exactly what he expected to achieve by it was anyone's guess. There was, Kraut had told me in confidential tones, not a Nazi's chance in Nuremberg that anything would come of it except a loss of face for Gene when the *consigliere* ruled against him.

The door opened, admitting a breeze that ruffled the Italian and American flags mounted on the wall behind the espresso bar. Don Cheech swaggered in, still wearing his sunglasses, with Clean a step behind him, holding the door.

For a guy who had done three and a half years on a five-year sentence, he looked pretty damned good. His thinning silvery-gray hair was as neatly trimmed as a golf green, and his deep-set blue eyes, staring out of a shiny, hard-cheekboned, square-chinned face were restless with energy and intelligence, assessing and appraising. I had forgotten how short he was, but his posture was ramrod-straight, and the body beneath his custom-made Male Attitude suit – gunmetal gray, with just the faintest sheen of silk – looked stocky and hard.

"Hey, bo," Kraut said. We put down our saucers and greeted him the way we were expected to, with a handshake and a kiss on the cheek. His skin was coarse and tasted strongly of some lemony aftershave. "Good to see you again."

"*Como se va?*" Don Cheech's voice had gotten more gravelly in the time since I had last seen him. I could almost see the polyps on his vocal chords, and I wondered how many contraband Chesterfields had contributed to its particular rasp. "You still skimming from my fucking club, you Nazi prick?"

"Yep," Kraut said. "I'm a born thief."

"I can testify to that," Clean said with a smirk. "Every time these two get together, my bag feels light."

"Don't let my nephew bust your balls, fellas," Don Cheech said, in a tone that said clearly, *Let my nephew bust your balls all he damn well wants and like it.* Abruptly he turned to me, the flesh around his eyes tightening in recognition. "Well, well, well. Look who we got here. Mickey Watts. Christ, how long's it been?"

"Five years, easy," I said.

"Longer than that," Clean said. He stood slightly behind his uncle, one hand casually in his pocket, a thick cigar between the fingers of the other. He looked as if he were posing for *Gentleman's Quarterly*. "He was still in the amateurs back then."

"And now he's a pro." Cheech looked me up and down the way a hunter examines a brand-new rifle. "Fighting in a fuckin' *cage*, no less. How's that treating you?"

"Rough," I said.

The door opened again, this time with a bang. Gino Stillitano strode in on a shaft of sunlight. His wraparound shades were pushed up over his forehead into thick straight brown hair blown careless by the wind. He was wearing a black leather racing jacket with a narrow red stripe over an open-collared black sports shirt, black jeans tight enough to show off the muscles in his thighs, and thick-soled black leather shoes. I thought he looked like Darth Vader without the helmet.

"Hey!" he said with malevolent good cheer. "The gang's all here. So to speak. How the fuck are ya, Cheech? Long time no see, huh?"

He brushed past Clean and took Don Cheech in a rough embrace, actually lifting him off his feet. "Jeez, you're getting' heavy, you little *cazzu*. What did they *feed* you upstate? When I was there it was joot balls and cold water." He set Don Cheech down and kissed him on the cheek with a loud, vaudevillian smack.

Don Cheech smoothed his lapels and hair with careful, dignified movements and stared at Gino with a distaste he probably would have hidden better under different circumstances. "Gene. Nice to see you're still a world-class prick."

"Oh, indeed. Indeed!" Gino grinned brightly. I had never seen him grin before and the effect was like watching someone carve a smile into a jack o'lantern. "How's that little faggot nephew of yours? Oh, shit – Clean! I didn't notice you standing there." Gino swatted Clean playfully on the side of the head, ignoring the wide-eyed look of indignation on his face as well as the spray of cigar ash onto the floor. "You look like a million fucking bucks, you know that?"

"Yeah, I do," Clean said, clearing his throat. He moved up to kiss Gino on the cheek, but the taller man took a quick step back, hands up.

"No, no, no. You kiss me I'll get a fuckin' hard-on, an' you know how that is in a pair of jeans – it's like tryin' to hide a ten-pound salami in a five-pound bag. You're so goddamn cute, Clean, I swear I don't know whether to take a picture of you or make you my *goumada.*" He turned to Don Cheech. "Pickle of a fuckin' situation we got goin' here, eh, old buddy?"

"Not really," Cheech said coolly, moving to the espresso machine. "I think it'll be cleared up real quick when Joe gets here."

"Oh, me too, me too," Gino said. He followed the older man to the bar, hopped on the stool and rested his leather-clad elbows on it, lowering his chin until it sat on the back of his hands. "If there's one thing that old greaseball is good at, it's this kind of Mickey Mouse hair-splitting shit."

"I wouldn't call it hair-splitting, Gene." Cheech said, pulling at one of the espresso machine's handles and squinting through the steam. "It's pretty much an open-and-shut case. I think you're wasting your fucking time being here."

"Hey – it's my time to waste, right?" Gino said. Cheech filled a cup, added milk, put it on a saucer and slid it across the bar. *"Grazie,"* Gino said.

"Gradito," said Don Cheech.

"I thought it was *benvenuto."*

"That's 'to welcome.' Not 'you're welcome.'" Don Cheech drew himself a cup. "You're a fucking disgrace to the Italian people."

"No argument there," Gino sighed. He glanced over at Kraut and I. "Hello there, fellas. Or perhaps I should say, *Salve!* Is that right, Cheek? *Salve,* hello?"

"*Disgrazia,*" Don Cheech muttered. *"Infamante. Infamara."*

"Damn it," Gino said. "I think I'm bein' insulted. Either that or Cheech here is trying to order lunch. Where's my *Jiffy Phrasebook Italian* when I need it?"

"You know," Clean said, taking a seat on the end of the bar and turning his stool to face Gino. "For somebody who's so proud of being a Northern Italian, you know shit-all about the place."

"I'm proud of being a Northern Italian because it means I don't have no fuckin' nigger blood in me like all you nappy-headed Sicilian and Calabrian and Neapolitan motherfuckers, who are halfway to card-carrying membership in the NAACP. *That's* why. Other than that, I could care less." Abruptly he turned to us. "How are ya there, Kraut?"

"Okay, Gene, okay. Gettin' by."

They shook hands from the distance Gino preferred. (I had learned the hard way not to kiss Gino's cheek, since it fell into the category of what he referred to as 'old greaseball bullshit.')

"And I see you brought your sidekick." Gino pointed at me with his distinctive gesture – a single pinky finger. I knew from experience he saved his index for people who were in imminent physical danger, but there was a look in his eyes that was many miles removed from the pleasant, slightly fatuous smile fixed over his teeth. "Look at him, Kraut. All dressed up and doing the town like a big-shot wiseguy. When I met this fuck, he looked like he needed directions to the soup kitchen."

"He cleans up nice for an Irishman," Kraut said.

"Speaking of which," Don Cheech broke in, speaking over the rim of his espresso cup. "You got some balls breezing in here in that fucking outfit, Gene. You look like you just come from Amateur Night at Yonkers Raceway."

"Cheech, it's like this," Gino said, turning the pinky on him. "When you got two hundred eighty-three inches of fuel-injected perfection under your hood, you like to get out on the highway and let 'er rip. Especially on a day like this. And you can't do that in Armani. Which, by the way, is very flattering on you. Hijack load?"

"Last guy that waved a finger at me, I made him eat it before I cut his fucking throat," Don Cheech said conversationally.

Gino stared at the offending pinky, slowly retracted it into his fist as if by invisible winch. The winch rotated again and his middle finger slowly extended. "Here, try this one instead."

"Like I said," Don Cheech graveled. "World-class prick."

The door opened again. Cowboy Nicky clopped in. He was wearing his usual rig – zippered leather jacket, collarless raw silk shirt opened at the neck, leather belt with heavy silver Western-style buckle, and dark boot-cut denims with brown cowboy boots. The tint in his bifocals lightened somewhat as he stepped into the room.

"Speaking of world-class pricks," Gino said.

"I'm a what, now?" Nicky blurted.

"Jesus, you two need a fuckin' makeover," Clean muttered. "Both of ya. It's like the NASCAR invasion."

"Am I late?" Nicky looked at his watch. "The Garden State is a cocksucker this time of day."

"Garden State?" Don Cheech lifted scarred eyebrows.

"His *goumada,*" Gino said. "She's a Joisey Goil. You're not late, Nick. You're on time. Forget about it."

Nicky squinted at the espresso machine. "That smells damn good. Mick, get me a cup."

"Now just a second there, Cowpoke," Gino shook his head sorrowfully. "I don't think it's appropriate for us to order Mickey Boy around now that Cheech is back. I'm not sure, but I think he belongs to the Don. To whom we are all pledged in allegiance."

Nicky's brow furrowed. He sat down tensely at the bar next to Gino. "I just want a fuckin' cup of coffee. Should I have stopped at Wa-wa?"

"It'd just make ya jumpy," Gino said, pointedly slurping. "Nothing worse than a jumpy Sicilian. One minute he's spilling his coffee, the next minute he's shootin' you in the back of the fuckin' head. It's the nigger blood, I tell ya, the nigger blood. Makes a man uppity."

The door opened yet again. Judging by the way everyone sprang to their feet, the man who shuffled in could have only been Joe Rossi.

He was old. That was the first thing I noticed about him – old, ugly, and dressed in a dowdy Mafia-emeritus style that was better suited to a nursing home resident than a *consigliere.* A shapeless flat cap sat low on a corrugated forehead. Horn-rimmed glasses with Coke-bottle lenses perched on a hooked, varicose nose; dusty gray eyes swam red-rheumy under lowering lids. Gray cardigan and shapeless blue slacks. His shuffling pace was governed more by the certainty that events will wait on him than by the weight of his years. He limped to a table, and, sitting with a grimace that showed large yellow teeth, signaled for coffee with arthritic fingers.

"How you doin', Joe?" Don Cheech said. "How you feelin'?"

"Aggravated." Rossi's voice was so rotted with age, I half-expected dust to puff out from between his lips like cigarette smoke. "I don't *do* conferences. But the boss says I got to. So let's get this over with."

They sat down at the long table in the center of the room: Don Cheech and Clean on one side, Gino and Nicky on the other, Rossi at the head, his worn wood-handled cane clutched in both hands like a pharaoh's *ankh*. As for Kraut and I, nobody invited us to sit. Clean had ordered us there, near as I could figure it, for intimidation purposes; and based on what I'd seen, it seemed worse than pointless to try to intimidate Gino Stillitano.

"I don't wanna be here any longer than I got to," Rossi said. "Gene, you asked for this sit-down, so get to it. What's your beef?"

"We know what his beef is," Cheech said, iron coming into his voice. "He don't wanna give up my crew."

"It ain't *your* crew anymore, Cheech." Gino replied, staring back at him. The fatuous tone he'd been using until now was gone; his face was the cold, expressionless death mask I'd encountered at Presto Repairs. "You may have built it, but I've done a fuckload more in the last three years than keep it warm. Half the guys in it are guys I brought up and straightened out myself. As for earning, if you noticed our flag flying over half of Brooklyn and Queens, it's because *I* put it there."

"You want to give a history lesson," Cheech said. "Start at the beginning, where *I* straightened you and Nicky out back when. Everything you got in this *brugad* now comes from that. If you've earned this or that or put the flag here or there – fine. But you can only do any of that because *I* vouched for the both of you when you were still punk kids. It's my weight that got you made."

It went back and forth like this for some time, and after a few minutes my attention began to wane. Television and film had led me to believe that mob sit-downs were full of drama – twisted gamesmanship, finger biting, elaborate curses in Sicilian dialect. What I was seeing was essentially a grown-up, gangsterized version of I-Know-You-Are-But-What-Am-I conducted by people with an eighth grade education. It seemed obvious even to me, a mote of dust of an associate, that Gino had no chance whatever of getting what he wanted and had called this meeting simply to make a case that he was being wronged – something which could not possibly interest any self-respecting gangster, and in any case seemed decidedly un-Gino-like. Don Cheech was saying this rather more pointedly when the door opened about a foot and Philly Guido stuck his head through with an apologetic grin. "Sorry to innerupt, but there's a message for Nicky from–" He jerked a thumb at the ceiling as if to indicate someone very high up on the food chain. Moving quickly, as if in embarrassment, Nicky rose, crossed the room, and spoke a few whispered words to Guido. Don Cheech cast them an irritated glance over his shoulder and then resumed speaking. As he did this, Nicky hastened back to the table. My eyes, squinting against the sudden flood of white sunshine, had just registered that he was carrying a pistol with a tube silencer screwed onto the muzzle when he raised it and shot Don Cheech in the back of the head.

A silencer is not anywhere near as silent as you think it is. I was half-deaf and all blind because something hot and wet splashed into my eyes and mouth. I took two steps back, caught my heel on something hard and unyielding, and fell to the floor. Through the ringing in my ears, I heard a curse, footsteps, a door bursting open from somewhere behind me, chairs scraping abruptly away from tables, Philly Guido barking *"Don't!"* and then Clean shriek, in the high-pitched soprano of a small child, *"No no no no no Jesus no!"*

The silencer banged again. A flat hard sound, painful but without resonance, like a giant clapping cupped hands. I heard a horrible, wretched glottal noise of pain and shock, and then there were three more bangs and the faint jingle of brass on the linoleum, and then nothing but hard breathing. Sprawled on the floor with my eyes screwed shut, I froze in mid-crawl, my heart pounding so furiously in my chest I thought it might shatter my breastbone. No point in trying to get away. Just wait for the bang. Wait for it. It's coming, so wait for it. Clench your fucking jaws until your teeth crack but hold in that slobbering flood of pleas and screams that are trying to get out. You've wrecked everything else in your life, but you can still die like a man. If they shoot you now. Now. *Now.*

But the next sound I heard was myself.

"Jesus Christ," I screamed. "Jesus Christ, Jesus-fucking-Christ *will you get it over with!*"

"Shut up," someone said, and kicked me in the ribs.

I wasn't expecting a kick. A bullet to the brain, yes, not a kick. I knuckled gore out of my eye sockets with trembling fingers. "I can't fuckin' see."

"Shut the fuck *up.*" Gino's voice.

"It's in my mouth." I spit and spit until I couldn't do it anymore. My eyes were burning and watering furiously, and my ears were ringing. "It's in my fuckin' *mouth.*"

"If he doesn't shut up, kill him." It was Old Man Rossi.

I heard the scuff of feet and someone had me by the lapels. In an instant, I was on my feet, head swimming.

"Mickey, shut your cocksucker." Gino again, oddly businesslike.

I stopped talking, but I could not stop whimpering. It was terrible to hear, but I could not stop. I heard Philly Guido say, somewhere off to my right: "Take a seat, Kraut, nice and slow. You packing iron?"

"No." Kraut's voice was shivery with shock, but controlled. I heard another chair scrape.

"All the same, keep your hands on your knees." Guido said. "We got no beef with you, so don't make one. *Capice?*"

A brief silence descended. My heart was now beating so furiously I thought it must be rippling the espresso in the cups, like the footfalls of a Tyrannosaur.

"Jesu Christo!" Rossi said suddenly. "Nicola, you got blood on my fuckin' sweater."

"Sorry, Joe."

"Sorry? I'll show you sorry." I heard the *whap* of a cane on flesh. "Stupid bastard. I tole you to wait 'til I was clear of him."
"We was sitting at the same table, Joe!"

The next *whap* sounded harder. "Don't talk back to me, you *figlio un cane*. Get my driver."

Gino handed me what felt like a bar towel. "Here. Clean yourself up. And stop whining. You sound like a cunt on Prom Night."

I got my eyes open and saw the world through a soapy lens. Don Cheech was face-down on the table, arms dangling towards the floor, the back of his head smashed open like a rotten fruit. There was a tremendous amount of blood on the blond wood of the table and on the gray-green linoleum floor, more blood than I would have imagined so small a body to have had I not killed a small man myself. But I didn't give a damn about the Don. My gaze jerked about the room until it found what it was both looking for and desperate not to see.

"Oh God," I said.

Clean lay on his back not ten feet from me. From the untrammeled heels of his thousand-dollar Farragamo loafers to the starched white collar of his Charles Tyrwhitt shirt, everything was intact. Where his face had been there was simply an enormous bloody crater, a glistening red-black mass studded here and there by the white gleam of a broken tooth or a yellowish shard of cartilage or bone.

I didn't quite scream, but something wrenched itself from my throat – a horrible gagging sound, as if I were trying to eject a bolus of grief, horror, and shock and were choking on it instead.

"Why are you talking?" Rossi said, pushing himself to his feet with a staccato crackle of tendons. "I *tole* you to quiet."

"Fuck up, Mickey," Gino said. He was leaning over Don Cheech's body, examining it with the clinical interest of a homicide detective. "Don't make him mad."

"I'm already mad," Rossi said, leaning on his cane so that the purple veins between his liver-spotted knuckles stood out. "This whole thing ain't right. I'm the *consigliere*. It ain't right for me to be involved in this kind of thing. It ain't *Cosa Nostra.*"

"We've been through that," Gino said absently. "Anyway, all you lost is a fuckin' sweater."

The door opened and the Tragedy Mask that was Face Fondozzi's head appeared. His voice was an apologetic slurp. "Joe, your car's here."

Rossi stared indignantly at all of us. He settled his cap on his head and shuffled toward the door. "No good gonna come of this," he said, rapping his malacca cane on the floor for emphasis. "Mark my fuckin' words. It ain't right. It ain't *Cosa Nostra.*"

"Didya have to shoot the fuck with the old man so close?" Gino demanded after Joe had left. "We're never gonna hear the end of this. He's probably had that fuckin' sweater since before we were born."

"Stop bustin' my fuckin' balls," Nicky snapped. "I'm the one got hit with the cane."

Gino poured himself a glass of Strega at the bar and downed it with a single jerk of his elbow. Then he went over to Don Cheech, grabbed him by the back of the collar and shoved his body noisily to the floor, where it flopped, slack-limbed and bloody, in the improbable attitude of the newly dead. He turned to Kraut, who was sitting stone-faced and narrow-eyed in a chair under the watchful eye, and even more watchful muzzle, of Philly Guido. "Kraut, you're an old warhorse, so I'm gonna do you the respect of asking you a straight question."

"Thanks," Kraut said.

"Is the house clean, or can I put away the broom?"

"You can put it away."

"You sure?"

"I am absolutely sure."

Gino nodded. "I figured. I mean, what goes on between the macaroni don't concern the sauerkraut, does it?"

"Not a bit," Kraut said.

Philly Guido sighed. I think it was relief. He didn't lower the pistol, but the muzzle dropped a few inches.

"Go home, Kraut," Gino announced, in the friendliest tone of which he was capable. "Crack yourself a Rheingold. Nicky will be by the Joint to explain the new regime later."

Kraut nodded and stood. After a moment's hesitation he said, "About the kid—"

"I need a few words with him," Gino replied. "Now be about your business."

Kraut went to the door. In spite of everything, I admired the steadiness of his legs. As the sunlight flooded in, he looked at me for perhaps one full second, and in that second I came pretty close to believing in mental telepathy, because I swear I heard his voice inside my head.

Tell him what he wants to hear, it said.

The door swung shut, but the breeze swirled away the smells of gun smoke and blood and replaced them with a warm summery scent that made my heart ache. Gino pointed to a chair. He used his index finger. I sat where I was told.

"Look me in the eye. Look at me."

I looked.

"You may be wondering why you're not dead. You are right to wonder. The answer is that between you and Kraut, the Grind Joint is running like a Swiss watch, and I never kill a golden goose, even a small one. Now, what happened here isn't none of your business. There's things going on all over town that are way above you and don't concern you. Only thing concerns you is you do what I say. You do what I say, you got no problems. You cross me, you die screaming. Understand?"

"Yes," I said.

"Good." Gino said. He stood up. The heel of one of his shoes rested in Don Cheech's blood. "I'm glad we understand each other. You clean yourself up and go home. Get yourself laid. Do some fuckin' thing. As of tomorrow, you're with me. Understand?"

"I understand."

"Good," he repeated. "Don't feel bad about Clean. He died for a good cause." He paused and tapped a finger to his chest. "Mine."

Chapter Twenty-One

The rain came and washed summer away.

It began as mist, softening the dusty yellow glare of the September sun, blunting its anger and its edge. As if by an invisible signal, the pace of the city seemed to slacken: traffic died away, the sidewalks emptied, the sounds of doors slamming echoed and re-echoed down the street and then stopped. A wind rose, rustling the gauzy curtains over my open windows and stirring the leaves of the philodendron on the sill. It drove in the heavy clouds lurking over the Hudson, and the light began to fade slowly, as if God were turning down a rheostat. Thunder cracked hard enough to vibrate a loose pane; the first drops of rain spattered against the screen. Two stories below, a gaunt black alley cat paused in the middle of the street, glancing about warily, unsure of which way to run.

"I know how you feel," I said.

The gloom in my apartment was as heavy as that outside. No lights burned. Three empty beer bottles stood on the scarred coffee table; several of Tina's dead cigarettes lay crushed out in the ashtray, her silvery lipstick on the butts. The bronze clock over the darkened television ticked off the seconds. Stillness hung like a moldy tapestry.

It rained hard for an hour, a steady downpour that turned the gutters into streams, stripped small branches from the willow trees, and sprayed a fine cold vapor through my screens. I stood by the windows and watched it all, trying not to look at my reflection in the flyspecked glass.

Death was with me every second of every day. It went to bed with me at night, woke up with me in the morning, and haunted my dreams in the restless hours between. It played itself on the inside of my skull like an endless loop of film. There's Don Cheech at the blond wood table. He's talking, hands accenting each word with neat New York gestures – chop of splayed fingers, an upturned palm, the thrust of an index finger. And behind him is Nicky Cowboy, the silencer like a tumorous growth on the muzzle of his pistol, hovering over the shiny bald spot on the back of Don Cheech's scalp.

A flex of tendons and a stab of pain in my eardrums. Somewhere amidst the ringing, the jingle of a spent brass casing on the floor. And Don Cheech is dead, his unfinished sentence trapped in a pinkish-gray streak of brains on the table, drying there, hardening there, never to be spoken, never to be heard. His lips to God's ears. And my mouth.

Dead. Gone.

Just like that.

It was this brute fact that clung to me. Stung my face and eyes like pulverized bone. Burned in my mouth like blood.

As long as I could remember, Don Cheech's name had been hard coin on the streets. Gangsters came and went, but Don Cheech stayed. He survived Family wars, government prosecutions, internecine feuds. Nothing stopped him. Not even Ho Chi Minh. The years passed, he got older and heavier, his skin hardened, his larynx filled with sediment, but he was always there, a weather-beaten figure that towered even in the shadows. *Pax Immaculata.* It would reign forever. Or until Nicky Cowboy blew his brains into my face. Whichever came first.

After the visuals came the sounds. The sound of Clean scrabbling on the floor. The sound of his panting, frantic breaths. That horrible piercing scream: *No no no no no Jesus no!* The clap of the silencer and the sound of his retching agony. Then the *coup de grace,* a triple-tap straight to the face. The mob loved symbolism. Two in the heart was a sign of respect. Three in the face was like pissing on the corpse.

A thought circled around my throbbing head like a carrion bird. *If they treat their own that way, what chance do I have?*

The thunder faded into silence, and the downpour slowed to a gentle farmer's rain. The air drifting in through the windows had the salty-metallic taste of the Hudson. The street, puddled and leaf-strewn, looked desolate in sullen gray light. Somewhere in the distance, I heard sirens.

"I'm right here," I mumbled into the window. My breath condensed on the pane, forming a small cloud. I traced a finger through it: *C* for Cheech. *C* for Clean. "Come and get me."

The sirens faded. No one was coming to my rescue.

"Damn."

I lifted my forehead off the glass. It left a print there, a suggestion of a face, the *C* forming half a set of lips. I traced the other half, forming an *O,* and instantly regretted it. Now the face was screaming. I stared at it for a moment and then wiped it away. No good. The smear of oil and water was too reminiscent of something else I had seen, dragged and smudged on the floor of the Friends of the Friends.

"Son of a bitch."

I turned and walked aimlessly around the apartment. I felt a strange sense of disconnection, as if it were no more than a dusty museum and I the night watchman, wandering about inside. Surely those were not my boxing trophies on the shelves hanging over the bar nor my battered sneakers on the faded hallway carpet by the front door. Surely that was not my dog-eared copy of *On the Marble Cliffs* by the nightstand, next to the lamp and the glass that still held two inches of flat beer. Surely this was someone else's place, someone else's things, someone else's life….

"Someone else's mess."

But it belonged to me. So I did the only thing I could do: I went into the bathroom and threw up.

I had vomited twice since yesterday, and it was all over very quickly. Afterwards, I rinsed my mouth out over the sink, blew my nose, brushed my teeth, and washed my face and the backs of my wrists in the coldest water I could stand. I looked at the man in the mirror. His eyes were blood-lensed slits, his mouth framed in stubble, and his hair hung down over his reddened forehead in matted strings. He looked very much as if he had gone fifteen rounds with a bottle of Jameson's Irish Whiskey and awoken face-down on the carpet.

"Good guess."

I walked back out into the living room. The clock said that it was not quite noon. The thought of spending any more time here suddenly became intolerable.

Outside, it was windy and cool under a close-pressing sky the color of greasy coins. The rain was steady. I took one look at my car, plastered with leaves and leaning slightly on one soft tire, and splashed off in the other direction, zipping up my windbreaker and digging my hands into its pockets. My left bumped up against the pair of brass knuckles that sat there like a sash weight. Of course, they were not actually brass; Kraut had pounded them together in his machine shop from strips of scrap metal and given them to me with a frilly yellow bow tied to the loops. His idea of a joke. I took them out and laid them on my palm, feeling their grim heaviness, their ugly solidity. I had broken three jaws with this slab of iron. Three jaws and at least one sternum. There was a figure for the books. If anybody in this business kept them.

I plodded westward, with my head down and my left hand clenched over the obscenity in my pocket. The rain soaked my hair to the roots, and before long, my sneakers pumped water out of their soles in a rhythmic, arterial spray. On the corner of Sackett and Van Brunt, I slipped into a bodega and, dripping solemnly, bought a twenty-ounce bottle of Beck's Dark from a stoic-faced Arab with a cat on his lap. Walking back out into the rain, I wondered if the cat knew how lucky he was, and doubted it. Nobody knows which side his bread is buttered until Nicky Cowboy spreads brains in with the butter. And then it's too late.

The sun was making a concerted effort to prospect among the clouds, but the best it could manage was a few veins of pure silver in an infinity of tarnished nickel. Ahead, through a maze of dun-colored buildings and rusty chain-link fences, I could make out the tidal straits that flowed between Brooklyn and Governor's Island. A freighter moved peaceably down the channel, preceded by a tugboat bedecked in old tires. The rains had swollen the East River as it rushed between the boroughs and out into Upper New York Bay. Its waters, so opaque they looked metallic, broke hard on either side of the ship's spreading wake, forming a shape that looked vaguely like two fish trying to swallow each other.

I wiped rain from my face and continued on, cutting across a trash-littered railroad spur on whose far end idled a half-dozen boxcars. Part way down the gravel escarpment on the other side, I was as close as I could come to the Buttermilk Channel without climbing the seawall and diving in. Breathing hard, the remains of my hangover thumping obnoxiously in my temples, I found a concrete piling and sat, watching the freighter as it nosed out into the bay.

Ever since I was a kid, when my grandfather used to take me fishing in Long Island Sound, I had done my best thinking by the water. I had even fallen in love with Anne on the ferry to Martha's Vineyard. There was something about the waves that produced a clarity in my mind, a stillness that seemed to court epiphany. Christ knew I needed one now. I took a long pull of Beck's and waited for it to come.

Mostly I thought about Gino. It is no easy thing to have your existence dependent upon the whim of a man to whom killing came as naturally as making love. No easy thing to realize that you knew too much – had *seen* too much – to be allowed to live if even the slightest doubt were ever raised about your character. Tomorrow, next month, next year, Gino might glance over at me as I lugged a stolen microwave into the back of the Friends of the Friends and think, *Why take the risk?*

I could feel his hook in my lip, and it tasted like Don Cheech's blood.

There had to be a way to cut the line. I could see only one, and it was barred by impossibility. Snitch. Pick up a phone and dial the FBI office in Rego Park. Ask for the tall, mustachioed son of a bitch who sometimes prowled around the Friends of the Friends in his gray clone suit and slightly scuffed shoes. Have him come pick me up in his maroon Crown Victoria with the whip antenna on the trunk. And the next time anyone saw me, I'd be taking the stand in the matter of *United States v. Eugene Stillitano, et al.*

It was a nice, easy way out, but I couldn't take it. I could not give up my name, my identity, the city of my birth. I could not turn my back on everything I knew, everything I loved. I could not leave and live out someone else's life, punching cash register keys in Norman, Oklahoma, and jumping every time a car backfired. I couldn't get out that way, even if it cost me my life.

But I didn't want to die, either.

I took another swallow. A good thinking beer, Beck's Dark. It lingered on your tongue like a kiss. I tried to remember who had introduced me to it. Certainly not my grandfather. The last object of Teutonic manufacture that had entered his body was a rifle bullet. The damage to his clavicle had ended a promising boxing career, and he was not the forgiving type. I liked to kid Kraut that his father had probably done the deed. Kraut's usual reply was that it was indeed a shame, as better aim would have rid the world of all future generations of Watts.

The bottle stopped halfway to my lips. Kraut. Something he had told me once…a story about a loan-shark from Canarsie, a big, Harley-riding sonofabitch who had found religion.

I stood, bit my lip. The story was important. Vital, even. But I didn't know why. Couldn't even remember the point. *Think*. Where were we when he told it to me? His construction business in Little Neck. Cutting planks of wood for the bar in my apartment. Smells of cigarette smoke and sawdust. Kraut's work-roughened hand putting down the circular saw and picking up a Rheingold. *Fssst* as he pulled the tab like the pin on a hand grenade. He was smiling out of one corner of his mouth. I screwed my eyes shut and tried to listen.

Craziest thing I ever saw. Big Eddie Maniscalco. Loan shark, and a nasty one. He was on the record with Joey Salerno when Salerno was just a soldier. Two hundred fifty pounds, tats from wrist to elbow, big waxed mustache. His favorite trick was dragging a son of a bitch behind his tailgate on a chain. Had a clawhammer in his saddlebag, too. Anything to get the money. Anyway, Eddie goes away for a year, and in the can, he finds Jesus. Nothing weird there. Lots a guys find Jesus in the can. Thing is, they lose Him a half-hour after they get out. Not Eddie. He's through with shylocking, through with the brugad. And he wants out. Tells Joey he wants to start a church in

Canarsie and preach the gospel. Thing is, he's on the record with a crew, and when you're on the record with a crew, you don't just give your two weeks' notice. You leave when you die. And Eddie, he was a big earner. So Joey tries to talk some sense into him. When that fails, he realizes Eddie has to go. And probably anybody else would have went. Thing is, Joey, he's got a soft spot for the guy. He don't want to whack him. And he realizes that since Eddie ain't made, maybe there's some wiggle room here. So he calls Eddie in and says, "You want out? I'll let you buy your way out. You pay me fifty thousand in cash, and I'll take you off the record. I'll release you from my crew, and you'll be a civilian." And Eddie, he just smiles and says, "God bless you" and walks out the door. Of course, most of Joey's crew, they figure they'll never see the fucker again. But a couple of weeks later, he shows up in a cab at Joey's social club with a shoebox fulla cash. He sold his two Harleys, pawned his gun and jewelry, emptied out his private stash, got a second mortgage on his house, and came up with the bucks. And Joey, he was as good as his word. He gave Eddie a kiss and told him, "Next time you talk to Jesus, put in good word for Joey, okay?"

I opened my eyes, momentarily disoriented, and took another slug of beer to clear my head. The freighter had passed to my left; it was close enough so that I could almost make out the big white letters under the bow railing above the hawsehole, and watching the little tug in front of it, I was reminded of a garden ant dragging a Japanese beetle. Every problem contains its own solution, but when the solution was too hard or too painful or just too damn risky, most people put on their blinders and said they couldn't see it. I no longer had the luxury of blinders. I had been blind too goddamn long.

In the months after I'd broken Tommy Battaglia's jaw, I had dragged blame around me like Marley's chains, rattling them at everyone I knew. At Clean for starting it all. Don Cheech for holding my marker. Anne for leaving me. Dago Red for making me a murderer. Kraut for teaching me the subtleties of earning. Tina for giving me a reason to earn. Gino for the hook in my lip. But it was I who had taken the bait. The Life had seduced me as certainly as it had seduced Linda and every other no-hoper at the Grind Joint, every other would-be hustler who thought he could flirt with the darkness and not have it swallow him whole. Blaming anyone but myself for what had happened was like Marley blaming the

Stock Exchange for his own greed. The question was: Could I do what Big Eddie Maniscalco had done? Was there a figure large enough to persuade Gino into releasing me, knowing what I knew, and seeing what I had seen?

What price freedom?

The rain began to pick up again. The red-brick buildings on Governor's Island blurred in the mist; beyond them, the towers of Lower Manhattan shimmered like a menagerie. I was soaked to the marrow and most of the beer was gone. It was time to head back. Stay out here much longer and I'd get pneumonia. I needed to go home, take a hot shower, towel myself until my skin tingled, and put on some soup. I needed to be safe and dry and warm and think about nothing at all.

That's what I needed to do.

But for now I just sat on the piling and watched the summer wash away in the rain, leaving the fall behind it.

Chapter Twenty-Two

The Grind Joint. A steel-gray Tuesday afternoon. In the back, where Kraut had knocked out a wall to expand the gaming area, workmen were hammering. They had opened the back door and gusts of air, moving like agitated spirits, stirred last night's cigarette ashes and carried away the odors of spilled beer and cheap perfume. Kraut and I stood by the new slate-topped pool table in the lounge, cues in hand. He was drinking Rheingold from a quart milk jug; I nursed Alka-Seltzer in a plastic cup.

"Buy a release?" Kraut said for the third time. His tone was wonderment tinged with horror, as if I had suggested that the true secret of weight loss lay in cannibalism. "You want to buy a fucking release from Gino Stillitano?"

"That's the plan."

"Forget the plan. It's the worst goddamn plan in history. And you're talking to a guy whose father helped put together the invasion of Russia."

"Kraut, I want out."

"Of the Grind Joint?"

"Of the Life."

Kraut looked at me with furrowed brow and narrowed eyes. Leaning forward for emphasis, his head came under the edge of the shaded lamp over the table. The thick bristles on his scalp gleamed in the yellow light like freshly polished brass. "Mick, I get that you're upset by what happened. It wasn't exactly fun for me either. But that stuff is strictly between the guineas. It's how they operate. You...." His voice trailed off.

"Get used to it?"

His frown turned into the familiar Kraut scowl, which deepened the creases on his forehead. "No, goddammit, you don't get used to it. You don't get used to brains in your mouth or your friend getting hit in front of you. But this is the Life."

"Exactly. And it's why I want out. I'm not cut out for this shit."

Kraut looked at me coldly, then lit a cigarette with the stylized movements of a lifelong smoker, his left bicep flexing as he flicked his Zippo with a calloused thumb. "I know a redhead says different."

It was as close as he had ever come to mentioning Dago Red since the night I had killed him, and I had to unclench my teeth before I could speak again.

"That's not fair."

"Fair? What the fuck is fair?" He hefted his cue and bent over the table, not troubling to take the cigarette out of his mouth. "We ain't playing Marquis of Queensberry rules here, Mick. We ain't playing at all. This is Gino Stillitano you're talking about. Three ball, right corner pocket."

"I know what Gino is. I've seen him at work."

"All the more reason to abandon this plan of yours." There was a clack, and the three vanished into the pocket in a flash of red and white. Kraut straightened, rested his cigarette carefully on the edge of the table, and reached for the chalk. "You know, they just as easily could have hit *you* that day. One less pair of eyes at the scene."

"You keep making my point for me."

Kraut made an exasperated sound in the back of his throat. "*My* point is that there's nothing preventing them from doing it now, either. You get on Gino's bad side, you raise any doubts about being a stand-up guy – you're gone. Best thing you can do is lay low, hand up your end every week, and keep your mouth shut."

"Until when? When does it end?"

He shrugged. It was an elaborate gesture – grim, fatalistic, full of resignation but also stoic acceptance. It communicated an entire philosophy of life in a single motion of his shoulders. "When you go like Cheech and Clean did. Or you go away to the can. Or, if you're goddamn lucky, you live to retire like Ernie the Coffee Boy. That's when it ends."

"It wasn't that way for Big Eddie Maniscalco."

Kraut's irritation showed in the arteries which stood out under his right ear. He put down his cue and took a long drink. "I shoulda never told you that story."

"Well, was it true or wasn't it?"

He glared at me. "Of course it's true. It's also twenty years old. And it happened under Joey Salerno. *He* had a heart. Gino's got a fucking switchblade where his heart should *be*. He'll never release you, and he'll probably whack you out for even asking."

"But there's a precedent," I insisted. "It's been done before. So I got a leg under me."

"Doesn't mean Gino won't cut it off."

"I know it's a big risk. But there are risks all around. And I got one ace up my sleeve."

Kraut picked up his cue, choked up on it one-handed. "Oh? And what's that?"

"Greed. Gino is the greediest son of a bitch that ever got his finger pricked. You said so yourself. He'd fuck money if he could find a way. When he thinks about it, he'll realize he stands to make more money off me leaving than he does by me staying."

"How is that, exactly? The kind of money we're talking about, you don't have."

"I can get it."

Kraut's tone sharpened further. "Not without going on a fucking crime rampage that will probably land you in the joint for twenty-five years!"

"I'll do what I have to do."

"Mick, think about what you're saying here. You want out of the Life, and your way is to go deeper in?"

I drank the rest of my Alka-Selzter and tossed the cup into the wastebasket in the corner. "It's like the song says. Sometimes you gotta go through hell to get to heaven."

Kraut did not even speak when he called his next shot, merely gestured angrily with the pool cue. In his agitation, his aim was poor, and the cue ball vanished into the pocket. He threw the stick to the floor.

"Hey," I said. "That's brand new."

"Fuck the stick," he snapped, advancing on me. "You got bigger things to worry about if you try to pull this hairbrained scheme."

"Kraut, my mind's made up. It's been made up since Don Cheech's mind got pasted to my face. Are you gonna help me, or are you gonna throw a tantrum and break all this crap we just bought?"

"You want help?" He said in sudden fury, the arteries in his neck matched, now bulging grotesquely. "I'll give you some help. Here's your help. Maybe it'll clear your fucking head!"

Kraut was an experienced streetfighter and he knew how to throw a hard punch on the inside with no windup. I had just enough time to realize what he was about to do, and then my ass hit the floor, followed immediately by my shoulders and the back of my head. I got an excellent view of the laces of my sneakers as they pointed momentarily at the ceiling. When my feet landed, I began to get up.

"Do yourself a favor and stay down," he snarled, looming over me with fists bunched at his sides. When I discovered that I was not angry, I did as he said and lay on the floor, propped on my elbows. My jaw throbbed, and I could taste blood on my tongue, but these sensations were hardly novel.

"Feel better?" I asked after a long moment.

"No."

"Good." I extended my hand to him. He stared at it for a moment, then took it in his and pulled me to my feet. My head swam momentarily and was still.

"I'll get you a towel," he said.

"Not necessary. You hit like a girl."

He looked down at his boots. His face was still red, but it was embarrassment and not anger.

"Kraut," I said, licking blood from the corner of my mouth. "I appreciate the concern. Even if you have a strange way of showing it. But it's my life. And I want it back."

"Even if it gets you killed?"

"Even so."

He turned away, picked up his cigarette, and drew on it. In the back, the hammering continued; one workman called to another for an extension cord. I brushed grit off the seat of my pants and washed the taste of blood out of my mouth with a swig of Rheingold. When Kraut's cigarette was down to its last quarter-inch, he crushed it out in a scuffed bronze ashtray and looked at me. There was nothing recognizable in his face now except weary, defeatist calm.

"What can I do?" He said.

Chapter Twenty-Three

Gino Stillitano had the only boat in Sheepshead Bay without a name. It looked decidedly odd, bumping gently at its slip with a stern as blank as a fresh sheet of typewriter paper, but no one ever questioned it, any more than his neighbors questioned why his house on Hemlock Street had no number, or his postman asked why the mailbox bore no name. To know Gino at all was to understand why all of his cars, including his pride-and-joy midnight black Rally Sport with the yellow primered flames running down the panels and a supercharger rearing out of the hood like a great chrome-gilt stallion, were registered to his *goumadas,* or to his vending-machine company, or some other legitimate business he owned or had an interest in. Gino never put his name on anything, and he liked to brag that the only written evidence of his existence were his birth certificate and his rap sheet.

"And I ain't sure about the certificate," he liked to say, in the proud tone of a man whose son just pitched a no-hitter. "Matter of fact, I don't even know when I was born."

Gino's mother had given birth to him during an alcoholic blackout in her cold-water railroad flat in Alphabet City and didn't go to the hospital until almost a week after the birth. The doctors had assigned him a birthday along with his surname before they called Social Services. He had been raised in orphanages, foster homes, and juvenile hall. Stillitano was his mother's name, and he was quick to say that he had not attended her funeral. Neither did his father, whom he had never met.

"Never want to, either," he would add. "If I ever do, I'll show him what his blue-eyed baby boy is all about. I'll slit his throat and fuck the wound."

Nobody doubted it. The unofficial estimate of his body count was thirty-one, and this figure was disputed only by those who considered it too conservative. What distinguished Gino from other Family heavyweights, however, was not the number of scalps on his belt but the uniquely personal way in which he handled his affairs. His empire was constructed not in the classical mob style – the Aztec pyramid – but rather honeycombed like a guerilla movement, with each cell largely independent of the others. Only he knew its full extent, and it existed almost entirely for his personal benefit. As the skipper of a work crew consisting mainly of enforcers and killers, he was not subject to the same economic pressures as the captains who ran the street crews – the men whose criminal doings kept the Administration in silk sheets and their *goumadas* in blue boxes. Beyond the usual tithe he had to kick up to the boss, underboss and *consigliere,* maybe twenty percent of his weekly gross, Gino's personal holdings – his legitimate businesses, his gambling joints, his whorehouse, his vending machine company, his loan-sharking and bookmaking operations, and God alone knew what else – were his own concern. In return for this freedom from taxation, he provided the Family with a reliable killing squad, men who would burn down buildings, intimidate witnesses, pulp troublemakers, and kill enemies real or perceived with speed, skill, and precision. Gino being Gino, he was as likely to execute a contract himself as delegate it. Where his crooked flag flew, his bottle-green Mustang GTO was as familiar a sight as the neighborhood delivery truck, with the exception that the appearance of a delivery truck did not generally cause grown men to wet their pants.

Over time I had heard all the stories. How Gino had doused a loan shark with gasoline and set him alight in front of a public tavern. How he had stuffed the hand of a recalcitrant debtor into a garbage disposal and thrown the switch. Of how he had sodomized a *cugine* who had slept with the wife of a made man and then thrown him off the George Washington Bridge. It made no difference if the stories were true. If not, something just as bad undoubtedly was, for Gino was that rarest of creatures in the *brugad:* the man who inspired fear not because he was made but because he was self-made. The murderous glow that surrounded him was not the reflected power of the Family but intrinsic, radiating outward from some deep primal core. People tend to enjoy things they are good at, and Gino enjoyed earning and he enjoyed killing. Which he enjoyed more was open to speculation.

All of this loomed large in my mind as I walked under the elevated tracks that shadowed Sheepshead Bay Road. The trestlework under the tracks was caked with rust, savage-looking weeds had broken up the pavement, and the long gray cinderblock wall that ran parallel with the tracks was covered in a patchwork of graffiti. Only the marina beyond was pretty.

I had chosen the location of this meeting with particular care. Gino had a mild dislike of social clubs – indeed, with anything he associated with "old greaseball bullshit." He preferred to do business in one of his cars, or in "walk-talk" on the street, or in the office at Presto Repairs. In those places he was all business, a money-making machine whose gears were lubricated by blood. Trying to approach him under those circumstances was like fumbling for a butcher knife in the dark – whether you got the handle or the blade was largely a matter of luck. On his boat, a cold beer in his hand and the sun hot on the back of his neck, I was sure I could find some polyp of humanity.

Well, not exactly sure. Hopeful. If I was sure, Kraut's .38 Detective Special would not have been sitting on my tailbone.

The rain and gloom of the last two weeks had blown out on the same winds that had carried them in. Sheepshead Bay languished in a yellow-lit calm that belonged to neither summer nor fall, but rather the clove that lay between them. Sunlight glittered amidst the whitecaps on the water, throwing the long array of boat masts along the quay into hard silhouette. Gino's Rampage Express was easy to find. At thirty-nine feet, it was the largest boat in the marina and occupied the extreme right-hand slip at the end of the dock – the nautical equivalent, I supposed, of having your back to the wall.

A beautiful boat, white on white fiberglass with aquamarine windows in the pilothouse and all the brightwork freshly polished. There was no one on deck, but I did see a figure on the pulpit, looking like a cameo against the sun. Long hair, careless in the breeze, hourglass curve of waist, knotted strands of a bikini bottom at the hip, endless legs. A *goumada*. No ordinary female had a shape like that. As I approached, I heard music playing in the cabin. It sounded like Nancy Wilson. A good omen. Better than Black Sabbath, anyway.

I called out when still well away from the boat. It didn't pay to surprise Gino Stillitano. The *goumada* turned languidly, one slender arm resting on the whitewashed rail, and looked down at me. Then she called for Gino in English not quite heavily accented enough to disguise her irritation.

I heard thumpings and mutterings from below, a mumble of conversation. Gino emerged from the cabin carrying a blue and white picnic cooler in both arms. From the way the tendons stood out on his forearms, I could tell the cooler was full. He put it down on the deck and straightened up to look at me.

He was wearing mirrored sunglasses and a short-sleeved shirt of white linen unbuttoned to reveal abdominal muscles as hard as armor plating. His khaki slacks bagged around the tops of his yachting shoes, and he did not appear to be armed. "Fuck do you want?"

His tone was so neutral a stranger to our language might have taken it for a greeting.

"Five minutes," I said.

Gino stared at me for a moment, his face unreadable. Then he glanced at his watch, its polished crystal momentarily dazzling me as it heliographed the sun into my eyes.

"Five minutes," he said at last. "You take any longer than that I'm using you as shark bait. And it better be good, whatever it is."

I made my way around the mooring lines and stepped onto the deck, feeling the slight sway beneath my feet. As I did, the girl leaned over the pulpit and called out in a pout: "Gino, you say no business today!"

"Shut your yap, or I'll send you back to Latveria."

"Latvia!" she said. "I come from *Latvia.*"

"You can shut your mouth in any language." He pointed a pinky, directed me down the steps. After what had happened at the Friends of the Friends, I was hesitant to turn my back on him; I felt my throat tighten involuntarily as I descended, ducking my head to enter the cabin.

It is disconcerting to see a hotel room, tour bus, or trailer that is more luxurious than your own home. The cabin of Gino's yacht, a little smaller than my living room, was fitted out in a style befitting a Mafia prince – varnished redwood cabinetry, gold-plated faucets, leather upholstery, granite tabletop, and a thick white carpet that swallowed my sneakers. A small flat-screen television had been installed over the dinette, and the lights of an expensive sound system winked from one of the cabinets. The door to the forward berth was open, and through it I saw a spacious bed bedecked with gilt-brocade pillows and a heavy silk-trimmed ivory comforter. The door to the head was closed; I could hear water running.

Nicky Cowboy stood in the galley, clinking ice into a tumbler with Gino's initials worked into the glass. He was wearing a turquoise sports shirt that revealed deeply tanned, surprisingly wiry forearms. His hands were for once bare of driving gloves, and I was surprised to see a gold wedding band on his left hand. His brow creased when he saw me. "We don't need a cabin boy," was his only salutation.

Gino climbed down after me and sat down at the table, one arm resting on the leather banquette. He took off his sunglasses and rubbed the small pink spots they had left on either side of his nose. His gray-eyed gaze rested on the bruise on the corner of my mouth, and I thought he might ask how it had come about. Instead: "Clock is ticking."

No one had invited me to sit, and I had never known what to do with my hands when I was nervous except shape them into fists. My mouth was suddenly dry as powder, and I cast a longing glace at the rum Nicky was pouring over ice. "Did you ever hear of Big Eddie Maniscalco?"

Gino and Nicky exchanged a look. Nicky pushed his tinted prescription lenses up the bridge of his nose and nodded. "Sure. Shylock muscle used to be with Joey Salerno. I think he was at Green Haven for a while when I was there. So what?"

"It's my understanding that he bought his way out of his, uh...commitments."

Nicky put down his rum and reached over to the fruit bowl on the counter, selecting a large Florida orange. He popped the button on the leather holster on his belt and removed a bone-handled folding knife with a Flickett on the handle. A movement of his thumb and the blade appeared with a flash and a click. "And?"

I shifted my feet slightly. The pistol seemed to weigh an immensity. I wondered if I could get to it before that knife buried itself in my windpipe. "So, I was wondering if I could do the same."

Silence. Motionless faces. Nicky's blade had frozen a quarter of an inch deep in the skin of the orange. Patsy Cline began to sing "Never No More" on the radio. That gave me a bit of a turn. Anne loved Patsy Cline.

Finally, Gino said, as if he had just woken up out of a deep sleep: "You were wondering…."

"If I could buy a release."

More silence.

"Buy my way out," I said, and coughed. "Like Big Eddie did."

It is not an easy thing to leave Gino Stillitano speechless. He stared at me for so long I felt his attention like individual pinpricks on every nerve in my face. It was agony trying to hold his gaze. Finally, he said, in a tone half between a laugh and a growl: "What, you ain't happy in your work?"

"It's nothing personal. I'm just not cut out for this life."

Gino picked up his sunglasses, and with great deliberation polished their lenses on his shirttail, not looking at me. His voice was cold but not hostile. "Other day rattle your cage, is that it?"

"That's part of it, yeah. But not all. The truth is all of this was a mistake. What got me hooked up with all of you in the first place was an accident. If there had been another way to get out of it without having you carry my marker, I would have done it. But there wasn't any other way. And then, when Anne…when my girl kicked me to the curb, I wasn't thinking clearly. I don't know what I was thinking. When I bought into the

Grind Joint – hell, I guess I just needed something to hold onto." I stopped. Nicky was glaring at me incredulously from under his umber lenses. Gino's face still held nothing I could recognize. "But it was a mistake, too."

"Kind of mistake prone, ain't you?" Gino said, still polishing. The very flatness of his voice began to frighten me a bit. It had the quality of the stillness which precedes the storm.

"That's my whole point. I keep making mistakes. Sooner or later I'm going to make one that's gonna get me killed."

Nicky's voice was low and hard as a kick to the shin. "Maybe you're doing that right now. Did you think about that?"

"All week," I said, looking directly at him. "But here I am."

This remark pleased or amused Gino in some trivial way. He huffed air out of his nose, which was as close as he generally came to laughing. "Carrying, too, I bet. What did you pack?"

I hesitated a moment. Now was not the time for dissembling. "Thirty-eight snub. Detective Special."

"Wadcutters?"

"Hollow points."

Gino smiled fleetingly. It in no way involved his eyes, which were like portholes opening onto some desolate landscape. "That alone could get you killed, showing up packing to a sit-down with your boss."

Nicky was looking at me carefully, trying to figure out where I was carrying the pistol. He began to peel the orange with elaborate nonchalance, the skin curling over his thumb like a ribbon.

"Tell me, kid," Gino said, smiling wider now. "If I said 'no,' were you planning on lettin' us have it?"

"There's all sorts of ways to say no," I said.

"And you thought I might wish to say no by, oh, having you cut up and thrown off the fantail?"

"Thought crossed my mind."

Gino tilted his head to one side, a gesture I associated with contemplation and not anger. "You're right. But since you're showing some balls here, I'm inclined to leave it to this." He stood up slowly, coming to his full height about nine inches below the cabin's paneled ceiling. When he spoke, his voice was cold but without inflection, like the voice of some intelligent war machine. "Nobody gets released from my crew this side of hell. You came into this crew under Gino Stillitano, and you will die under Gino Stillitano. Do you understand?"

Nicky had stopped peeling. The skin of the orange hung in a ribbon below the blade of his knife. He stared at me warily and jumped a bit when the bathroom door opened.

A second *goumada* appeared, in a purple bikini top and matching fringed sarong, holding a toothbrush. She was short and big breasted, with thick dark hair, perfectly sculpted eyebrows, and a porcelain complexion. Her large, liquid Italian eyes glimmered at me without interest before she spoke. "Nicky, where's my drink at? You waiting on Christmas, or what?"

Nicky glared at her. "We're busy here. Go wait in the bedroom."

"I'm thirsty now."

"I said wait in the goddamn bedroom."

"Keep it up," she said darkly, sweeping past him in a flutter of purple cotton. "You'll be humping your hand for the rest of this voyage." The door to the forward berth shut with a thud.

Silence descended. Patsy Cline finished insisting that never no more was she gonna cry about that other fella, on account of the fine new man she had in her life, but she didn't sound very convincing. I looked back at Gino; he stared after the *goumada* with the nonplussed expression of a man interrupted at the climax of an important speech. I saw the opening and took it. "What am I worth to you, Gino?"

"Fuck do you mean, worth?"

"If somebody offered you money for me, what would you ask for?"

A muscle in Gino's jaw clenched. "Your five minutes are up."

"Big Eddie Maniscalco was worth fifty grand to Joey Salerno," I said. "How much am I worth to you?"

"Your life won't be worth a fucking thing I don't see your back in about five seconds."

"I'll give you what Eddie gave Joey," I said. My heart was pounding. "Fifty thousand. Cash."

"Get out," he said.

"Seventy-five."

Gino said nothing.

"A hundred."

Nicky had finished peeling the orange. He broke it in half and put two slices into the tumbler of rum. "You're full of shit. You don't have that kind of dough."

"Supposing I could get it." I said. "Would a hundred take care of my obligation?"

Gino was looking at me speculatively, as if he could not decide whether to be angry or intrigued. "No," he said at last, and sat slowly back down in the booth. "But it does get my attention."

Nicky looked at him in bafflement. "Oh, come on, Gene, you're not seriously listening to this bullshit, are you?"

"One twenty-five," I said.

Gino sat back. Stared at me. Drummed the fingers of his left hand on the polished granite. After what seemed like an hour he began to speak. "Everybody knows I got, shall we say, a fascination with numbers. But that don't mean I can be bought easy. The kind of green you're talking about takes time to put together – a *lot* of time, if you ain't a big earner. Which up to now, you ain't been. So, it would take you months, even if you got money saved away to start you off. And in that time, you won't be earning for me, because you'll be too busy earning for yourself to pay me down the road. So I got to factor in the money I'm losing week by week because you're not kicking up your shares to me like normal." His fingers paused momentarily in mid-drum; then fell flat on the table as if exhausted. "And when I do that, I can't say one twenty-five rings the greed bell."

Yet another silence. Nicky appeared to be relieved. He took a long drink of rum, nodding. But something in Gino's face, some infinitesimal lessening of tension around his mouth, told me that if the greed bell wasn't yet ringing, at the very least my hand had found the rope.

"All right," I said quietly. "What would?"

Gino's eyes were half-closed, as if in meditation. He patted his shirt pocket, produced a short brown cigar the width of a roll of nickels, and unwrapped it carefully. From his left pants pocket emerged a guillotine cutter. He snipped the end and planted the cigar between his teeth. I dug out the lighter I had learned to carry and held the flame until he had it going. When he settled back, he had the air of self-satisfaction that I usually associated with a cat who has just broken a bird's back and is about to settle down to eating. "We do this," he began, speaking around the cigar. "We do this the way we'd do a shylock loan. I'll take the one twenty-five, but since I know you don't *got* it right now, I'm considering it a debt and charging three points vig weekly. You understand what I'm layin' out? Every week I don't see my hundred twenty-five Gs, we tack on thirty-seven fifty to the principal."

I did some fast mental calculations while Gino puffed pepper-scented smoke at the ceiling. "At that rate, I'd owe you two hundred grand by the end of the year."

"Two hundred fifteen," Nicky mumbled, staring at his fingertips as if they held a calculator.

"It's a lot of money," Gino said. "But that's okay with me. I like money. And because I'm the impatient type, I'm gonna give you until Christmas to pay up or the deal's off. By which I mean you still owe me every penny of the hundred twenty-five grand plus the interest, just for bringing it up, but you *don't* get a release – unless going over the fantail counts."

This added condition seemed to satisfy Nicky. He smiled a bit and drank off half his rum, the oranges bobbing in the glass.

When I did not immediately reply, Gino's look of predatory geniality vanished. "Your time is up, times three. You know the deal. You want it, those are the terms. You don't, get the fuck out of my sight and never mention this shit to me again, or I'll hang you on a meat hook by your asshole."

"You should do that to him anyway," Nicky said.

I said nothing. It was so quiet I could hear the crackle of the cigar's binding as it burned. Gino looked at me expectantly.

"I'll take the deal," I told him. "But I've got to tell you, I don't know if I can pay you off that fast."

Gino removed the cigar, turned up one corner of his mouth in something that was half-smirk, half-smile. "Then I suggest you get your ass out there and start earning."

PART III
Chapter Twenty-Four

September burned away like a fuse, leaving only smoke-shrouded memories and mingled scents of sweat and desperation. The images left behind were jagged and fragmentary, often without context, belonging to no particular time or day.

It seemed to me that I lived at the Grind Joint – lived and re-lived the same experiences over and over again until a permanent and numbing sense of déjà vu settled over me. When dawn showed its golden face over Queens, Kraut and I were in his office, counting out the night's take with fingers trembling from fatigue. It always looked like a great deal of money at first, mounded on his desk so that individual bills sometimes spilled out over the sides like sheets from a broken ream of paper, but gambling is a business with surprisingly large operating costs – overhead, payoffs for the borough cops, tribute to Gino, the necessity of refilling the house bank. Looks could be deceiving, especially to someone who wanted to be deceived. In the morning, I seldom had the energy to drive home, electing instead to collapse into one of the small upstairs bedrooms for a few hours of oblivion. When I woke, sweating in the heat of Indian summer, my tongue furred and my eyes gummed shut from exhaustion, flashes of light from the windshields of cars passing on the Clearview Expressway sparkled in front of my eyes like cartoon stars.

Back at my apartment, I would sit under the shower and imagine the hot water scouring layers of grime off of me in slow succession: sweat, cigarette smoke, cheap perfume. On more than one occasion I fell asleep in that position, the water coursing down and down until the steam fogged over the mirror and condensation puddled on the floor.

Often I forgot to eat, and when I remembered I usually discovered there was nothing in the fridge. I would stand staring stupidly at the grimy metal shelves for some minutes, as if by doing so I could conjure a meal from the packets of soy sauce and empty pizza cartons that lay within. In those moments, I would remember how Anne sometimes used to surprise me in the foul-weather months with an indoor picnic – there, where the sun now dappled the empty carpet by the windows, we would lay on a red-checked blanket, the wicker basket opened between us, eating her cold pasta salad and drinking white wine while the rain beat against the windows and Patsy Cline played on the stereo. But that was only the longing of a man dying of thirst for every drop of water he had ever squandered. Inevitably, I would come back to the present, the taste of the wine evaporating on my tongue and replaced by the metallic film of deep-down hunger…and the knowledge that wherever Anne was picnicking, it was not with me. Just as inevitably my fingers would close around the neck of a bottle of beer, reasoning that a calorie was a calorie no matter how empty the Surgeon General said it was.

Parking my car under the lightning-scarred poplar tree down the street from the Grind Joint in the late afternoons, already half-drunk, I would look up with red-rimmed eyes at the big old house with its soiled white siding and coal-black shutters, its lawn showing only feverish bursts of crab grass in bare earth, and long to see it in flames. Fire gushing from every window, its slate-topped roof caving inward, its upper stories collapsing in sluggish agony. But it never happened, and when the inner door swung open and the effluvium of last night's merry-making and money-taking swept down the stairs hard enough to puff the hair off my forehead, I always fought down the nausea that landed like a bare-knuckled blow somewhere between my gut and my gorge.

The hours before opening would pass in tedious monotony. There were always a hundred details to be attended to and never enough time to attend to them. Floors would have to be swept and mopped, ashtrays emptied, countertops wiped down, bathrooms scrubbed, the bar restocked with hijacked liquor, the big industrial refrigerator restocked with hijacked food, new sets of poker chips, cards, dice, racks, pool cues, chalk, napkins, plates, silverware, glasses brought up from the dank stone-walled basement, cases of beer opened and packed on ice, the roulette wheels tested and re-tested, the sound-system checked, the sound-proofing repaired, the row of slot machines maintained and examined for cheating devices, the security arrangements rehearsed, the grievances of various employees addressed, mollified, ignored. Bobby Tomascello was upset because a high-ranking associate from another Family was rude and insulting to him whenever he lost at craps. Linda the Bartender wanted the butter-ass businessman from Bayside beaten out in the alley the next time he copped a feel without permission. Gavin demanded a bigger cut of any poker game that lasted more than twenty-four hours. Kraut was angry because Jerry the Bartender had told him Antoinette the Hat-Check Girl was turning tricks in the upstairs bedrooms and the house wasn't getting a cut of her action. One of the Sicilians Nicky Cowboy had supplied us from the Gravel Hauler's Union as a bodyguard was having visa problems and was worried he'd be deported back to Sicily, where there was a price on his head over a botched diamond heist. On and on.

In these hours, when every door was open and the house rang with clatterings, bangings, thuds, creaks, curses, when everyone was bustling about in an ill-temper and treading on each other's toes, when workmen were hauling in cases of crab meat or whiskey or sacks of lettuce up the back steps, it always seemed that I was cold no matter what the temperature was. There was a dankness to the Grind Joint, a lingering chill that clung to my skin and stayed there, numbing my fingertips and making my nose run even when it was hot enough outside to bring out the sweat on my tailbone. At first I thought it was because I was shedding weight. Then I began to suspect that the Joint itself simply refused light and warmth, deflected them like a science-fiction cloaking device.

When the doors opened, usually with the day's last light casting a feeble glow on the big steel security door, I would stay in the front bar, greeting the customers. Trying to determine at a glance the rank, stability, and aggregate wealth of the newcomers. Trying to assess the moods and fighting abilities of the troublemakers. Scrutinizing the armpits and waists of their suit jackets to divine the telltale bulge of a pistol, the revealing print of a knife handle. My cheek grew reddened and fragrant from the greeting kisses of the fringe players – the lower a man's standing in the mob, the more likely he tended towards formality – and my palms swollen from shaking hands with men who wore size fourteen rings. My head swam with booze and booze and more booze as I stood chronic losers to drinks, and accepted the condescending largesse of the big winners. My ears rang with the din – music, shouting, drunken laughter, the distinctive rattle of the roulette wheel and the mechanical click-and-whirr of the slot machines.

My body grew steadily more battered, fresh injuries blossoming over the half-healed ones. A punch to the ear. A knee to the ribs. A pool cue broken over my forearm. Scrapes on my knuckles, my knees, my elbows, my collarbone. Bruises in fading yellow, gangrenous purple, putrescent green. Sometimes the shadows of exhaustion under my lower lids only looked like black eyes; sometimes they really were. The rope that bound my temper, frayed to strings by sleeplessness and the never-ceasing pressure to earn, snapped as often as it held, with the result that I was held back from starting fights almost as often as I intervened to break them up. Kraut, tired of bailing me out with his fists, told me in no uncertain terms to reign it in or start packing.

I bought a pistol the next day.

There were pies cooking everywhere in the Joint, and I tried to keep a finger in every one. With great difficulty, I memorized the tables of probability and made side bets on the crap games, spending hour after hour with sweat-dampened bills crushed in one hand and my mind racing ahead of my mouth as it never had in math class. From Alton, I obtained inside information on many New York-based fighters – whether they were making weight properly or using drugs, whether they were doing their roadwork or sleeping in, whether they were shipshape or hiding injuries from the Athletic Commission – and with that information placed action with a bookie who was into the house for eight grand. With Kraut's approval and backing, I increased the tax on the small-time loan sharks who had circled the big-stakes poker games, nursing their Seven-and-Sevens and sizing up the losers with predatory smiles. I even approached Kraut about going into the shylock business ourselves.

The hours of darkness passed like fever dreams, rambling, disjointed, exhausting. Sober despite a steady inflow of alcohol, I prowled around the Joint like an insect through clockwork, in the action but not of it, my heavy-lidded gaze moving over every face and classifying them not by name but by profession – stripper, bookmaker, cowboy hijacker. Many times a night I slipped into Kraut's office and estimated the take, scribbling my calculations on flash paper and then igniting them in the big bronze ashtray on the desk. Sometimes I slipped out through the kitchen in back and sat on the steps that descended into the muddy, neglected yard, a shadow among shadows, the faint pulse of the speakers pressing against my back like the heat of a fire. There I would breathe in the clean night air and rest my head against the cool iron railing, muscles aching with fatigue, eyes stinging, trying to imagine myself as one small step closer to freedom with every moment that passed. But it wasn't that simple. There were bad nights, nights the dealers raised when they should have held or folded when they should have called, nights when the slots vomited quarters in clanging, jangling torrents, nights when the dice were so hot they seemed to leave scorch marks on the felt and even the most inveterate losers took us to the bank. And for me, those were very long nights indeed.

The Joint was not open every night of the week, and on my days off I often lay motionless for four or five hours at a time even when I was not sleeping. Too tired to move, to eat, even to shave, my mind gelatinous and inert. But even in these still moments, when the clock over the television ticked quietly into the silence and the sunlight swam on the ceiling like reflections from a pool, I could find no easy peace. Always the knowledge of the vig plagued me, sometimes lurking on the edge of my thoughts, sometimes shrieking in the midst of them. The vig. The hideous, perfidious, insidious vig that worked as a metastasizing nemesis against every move I made, every dollar I scored. Its number pressed into the flesh of my mind like a brand – thirty-seven fifty, thirty-seven fifty, thirty-seven fucking fifty. Every week, I had to pocket $3,750 as a hedge against the vig before I could move a penny towards the principal.

I tightened my belt as best I could, but I had never lived extravagantly to begin with and there was very little fat to trim. Lying in bed with Tina one afternoon, I asked her in a hoarse, cracked whisper if she wouldn't be better off rid of me, since I could no longer afford the nights on the town, the ringside seats at the Garden, the expensive little gifts from Saks Fifth Avenue and Victoria's Secret. Hell, I could not even spring for a chocolate Martini at her favorite club. She could have the pick of the litter: why settle for washed-up Faust trying to buy his soul back from the devil?

Tina shared a habit with Gino of rarely smiling except at someone else's discomfiture. She smiled now, the bleached-white teeth gleaming between the silvery-pale lips, one perfectly-plucked eyebrow arched in an expression of amused condescension. Sliding her press-on nails down my abdomen, she asked me if I really thought she was with me for my money. Are you kidding, she said? I've got more money than *you* do. A *lot* more. I'm in this for the *sex*, you punch-drunk jackass.

Much later, lying next to her on her rumpled Ralph Lauren sheets, my battered body showing off its bruise-mottled ribs to the overhead mirror, I propped myself up on one elbow and asked her: How much money *do* you have?

The next morning, with a gravity that would have impressed the Pope, Tina handed me a heavy manila envelope containing five thousand dollars in cash, and became a silent partner in the Grind Joint's newly minted shylocking operation. Kraut took the news with a wry, slightly salacious smile. You can never have too much pie, he said.

October arrived like a weak jab. I registered the change of months in terms of sensations only – coolness in the evening air, dew on the windshield in the morning, shorter days and longer nights. Running on nerves and willpower and driven by desperation for yet more ways to make money, I forced myself to commit my few off-hours to training. After the first session with Alton, I fainted and had to be revived with cold water and smelling salts. By the third, I was only vomiting. Gradually, a semblance of my timing returned, and the Hard Knox echoed with the staccato crack of fists on handpads, on speedbags, and eventually, on sparring partners. My weight continued to drop; from a bloated and beer-bellied two hundred twenty pounds, the needle retreated to the area of my fighting weight, as much from malnutrition as exercise. Alton scolded me like a mother hen and stood by, glowering, as I dutifully ate the protein-heavy breakfasts he cooked me. Sometimes the fork trembled on the way to my mouth, but to my half-starved and neglected body, the cholesterol had the effect of morphine on a burn patient, and before too long the strength returned to my limbs. Mostly.

One night a few weeks before Halloween, I counted out my bankroll to the last quarter and afterwards sat on the edge of my bed with my head in my hands. More than eighty grand separated me from manumission, and the sands in my hourglass were beginning to dwindle. In that moment, my hatred for Mikhailis Morganstern rekindled and blazed as never before. If only he'd signed me after Kreese, I might have been able to pay off this debt in the cage, where at least I had the advantage of long experience.

It struck me then that between fight promoters and professional criminals, the edge in business ethics actually went to the crooks. A man like Kraut could rob a bank, burn down a building, or massacre a roomful of enemies without batting an eyelash, but the idea of coming at someone sideways, undermining him by working through his girlfriend, systematically engineering his downfall while shaking his hand – this literally would never occur to him. If there were no honor among thieves, the so-called legitimate businessman seemed to be deep in negative numbers.

I thought about that for a while. Maybe the past ten months, spent in the greasy bosom of the *brugad,* had further warped a sense of values already bent out of shape by the streets of Hell's Kitchen, but it seemed to me I was growing more comfortable among illicit evil than the type society had lent its stamp of approval. Crooks, conmen, hustlers, hijackers, and whores – those I understood and could deal with, if only clumsily. M.B.A.'s in Bill Blass – with them, I was out of my league. What I needed was a bridge *between* the worlds, a way I could play to my strengths somewhere Mikhailis Morganstern had no dominion.

I went to my telephone and called Kraut. To make all the arrangements for what I wanted to do took less than two hours.

Better the devil you know, right?

Chapter Twenty-Five

"You sure you want to do this?" Alton said for the twentieth time. "I mean, are you really *sure?*"

"It's not a question of want," I said quietly, sipping water from a plastic bottle wrapped in medical tape. "I don't have a choice."

"Course you do," he replied, pointing a finger at the exit. "Walk through that muthafucka and your choice is made."

"I don't think they'd let me, at this point."

"Your friend here could persuade 'em."

Kraut nodded slowly. His leather jacket was unzipped, and I could see the butt of his Walther under his left arm. "You want to back out, I can't say as to what happens tomorrow – but nobody gonna stop you from leaving tonight. I fuckin'-A guarantee you that."

Kraut's voice reminded me of a muffler dragging on asphalt, all flying rust and yellow sparks. When he took that tone, you could count on the fingers of one hand the number of people on Earth who would have dared to cross him. In spite of everything, I felt myself smile – slightly.

"I believe you," I said, shaking out my hands. "But it's tomorrow that I'm worried about."

"This is crazy," Alton said.

"This is money," I said. "And the clock is ticking."

The room around us looked like the set of a horror movie – smutty cinderblock walls, exposed pipes caked with rust, chipped concrete floor sheened with old oil stains. The only light came from an exposed forty-watt bulb in the ceiling. I sat on a heavy machine table, sweating lightly despite the chill, trying to focus only the grime-streaked door and not what lay beyond it. Trying to summon up the images that had always sustained me, settled me, given me courage before the bell rang. As a Golden Glove boxer fighting Puerto Ricans from Spanish Harlem and blacks from Brownsville, I learned a lot about fear at a young age and the different ways to conquer it. There was no need for me to be afraid now. I was an old hand at this game. Between the amateurs and my MMA career, I must have fought in close to a hundred and fifty bouts. Old hand? Shit. When it came to the fisticuffs, I was Methuselah.

Of course, in most of those fights, my fists were wearing gloves.

"I seen some fucked-up things in my time," Alton said finally, putting his hands on his hips. "But this is the most fucked-up of all of them."

"You went to Vietnam," I said.

"I got drafted," he said. "Who the fuck drafted you?"

"*La Cosa Nostra.*"

Kraut turned his blue-gray eyes on me. "Do us all a favor. Don't mention those words again. In this place, you can get killed for using the *La.*"

The big steel door opened with a creak and a jerk. A squat, fat-cheeked *cugine* in a black warm-up outfit thrust his head inside, the ornate gold crucifix around his neck swinging forward to catch the light. "You're on, tough guy," he said in a nasal Bronx accent. "You ready?"

He swung the door open without waiting for an answer, filling the room with a spill of weak florescent light. I slid down off the table, handing the water bottle to Alton, who wore an expression somewhere between incredulity and a grim determination to see a fool through his errand. Kraut stood back, jaw muscles clenched, the hollows in his face pooled in theatrical shadow. In that pose, he strongly resembled the pictures of his father that hung in the front hallway of his home, taken on the Eastern Front during the Second World War – that same mixture of fatalism and determination.

I wondered fleetingly if my face wore the same look, and if so, which quality was more dominant.

The hallway was as ugly as the waiting room; one of the florescent bulbs was dying, and it buzzed and crackled insistently above us. The *cugine,* who had identified himself as Mario, walked ahead with a brisk, swaggering stride, his portly acrylic-clad thighs brushing together with a noise like an insistent whisper. "Last fight didn't go very long. Carmine's kinda pissed off. You don't give the crowd a good show, he'll hang you from the fuckin' ring ropes."

"I'll keep that in mind," I said.

"You know the rules, right?" His voice was breathless from the dual effort of walking and talking. "No biting, fish-hooking or eye-gouging. No nut shots. Stay off the floor if you can. Other than that, go crazy."

"Crazy is right," Alton muttered.

"Dude you're up against is good," Mario continued. "Real good. Won his last eleven fights. Most of 'em he sent out in stretchers. Won't nobody on the regular circuit get in with him no more."

"Great," I said.

"You remember what we talked about, now," he said in a pedantic tone. "Carmine ain't lookin' for a miracle here. He don't expect you to win or nothin'. But if you can get past the over-under, he stands to make a pile tonight, and he'll give you a taste."

"Fine," I said. "But I came to win."

"So did Custer."

I heard the noise of a crowd up ahead – mingled voices, music, shuffling feet, the drone of space heaters. Smelled the first cigarette smoke. Felt my fists clench involuntarily under their gauntlets of sweat-hardened tape. The first fear arrived. It felt like winter sunlight – cold, bright, harshly insistent through your windshield. We came out of the hallway into a large, well-lighted storage room with an enormous ceiling and walls of corrugated metal. Against one of the walls, a deejay booth had been set up between powerful speakers; a young man in a soft black cap and headphones worked the turntables, nodding his head to the beat. On the opposite wall stood a full-service bar, behind it a stolid-looking black man with graying herringbone sideburns in a white tuxedo jacket. Before us a crowd of perhaps a hundred people stood in a loose ring around a bare patch of concrete floor. A number of others milled about here and there in small groups.

I had been expecting rough trade and a lot of it – bikers, gum-chewing sidewalk soldiers from the local mob, rent-a-thugs and their whores. But the crowd was largely Manhattan and upscale – attractive young women in Dolcé cocktail dresses and three hundred dollar heels, middle-aged men in Byblos jackets and buffed shoes of patent leather. The overhead lights glittered on gold cufflinks, pearl clasps, silk ties, and a small constellation of diamonds. Flavored tobacco smoke mingled with the scent of perfume and wine. Even the haircuts looked expensive. The only muscle seemed to belong to the house – standing here and there in designer warm-up suits or heavy leather jackets, some clutching small hand radios, trying in the timeworn manner of bouncers everywhere to look at once menacing and discreet.

Mario gestured for us to halt just outside the threshold with a fat-fingered hand and strutted over to a spectral-looking man with thinning silver-gray hair and a Scrooge nose, who was drinking mineral water from a small green bottle. The specter was probably the shabbiest dresser in the warehouse. In his granny glasses and tweed jacket, he looked for all the world like a rumpled college professor – all that was missing was the pipe and the leather patches on his elbows. Yet in his presence, the *cugine*'s body language immediately turned servile: he folded his hands, lowered his head, and looked at the tips of his brand-new sneakers while he spoke into the old man's ear.

"The man himself," Kraut said.

Alton narrowed his eyes. "Who?"

"Carmine Spina." Kraut was speaking in what I thought of as his Prison Exercise Yard voice – a low murmur that was distinct at four feet and unintelligible at six. "Made guy. Controls the underground fight circuit. And look who's with him."

I looked and suddenly felt as if the fight had already commenced, because seeing Mikhailis Morganstern take his place next to Spina hit me like a fist to the breastbone.

He was dressed in his trademark Saville Row, and his smooth-shaven head gleamed in the overhead lights like the crown of a helmet. As he lifted a brimming flute glass to his lips, I felt his dark deep-set gaze upon my face, saw the cupid's bow mouth bend ever so slightly in a smile.

"Easy," Kraut said, looking closely at my face. "You slug him and they'll never find our bodies."

I was trying to return Mikhailis's stare, but hatred was sparking my heart along with such fury that my vision blackened with every beat. The mocking half-smile, wetted briefly with champagne, wavered in and out of that blackness. "He's no wiseguy."

"He's Spina's guest."

As if to confirm this, Mikhailis leaned in close to Spina, so close his lips almost brushed the older man's ear, and spoke a few unhurried words, as one would speak to a *compare*. The king of the underground fight circuit settled his spectacles on the gaunt blade of cartilage that was his nose and squinted at me the way you would squint at a racehorse you had heard good things about but never before seen. He said something to Mario, who turned and peacocked his way quickly back to us.

"He wants to meet you," the *cugine* huffed. His baby-fat features held an expression of almost comical surprise, but they tightened when both Alton and Kraut stepped forward with me. "*Just* you, cowboy, not your posse."

I hesitated for a moment, then started toward the two men so abruptly that Mario had to hustle in my wake.

I hadn't seen Morganstern since the Suba fight, and I had forgotten how big he was. Not just in height or breadth but in impact. Everything about him was solid and heavy – skull, frame, musculature – and every gesture he made, even the intonation of his voice, had the repose of wealth, power, self-belief. He looked like an idol consecrated to the gods of arrogance.

Damned if I would bow.

"Mickey," he said. "Good to see you again."

I looked down at his proffered hand. Probably fresh from the small of Anne's back. Or somewhere else. Had a brief vision of turning it clockwise and pushing until the big son of a bitch fell to his knees in agony. It was one of the simplest moves in aikido, and one of the most painful. But as I reached for it, I glanced up into those fathomless heavy-lidded eyes and in that instant I knew – not thought, *knew* – that this was precisely what he was expecting. I was a fighter, after all. All balls and no brains, driven by my impulses as thus easy to predict. To manipulate. To destroy. For the price of a moment's humiliation and discomfort, he could see his only romantic rival jumped by half-a-dozen of Spina's thugs, beaten and broken, perhaps dragged down into the basement to be murdered. If he hadn't actually planned it he was certainly smart enough to have recognized the opportunity when it walked up to him, glaring. It was all there in his subtly smiling face.

Go ahead, the smile seemed to be saying. *Take a shot and see what happens. Or don't, and live with knowing you passed up the chance.*

I hesitated. No more than the time it takes to draw two or three breaths, but it seemed like eons, epochs, ages, during which a thousand muscle-memorized techniques for taking human life trembled on the edge of my nervous system. Then, with a mingled mental cry of relief and anguish, I shook his hand and let it go, but not before I saw disappointment shallow briefly in his eyes."I was just telling Carmine how surprised I am to see you here," Mikhailis said. He had a voice to match his appearance; deep, powerful, somewhat drawling, the voice of a man who knew people and events would wait on him. "Pretty far off Broadway, isn't it?"

"For both of us," I said.

He shrugged. "A fight's a fight to me. As long as someone's bleeding, I'm happy. But don't tell Anne that."

With immense effort, I kept my expression set, my voice unchanged. "I don't see much of Anne nowadays."

He made a *tisk* noise with his tongue. "That's rough. But you have to understand something about girls, Mick. You see 'em in the winner's circle, but you'll never find horseshit on their shoes. They like money and power and fame, they like to see their reflections in the gold cup, but they don't want to know how you got it. They don't want to know about what goes on in the stables and the glue factory, and God help you if they have to smell 'em. You want to keep a lady like Anne, you've got to convince her that business is Marquis of Queensbury rules, not a street fight with switchblades and steel-toed boots. That's why I like these little soirees of Carmine's so much. It's like 'The Most Dangerous Game' in here. Like what I do with the League, but with all the sanctimonious safety bullshit scraped away. No rules, no restraints…just reality."

We stared at each other. We were so close I could smell the aftershave under his collar, so close that the tips of my old boxing shoes almost touched those of his reindeer-hide loafers. Along with the coiled-spring tension in my body, I had a strange, almost surreal sensation of being caught in a James Bond movie at the point where he and the villain come face to face but are not yet ready to commence hostilities, settling instead for veiled language and double meaning. It might have been comforting, had I been sure which of us was the hero and which doomed to play his foil.

"This was one of yours, eh?" A raspy, Bronx-accented voice to my left turned my attention from Mikhailis's looming face to that of Carmine Spina. Behind the glasses, his eyes were pale gray and held as much warmth as a guillotine blade. "He don't look like all that much."

"Don't sell him too short," Mikhailis replied, still looking at me. "He takes a good beating."

"He better do more than that," Spina said. "I want a *fight,* not a public execution."

"Six of one, half-a-dozen of the other," Mikhailis said, and winked.

Carmine turned abruptly to Mario and made a negligent gesture with his chin.

The *cugine,* who had been staring at his master with doglike eagerness, turned to me at once. "Okay," he said, a bit breathlessly, with a wave to the deejay. "Follow me."

Turning away from Mikhailis, I waved to Alton and Kraut, and we made our way to the center of the warehouse, the crowd parting before us, faces eager, expectant, pitiless. A few of the women looked me up and down with chilling frankness, the way men look at strippers or the contestants of bikini contests. We arrived at the bare patch of concrete in the center of the room, a rough circle about twenty feet in circumference demarked by swaths of electrical tape. The concrete was spattered everywhere with blood. Amidst the innumerable smears and flecks, some rust-brown, others ruby red, I saw a fragment of slightly yellowed enamel – the broken crown of a tooth.

Alton said, "Ring ropes?"

"Figure of speech," Mario replied, turning fat-enfolded eyes on me. "About the hangin', I'm bein' fairly literal. You get an urge to dog it in there, take my advice and don't."

"It's winner-take-all," Kraut said. "Why the fuck would anybody dog it?"

The *cugine*'s mouth drew back in a boyish smile. "I guess some people think it's better than gettin' beat to death. But trust me, you dog it, you get beat to death just the same."

A whine of feedback cut through the gabble of conversation around us, and the wattage in the overhead lights dimmed to a mellow glow. The deejay's deep-yet-mellifluous voice flowed out over the speakers as he moved smoothly through his pre-fight shtick. I hardly heard a word of it. Standing still with Alton's hand on my shoulder, I felt as if the pounding of my heart were loud enough to ripple the champagne in the spectators' glasses.

Now the crowd began to move on the opposite side of the room. I saw the gleam of light on a shaven head and tracked it the way you track a shark's fin from a shallow-bottomed boat.

"Here comes the judge," Mario smirked.

My opponent stepped over the tape into the circle accompanied by a single handler carrying a towel and a water bottle. He was of indeterminate race, possibly Brazilian, with a round skull, battering-ram jaw, and ears like a dog's chew toys. His nose was almost flat, and the shiny scarring over his eyebrows and cheekbones was so extensive he looked as if he put out a small brush fire with his face. His bare upper body was a relief map of muscle, with heavy vein-work in the forearms. Tattooed in an arch across the top of his abdominals in Gothic lettering was the word *MONSTRO.*

"Jesus Christ," Alton said to Mario. "Fuck did you find this fool, a kennel?"

"Kennel wouldn't take him," was the laconic reply.

There was some applause and a few whistles, but not enough to drown out the rustling sounds of money changing hands. I glanced over at Spina, who stared at us without expression, and at Morganstern, whose sly little smile had resumed its place upon his lips. Above and behind him, standing on a dais of varnished wood before a huge scuffed-up blackboard, an oddsmaker in a red-shaded visor cap insulted me with a brisk movement of chalk. Apparently, I wasn't supposed to last longer than five minutes. But if I did, and I won, I'd pocket ten thousand dollars.

However, as someone had once remarked, *if* is the longest word in the English language.

The deejay wrapped up his introductions and put on some music – a frantic yet coldly mechanical dance beat of the type you find in clubs where the girls wear black lipstick and have their nipples pierced. I pulled my hooded sweatshirt over my head and handed it to Alton, leaving me clad only in camouflage trousers cut raggedly above the knee and my old red boxing shoes. The air around me felt cool against the sweat on my skin. I was acutely conscious of the contrast in our bodies – mine pale and scuffed at the knees and elbows, showing too many ribs and not enough muscle; his dusky and hulking, the veins standing out as rigidly as strings of catgut on his biceps and forearms.

Mario walked out to the center of the ring and gestured us towards each other. I took a last sip of water to wash the metallic taste of fear out of my mouth and met the Brazilian center ring, bumping chests with him, noticing for the first time that I was about two inches taller. Staredowns were generally easier with a height advantage, but Monstro's eyes, so gray as to be nearly white, glared up at me from under his shelf brows with a blazing, animalistic intensity that spoke of psychosis or cocaine.

"You're nothing but an old bitch!" Monstro hissed in a high, hoarse voice, the sweat-oiled flap of his nose brushing my chin in hideous intimacy. *"Voce e uma cadela veia!"*

"Right back atcha, Sparky."

Our referee pushed us apart, gestured for us to move to opposite sides of the ring. As I did so, Alton looked at me and cried: "Mick – don't take it to the streets with this muthafucka. Do what you *do.*"

"Youse guys ready?" Mario shouted theatrically. I nodded a few times before I realized he was talking to the crowd. "Let's get it on!" he roared in response to their cheers, sounding like a cross between Mills Lane and Big John McCarthy. It was the closest thing we had to a bell.

Monstro sprang at me with a flying knee. I slipped to the left and he landed a few feet to the side of me in a thud of bare feet, then pivoted with his fists clenched inside their mantlets of tape, grinning ferociously. I punched into the grin and felt lips like sweat-hardened leather under my knuckles, teeth rigid beneath them, not much give at the neck. No sooner had my fist landed than he swung out his right hand and struck its back against the edge of my cheekbone just in front of the ear. The whole right side of my face went numb, and I had just enough time to register that sensation when his shin caught me flush in the ribs.

"I gonna fuck you like a rooster fucks a chicken!" he shouted in Portuguese, raising his arms in triumph as I staggered backwards. I wanted to respond with something cute, like, *Speak English or die!* but the pain in my ribs prevented me from speaking. In any case, he didn't celebrate long, but made a couple of mocking feints as I circled around to his right. Every time he feinted, I sprang back a foot like a startled cat. His grin had blood on it now, but that only served to make him look fiercer.

Monstro came in again, swinging wildly with his right, and I caught it on my left forearm and hit him hard in the jaw, feeling bone and beard stubble, and followed it up with a knee to his midsection. It was like striking a padded statue, but I heard the air come out of him in a startled grunt, and as I shoved him backwards, I noticed the grin had left his face. I kicked him in the left calf, and when his hands went down instinctively, I put all my weight on my left leg and kicked him again in the pit of his stomach. He fell backwards, legs going up over his head in a reverse somersault, but was up again in a single motion, the crowd raising glasses and cash-filled hands in delight, the deejay roaring. He seemed to bulge with a sudden infusion of rage, veins standing out from wrists to temples, and then he was flying through the air and the last thing I saw before I hit the floor was his calloused, dirty-yellow foot as it landed on my collarbone.

The concrete was cold and gritty, and I saw more feet, a forest of lower legs around me, trouser cuffs resting on polished leather shoes, silk stockings sheening lovely calves, a superb pair of Gucci slingbacks, and then Monstro was standing over me, bellowing, slobbering, and I took a kick to the head and another to the side. I rolled and rolled, propelled by his feet, and in desperation I clutched at one of them and wrenched it with all my might.

Monstro screamed in pain, an oddly effeminate sound from such a beast, and fell next to me. My fingers sank a half-inch deep into the flesh of his foot, turning it, feeling the ridges of the tendons beneath my fingertips, the protesting creak of his bones. He screamed again and stomped me between the eyes with his free heel, and I let go as the crowd shrilled for blood.

He stood, spit running out of his jaws like a rabid dog, hobbling now, and I got up too, blood on my mouth and running down my chest and my eyes watering and Monstro blurring, trebling in my vision under the hot lights. We were both breathing hard and circling each other slowly, warily now, animals who have taken each other's measure and found nothing reassuring in the taking. My right ear felt like a leaky hot water bottle and my nose as if it had been crushed. Monstro didn't feint any more, and he didn't grin. His eyes had taken on a vitreous glaze, and his mouth was a branded snarl. Every time he gulped air, the muscles in his stomach contracted like paving stones in an earthquake.

He came forward and spun a kick at me, a sweeping wheel kick that batted aside my hands. I tried to kick him in the side in return and he trapped it with his left hand, his thick fingers clutching at the uppers of my boxing shoe, and struck me in the mouth with his right. One, two, three times. For a moment we danced this way before he punched me out of his grip and I stumbled backward, spitting blood, my back butting up against the crowd, champagne spilling cool down my side, and then rough hands propelled me forward. Monstro's big tattooed fist whistled toward me in a flat arc, and I ducked my head and took it just above the ear. I felt the joints in my legs go and his hand snake through my sweat-soaked hair. He kneed me in the chin, struggled with me, kneed me again, grunting and cursing in Portuguese. I slipped an arm around his waist and smothered him, but he got his feet planted and rolled me over his hip just as easy as you please. I hit the concrete like a sack of pancake batter.

The crowd pressed in around me, shaking their fists and screaming. A twenty-dollar bill shook loose from one pumping fist and side-slipped through the air as if in slow motion, executing a loop-de-loop and settling on the blood-speckled concrete just below my chin. The crumpled face of Thomas Jefferson looked up at me in august disapproval, turning on the current of my breath, turning the way the hands of a clock turn, and somewhere in my throbbing skull I heard the ticks, the tocks, the ceaseless drumbeat of time and the vig that marched to it. I felt rather than saw Morganstern's smirking face, and Gino Stillitano's, and Nicky Cowboy's, and even Anne's – everyone who had ever wanted me to fail, needed me to fail, been absolutely certain that I would fail and must therefore be cut loose to drift in that failure alone. Rage suffused my veins again, a great red rage that lifted me off the floor as Monstro bore down, just in time to meet my fist with his mouth. His lips gave way in a crimson gush, and he staggered and snarled and punched me in the ribs, and we stood there, left hands clenched at the backs of each other's necks, punching away with our rights, blood mingling in the space between us, no technique, no thought at all, just the mutual, mindless desire to destroy.

Somewhere amidst the thuds of impact and the stabbing agonies in my arms, my ribs, the side of my head, I heard a voice shouting over and over again, as insistently as the notes of a bugle through the din of battle: *"Don't take it to the streets with him! Do what you do! Do what you do! Do what you DO!"* And I thought: but this *is* what I do. I do it every night. Swap elbows and foreheads with Grind Joint goons. But none of them built like this.

Another thud, this one to the temple, and a memory shook loose, floating down out of the rafters of my mind: the face of Dem'yan Suba, full of cold confidence that I had no other method than to try an overwhelm him with savagery. That I was too stupid to use my mind and, locked in a cage with a cold-blooded assassin, would simply try to out-savage him and fail. And here, now, Monstro knew it too.

Because I was fighting like a thug. Like an animal. The way Gino would have fought. The way Monstro was fighting now. No longer did I try to outthink my problems; I simply attacked them, mindlessly, like a beast, and even when this method failed, I continued the attack, because I had forgotten any other way. The devolution was complete, and I was one of them. Shit, maybe Clean was right. Maybe I always had been. Maybe at my essential core there was nothing in me worth keeping. Worth saving. Worth loving. Maybe that was why Anne had left me. Because she had seen through my collegiate façade to the thing that hissed and slithered inside. The gangster. The monster. The murdering beast.

"Like hell!" I screamed through smashed lips, and drove my shoulder into Monstro's chin. His eyes registered surprise, and I punched between them, a good, hard, old-fashioned jab, a right to the chin after it, and I pivoted smoothly as his counterpunch struck empty air. I hit him with two more jabs high on the jaw, his beard stubble raking my knuckles where the tape didn't cover them. He swung again, and I noticed for the first time how short his arms were, how easy it would be to control the distance if I just kept the stick in his mouth, just used my brain and boxed the way Old Sam had taught me to. And so I did, two more jabs and a pivot to the right, and he missed again, fist whispering past my ear, and I crossed him hard, turning his head in a spray of blood and sweat, feeling the impact rattle up my arm.

He chased me around the ring, dragging his bad leg, the muscles in his arms bunched to grotesque proportions as he swung and swung and caught nothing but air. My fists, on the other hand, could not miss his chin – it was a magnet that drew them as jabs, straight rights, hooks that painted the floor with spatters of his blood. My shoulders were quivering with exhaustion, my hands felt like sacks of broken glass and still he came, one eye puffing shut, one cheek blown out pink and shiny, his canvas pants drenched in red, breath coming in shuddering gasps.

Oh, he was a tough motherfucker. I don't have to give him that because he took that title fair and square. Took it with a dozen, two dozen, three dozen hard shots, and still kept coming, lurching forward, ignoring the fists on his jaw, the gunshot impacts of my feet against the thigh of his injured leg, the elbows that crashed against his scarred cheeks. He came forward like the rebels at Gettysburg, like the Union boys at Cold Harbor, and like them was massacred for his pains.

"Go *down!*" I shouted, and popped him with another jab. "Go down." Another. "Go down." Two more. He swung again, so wildly he nearly left his feet, and I blocked it with my elbow and punched him hard in the sternum. "Down," I said. He spit blood at me and swung again, kicked, hit nothing, caught a knife-hand to the side of his neck for his efforts. *"Down."* He was weaving now, running on rage, nothing left on his punches, his kicks swats against my thighs. I hit him and hit him and hit him again, and his handler was screaming something in Portuguese, and Monstro just stood there with his mouth gaping and his arms dangling at his sides. I hesitated just a moment, thinking in that splinter of a second that one more head shot might kill him, and I thought of Dago Red and turned my fist southward into the pit of his stomach. He folded over it, his breath and blood and spittle hot on my bicep, and then fell to his back, gazing up at me with white, uncomprehending eyes. He was finished.

The crowd noise and music were deafening in my ears, but I was aware of it only distantly as I looked down at him, unsteady on my own feet. I put my hands on my knees and gulped in the air until the overwhelming urge to faint weakened to a mere suggestion.

"Don't call me *cadela,*" I told him.

Mario leapt into the ring, gold crucifix bouncing. Monstro's handler ran out after him, and in an instant the circle dissolved and was filled with people, shouting and laughing and cursing. I felt many hands slapping my back, and a lovely redhead in a sequined top and expensive shawl leaned in and kissed me on one feverish cheekbone. Then Alton had me by one arm and Kraut by the other, and they were dragging me through the crowd.

"I *told* you to box the man," Alton said, shouldering patrons aside with more violence than was necessary. "I swear to fuck, you're the longest distance between two points, Mickey!"

Kraut was staring at me in open-mouthed admiration. "That was the goddamndest thing I ever saw. Who'da thunk it? Who'd a fuckin' *thunk* it?"

I expended some effort for a look over at Mikhailis. He was watching me *sans* expression, his head tilted to one side, the lights setting the fire opals in his signet ring ablaze as he lifted his champagne glass in something that was more than an acknowledgement but not quite a salute. Then the crowd blocked him from view.

Alton, Kraut, and I moved back down the corridor like a trio of drunks. Mario ran after us. "You cost a lot of people a lot of fuckin' money," he panted. "But son of a bitch, that was a good fight! Carmine's real happy."

"I can tell," I said, lisping the way you do when you can't bring your lips together. "Where's my money?"

"Ho! Listen to fuckin' Robert De Niro here. You'll get the money. Carmine don't welch on nobody. Eight big ones, just like we said."

"*Ten* big ones," Kraut said, showing most of his teeth. "The payout was ten."

"Bet price is two thousand. I musta mentioned it before. Anyway, you take it easy, kid. Congrats on the win." He slapped me lightly on the cheek, frowned at the sweat and blood on his fingers, and wiped them on my pants before he left.

"Son of a bitch," Kraut hissed as we went through the doorway into the dressing room. "I shoulda known that old spider woulda found a way to fuck you."

"Forget it," I said, thinking maybe there wasn't much difference between businessmen and gangsters after all. "Just get me to a hospital."

They lifted me onto the machine table so that my feet dangled above the floor: Alton steadied me with one hand and up-ended the water bottle over my head. It was the first pleasant sensation I experienced in what seemed like days. Kraut vanished in a jingle of car keys, the door creaking shut behind him, and the noise of the crowd cut off as if by a switch. Alton let me drip for a minute and then began to sponge me down with a towel, clucking his tongue like an old mother hen.

At some length, as if pronouncing a medical diagnosis, he said: "You are one sorry-ass muthafucka."

"Don't I know it."

"By the way, what the hell's a *cadela?*"

"Honestly, Alt," I said, shutting my eyes. "I have no idea."

Chapter Twenty-Six

I got home from the hospital shortly before dawn. The orange paper lamps my neighbors had put out for Halloween were still lit when I opened the lacquered iron gate of my building and limped up the steps to my flat. I myself was not feeling the Halloween spirit. I felt more like a jack o'lantern on the first of November, broken on the pavement and awaiting the broom. Everything hurt, and my mouth tasted like blood. When you swallow too much, it has to come out, so they pump your stomach. What they don't do is give you an after-dinner mint.

I went to the bathroom and left the lights off when I urinated. I knew there would be blood in the bowl and did not want to see it. I couldn't close my right hand over my toothbrush, so I sipped Listerine from the bottle until the raw steak taste was gone. When I spit, I could feel the charcoal they'd used to make me vomit pass between my lips.

There was ice in the fridge, which was useful, and Tina's Grey Goose vodka, which was more so. I sat down on the couch, feeling stupid and empty. Sometimes you expend so much of yourself in a moment that there is nothing left inside of you afterward. The only thing that bothered me, aside from the pain, was not being able to close my hand, but I knew that wouldn't last. In the meantime, I could always drink with my left.

I wanted more than anything to sleep, but the knowledge that I still owed Gino a fortune kept lifting my chin from my chest with a start. I was a fast healer; a few days lying in bed and I would be strong enough to resume light duty at the Grind Joint, but to what end? Covering the vigorish soaked up most of my weekly profits; the remaining money was having about as much of an effect on the principal as a chisel would have on the Rock of Gibraltar.

I was still brooding on this when the phone rang, a shrill sound in the gloomy early-morning silence. I picked up my phone with my less injured hand and stared at it until the name on the caller identification came reluctantly into focus.

ANNE CLAYBOURNE.

A glad shock coursed through my body from head to heel. Pain, exhaustion, and despair were banished in an eye blink. In something approaching a joyous panic, I surged to my feet and all but shouted, "Hello?"

"It's Mikhailis."

If seeing him at the Fight Factory had been a punch in the sternum, hearing his voice on Anne's phone was a knee to the groin. My knees buckled, and I sank back into the couch as fast as I had risen. It was one thing to suspect your worst fear, another to have strong circumstantial evidence, but to *know*, to know as certainly as you know the sun is about to rise, that the woman you love is sleeping with the man you most despise – oh, my friends and Romans and countrymen, that is a different animal, and it has very large fangs.

"Sorry to ring you so early, especially after the night you just had, but I've been doing some thinking. About your career, I mean." His tone was friendly, not the faintest trace of smugness or taunt. "It really bothers me to see a fighter of your caliber getting busted up for the sort of chicken feed Carmine pays – especially considering the fight won't count on your record. I know you've got money problems, but this isn't the way to solve them." There was a short pause. "I didn't want to bring this up, but I have to tell you that Anne's very concerned about your, ah, situation."

I heard a squeak by my ear and realized I was holding the phone tight enough to crack its plastic case. When I spoke, my voice had a strangled, savage quality that frightened me. "What. Situation. Is. That."

"There's no need to stonewall. She told me everything. About the mess you're in. About what you did to get there and what you're doing to get out of it. Working with that crowd from The Friends of the Friends. They're bad news, Mick. Even Carmine thinks they're bad news."

I took a breath deep enough to set off the pain in my ribs; it served as a counterweight to the rage and allowed me to speak almost normally. "What do you know about The Friends of the Friends?"

"Mick, I cut my teeth in this business promoting underground shows with Carmine. I know all the players. Anne doesn't know *that,* of course." He uttered a low, worldly chuckle, as one man to another. "You could fill books with what Anne doesn't know, but that's another subject. The point is she's concerned about you, and so am I. Whatever, ah, differences we may have, I'm a businessman at heart, and my business is fighting. So I'd like to make you an offer. The League is holding a card at the Garden a week before Christmas, and I'm having trouble filling out the undercard. How would you like another shot at the Big Show?"

I shut my eyes. I had a dreadful feeling of being toyed with by a cold cruel intelligence, danced about like a wooden puppet over an open flame. In spite of everything I heard myself say: "Against who?"

"Wilson Kreese."

"I *beat* Kreese."

"He wants a rematch, and I'm inclined to give him one."

"Why?"

"Wilson's an old friend. And one of the joys of being me, Mick, is that I can help my old friends."

"And screw your enemies."

"When the occasion arises."

"What's the deal?"

"Standard."

"Ten to show and ten to win? That's an insult."

"No, it's an offer. You won't get a better one anywhere else."

"I made a lot more than that for Suba."

"Suba beat you."

It grew very quiet. I could hear the old bronze clock I'd mounted over the television ticking into the silence. Every movement of the seconds hand represented a minute increase in my debt to Gino. Handfuls of pennies that grew into heaps, into hills, into small mountains of greasy copper. A hundred thousand dollars' worth of interest, and me buried beneath it. To take the fight meant getting back into the gym as soon as I was ambulatory. It meant imposing the self-discipline of a warrior-monk, committing to four or six or even eight hours of training a day, five days a week, right up the sound of the opening bell. It meant taking my foot off the Grind Joint's accelerator and becoming a fighter again, for money that could no more break Gino's hold on me than a plastic sword could break a slave chain. And Mikhailis, whose contacts seemed to reach as deep into the underworld as my own, who seemed to know everything, must have known this, too. Negotiating with him was like playing chess with the devil.

"I've got a counter-offer," I said at last. "Take your ten-and-ten and go fuck yourself with it."

Again the chuckle. "Is that any way to talk to your benefactor?"

"You've a better shot at becoming my pimp."

"Six of one," he said easily. "Tell you what, Mick. I know you're a hardheaded Irishman, so I'm going to hold the space open for you. I can't hold it *too* long, but if you change your mind, just give me a ring." He paused and chuckled again. "You know the number."

The line went dead. I took a sip of vodka, grimacing as it sluiced over the cuts on my gums, and stared resolutely at the gloom outside my windows. I didn't scream or overturn the coffee table or crush the phone beneath my heel. I didn't put my fist through the window or smash the shelves over the bar that contained my amateur boxing trophies. I didn't fall down to my hands and knees and weep out of grief and humiliation and despair.

But Christ I wanted to.

Chapter Twenty-Seven

"You know," Philly Guido said, brushing snowflakes out of his eyebrows. "I don't like you very much."

"Then why'd you call me here?" I asked.

He wore a hooded warm-up jacket in the colors of the Italian flag over a turtleneck of soft black wool and brand-new designer jeans tight enough to show the *fazool* in his right-hand pocket. When he signaled the waiter for coffee, I thought I saw the imprint of a pistol beneath his armpit.

"Because I hear you need money," he said, peeling off his gloves. "Because you can keep your mouth shut. And for another reason, too. The best reason there is."

"What's that?" I said.

"The hate-fuck is one of life's great pleasures."

The waiter brought a mug of coffee and set it down with some silverware rolled in a napkin that was held together by a green paper band. Maybe it was a sign of how far gone I was that it made me think of the bands banks use to bundle money.

"Go on," I said.

Philly ripped the band open and used the tarnished-looking spoon within to stir an astonishing quantity of sugar into his coffee. "You have a problem with Tommy Battaglia. True or not true?"

"Tommy had a problem with me." Outside the snow was falling hard, a wet, clumpy snow that stuck fast to everything it touched and gave Queens Boulevard a whitewashed charm it lacked in everyday life. "But it was a long time ago."

"You think he's forgotten you?" Cream was turning his coffee the color of a mud puddle. "Guy who sent three of his teeth into the cheap seats?"

"I haven't forgotten him. It's his goddamn fault I'm stuck in this business."

Philly's spoon rang repeatedly against the inside of his mug, as if he were about to make a toast. "Point is, if a chance came by to say, open up his ass, you wouldn't pass it up?"

"Philly. Look at me. Does it look like I need any more trouble than what I already got?"

I didn't have to look at my reflection to know what he was taking in. Deep red score marks on my forehead and cheekbone. Purple bruise under my left eye, turning a sickly greenish-yellow at the corners. The eye itself misted pink. Lower lip still showing stitch marks, and surgical tape on two fingers of my left hand. That was just the stuff he could see.

"It's true," he said cheerfully. "You look more beat-to-shit every time I see you. But you still need money. A lot of money, and you need it fast."

"Not bad enough to knock over a made guy for it. And Tommy is made now. Finger pricked, name on the books, button-in-hand made."

"Yeah. But he's also stupid. And sloppy."

"So?"

"So, his father put him in charge of a numbers bank in Coney Island, and a little birdy told me that he don't do much of a job of it. Too much coke up his nose to dot his *I*'s and cross his *T*'s. Especially when it comes to security."

"No."

"No, what?" Philly's normally expressionless mouth composed itself into a smile of surprising charm. "We're just two guys talking here."

But for a long time we didn't talk. He watched me through the steam from his coffee, the smile resting comfortably on his face. I stared back at him, my own muscles far too stiff with bruises to register an expression.

"Philly, I'm not interested."

"Your share would be big. Maybe fifty grand, maybe more."

I fell silent again, wrapped my hands around my mug, feeling the warmth against my palms. I tried to concentrate on the warmth and not the fact that fifty big ones would put me damn near over the top. "Let me ask you something. How many guys from Gino's crew have you approached about this?"

His smile weakened at the corners, fell away into a frown. "What's that got to do with the price of pussy in Peking?"

"Phil, I may be punchy, but I'm not a complete fucking idiot. Those guys are cowboys. If they turned you down, it's because they don't think you've got a snowball's chance in hell of pulling this off."

"Listen to me. This is a golden fuckin' opportunity I got here. A first-class score. And I got everything I need – times, places, layouts, the whole 411. I even got a man on the inside to unlock doors for us. What I *don't* got is an 'us' to pull the damned job."

"Face isn't in on it?"

"Of course he is," he said, showing surprise, as if I'd suggested that he leave one of his legs at home the next time he went jogging. "But that's it."

"If it's so golden, why'd everybody else say no?"

"You know why!" Philly hissed, and then looked guiltily around the diner. His voice dropped to a harsh whisper. "They don't have the balls to cross a made guy, much less a fuckin' Battaglia."

"But you think I do?"

"I think you're fuckin' desperate." His telltale smirk asserted itself. "To me it's the same damn thing. Anyway, it's not like we'd walk in there with fuckin' nametags, you know what I mean? God invented the ski mask for a reason."

"And if Tommy finds out?"

"Then you got problems. But it seems to me you got problems now. Word on the street says you need to come up with two hundred large by Jesus's birthday, and by the look of your kisser, I'm guessin' you don't have it."

It is very annoying to be out-argued by someone who can barely complete a sentence without using the word "fuck."

"Who's the little birdy?" I said at last.

Philly's smile returned. I noticed that the snow in the fabric of his flat cap was beginning to melt, but I knew he wouldn't take it off – it would have spoiled the carefully crafted air of criminality he worked so hard to cultivate. "Oh, nobody special. Just the guy who used to run the bank before he got bounced to make way for Tommy."

"His name, Phil."

"Why the hell should I tell you if you ain't signed on?"

"I ain't signing on *unless* you tell me. You can make book on that."

We engaged in a brief staring contest, but since he was a gangster and I was a fighter, there could be no winners. At last Philly said, in that queerly subaural voice only criminals seem to use, "Johnny Wheels."

It took me a moment to recall the face. "The guy with the scars, always playing poker at the Joint?"

"That's the one. He wasn't too happy getting demoted to make way for that retard Tommy, so he's decided to retire."

"To a tropical island, I take it."

"He ain't gonna stick around here, that's for sure. Top of the suspect list. But what's that to us? Only connection any of us have to Johnny is through the Grind Joint, and that's like the Grand Central Station of wiseguys."

I took my first sip of coffee. It was hard to drink coffee with a split lip, even though the emergency room doctor had done a fine job of stitching it back together. I drank a milliliter's worth and looked out the window, watching the snow collect in the dent on the hood of my Maverick and in the cracks on the sidewalk in front of it. April showers meant May flowers. Snow in November meant – what?

"Okay," I said. "Now tell me the rest of it."

"Rest of what?"

"Taking down a numbers bank ain't like knocking over a candy store," I said, feeling very much like a criminal as I said it. "And unless Martin Scorsese and Michael Mann are big fat liars, there's gonna be security. Even with the inside scoop, it's not a three-man job. Who else has signed on to this little escapade?"

"So far it's just you and me and Face."

"You mean just you and Face," I put my cup down and steepled my fingers under my chin. It was harder than it sounds with two of them taped together. "Y'know, a cynical person might ask why you want me on this job. Being that I've got no experience what-so-fucking-ever. He might even ask if the person you really want isn't me, but somebody who'll only go along if *I* go."

"Aw, come on," Guido tugged at the neck of his sweater as if it were on too tight and smiled again, a bit uncomfortably this time. "Everybody knows you and the Kraut are tight."

"And you want me to sell him on this."

"He was a great stick-up guy in his day. Good at the wheel, good with a gun."

"And sharp as a tack. I don't think he'd go for it in a million years. Too risky."

"He'll go if you go. He talks about you like you're his fuckin' kid or something."

"Philly, I'm liking this conversation less and less. I think maybe I should leave."

He regarded me coldly for a few moments, then shrugged. "There's the door."

I looked at it but did not move. Instead, I sat in the chair and let Guido smirk at me.

"Well," he said at last. "You gonna talk him into this, or what?"

"He'll come with us or he won't," I said, hating that I was using the word *us* without ever having said *yes*. "I don't think I'll talk him into anything."

"Whatever. Just so he comes. We can do it with three, but a fourth wouldn't hurt."

We stared at each other. I heard a cook whistling "Feliz Navidad" over the sound of frying bacon. I would have said it was too early in the season, but in recent years the boosters had been putting on the Christmas cheer before the Halloween decorations were down. Given what sort of Christmas I was likely to have, this didn't exactly make my spirits rise. But if Philly was telling the truth – a big *if* – I now had an opportunity to fill the hole I was in with a single turn of the shovel. The idea of freeing myself from the claws of the *brugad* had obsessed me so much in the last few months that for a moment my heart jogged gladly in my chest at the prospect. Then I remembered that what I was being offered was a gangland version of *Let's Make A Deal.* Behind Door #1 lay the cash – and my freedom. Behind Door # 2, a cell in Attica, my payoff for a conviction for armed robbery. And behind Door # 3? A morgue slab. I heard Kraut's voice in my head: *You want out of the Life, and your way is to go deeper in?*

"You've thought this all out, haven't you?" I said finally.

"A score like this don't come along every day. When it does, you grab it. That's what separates the wannabes from the wiseguys." He tugged back his sleeve and took a look at his watch. "I got places I gotta be. You gonna talk to him, or what?"

I nodded very slightly, as if to demonstrate my reluctance.

"Good," he said, and rose to his feet. "You get him on board, you call me, and we'll get into the details."

"I can hardly wait."

Guido drank off the rest of his coffee and paid for it with some change in his pockets. He did not leave a tip. "Don't look so fuckin' mopey," he said pulling on his gloves with a taunting smile. "What could possibly go wrong?"

Much later, thinking of this conversation, I was reminded of a line from Hemingway: *And like a fool he did not knock on wood.*

Chapter Twenty-Eight

The warehouse would have been ugly and cheerless even in daytime. At three in the morning on a starless winter night, it looked like a repository for every damned soul the City had ever produced.

Chain-link fence topped with spirals of rusted barbed wire. Dirty No Trespassing signs clanging off the links every time the wind took a breath. Vast blacktop lot, gleaming here and there with pools of dirty ice. Then the great shadowy bulk of the warehouse itself, a football field of soot-blackened brick three stories high, showing rows of unlit windows. Ugly, but anonymous. Thousands of people passed it every day on their way through Coney Island without suspecting that this heap of soiled brick on the end of Stillwell Avenue was home to the biggest Mafia numbers game in all of Brooklyn – a game that employed over a hundred runners and paid a quarter of a million dollars for a winning ticket.

Johnny Wheels pulled the minivan up to the warehouse gate, sleet flickering in his headlights. From my vantage point in the back, all I could see of him was the outline of his head and the jeweled hand he'd rested on the steering wheel, feebly illuminated by the glow of his cigarette.

"All right," he said to no one in particular, speaking in a low, controlled tone. "He'll be out in a minute to open the gate. Remember, *no shooting*. Any shooting and this is over before it fuckin' well begins."

"Don't worry," Face whispered next to me, his trollish features sheened and flattened by his nylon stocking mask. "I'm a maestro with the sap."

"You better be," Kraut said. He was directly behind me, a Mini-14 carbine cradled in the crook of his left arm. "You been bragging about that sap long as I known you."

"It ain't *bragging* if it's true," Face said.

"Shut the fuck up, all of you," Johnny hissed. "Here he comes."

Any member of a crew who pulled guard duty in weather like this was bound to be a loser, and the man who lumbered out the guard shack holding a newspaper over his head lived down to my lowest expectations – balding, pot-bellied, and at least a week from his last visit to the razor. Walking on the pale yellow carpet of light that spilled out of the shack, he made his way awkwardly to the gate, newspaper wilting in his grubby fingers, and squinted into the headlights. "That you, Johnny?"

Johnny rolled down the window to his shoulder and spoke to him through the diamond pattern of the chain-link fence. "No, it's fuckin' Elliot Ness. Open the goddamn gate."

"What you doin' back here?"

"What is this, Twenty Questions? Let me in, you fat fuck."

The guard frowned and tucked the newspaper under his arm, revealing a nearly bare scalp plastered with strands of greasy brown hair, and fumbled with a keychain. "You don't got to be abusive," he said. Then a crafty smile appeared on his face, the type which invariably proceeds some witless witticism. "I seen this ride, I thought maybe you was a soccer mom got lost and needed directions."

"Lincoln's in the shop," Johnny said, chewing the cigar. "So I borrowed my girl's wheels. That okay with you?"

The guard shrugged, unlocked the big chain wound around the gates and pushed them open one at a time, huffing a bit at the effort. Although I knew he could not see through the tint of the minivan's window to the darkness of the back, it was still disconcerting to have him looking almost directly at us. "You know, John, you're a real fuckin' prick sometimes."

"Yeah? Well, you're real fuckin' stupid *all* of the time.". He took his foot off the brake, and we rolled forward slowly through the gates.

"Hold up a minute 'fore you lock," he said out the window. "I got somethin' to show you."

The guard's voice, muffled by the sound of the minivan's engine, took on a petulant note. "Fuck's sake, it's rainin' out here."

"You could use the shower."

I heard the jingle of a keyring. Footsteps by the side of the van. Heavy breathing. "What's so goddamn important?"

"Now," Johnny said.

In one practiced motion, Face wrenched the handle of the minivan's sliding door and shoved it to one side, exposing the startled-looking guard. He had exactly enough time to draw a breath before the sap caught him on the temple just above the right eyebrow with a sound like a raw hamburger patty hitting ceramic tile. It was an expensive sap, double-stitched leather over whalebone, and it did the job in one shot. The guard went down, not the way they do in movies, with a dramatic flail of arms and legs, but stiffly and all at once, like a tree cut at the base.

I jumped down after him, the sleet prickling the back of my neck as I seized his meaty forearm. His body was rigid, not limp, and one hand still clutched firmly at the now sodden copy of the *New York Post*. "Philly," I said. "Get your ass down here and help me."

He emerged in the doorway at a crouch. In the flat glare of the streetlamps, his coppery brown eyes shone like a cat's out of the holes in his hockey mask. He jumped down smoothly, the flash suppressor on his Mac-10 swinging against his leg.

"Fuck did you have to bring that cannon for anyway," I whispered, pulling on the guard's arm. "You expecting World War Three?"

Philly didn't reply. He was already lifting the guard up by his armpits. Together we manhandled the body back into the guard shack and laid it where it couldn't be seen from the street.

"All right," Johnny said. "Tie him up good, but make sure he can breathe when you gag him."

Face was already yanking off swaths of duct tape. "Fuck do you care?"

"He's my cousin," Johnny replied matter-of-factly.

I had no sooner slid the door shut when Wheels started the minivan slowly toward the warehouse, winding us around phalanxes of rusty oil drums to a loading dock that looked as if had not seen any action since the Carter administration. One of the big bay doors was open and Johnny drove through it, headlights revealing a vast, high-ceilinged room of corrugated metal and oil-soaked concrete. The minivan stopped.

I peered out the windshield. There were eight cars parked in a neat line by a flight of concrete steps that led to a doorway: two black Lincoln Navigators, a silver Cadillac Escalade, a red Camaro with a broad white racing stripe down the hood, and four lesser sedans. Johnny parked the van on the end and methodically crushed out his cigar in the ashtray. He opened his jacket and removed a hammerless .38 revolver, broke open the cylinder, checked the rounds within, and snapped it back in place. "Okay. We are ten minutes from the biggest fuckin' score of any of our lives. You guys all do like I say, and it goes down like cream. You fuck up, and none of us are walkin' out of here."

"We'll hold up our end," Kraut said, rolling his black ski mask down over his face. "Just you hold up yours."

Johnny got out of the car and shut the door. Buttoned his jacket to conceal the butt of his pistol. Tugged his cuffs until the links were visible and took a deep breath. "Everybody sit tight. I'll be right back. Stay in the van and keep quiet."

"Fuck are you going?" Philly said.

Johnny smiled – the nasty smile of the inside joke. "To see if my diversion is working."

He mounted the steps and went through the metal door, which shut behind him with an ominous clang.

Silence descended, broken only by the rumble of the van's engine and Face's somewhat labored breathing. I lay perfectly still, unwilling to move a muscle, unwilling to let myself think. To think would be to reflect on the monolithic stupidity of what I was doing, and I couldn't have that. Nor could I look at Kraut. The eyes glinting from holes in his ski mask were the eyes of a hostile stranger. He hadn't wanted any part of this caper, had argued violently against my participation, and had only signed on at the very last moment for reasons he refused to explain. Since then his demeanor had changed.

The Kraut I knew was a rough-and-tumble saloonkeeper, the sort who would kick your ass and then buy you a cold one to show there were no hard feelings. This new Kraut seemed to be composed entirely *of* hard feelings. His face read menace from glare to sneer, his movements had acquired tension and economy that reminded me of a commando, and he radiated that same sense of being ready to kill at any moment, viciously and without remorse. I'd been a fighter my whole life, and I knew fighters when I saw them – streetfighters and technicians, wrestlers and grapplers and strikers, guys who were point karate experts and guys who fought in unlicensed bare-knuckle boxing matches. This man was not any of those things. He wasn't a fighter at all. He was a killer, and he scared the shit out of me.

So I just sat there, trying not to think, conscious of the faint scent of Philly Guido's cologne in my nostrils and the cold weight of the .357 in my lap, enduring the passage of time like a dentist's drill, until at last the door clanged open and Johnny emerged, grinning.

Ten minutes, Mickey, I thought as I jumped out of the van, faintly pleased that my knees didn't give way when I landed. *Ten minutes against the rest of your life. Don't think – go!*

I went. Followed Johnny and Kraut and Philly Guido through the doorway into the hall. It was unheated, unlit; the pencil-beam of Johnny's flashlight revealed a tunnel of glazed cinderblock and institutional linoleum. Moving quickly on sneakered feet, we passed rows of darkened office doors, none of which looked as if they'd been opened in years, rounded a corner, climbed three short steps. I was already disoriented and tried to remember the layout as it had been described to me at Kraut's kitchen table during our planning sessions. No use. It was all I could do to keep my legs working. Some fucking armed robber. But it didn't matter. I wasn't planning on making a career of this. Quite the contrary. If I got out of here alive, I swore never, ever again to do so much as jaywalk so long as I fucking lived.

At last we came to an opened doorway dead bang in the center of an enormous hallway. Johnny rubbed his thumb and forefinger together, still grinning. Inside I saw counting and adding machines, cardboard boxes filled with disposable cell phones, paper grocery bags overflowing with policy slips, mounds of newspapers, boxes of grease pencils, ashtrays flinched from a dozen different motels, water glasses, half-eaten sandwiches, even a twelve-gauge pump shotgun leaning against a wall. None of it interested me in the slightest. What did interest me lay on an enormous conference table in the center of the room. In stacks, in bundles, in loose and careless heaps.

Cash.

More than I had ever seen in my life.

At least a quarter of a million dollars' worth.

And not a soul around to guard it.

There was no need for conversation: we all knew our roles. Face was the wheelman; Johnny, Kraut, and Guido were on collection. And me, I was to stand at the end of the hallway with Magnum in hand, just out of sight, and make sure nobody was coming.

Not exactly rocket surgery. But as Philly had put it: "It's the one thing that needs to be done that I'm absolutely sure you can't fuck up."

And he was right.

For at least three minutes.

That's when I heard the noise. I'd been standing in the T-junction, listening to the sound of my own breathing through my itchy wool ski mask and wondering just what the hell kind of diversion Johnny had arranged that could possibly cause Tommy Battaglia to abandon his post, when a sound assailed my ears. Long, high-pitched, full of terror and pain. Magnified and distorted by the tunnel-like hallways, but unmistakable.

A scream.

I felt gooseflesh break out over my arms. The last time I'd heard someone scream like that had been at the Friends of the Friends. And they'd had to bury *him* in a closed casket.

There was a long silence. Then a secondary noise, not anywhere near as loud, that was harder to identify. It took perhaps thirty seconds before I recognized it.

Laughter.

Then a sharp, buzzing *crack* and another scream, louder and longer than the first, sputtering out last into a string of pleas, curses, sobs.

I looked back down the darkened hallway to the faint glow that indicated the count room. Just five more minutes and it would be picked clean. Five more minutes and I could strike off the chain that bound me to the *brugad* and get on with my life. All I had to do was nothing. Just stand here, gun in hand, and pretend I was deaf.

Another shriek. More laughter. Hysterical. It sounded like a comedy club in there. If they had comedy clubs in hell. A lot of people were having a very good time down the way…and one man was having the worst night of his life.

And the last.

Hell with it. It didn't matter. People die every day in this city. They die of old age and smelly squalid diseases, they get spattered in car wrecks and electrocuted by toasters and poisoned by jealous wives and shot by jealous husbands, they fall down elevator shafts and get crushed by falling girders and swallow the wrong pills and just die, die in droves, and that's the way the world is wired. Five, six murders every day in the Big Apple, and whoever was screaming those screams was just one more victim. Except unlike that old lady who got bashed for her pension check, *he* probably deserved it. And even if he was innocent as a lamb, it wasn't my fucking problem. The sensible thing, the right thing, the non-insane thing to do was to stay where I was. At my post. Wait here rigid as a statue until Johnny told me to move, and then run for the van. Don't do what that little voice is demanding. Don't, under any circumstances, take one step toward that godawful sound.

Or another.

Or twenty more.

Thirty.

Forty.

Freeze when you hear the screams again, much louder, more distinct, so that you can almost picture the man uttering them.

Round the corner.

Disappear into shadows so deep they look solid.

Smell the dust, the petrified rat droppings, the chill overlaying them all.

Taste the fear, a bright hot taste like fresh blood in your mouth.

See the faintest glow of light, like the light of a radio dial, outlining a doorless doorway.

Turn into it, Magnum out front, as if challenging the darkness to a duel.

See an old office, long abandoned, the blurred outline of an old steel desk, now cloaked in cobwebs, and at the end, another door whose frosted glass window had been busted out, the jagged remaining pieces forming the shape of a porthole. Better light through the porthole, a clear view into the next room.

I said a *clear* view. Not a good one. Because what I saw was Tommy Battaglia standing not a dozen feet from me. From my vantage point, I could see only the back of his head and one sharp cheekbone, but I remembered his face clearly – gelled hair, hawk nose, eyes like bubbles of fresh tar, a thin-lipped mouth with sneer lines at one corner. He was wearing a shirt of chocolate-colored silk over black Armani slacks and held an alligator clamp in one hand.

And as crazy as it sounds, he was giving a lecture.

"Come to think of it," he said, in that harsh, grinding voice I had first heard in the nightclub a year before. "The only problem I have with you, Lenny, is that I can't kill you twice."

Holding my breath, I took another step forward. Directly opposite Battaglia, a shirtless young man sat, his arms and legs bound by lengths of yellow nylon rope. A few hours earlier, it had probably been handsome. Now, with one eye swollen shut and the lower lip smashed like a rotten piece of fruit, it was scarcely recognizable as human. He stared wretchedly at the floor, tears streaking through the blood on his cheeks. Across the muscles of his chest and belly were hideous red weals where the clamp had found purchase. Beneath the chair, a puddle of urine glistened in the harsh light of an electric lamp.

"Now, I don't wanna seem like a hypocrite here," Battaglia said, opening and closing the clamp a few times for effect. I could see the heavy cables running from it, down to what must have been a car battery. "So I got to tell you, Len, I'm not mad that you stole. I mean, I'm a thief, too, y'know. So in theory I got no problem with it. Knock over the church poor box, steal the Jerry's Kids penny jar – fuck do I care? The issue I have – can you guess the issue? – is when you steal *from me.*"

"I didn't," the man in the chair blubbered. "I didn't, I didn't, Johnny's fulla shit, stop, please stop, *please*—"

Somewhere out of view, a voice with a Brooklyn accent thick enough to spread on toast began a ghastly imitation of a baby crying. Tommy's face lit in a lurid, hateful grin, and he knuckled imaginary tears from his eyes. There was braying laughter from all sides. Sounded like half a dozen men in there, and that fit the pattern. Battaglia hated people but he loved attention. And for a torture job, he'd want the biggest audience he could get.

"Hush," Battaglia said, his face growing serious and sober. "And answer me this question. It's a very important question, Len, and I want you to be very truthful in your answer. Can you do that for me?"

Lenny sobbed in the affirmative, snot running in a clear stream around his upper lip. Battaglia leaned in very close, and in the most intimate way imaginable, whispered:

"What do you think your mom will say when I stuff your nuts in her mailbox on Christmas Eve?"

More laughter. Lenny convulsed, but with his wrists and ankles bound there was nowhere for him to go, and with his smashed lower lip he couldn't even plead coherently.

Tommy grinned again and snapped the clamp once, twice, towards Lenny's nose. "It's still early, Len, and I got plenty of fuckin' juice in the battery. So why don't you save yourself a bit of pain and confess to what you done? It may not help your body much, but it's good for the soul!"

I crept closer to the window and slowly raised my revolver until the front sight bisected Battaglia's eyes. It was an involuntary motion, as if my hand were hooked to a guide-wire. Tommy had no idea I was here. No one did. I could still walk away, just turn around and leave these fools to Johnny's idea of a diversion.

If I walked away, it was over.

I'd have the money…my freedom… and Lenny's screams to keep me company on those cold winter nights to come.

What do you care? A voice sounded from inside of me. *What the hell do you care?*

I shouldn't. I didn't know the man from Adam. He was one more fringe player on his way to becoming a police statistic, a patsy-cog in the engine of Johnny's revenge. His death would give me back my life.

All I had to do was walk away and let it happen.

Instead, my finger tightened on the trigger.

It was *Let's Make A Deal* all over again, but now there were only two doors.

Leave…or stay. And fight.

I realized I'd made my choice when the hammer fell, and I shot Tommy Battaglia in the face.

Chapter Twenty-Nine

Tried to, anyway.

I never was much of a shot. A gout of flame the size of a basketball exploded what was left of the old office window, and I saw Tommy's right hand vaporize in a cloud of blood and severed fingers. The clamp windmilled out of his hand, glittering amidst the arterial spray, and the heel of my shoe was hard against the flimsy old door, smashing it open as I rushed into the room with the Magnum ahead of me.

It was like kicking over an anthill. An anthill filled with cigarette smoke and wiseguys. There must have been half-a-dozen of them around me – some standing, some sitting in hard-backed wooden chairs, one reclining on a green vinyl couch with a copy of the *Daily Racing Form* spread out in front of him and his Bruno Maglis resting comfortably on the armrest. Tommy's crew, compelled away from dice games and strip joints and the saline-filled breasts of their *goumadas* to watch their skipper exact personal vengeance. Battaglia style.

I swept the room with the revolver. Everywhere there was violent motion – people scrambling to their feet, flinching, cursing, bleeding from flying glass, the natty gangster on the couch swinging his loafers to the floor and grasping for the nickel-plated semi-automatic that lay on the coffee table in front of him.

"Nobody move!" I roared, but if my ears were ringing from the shot so were everyone else's, and the Dapper Don's manicured fingers curled around the butt of his weapon and hefted it off the table. I had one glimpse of its muzzle, brimming with malevolent shadow, and my finger

convulsed on the Magnum's trigger again. The Don's white Charles Tyrwhitt shirt flapped as if in a gale, and he folded up hard, clutching what looked like a wet red rag on his ribcage, and rolled to the floor.

Another man lunged at me from the left. Stocky. Thick gelled hair. Jaw like an anvil, supported on a mass of gold chains. In a flash, I realized I knew him: Tommy's right-hand man, the Chin. Stupid as a pit bull and twice as fierce. I'd have to put him down. But as the smoking muzzle of the Magnum whirled to meet his charge, something remarkable happened. The expression on his face went in a blink from murderous rage to pants-pissing terror. He jammed a heel against the linoleum and managed to stumble to a stop four feet away from me, his thick-fingered hands rising of their own accord. *"Don't!"* He screamed, sounding not at all the tough guy.

For just a second, I almost shot him anyway. Then I planted a foot on his belly and knocked him on the seat of his pants. "I said *nobody fuckin' move!"*

Nobody did. Not much, anyway. The Chin lay on ass and elbows, fat face pale under its Levantine sheen. Tommy was on his knees, left hand gripping his right wrist, arm sheeted in blood to the elbow, face all veins and cheekbones and bulging, incredulous eyes. The Dapper Don lay in a fetal knot on the floor, writhing and moaning through clenched teeth. The remaining wiseguys stood frozen in place, mouths agape. One of them, sporting a scarred lip and a jacket of roan-colored leather, had his hand on the butt of a pistol tucked behind his belt buckle. He looked at me, looked at it, and then, with torturous slowness, almost as if he were handling a sweaty bottle of nitroglycerine, tugged it free of his waistband and lowered it gently to the floor.

"Kick it here," I said.

The automatic made a six-foot streak on the dusty linoleum and came to rest a few inches from the tip of my shoe.

"All right," I panted, and gestured at Lenny, who was sitting stock-still in his chair atop a puddle of blood and urine. "Untie him. Now."

No one moved. Chin swallowed audibly and licked his lips. I turned the Magnum on Roan and thumbed back the hammer with a satisfying *click*.

"I wasn't asking."

Roan came forward and began to work clumsily at Lenny's bonds. It is a lot easier to tape a man up than it is to free him. A few feet away, Tommy, slumped against the wall with his face lensed in sweat, bared all of his teeth at me. "I'm gonna kill you," he said in a vicious, spittle-choked voice. "I'm gonna…fuckin'…*kill* you."

Roan had freed Lenny's hands. He was now working on his ankles, pausing every few seconds to cast a frightened glance at the muzzle of the Magnum. At this distance it probably looked like the entrance to the Holland Tunnel. As he fumbled, Lenny was gazing at me with his one good eye in a baffled stupor, the gag sprouting like a weed from his split and bleeding lips.

"Dead," Tommy was growling over and over again. "Dead. You're fuckin'…*dead!*"

Again, my finger tightened on the trigger, hard enough to move the cylinder a quarter of an inch. So easy to finish him off. But I had already fired – how many times? If I shot Tommy when he was helpless, the others might assume they were next. Might rush me. I might get off a single round before they wrestled me to the floor.

And I'd be lucky to get out of here alive as it was.

Roan freed Lenny's ankles and backed away, holding the blood-smeared nylon rope in front of him as if it could ward off bullets. Slowly, with a kind of pathetic dignity, Lenny stood, but he had to steady himself on the chair back before he could take a step.

"Gonna kill you." The words were slobbering from Tommy's mouth in a hateful mantra. His gaze was fixed somewhere past us – to the day of vengeance already taking shape in his fevered mind. "Gonna fuckin' kill both of you. Kill your *families*. Kill your *mothers*. Kill–"

Lenny reached Battaglia and very deliberately trod on his wounded hand, cutting off the flow of curses and producing a shriek of agony that made the hairs on my neck stand up. Then he turned toward me.

"Run," he said.

Chapter Thirty

We ran.

Or rather, I did, shoving Lenny ahead of me. The cold-blooded courage that had come over me moments before had evaporated. In its place was the horrible fear that the others had left me behind at the sound of the first shot. Just stuffed as much cash as they could manage into the bags and legged it.

If that were the case, Tommy would be getting his revenge, and a lot sooner than either one of us planned.

Lenny's back was as muscular as the hindquarters of a horse and felt like wet cement under my palm as I urged him on, my pistol leveled clumsily behind me. Through the door I could hear Tommy screaming, the stamp of feet, and the distinct sound of the slide being pulled back on a semi-automatic pistol. Then, in a huge, roaring voice, I heard the Chin yell: *"We're comin' for your ass, motherfuckers! WE'RE COMIN' FOR YOUR ASS!"*

It was like two nightmares at once – blundering through a darkened maze, pursued by vicious beasts. Far behind me I heard the outer office door crash open and the squeak of soles on linoleum. Still shoving Lenny forward, I turned and fired a round at the shadowy man-shape that had emerged from the doorway. In the close-pressing hallway, the roar was monstrous, the flash blinding. For an instant, I saw everything with perfect clarity, right down to the grouts in the cinderblock wall beside me. Then I was blind.

Three nightmares. Lost, hunted, and in the dark.

I stumbled on, breath coming in ragged, panicked gasps, ears ringing, the smell of cordite thick in my nostrils. Lenny could manage no more than a trot and groaned like an animal with every step, elbow clamped hard against his ribs. Behind us there was a roar and a flash, and something whipped past my cheek and buried itself in the wall somewhere ahead.

The turn was up here somewhere. The lovely, God-blessed turn. It hadn't seemed nearly this far when I had walked down it a few minutes ago. Of course, a few minutes ago nobody was shooting at me.

BAM. Another bullet. It skipped back and forth between the walls with a horrible whining sound that made every nerve ending in my body tingle with anticipation. I slung the pistol behind me and fired again, not troubling to aim, not even to open my eyes, and kept going.

At last! The corner ahead. Lenny rounded it, moaning, his head nearly parallel to the floor. I felt myself grinning in idiot relief, was still grinning when I heard him run smack into someone. A meaty sound, a thud to knock the breath from your lungs. Then I was tripping over Lenny and the Magnum was flying from my hand.

So much for playing hero.

I hit the ground hard, slid a few feet on dusty, rat-pocked linoleum, and was promptly stopped by the wall. There was a flash and then everything went quiet around me. Even the ringing in my ears died away. I was sinking into unconsciousness, being pushed down into warm quicksand by gentle, almost loving hands, and it wasn't so very bad. Just close your eyes, I thought, and this will all be over. You'll wake up from *this* nightmare into….

Hell itself.

If Tommy was pissed at me for breaking his jaw, how would he take this?

Groaning, I scrabbled the floor for the pistol. It seemed to have vanished, and in its place were thick bundles of heavy, finely textured paper. Fuck was this shit? Oh yeah. Money. The money we had come to steal. All over the damned floor.

I rolled onto my back, stomach rolling with nausea, and caught a glimpse of Philly laid out on the ground, his canvas sack spilling cash every which way, his submachinegun a yard from his outstretched hand. He was groaning, too. You groaned a lot when you did business with this guy Lenny.

A bullet struck the wall five or six feet above me, powdering my face, my chest, my arms. Not much of a roar behind it. Either I was deaf or Roan was firing the small-caliber pistol I should have picked up on my way out of the room. Shoulda, woulda, coulda. For the want of a pistol, a Mickey was lost.

Footfalls were thundering on the linoleum. In a few seconds they'd be on us, and that would be it.

If we were *lucky*.

Kraut swung around the corner, the wire stock of his Mini-14 carbine socked into his shoulder, his right hand wound around the grip. He did not speak. He did not even aim. Standing above me, his boots braced on either side of my legs, he fired.

TOW TOW TOW TOW TOW TOW TOW

He swept the hallway like a fireman with a hose; coldly, systematically, the carbine's barrel exploding in huge stabs of whitish-yellow flame, stab after stab, round after round. In the stuttering flashes of light I saw bodies falling, heard fragments of a scream, and then everything was consumed in a roaring cacophony of sound.

My God, the noise! The noise was worse than the fear. It was worse than anything I had ever imagined. It passed through me like a violation, jarring every tissue, pulping every cell. Before it I was puny and small. I screamed and writhed, palms jammed to my ears, knees jammed to my chest, spent shell casings jangling about me on gushes of burning air.

"Stop!" I heard myself screaming. *"Stop! Stop! Stop!"*

At last it did, but only because he ran out of ammunition. Half shrouded in cordite smoke, Kraut hit the magazine release. It clattered to the floor between my feet. With a single smooth movement, he fished a second clip from his waist pocket and jammed it into the receiver. My whole body tensed involuntarily, expecting another eruption. Instead he stepped over me, turned, and yanked me roughly to my feet.

Move your ass, his lips said.

I moved nothing. Just stood there feeling as if I had been lobotomized and my brain-pan stuffed with soggy cotton. Except for a hellish ringing, like the vibration of some gigantic tuning fork, I couldn't hear a damned thing.

Down the hallway, shadows flitted behind the smoke. An angry spurt of light revealed that what was left of Tommy's army wasn't quite ready to call it a night. I stumbled away, back towards the count room, feet kicking aside the bundles of cash that just minutes ago had seemed like the most important thing in the world. I dragged Lenny to his feet.

Guido was up to his knees, looking shell-shocked under his nylon mask. With the instinct of a born hoodlum, his fingers clawed at the money on the floor, stuffing one brick after another into his canvas sack. Then he was rising, turning, leaving his gun where it lay and running ahead of us, weaving like a drunk, rebounding off the walls as he ran.

Another corner and we were at the count room. I saw Johnny at the doorway, holding a revolver in one fist, an overstuffed sack in the other, his face empurpled with rage. He was screaming at me, the cords in his neck standing out in bundles, screaming as we passed him leaving money fluttering in our wake, screaming in fury and frustration, and he was still screaming when the hallway lit up with gun flashes again behind us – two, four, five. I felt rather than heard him fall.

We burst out the door into the sleet-soaked night, slipping on the icy concrete, stumbling down the steps to the idling van. Face had heard the shots and flung open the sliding door, and Kraut leapt in as nimbly as a panther, reaching out for Philly's hand. Philly tossed the sack in first and then hopped after him; I shoved in Lenny and shouted for Face to move, move, move and he was in the seat and moving.

Everyone was yelling, the van was rocking as we shot out the gate into the street, big gusts of cold wind blasting through the open door, and I caught one blurry glimpse of the Coney Island Ferris wheel burning like a man-made constellation against the horizon before Kraut reached over and slammed the door shut.

"What the fuck happened?" Guido kept repeating, still too dazed to be angry. His sack had spilled open and bundles of cash, some speckled with blood, lay everywhere. "What the fuck happened? What the fuck happened and *who the fuck are you?*"

He was staring at Lenny. As was Kraut. Even Face, hunched behind the wheel, cast rabbity glances in the rear-view mirror as he drove.

"I'm Lenny," he said with great difficulty, staunching his lower lip with a sheaf of twenty-dollar bills. At some length he turned his good eye on me. "Who're *you?*"

I was still nearly deaf. My head and neck felt as if they had been pulped by a meat mallet, and I was powdered from head to toe in pulverized cinderblock. One of my eyes had stopped a grain of gunpowder and watered furiously. I had to pull off my ski mask and gloves to knuckle it away.

"Santa Claus," I said. "Merry fuckin' Christmas."

Chapter Thirty-One

It was a tragedy of a day. As if someone had murdered the sun and lain a chainmail shroud over its corpse. I woke to the sound of sleet beating against my windows, and the metallic gloom that showed through my blinds gave me no indication of the time. It might have been five in the morning or eight in the evening. I stared at the alarm clock for a few moments, but the blurry red numbers stared back at me meaninglessly, like letters printed in a foreign language.

I lay in the semidarkness for perhaps an hour, in that peculiar state of deep-body torpor that follows a near-death experience, staring vacantly at the patterns of water-damage on my ceiling. My brain felt like a badly rusted clockwork – intact but incapable of movement. It seemed to me that fatigue had settled into every particle of my being: the pores of my skin, the roots of my hair, into fat cells and muscle fibers, into my aching bones and the marrow that lay inside of them. I felt that if I had possessed the energy for movement, I would have sweat out a pallid yellow liquid that smelled of cigarettes and beer, unwashed bodies and desperation. Movement seemed neither desirable nor possible.

I felt nothing. No fear, no disappointment, no anger or self-pity. Just the great, windblown hollowness that accompanies failure. Perhaps in time there would be relief as well. One of the cold comforts of coming up short is the stark certainty of it. It has the hardness and weight of a tombstone.

Eventually, someone knocked on the door. It would have startled me had I been capable. As it was I simply waited for it to go away. It did not. I looked at my revolver on the nightstand, but I did not pick it up. Fear is a luxury of the energetic. "Who is it?"

"Kraut."

I peeled back my covers and climbed out of bed. The apartment was very cold and smelled like last night's cigarettes. I stuffed my feet into my worn-out slippers and turned the valve on the radiator. When I knelt, my knees cracked like an old man's.

Kraut's jacket was crusted with melting ice, and he had to shake out his wool cap over the kitchen sink when he came in.

"How short are you?" he said by way of greeting.

"Too short. And no way to get it before the deadline. Game's up, Kraut. And I lost."

"You got no one to blame for it but yourself."

"I know."

He emerged from the kitchen with his jaw muscles working. Something in the flatness of my tone seemed to rankle him. "You know, if anybody else did what you did back there, I'd have fucking killed them." His eyes were red-rimmed with exhaustion, and the gray-flecked stubble on his chin was nearly as long as the hair on his head. In the sallow light, his face looked drawn and pale, and his hand shook while he lit a cigarette. "And I do mean anybody. You're lucky all we took from you was your share. Such as it fucking-well was. Do you know I had to kick most of mine over to Philly just to stop him from clipping you?"

"I appreciate that."

"Do you?" He squinted at me through the blue-gray smoke. "Do you appreciate the fact that your bullshit heroics nearly got me killed?"

"I'm sorry."

"And you think that makes it all right?"

"I don't know what else to say."

"You could start with a fucking explanation."

"Of what?"

"Of *what?*" He leaned his head toward me, close enough so that I could see each broken capillary in the whites of his slitted eyes. "Of what motivated you to risk all of our asses – not to mention the *score* – for some prick you never met!"

"I don't know."

"That's a crock of shit. You *do* know. You just don't want to say."

"You wouldn't understand. You wouldn't let yourself understand."

"Try me."

The apartment was silent except for the sound of the sleet, mingled with rain, on the sidewalk. Almost aimlessly I walked to the windows, feeling the cold that radiated through them. When at last I spoke, it was as much to my reflection as to him.

"Ever since I came into this business," I said slowly, "there hasn't been one day of my life that belonged to me. First I owed Clean, and then you, and then Gino. The names changed, but always there was somebody out there pulling my strings, telling me what to do, what to think, what to feel. Even when I went against them, I was still in this world, still in the *brugad*, following their rules, playing at their game. Everything I did, every score I took, every night I spent at the Grind Joint, every time I stepped out with Tina – it was all the *brugad*. Day and night. All the time. The fucking neighborhood. They call it *Cosa Nostra,* but it's not 'our thing,' Kraut. It's never been ours. It's *theirs*. Their world. And I've just been living in it. Trying to please them. To be the good soldier. The stand-up guy. Because after Anne, I didn't have anything else."

Kraut said nothing. The rain crawled down the windows, making the outside world waver and blur. There was no color in that view, no warmth. The trees were bare of branches. The apartments across the way had a drowned look. Brooklyn on the knife-edge of winter.

"Even since I decided to get out, I've been playing by their rules. Hustle. Put money on the street. Take scores. Like some kind of fuckin' animal, a machine that can't do anything else. Other people? Fuck 'em! I got a mission here. And nothing was gonna get in the way of my mission. Nothing. No matter what, no matter who got hurt, I was gonna make that money and be free.

"But last night, when I heard that poor son of a bitch screaming…something happened to me. Just for a moment, I got a glimpse of who I was before all this happened. Before I slugged Tommy B. on the jaw, before I got stuck at the Joint, before what happened with Red. I saw who I'd been before. And I thought, how much dirt can a man do in his life before it won't come off? How much blood can he spill, how much money can he steal before there's nothing left of who he used to be? Before he's nothing but a gangster, not just in what he does but what he *is?*"

I heard Kraut's breathing behind me. Wondered idly if he were reaching for a knife as I spoke.

"Maybe I've already reached the point where I can't go back. Maybe I passed it a long time ago. Maybe for the rest of my life I'll never be able to stop thinking or acting or doing like you do. I just know that last night I felt something in me I thought was gone for good. You call it bullshit heroics? I call it a heartbeat. Some hint, some fucking clue that maybe there's something left in me that doesn't belong to Clean or Gino or you. So no, I couldn't just walk away and leave the son of a bitch there to get tortured to death. Not if it meant losing all the money. Not if meant getting all of us killed. Not for any reason. I didn't just want to save him. I wanted to save *me.*"

Kraut made a scoffing noise somewhere in the back of his throat. "You wanted to get saved, is that it? Like your hero Big Eddie Maniscalco? What's next for St. Mickey? Want to go open up a neon-window church in the Bowery? Quote psalms to the crackheads?"

I turned away from the windows to face him. It felt as if the muscles over my skull had frozen solid – eyelids, cheeks, jaw all jammed tight with fatigue, so that I could speak only in a monotone, as if the words I were saying were in no way connected to the emotions that drove them. "Why'd you take this score, Kraut?"

"Fuck do you think I took it for? It figured to be a big payday."

"Sure. But that's not why you took it."

"Oh?" His face was flushing pink to the roots of his close-cropped blond hair. "Tell me why I took it, Dr. Melfi."

"You took it," I said deliberately, "because you know that Philly and Face are cowboys. You figured it would go bad, and that I had a better shot of making it out alive if you were along for the ride. You took it so you could be there to watch my back when it all went down."

I paused for a moment. The muscles in Kraut's jaws were standing out like walnuts, and the pink of his complexion was shading to a deep, dangerous red – the type of red that precedes a stroke or an ass-kicking.

"You took it because you wanted to look out for me," I said finally. "You took it because you heard your heart beating. So if you want to go down to the Bowery and quote psalms to crackheads, maybe we should split cab fare."

"You got maybe a month before you come due," he said in helpless, clench-fisted fury. "And since you ain't got the money, I suggest you start packing your bags."

"No."

"No? You owe Gino everything you've made in the last six months. And he'll take it from you if you stay. You won't keep a penny."

"I know."

"He may even kill you. It's a fucking insult to ask for a release from a crew, much less come up short with the cash."

"I know."

"Even if he doesn't, you'll still be *in*." His voice took on a kind of enraged satisfaction. "You'll still be one of his good little soldiers. Just beat to the bone and broke. You'll be picking poker chips off the floor at the Grind Joint for the rest of your fucking life."

"I know."

"Stop fuckin' saying that!"

Kraut would have made a hell of a drill instructor for Frederick's fusiliers. He screamed out of his diaphragm – a huge, primitive sound somewhere between the blast of a foghorn and the rumble of a bass drum. I waited the decent interval before I spoke. "What do you want me to say?"

He ran a hand over his face; the sound of his calluses against his beard made its familiar rasp. Then he dragged deeply on his cigarette, as if he were trying to imbibe strength out of its filter. "I want you to tell me what the fuck you're going to do."

I've said it before: every problem contains its own solution. It occurred to me in that moment, as I stood there in my threadbare flannel pajama bottoms and worn-out slippers, with my back turned to the iced-over windows and the chill creeping up my spine, that the answer to mine lay within me. Had for many months, buried beneath the surface of my thoughts like a sliver of old shrapnel. It was simply a question of facing that fact. Of picking up the scalpel…and cutting it free.

"I'm going to fight," I said.

Chapter Thirty-Two

Madison Square Garden in the fading December light. Flurries of wind-driven snow flicker in the blaze of red and green Christmas lights bedecking Eighth Avenue. Crowds thick on the pavements, cabs thick on the streets, smells of cold and ozone. In the background, horns, sirens, jackhammers, the barks of hotdog vendors. Citysong.

A strange name, has the Garden. It's not square at all, but curved like the Flavian Amphitheater where the gladiators found death and glory. A circle amidst the edges that make up Manhattan. When I was a child, we'd drive past the place in the family car, and my father would lift a broken-knuckled hand and wave at it and say in that voice of his, that harsh voice made harsher by innumerable broken noses, *Someday.*

But someday never came. Not for him. His boxing career had guttered in smoke-smeared ballrooms and poorly ventilated clubs whose rings contained canvases gone brown with old blood, fighting on cards nobody remembered, for money that didn't quite cover his medical bills. The only times he set foot in the Garden were when he paid cash money for a ticket.

Top of the world, Pop.

Sure. But even if he were alive he wouldn't be here. Mixed martial arts was to him on par with cockfighting or bear-baiting. The idea of his son fighting in a cage made him physically sick. No, he had a different plan for me entirely. It was *his* plan, dog-eared and well-thumbed, handed to me like a roll of blueprints at the moment of my birth. The Olympic trials, the Games, the gold, and then my face on a Wheaties box and million-dollar offers from boxing promoters with Vaseline smiles. That was what he wanted. What he expected. What he *demanded.* But things didn't work out that way. Mainly because I didn't want them to. Didn't want to compete with his dreams. Wanted to chase my own.

Inside now. The hallways describe long shallow arcs that follow the course of the building. Sense of vastness, of sterility, as of being inside some gigantic but seldom-used showroom. The lights are bright, the surfaces hard and polished and cold. At last an official hustles us into the dressing room. He doesn't seem impressed with me. Maybe it's the hollows in my cheeks, the fading yellow bruises around one eye, the trace of a limp from the injury in my all-too-brief training camp. I don't look like a guy on his way to a fight; I look like a guy coming from one.

In the corner of the dressing room, a monitor shows the cage. In it, the lean and loose-limbed Quintino Laca is fighting the tight-muscled Darius Dächer. Dächer is playing *murmillones* to Starza's *retarius* – using his long leg-kicks like a sword to ward off the net that was Laca's jiu-jitsu. It's a classic confrontation, striker versus grappler, and the striker Alton and the grappler Massimo pause to watch it, even as Sam presses a jump rope into my hand and tells me to git along with my warm-up. Good old Sam. There ain't much you can count on in life, but you can count on those rheumy brown eyes to glare at you disapprovingly. He used to glare at my father in just the same way when he failed to slip a jab, which was often. Dad's method of stopping a jab involved taking it square on the face. Not a lot of technique there. *I* was the one with the technique. He saw it early. Everyone saw it early. Oh, the kid is so *good.* So *strong.* So *slick.* A natural. He's gonna go all the way, Jimmy. All the way to the gold.

The sweat is trickling down my face, dampening my T-shirt, pitter-pattering at my feet. That's good. Laca has taken Dächer to the fence. Cramped up against that cold chain-link, the *murmillones* can't use his sword. He's in the net now, and soon the trident will pierce him in the form of a submission. Then it's my turn. I shouldn't be scared, but I am. And in a sense, I always have been.

Have you ever been to a truly foreign country? Foreign the way Kazakhstan or Bangladesh or Swaziland is foreign? When I began the transition from boxing to mixed martial arts, that's precisely the sensation that overtook me. The feeling of being a stranger in a strange and hostile land, one where nobody spoke my lingo and everyone wanted to beat the shit out of me. Of course, I knew the vocabulary of the Sweet Science. Shit, I was an *Encyclopedia Pugilistica.* Punch and counterpunch. Jab, lead, cross, hook. Clinch, slip, and shoulder-roll. You wanted to know how to cut off the ring? How to use a crab defense? How to shoeshine? How to go side-to-side? No problem. It was my language, and I was fluent.

Then I started training with Alton, and the language changed.

He started me on aikido. The Gentle Way. In essence, the opposite of boxing. No punches. No kicks. No strikes of any kind. Just easy fluid movements, designed to redirect the energy of the attacker. Painful as hell, but not injurious. That came later, with hapkido. The Way of Power. More grappling here, but also more violence. Techniques designed to end fights or even lives with a single movement, a single blow. Before too long I knew how to crush tracheas, shatter kneecaps, rupture testicles, pop out eyeballs. Throw pressure-point strikes that could leave a three-hundred-pound linebacker sobbing for mamma. Useful stuff for the street, but not for the cage. So began the Muay Thai. Shin kicks and spinning backfists and liberal doses of *namman muay* on the elbows so the flesh wouldn't tear when you drove the bone behind it into someone's face. Then the jiu-jitsu. Grappling down on the ground where it gets really ugly, submission holds with bizarre names like Americana, Gogoplata, Heel Hook, Anaconda Choke, Kimura. But I was good at it. Good at *all* of it. Some people are good at drawing and others at singing and others at crossword puzzles or discus or building scale models of the *Mary Celeste*; I was good at physical violence. It came naturally. Like disappointing my father.

The warm-up's over. Dächer's handlers are helping him off the mat. His mouthpiece had come unstuck and hung over the spit-sheened ball of his chin like a row of broken teeth. Poor sonofabitch probably didn't even know he'd tapped to a guillotine choke. That was Laca's specialty. I knew this because he'd damn near finished me with the same move two years previously. Luckily for me, Massimo had shown me the escape. Back in those days, escape was second nature to me. Nothing could pin me down. Not fighters, not women, not Pop's expectations reaching out from the grave.

Walking to the cage now. Christ this crowd is big. How many people can the Arena hold? Must be close to twenty thousand. The population of a small town. And yet this is small potatoes compared to what the Roman Coliseum would hold. Oh, I know the *Amphitheatrum Flavium.* Went there to scatter Pop's ashes. It was his last request. Rome was where he'd honeymooned with my mother, and as a fighting man, he'd been drawn to the arena. In our frowsy little cold-water walk-up in Hell's Kitchen hung a yellowed picture of the young couple, standing on the wooden walkway over the *hypogeum.* That was where he wanted to go when he died. I flew all the way to Italy to take him, and it was no easy task. Had to smuggle the urn beneath my coat on a drizzly dull Tuesday afternoon in winter, when there was nobody there but cats and postcard-hustlers and a few glum Japanese tourists. Had to tip the ashes discreetly over the railing amidst the whir and click of the Nikons and then hustle away as if I'd just committed an act of petty vandalism. When I told Anne that story, she'd wept into my shoulder. I'd felt the tears hot against my neck and was grateful for them. She could do what I never could. Weep for my father. And in that instant, I'd known that I loved her.

At first, I can barely hear my entrance music over the cheering, the booing, the whistling and shouting and stomping. Then like an antiphonal choir, the lyrics roll over the crowd: something about razors and dying roses, demi-gods and hungry ghosts. Appropriate. The referee gives me the onceover. I nod when he speaks, not listening. My gaze is cageside. Five rows back I see the gleam of Tina's blue-black wig. Her eyes glitter expectantly beneath the sheen of her colored contacts; her heavy breasts, exposed by a plunging neckline, rise and fall as if she's already on the precipice of orgasm. Next to her, glooming like a chaperone or a bodyguard, is Kraut in his black leather jacket, his face as immobile as a gladiator's mask. Some yards away, reclining at the end of a long line of obvious wiseguys, are Gino Stillitano and Nicky Cowboy. Their eyes track me coldly in the blue light, and the faintest trace of a smirk is chiseled between Gino's lips. I wonder fleetingly if his ancestors didn't wear that same look when they watched the Christians being fed to the lions.

Ahead of them all, Mikhailis is in his usual place of honor in the front row, smiling genially. And why not? Look at his date. Her golden curls. Her smoke-green eyes and sun-honeyed skin. Her beauty as easy and natural as Tina's was painstakingly affected. A delightful touch of cruelty, bringing Anne here. Even the sadness in her face didn't ease the pain of her presence on Mikhailis's arm. I'm not even in the cage yet and I'm already bleeding.

Inside, Kreese is pacing like a caged tiger, fists clenched so that I can see the muscles of his forearms standing out in bas-relief. His glare, an immensity of hatred behind it, could make a face bleed. He doesn't even raise his arms when the announcer calls his name. Too focused on me. On what he wants to do to me. One of his handlers is trying to insert his mouthpiece, but Kreese shakes his head. There's something he wants to say, and I'm about to hear it, because the time has come for the prefight instructions. We come to a stop at a foot's distance from each other, and the referee goes into his shtick, telling us what's legal and what's illegal and all the other shit we should know already, and all the while my opponent is edging closer to me, an inch at a time, until I can see each crystalline bead of warm-up sweat glistening on his naked scalp, until we're almost nose to nose, and he growls, *Did you like the flowers, you fuckin' cunt?*

Then we're backing away, and the seconds are out of the cage and the bolt on the door slams home and I can hear the commentator bellowing, *Here we go*…and just like that the blue-gloved fist of Wilson Kreese is blurring toward my head. I feel the thud of impact, the burst of heat, the odd clarity that comes afterward. Feel the texture of the mat beneath my bare feet and the heat of the lights on my scalp. My own heart beating, pushing the hot blood through the fine threadwork of veins in the muscle, and the muscles move and I bury my left fist into Kreese's ribs, feel the puff of his breath grunting out in pain. But my mind, reeling already, reels faster now, forming a kind of vortex in which one thought spins around over and over again: *You're the one who jumped me outside the Grind Joint?* In retrospect, it was obvious, just as it was obvious

Morganstern put him up to it. But the view from Retrospective was always good. The view from Now was not. And the footing was terrible.

Kreese demonstrates this by bulling forward beneath my weak follow-up strike. By grasping my forearms, slamming me backwards into the fence, and landing a knee high on my flexed abdominals. It's no ordinary strike; he's not even trying to conserve energy for the later rounds. He doesn't *want* any later rounds. He wants to finish me quickly and pocket the big cash bonus that goes to the winner, the one I need so very damned desperately if I ever want to be free. And if he caves in my ribs en route, so much the better. Kreese wouldn't be Kreese if his dreams didn't involve trampling mine.

Knees. If I'd done what Pop wanted, I'd never have had to eat a knee, or an elbow, or worry about getting choked unconscious or kicked in the thigh or hearing the sound of my own ulna breaking. Could have made a lot more money, too. Enough to pay off Gino in a single night. But I didn't want to go down a half-beaten trail. I wanted to blaze my own. It was strange that nobody could understand it. Nobody except Clean. His own grandfather was a kingpin in the dry-cleaning business. A straight civilian, law-abiding and tax-paying. Couldn't understand why his son wanted to be a gangster. I remembered a time long ago, Clean and I were drinking in Eamonn Broye's, and the rain was crawling down the big plate-glass windows overlooking Flatbush Avenue, and he stubbed out his English Oval and said, *It ain't easy to be your own man when your dad is* his *own man, is it?* Anytime people questioned why I palled around with Clean, I thought of those words, uttered back when he was a Camaro-driving *cugine* and my only endorsement came from a muffler-and-brake shop three blocks down the way. We were both rebels in the wrong, and knew it, and refused to renounce our rebellions, and this was what had made us brothers. And look where we were now. Clean was mummifying slowly under six feet of unhallowed earth, and I was eating knees against a chain-link fence.

Oh, it hurt all right, but there's pain and there's pain. My mother died when I was twelve years old. We hadn't been in Brooklyn for six months when she found the lump. My father had been making better money then, which meant that we were still poor but could now afford to live beyond our means, and we moved over the river to the little yellow house in South Brooklyn, and my mother planted tomatoes in our garden. Before the pale green vines had climbed the trellis, the priest was saying thus do I commend thee into the arms of our lord of the earth, our lord Jesus Christ, preserver of all mercy and reality, we give Him glory as we give you into His arms in everlasting peace, amen amen amen. Big fight about cremation. Father Pulio said it was wrong, but the monsignor overruled him. Father Pulio didn't like that. He sulked all through the funeral mass. Shoved that urn in my father's hands like it was a sack of garbage. Said something, too. Don't know what it was, but it was the wrong something to say. Cost him three of his teeth. Nothing like being twelve and watching as they drag your dad out of the church with the priest's blood on his fists and your mother's prematurely scattered ashes drifting over the pews. That sets the bar pretty fucking high for pain. The knees of Wilson Kreese just don't seem to matter in comparison.

I can see the confusion in his seawater-colored eyes. This should *hurt*. But it doesn't. Not enough, anyway. So he wrenches me down to the mat. That's where he's happiest, anyway. A tenth of a ton of glistening muscle lands atop me like the lid of a coffin. I can hear my corner shouting advice, instructions, curses. Escape, they say. Fine. I toss Kreese off me with the strength of my hips and roll sideways, get my heels beneath me and stand, and Kreese is standing too, and as soon as his feet are off the ground, I drill him good with a *thip* to the solar plexus. A *thip* is what Thailanders call a foot-jab, and it sends Kreese windmilling across the cage. I follow it up with a lunging right hand that takes me clear off my heels, a Superman punch that just clips the edge of his chin. Clang! goes Kreese into the fence, but he's not hurt. I was a half-second too slow to do real damage, and as he rebounds off the chain-link, he gets in another knee along my ribcage, just under the armpit, and it's like a large-caliber bullet has struck me through the lungs, filling them with blood and hot lava. This must be what the lion felt like in "The Short, Happy Life of Francis Macomber" when Francis shot him through the guts. A sick, sapping agony. If I had the strength, I'd spare a glance at Gino through the fence. I bet he's smiling now. Some men like to win more than they like to get paid; if I fail here, Gino gets both satisfactions at once. All the money I've earned, and my everlasting servitude to his favorite cause, the cause of him.

My knees are buckling from nausea, and Kreese is muscling me back across the cage. My heels are actually sliding across the colorful corporate logos emblazoned upon it, and there's no time to reflect upon the irony of the makers of malt liquor and fast food and sugar-laden energy drinks sponsoring a League which contains some of the most perfectly conditioned athletes in the world, because one of those athletes has just smashed me across the cheekbone with an elbow. Through the haze of pain, the constellation of stars circling about my head, I hear the crowd's collective gasp – twenty thousand indrawn breaths all at once. I wonder if Anne's is among them. Wonder if it troubles her to see the lips that so often covered hers knocked bloodily to pieces.

We're in the clinch again, chins pressed hard into each other's shoulders. I can't get any strength into my muscles, and I can taste vomit as well as blood along with the slimy plastic of my mouthpiece. If I were boxing, I'd use this moment to rest, but this isn't boxing – in MMA the clinch is as dangerous a place as any other. More dangerous if your opponent is Kreese. I can hear Alton bellowing *knee, knee,* but when I strike it's no harder than a slap, and this time when I'm thrown to the floor I can't get back up. Have to go straight into the guard, but Kreese is twisting, twisting those monstrous muscles, trying to move into side control, and if he gets there, it's not so much a question of if as of when.

Ah, the hideous pantomime of intimacy. When I first began with jiu-jitsu I had trouble dealing with it. The press of sweaty flesh, the mingled breathing, the grunts of exertion and sudden shifts of movement were all too redolent of sex, and let's face it, Kreese is a poor substitute for Anne. Good old Anne. Was it really only a year ago I defeated this same fighter while she looked on and cheered? It seemed eternities ago. A vast period of decline and dissolution. What was that the Muslims said? That hell was not a place but the absence of God's love? Maybe it was simpler even than that. Maybe hell was just the absence of love, period.

Kreese has worked himself into side mount; our bodies now form a rough crucifix shape on the mat, with me as the crossbar. He's free to bring his knees into my ribcage and is exercising that privilege with abandon. I can't remember what the sack of membrane is that holds the organs in place; I think I'd been breaking up a fight at the Grind Joint when I should have been studying for my night-school Biology final. But whether it's the mesentery or the peritoneum or the Gut Bag, it's sure taking a beating now, and everything within it. I can't do much but flail like an insect pinned to a display case, and what little energy I had after the armpit shot is bleeding out fast. Once again, I can hear my corner screaming for a sweep – Massimo is actually screaming in Portuguese, which is never a good sign. Probably they can't believe how badly I'm performing here, now, when it's all on the line, down to the very last chip. In a way, I can't believe it myself.

I spend lavishly of my remaining strength to roll onto my side, which spares my throbbing ribs at the expense of my stomach. With my cheek pressed to the canvas, I see Anne staring at me through the fence not more than twenty feet away. The eyes are glistening, the oh-so-familiar lips aquiver. Morganstern seems to be holding her arm as much to keep her in her seat as to display affection. But his grip isn't strong enough. As another knee smashes into me, forcing my mouthpiece onto the mat like viscera from a wheel-crushed animal, she wrenches free and half stumbles, half runs for the aisle. Mikhailis doesn't follow. Doesn't even look. He's staring at me with unnatural intensity, his normally subtle smile spreading slowly into a triumphant grin.

Kreese tenses and shifts his weight as if to draw back his knee one more time, and then suddenly he leaps, a short hop over my body, and the next thing I know he's contorted himself around my right arm like an albino python. Panic suddenly jangles along my nervous system, obliterating the pain completely. Dear sweet Jesus, he's got me in an armbar. The same move I used to defeat him. The same move *he* has used to virtually cripple a dozen-odd men. And I know Kreese. It would be worth it to him to forfeit his entire purse, even to be expelled from the Cage Combat League, simply to hear my elbow pop.

Of course, I know how to escape from this hold. Just give the old arm a quarter-turn, as if it were a Phillips-head screwdriver, to relieve the worst of the pressure on the joint, then keep turning with the entire body this way and that until all the leverage he has built up works against him and viola, *he's* the one on the losing end of side control. It sounds easy. And if you practice it a few thousand times with, say, Massimo Raia, it actually even works once in a while. So I turn my arm. Try to, anyway, but Kreese has a mighty grip – once again, I can see every individual muscle bulging, see each individual vein. He's using everything he has, every watt of electrochemical power in that huge battery of a body to finish me right here and now. The pain in my joint increases, burns through the morphine-like panic, doubles and redoubles. Sweat stands out on my forehead – I can feel it rolling down my cheeks. My arm is now bent five degrees the wrong way. Six. Seven. Eight. The bones themselves are creaking within their strata of muscle, protesting furiously against this assault on their structural integrity. And yet I've managed an eighth of a turn. One more successful movement, one last effort from my hips, and he'll be wearing my noose. I know it. *He* knows it. And in that moment our gazes lock.

Kreese's face is a gleaming crimson. He's spit out his mouthpiece so he can gulp in the air he needs, and his mouth is contorted back over his teeth. We've reached that moment of the tug of war where strength cancels out strength and the issue turns on superior resolve. Who wants it more. And in that instant, I realize what the answer is. What the answer must be. And I accept it in my heart as I have already accepted it in my brain. I feel my hand flatten back on the mat and the pain spread up and down my arm, into my shoulder, into my head, to the innermost reaches of my mind, a great red surge of torment unlike anything I've ever experienced, so that the scream building within me actually chokes off into a kind of rattle I can feel but not hear.

And so breaks my arm.

Chapter Thirty-Three

I had been dreaming of snow in Hell's Kitchen; I woke up to cold Brooklyn sunshine. For a moment, I did not know why. Then the phone rang again, a shrill jangling that rippled the water in the glass I kept by my bedside. I slid my good hand out of the blankets and pushed aside the loaded revolver on the nightstand to pick it up.

"Good morning, fucko." It was Nicky Cowboy, his voice full of a kind of malevolent good cheer. "You know what day it is?"

"Yeah."

"Gene's having a little Christmas party at the Friends at noon. Attendance is mandatory. Especially for you."

"I'll come bearing gifts."

"You'd better." The line went dead.

It was nine in the morning on Christmas Eve. I threw back the faded green comforter and swung my bare feet to the floor, staring into the light that streamed in through my dusty blinds. From beneath the cast that encased my right arm, a slow, steady throb of pain commenced. No, not commenced. It had never left me entirely, no matter how many painkillers I swallowed. Even within my dreams it haunted me, like a modern-day substitute for the slave who used to stand behind victorious Roman generals and whisper, *All glory is fleeting.* Except that in this case the slave had added a line: *Defeat likes to stick around.*

I chased down a Vicodin with the water. For a while, I had only early-morning stupidity and pain. Then it occurred to me with cold sinking sensation that this might be the last day of my life.

I prepared as best I could with one arm. Soft body armor beneath a heavy cable sweater. Thirty-eight Detective Special loaded with hollow points on my left hip, just two practiced movements away from going off. A Derringer in the left pocket of my overcoat. And a shot of Jameson's for courage.

In the big plastic suitcase I'd purchased at a pawn shop was more money than I'd ever seen in my life or would likely see again, even if I didn't finish the day in a chum bucket. After it had been counted and recounted the previous night, I had locked it in the suitcase, then handcuffed the suitcase to the radiator and passed out. Now I inserted the handcuff key into the lock and released it with a metallic snap that was oddly satisfying. Assuming I lived through the day, they could go back to their primary purpose of securing Tina to the headboard.

Outside, the sun blazed in a harsh blue sky, and a wind that had men clutching their caps to their heads blew in ceaselessly off the East River. I slung the suitcase into my trunk, slipped on my sunglasses, and started out towards the Friends of the Friends, the rumble of the Maverick's engine vibrating the steering wheel like a tuning fork.

It is strange the effect that months of constant tension can have on the body. My mouth was powder-dry, my palms slick, my bladder pressing urgently although I had already twice relieved it. A cold sweat trickled persistently from under my arms. Yet I felt oddly detached as I drove one-handed across Brooklyn and into Queens. Perhaps I was making a mistake – one last, fatal mistake to top off all the others I had committed over the last year. It would be so easy to run, after all; to take Tina and the money and disappear into the sea-spray of some Caribbean island, never to be heard from again. The tantalizing imagery of that thought had been persistent enough these past few months, unfolding before my mind's eye like a centerfold. But in the end, this was just another form of surrender, and I was all through with surrender – with giving up, backing down, quitting. On the blood-soaked floor of Carmine Spina's fight factory, I had discovered a determination I had never known was there, and that spoke to me in the low, hard-timbered voice of my father.

It told me to finish what I'd started.

Even if it killed me.

The air was wonderfully cold and crisp, the sunshine insistently cheerful. It seemed far too beautiful a day to die. I wondered if my nerves would fail me when the moment came – whether I would stand there and let them kill me or fight. I had resolved either way that if I had to clench my teeth until they cracked, I would not leave the world with a plea on my lips. It seemed now like one of those promises that you make knowing damned well you're unlikely to keep it.

I parked at an Italian bakery two blocks away from the Friends of the Friends and lugged the suitcase out of the trunk, the effort of which brought the pain-sweat out on my upper lip. The air was full of the smell of fresh bread – a scent to make you mouth water, provided you can produce any saliva. On the street ahead of me, I identified those present by their cars: there was Gene's turquoise Newport Custom parked audaciously in front of a fire hydrant and glittering in the sunlight like a gigantic Easter Egg; Nicky's tint-windowed, hunter-green Caddy with the NRA license plate holder; Philly's fire-engine red IROC-Z Camaro with the big *cornu* hanging from the rear window; and Face's beat-to-shit Buick Regal.

I was still standing there, staring dully at the flat-roofed little building half-hidden by weeping willows and listening to the sound of my heart, when Kraut's dusty work van swung up to the curb.

He climbed down onto the street, adjusted the pistol tucked into his waistband and then buttoned his leather blazer over it. His thick blond hair had been recently trimmed and he was clean-shaven below his Ray Ban sunglasses, making him look younger and more formidable.

"What are you doing here?" I said.

"Spreading Christmas cheer. Fuck does it look like I'm doing?"

"You can't go in there with me."

"Why not?"

"You know why not. Gino might take it the wrong way."

"He can take it any fuckin' way he wants. You're my partner."

"I *was* your partner. You bought me out, remember?"

"Yeah, and at five grand more than your share was worth. What was I thinking?"

"Kraut, I appreciate what you're doing here, but this is my mess. It's always been my mess. And I'm the one that's got to clean it up."

He stared at me with graven-faced contempt. When at last he spoke, it was in the harried, slightly condescending tone of a long-suffering schoolmaster. "Mick, if you're Butch, you don't leave Sundance at the door. Understand?"

With that he turned on his heel and marched up the street, forcing me to hobble after him – money weighs a lot more than you think it does. There was no preamble, not even an exchange of glances as entrance of the Friends loomed; we simply went inside, with Kraut leading the way.

No lights burned within. There was no need for any; the smoked windows gave off a milky, ethereal glow. Face and Philly were sitting at the green-felt card table playing poker. Behind the bar, an old man with a crewcut was noisily slurping espresso from a glazed china cup. In the far corner, a scar-faced hoodlum with slicked-back hair and prison-built muscles flipped the pages of a pornographic magazine. The door to the back room was open; through it I heard the low babble of a television.

"Fellas," I said.

For a moment I felt as if we had walked into a wax museum instead of a social club. Everyone seemed to have frozen in mid-motion; not even the smoke from Face's Panamanian cigar seemed to move. Then the door swung shut behind us, sweeping in a gust of cold air that rippled the Italian and American flags tacked up on the opposite wall, and the spell was broken. Face, who was wearing a red felt Santa Claus hat whose jollity contrasted brutally with his trollish features, laid the card down on the table with a muted snap, and cleared his throat. "How you guys doin'?"

"Terrific," Kraut said, slipping off his sunglasses. "Chock full of holiday spirit."

Scarface put down the nudie magazine, stood up, and walked into the back room without another word. I felt my gun hand twitch.

"What's that you got there?" Philly said with feigned curiosity, nodding at the suitcase over the fan of his playing cards.

I set it down on the floor, breathing heavily. Every pair of eyes in the room followed it. "Stocking stuffers."

Another silence followed. The television over the espresso bar was dark, and the Rock-Ola stood mute and forgotten against the wall. Someone had set up a small Christmas tree in the corner; its white lights kicked on and off in a circular pattern, as if they were chasing themselves. Philly was regarding us both with an opaque look, his finger tracing the ridges on the edge of a poker chip. There was no recognition there, no admission of what we had done together, no anger at how I'd fucked it all up, nothing. I wondered whether he or Scarface had been tapped with the job of killing me.

"Somebody gonna offer us a drink, or what?" Kraut said.

The old man put down his espresso saucer with a clink. His voice sounded like a shovel-full of wet gravel, and I realized with a start it was Ernie, keeper of the whorehouse gate, looking somewhat more impressive in an old corduroy jacket and open-collared shirt than he had in his bathrobe and slippers. "I don't drink with people who keep *Mein Kampf* on the nightstand."

"Ernie! You old kike." Kraut crossed the room to shake hands. "I haven't seen you since...."

"Yeah," Ernie said, casting a rheumy-eyed glance at me. "Since."

The image of Dago Red's sheet-wrapped body flickered unpleasantly in my brain. "How have you been, Ernie?" I said, sidling up to the bar.

The old man produced a bottle of Strega and worked out the stopper with a four-and-a-half-fingered hand. His face was as I remembered it, brows still unnaturally dark below the iron-gray bristles, skin flecked with age and sun and hard-living. Yet there was an air of solidity, of deep-down hardness, that was oddly reminiscent of the Sphinx as he must have looked before Napoleon's cannoneers had their fun with his nose – an impression that time alone would never be sufficient to destroy him. "Not so bad since youse two stopped coming to see me."

He poured three glasses. Beside us, the poker game went on in a desultory fashion, with Philly and Face arguing over whether Ted Williams was the greatest pure hitter of all time. Everything around me contrived towards a relaxed atmosphere, and yet the undercurrent of tension was such that I could hardly swallow the fiery yellow liquid for the knots in my belly. Part of me longed for the explosion, but the greater part of me dreaded it. Who would make the move? Scarface was the obvious choice – entirely *too* obvious. They understood I'd be looking for the unfamiliar face. No, it would somebody I knew, and Nicky had to figure I'd never let him behind me, even for a second, after what I'd seen him do to Don Cheech. That went double for Gene. Smiling fixedly at Ernie, I used my peripheral vision to study the poker table. Face would have to jerk his chair sharply backward and stand up to get a clear shot, and he preferred the garotte to the gun anyway – an impossibility with Kraut at my side. Okay. It had to be Philly. He'd probably asked for the job after the stunt I'd pulled at Battaglia's. And he had the same motivation as Gene did for having me in the ground – one less loose end in a life that was tangled with them.

I smiled and sipped, sipped and smiled, keeping Philly's tanned, goatee-framed face firmly in the corner of my eye. Whatever his other flaws, Guido was a meticulous planner. His weapon was probably secured under the table with a swatch of packing tape. He had nimble hands, and he would have practiced the move all morning. It would take him a second and a half, maybe two, to yank it free and take aim. Three if he went for a headshot. In that time, I might be able to make his brains see daylight with a shot of my own – he wasn't the only one with fast fingers, and I was pretty good with my left. But maybe it would be better to move first? Spoil his aim? Then shoot before he could adjust?

I hardly tasted the Strega anymore, feeling only the pounding of the blood in my temples, the weight of the pistol on my hip, the odd gravity of the suitcase and a sense of anticipation which was almost unbearable. I was just putting down my glass with a shaky hand when Gino strode into the room with Nicky Cowboy hard on his heels

"Wel-l-l-l," he said loudly. "If it ain't the prodigal fuckin' son. And his suitcase."

I knew at once he'd been waiting to use that line since he had awoken that morning.

"Hello, Gene. Nick."

"I really didn't think he'd show," Nicky said, pushing his half-glasses up his nose and scrutinizing me through their lower lenses. "Not after he got his ass kicked in that fight."

"Such a cynic, Cowboy." Gino scolded him with a pinky. "Your problem is, you got no faith in human nature. Me and the kid here had a deal."

He wore his thick leather racing jacket with the narrow red stripe over a black Henley shirt, tight black jeans, and black motorcycle boots. The buckle of his belt was festooned with a sprig of mistletoe that sported two small red berries. This last touch did not greatly surprise me: it was difficult to picture Gino allowing anyone to kiss him on the mouth.

"Fuck are you doing here, Kraut?" Gino said, still staring at me. "I don't remember your name on the guest list."

"Funny thing about Germans, bo," Kraut replied in a low voice. "We make our own invitations."

Gino's eyes narrowed momentarily. Then the slightest of smiles shallowed in one corner of his mouth. "You almost make me want to buy a dog. Sit down."

Kraut unbuttoned his blazer and eased against one of the leather-topped stools facing the espresso bar. He made no attempt to conceal the walnut grip of the revolver that stuck over his beltline.

Philly laid his playing cards flat on the table and drummed his fingers on the felt. Once. Twice. Then they lay still.

"So," Gino said to me after a short pause. "What else did you bring me, aside from your pet Nazi?"

My fingers found the sweat-dampened handle of the suitcase. I walked it to the poker table and set it there on the wrinkled felt. "Like you said, Gene…we had a deal."

"Yeah," he replied, the unpleasant smile still glimmering in the corner of his mouth like a smear of blood. "And you didn't hold up your end of it. Came close, but couldn't *quite* bring home the bacon. Shit, they must have heard your arm snap in the cheap seats."

"Too bad, really," Nicky chimed in, folding his arms and smirking. "Youda pulled this off, even *I* woulda been impressed." There was a short pause. "Well, not really. But at least I wouldn't have wanted to paint your guts on the fuckin' linoleum."

"Funny thing about this deal," Gino added smugly. "You don't get no points for almost."

I popped the locks and opened the case, turning it with one hand until it sat before him like a clamshell. The distinctive smell of cash rose into the air, mingling with the scents of espresso and cigarette smoke.

"I'm all through with almost."

Gino's sneer seemed to have a certain momentum. For about five seconds, it clung stubbornly to his face even as his eyes widened. Then it unraveled and left his mouth in a flat, disbelieving line. "Holy shit."

Every eye in the room seemed to have taken on the dull glaze of hypnosis. Philly licked his lips. Face stared into the case as if it were a naked female body. Even Ernie, whose face yielded all the mobility of an Easter Island monument, wore a small, dreamy smile.

Nicky's lower jaw had slipped its hinge. For a moment, I could see the gold fillings on his back molars. "No fuckin' way."

I cleared my throat. "Two hundred grand."

"The hell you say," Nicky growled.

"Count it."

"You're fuckin'-A right I'm gonna count it." He declared. A moment passed. Then said harshly to Face: "Count it."

"Nah," Gino said quietly, and tipped his gray gaze up to meet mine. "No counting. If he was gonna stiff me, he never would have showed in the first place." Gino stepped forward, picked up a thick bundle of cash, flipped through its edges with his thumb. "You really pulled it off, didn't you?"

"Yeah."

He tossed the bundle onto the card table. He had recovered his poise and his voice assumed its normal, steely edge. "If I'd known you could be this big of an earner I'd never have made this deal in the first place."

"That's what I figured."

"Ah, I see." Gino's unpleasant smile returned. "And now I s'pose you think you're clever 'cause you got off cheap?"

"I don't think I got off cheap, Gene."

"Then maybe you think you got over on me. Outhustled me a bit?"

"No."

His voice rose a full octave. "Think maybe you're a big wiseguy now, 'cause you made a bet with me and came up winners? Is that what you think?"

I swallowed. Sweat trickled coldly down the hollow of my spine. "What I think is that we had a deal, and I kept up my end of it."

Gino stared at me without blinking for what seemed like a presidential administration. Finally, he said: "Oh, I'll hold up my end, jerkoff. But before I do, maybe you need a little reminder of who the real fuckin' wiseguy in the room is. Maybe–"

In my peripheral vision, I saw Philly shift slightly in his seat, and something inside of me, the over-stretched string of nerve that had been holding me together all morning, snapped clean. In a single motion, I yanked the .38 from its holster, arm blurring out like a whip as I thumbed back the hammer, and before anyone could move I had his head squarely in my sights. *"Don't move!"*

For the first time since I had entered the room, Philly's face registered a recognizable emotion: surprise. His eyes crossed a bit as he stared at the muzzle that stared back at him. Then the poker chip in his right hand fell to the table with a *plink*.

"What the fuck are you doing?" Nicky said, sounding more indignant than alarmed.

"Doing? I'm getting the drop on Philly Boy here before one of you can give him the signal to put two in my ear. Didn't think I saw that one coming, did you? Didn't think I was *wiseguy* enough."

Kraut's voice, low and gentle on my left: "Mick."

"No, Kraut," I shouted. My heart was pounding so hard it was actually distorting my vision. Philly's wide-eyed sun-browned face seemed to sparkle amongst stars, whorls, tiny black holes, like a bewildered cartoon character. "Gene thought I needed a reminder. Like I could ever forget what he is!"

"Mick," Kraut said again.

"*I kept up my end the deal!* I went through hell, put a fortune in your pocket, and all I asked was the right to walk out of here without you on my back! But you just can't stand to lose, can you? Even when you win!"

Gino was looking at me with complete calm. When he spoke his voice was low, almost pleasant, as if he were pointing out a wild rose growing in a weedy sandlot. "Reminder's over there, stupid."

"Mick," Kraut said insistently. "Look."

Keeping the Detective Special trained squarely on Philly, I looked without moving my head. Ernie had one gnarled, liver-spotted hand firmly on the back of Kraut's neck. In the other he held a small-caliber revolver. It was behind Kraut's head but pointed directly at me from a distance of about eight feet. On the thin slash of lips that separated Ernie's upper and lower jaws was what can only be described as a Mona Lisa smile.

"Nobody gets over on Gino Stillitano," Gene said after a long, charged silence. "We made a deal, and like you said, you kept up your end of it. So the deal is done. You're out. Scratched off the record. Released. You get your life back – whatever the fuck that's worth. But never forget what happened here. Never forget that I had you looking the wrong way. That I'll *always* have you looking the wrong way. Today it was Ernie you didn't see coming. Tomorrow it could be someone else, creepin' up behind you with piano wire or a twenty-two. All it takes is a nod, and you vanish off the face of the earth. And if it ever gets in your head to run your mouth about any of the things you seen since you been with me, if you so much as whisper my name out loud at night, I'll find out, and you will go…and you will never, ever see it coming. Do we understand each other?"

For a moment I said nothing. The muzzle of Ernie's pistol glared at me like the sightless eye of a skull. Then I eased the hammer forward on my .38 and slipped it back into its holster. "Yes."

"Good," Gino said. "Now get the fuck out of here. Both of you."

I looked down at Philly, who was staring up at me ashen-faced beneath his tan, his hands still frozen in a warding-off gesture before him. "Sorry about that."

"Get fucked."

Kraut went to the door and opened it, admitting a flood of cold sunshine that had Face reaching for his sunglasses. I took one last look around the room, breathed deeply. *"Bona fortuna,* fellas."

For a moment I thought no one would reply. I started for the door. Then Ernie lowered his pistol and said: "Take it easy, kid. Don't hook with no hookers."

"Right," Face added, picking up his playing cards. "And feel free to come back and terrorize Phil any time you get the urge."

"He'll be back," Nicky said unexpectedly, folding his arms across his chest and staring at me with hard, inscrutable eyes.

"No he won't," Philly said shakily, swallowing. "He comes back, I'm gonna fuckin' kill him."

"He'll come back," Nicky repeated. "Nobody walks away from this life."

I looked at him. For just a moment I saw Don Cheech in his place, sitting calmly at the table with espresso in hand. It had only been a year ago. It seemed like a thousand.

"Watch me," I said.

Chapter Thirty-Four

Afternoon had dulled into evening when I arrived at the Promenade. It was bitterly cold, and the insistent wind that hurled itself through the spans of the Brooklyn Bridge sounded like the latter stages of an Irish wake. For some time, I stood against the railing beneath a flickering streetlamp, watching the waters of the East River empty out into the Bay. It gave me an odd comfort to know that one of the lights twinkling feebly on the other side of that river belonged to me – a home that until a few hours ago I had been certain I would never set foot in again.

For a time, I followed the progress of a police helicopter as it chased its searchlight into the gathering darkness over the water. As if by unwilling reflex, I pictured a bloated white body bobbing in the surface current, caught in the cone of light like an insect in a spider's web. I could see it with unpleasant clarity – wrists and ankles bound with duct tape, mouth distorted by a sodden gag, throat offering an obscene purplish smile where the blade had sliced it from ear to ear. Every time the body surfaced in the choppy water it bore a different face – Dago Red, Don Cheech, Clean…myself.

I shook my head slowly and the image vanished, fading with the helicopter's running lights as it pushed southward along the Brooklyn coastline. The wind picked up again, rustling the boughs of holly that city workers had fixed to the lamps lining the Promenade. A long length of red ribbon, worked free from its wreath, swept past me down the deserted boardwalk. It occurred to me idly that it was Christmas Eve, and I nothing whatever on my person but a cigarette lighter, a pistol, and the St. Jude medallion my mother had given me on my tenth birthday. The sum total of my assets were a thirty-year-old Maverick and whatever loose change happened to be nesting in its seat cushions.

Would the toll taker on the bridge believe I had started the day with two hundred thousand dollars in cash? I could hardly believe it myself. It was like coming back from some failed Arctic expedition where the supplies had run out and you'd discovered that you would eat human flesh if you were hungry enough. You looked into the mirror and realized there was someone else within you, a person you didn't know. And he was capable of anything.

The bookies at the Fight Factory had made me a heavy favorite to beat Kreese in the rematch. After all, he was nearly forty, cage-worn, and I'd submitted him in our first meeting. The early betting action had been solidly in my favor, and since money moves the line, the odds were soon even more grossly on my side. Nobody seemed to think The Kapsule could pull it off. So you can imagine how the eyebrows went up when Tina sashayed up to the window the night before the fight and put twenty-five thousand dollars on Wilson Kreese at three-to-one. They went up even more when a busted-up hoodlum by the name of Lenny Longarone swung by an hour later and shoved a few dozen stacks of greasy-looking bills under the railing before clearing out with the look of a man who had a date somewhere in Florida and was running just a bit late. By the time Kraut appeared to place a third bet, Carmine Spina himself had been on hand to give him a pale-eyed stare through his half-glasses and ask a question:

You know something I don't?

Kraut wasn't afraid of Spina, but he wasn't stupid, either. He hesitated for a few moments, tapping into decades of experience to decide on how best to play it, then began sliding his cash across the counter.

Maybe, he said.

Spina nodded and walked off. He could have shortened the odds and saved his bookies a fortune, but then he wouldn't have been able to place his own bets in Atlantic City and Vegas and make a larger fortune for himself.

It all went down exactly as I'd planned it, right up to the last, when Kreese had made his little confession, and I discovered that I'd killed the wrong man. But even that knowledge didn't make a difference in the end. Defeating Kreese wouldn't have put me over the top. Betting against myself, and then letting him finish me, did.

It would have been almost anticlimactic if I hadn't been so damn sure Gino was going to kill me anyway.

Cradling my broken arm like a package, I walked aimlessly down the Promenade, thinking of the last time I had been here, a year previously, hand in hand with Anne. What had I been thinking about then? Keeping my weight down over the holidays. Whether the classes I had scheduled at City University would interfere with my training schedule. Whether I could afford to take Anne to dinner at a fancy restaurant on New Year's Eve. It was like looking at photos of yourself in an old family album – intellectually you understood that the chubby-cheeked kid in the rubber pants was you, but emotionally there was no connection. The thoughts, the concerns and feelings of that time were lost to you, dulled and ultimately faded out of existence by the passage of time. There was no hope of going back to the man I had been, no point in even trying. The album was closed, and the dust was already gathering. I had to make a new life, a new me, and I was literally starting over from scratch.

A laugh escaped me on a puff of steam. People dreamed about second chances, and now I had purchased one with a suitcase full of dirty money – hardly an auspicious beginning. But the chance was here. It was now. I should have been exhilarated, inflamed, reborn. What I felt instead was the shame-faced relief of an army deserter, mingled with an odd restlessness, a feeling that I was overdue somewhere – the Grind Joint, the Friends, some parking lot in Queens where I was supposed to meet that dentist from Bayside to collect the interest on his shylock loan.

My mind flickered back to something my uncle had told me about Vietnam. One day, he said, he'd been humping a paddy dike in the III Corps Tactical Zone with two hundred rounds of machine-gun ammunition bandoliered over his shoulders, mopping sweat off his mosquito-bitten face with a go-to-hell rag and listening for the telltale sound of an enemy mortar; the next, he was sitting on the plastic upholstery in his mother's tiny walk-up flat on West Forty-Eighth Street, drinking lemonade and listening to a Mets game on the radio. Physically, he was in Hell's Kitchen; mentally, he was still up to his shins in paddy water and waiting for the mortar's whistle.

They had taken my uncle out of Vietnam, but he had never been able to get Vietnam out of himself. It was always there, just behind his eyes – sometimes resting quietly, other times raging, beating its fists against the walls of his brain, intruding on his every waking moment until he could find no peace except in the bottom of a bottle. Did the *brugad* have a similar power?

I shook my head. That was a question for the future. For the now, I had problems enough, and problem number one was what the hell I was going to do with my freedom. The damage to my arm was serious; I'd be months in the cast and months more in rehab, and even then there was no guarantee I'd regain full range of motion. After that would come the long, painful process of torturing my body back into shape, and then testing it out on the road, in the undersized cages and blood-spattered rings of the minor-league promotions I'd thought I'd left behind forever. If I was patient and determined, maybe in two years I could get back to where I had been a year ago. Who knew? *If* is the longest word in the English language.

I had other problems. I had bought my way out of the mob, but there was no statute of limitations on murder. Dago Red's case was still open, and at least five people knew that I had killed him. The fact that they were bound to silence by the code of the streets wasn't much in the way of security. A year in servitude to Gino Stillitano had taught me exactly how much honor remained among thieves. Then there were the Battaglias to think about. From what I understood, Bruno was turning Brooklyn upside-down trying to find out who had ripped off his bank and shortened his son by a hand, and where he was concerned, there was no statute of limitations on anything. If I'd have to keep one eye cocked for the G. from now on, I'd need the other on permanent guard duty for Battaglia hitmen.

Then there was Morganstern.

When dear old Mikhailis discovered how he had unwittingly served as the tool of my deliverance, his rage would be devilish. Having Anne in his bed and blackballing me from the League would no longer be enough; he would come after me with everything he had.

Assuming, of course, that I didn't come after him first.

That was the trouble with murder. Once you get away with it, it becomes an option. If Morganstern pushed too hard…well, I hadn't planned on killing Red, either, but it had happened. And I knew under the right circumstances it could happen again. Clean had seen the monster in me before I had seen it in myself. The trouble was I now recognized that same kind of beast in Mikhailis. And so long as he remained the most powerful man in mixed martial arts, there was no avoiding him. Sooner or later we must meet again. And when that happened….

I felt the ugly weight of the pistol beneath my jacket. As a child, I'd been taught to despise guns. *Real men settle with their fists,* my father had always said, and I had believed him, only to discover the world wasn't exactly overflowing with real men.

On the contrary, it was brimful with cunning, cowardly sons of bitches who gave the orders for violence but were always somewhere else when the trigger was pulled. Against people like that, honor and even courage were nothing but weaknesses. As Kraut had said, there were no Marquis of Queensbury rules on the street. You had to beat them at their own game; had to match their slyness and savagery; to see their viciousness and raise it, until they understood they had no personal immunity. To do that, you'd need more than your fists. You'd need guns, and people were like guns in human form – people like Tina, people like Kraut. People who knew how to fight in the cage we called Life.

I knew what my father would have said to that. Don't go down to their level. Don't let them dictate your actions. Be who you are…and throw that goddamned pistol in the river.

My fingers brushed the coarse-grained wooden butt. Cold as an ice cube despite my body heat. A simple matter to yank it free and toss it into the water. There was no one out here to see.

Be who you are, son.

Okay, Pop. I will.

But it just means disappointing you one last time. You and everyone else who ever believed I was better than the streets that bore me.

I left the pistol in its holster and started toward my car, feeling lonelier than I ever had in my life. Night had fallen, and the wind howled through the cables of the bridge down the empty Promenade like the roar of a crowd. In a way, it seemed fitting.

A gladiator goes in alone.

He leaves that way, too.

ACKNOWLEDGEMENTS

Writing is a solitary process, yet no novel is ever written entirely alone. Special thanks go to Patrick Picciarelli, Detective Lieutenant, NYPD (Ret.), who was instrumental both in guiding me through the dark alleys of my first novel and in supplying expert commentary about the New York mob; to Michael Dell, my editor, whose eye for story and structure is second to none; to Kevin McMahon, co-owner of the UFC Gym in Santa Clarita, CA, for letting me use his facility; to Heather Carson, for being equal to the monumental task of shooting an author photo that made me look good; and to my family -- Evelyn, Jerry, Jerilyn, Cory, Brett, Pat, Beth, and Scott -- whose moral (and financial) support made *Cage Life* possible.

ABOUT THE AUTHOR

Miles Watson was born in Evanston, Illinois, and published his first short story at 17. He holds undergraduate degrees in Criminal Justice and History, and he made a living as a law-enforcement officer before moving to Los Angeles in 2007, where he works in film and television. A lifelong martial artist, he holds a black belt in Tae Kwon Do and has studied boxing, Judo, Aikido, and Hapkido. In 2012, he graduated from Seton Hill University with an MFA in Writing Popular Fiction. *Cage Life* is his first novel.

Instagram: TheMilesWatson
Twitter: @TheMilesWatson
Website: MilesWatson.net

96263596R00159

Made in the USA
Columbia, SC
27 May 2018